OMEGA TEAM
BOOK ONE
WILLOW'S WRATH

BOOKS IN THE
OMEGA TEAM SERIES

AVAFLORIANJOHNS.COM

OMEGA TEAM

BOOK ONE

WILLOW'S WRATH

AVA FLORIAN JOHNS

First Printing, September 2017

ISBN 978-1946195-05-0

Library of Congress Number: 2017954559

Cover and interior design by www.fuzionprint.com

AVAFLORIANJOHNS.COM

PROLOGUE

The year is 2083. Earth is the controlling planet in the ruling body called the Planetary Government (PG). There is a new Supreme Chancellor who rules the planets with an alien supremacy approach. The belief that humanoids are superior above all other races in the universe. The Alien Planetary Alliance (APA) is the new government power trying to rid themselves of the PG but so far have been thwarted at every turn.

The Planetary Government was founded on fear. The fear that 'we the people' were losing our comfortable way of life, the way of life that was pure and good. That 'certain' citizens were going to try to take something from us. The supreme chancellor and his followers did everything they could to make us fearful, of anyone that was unlike us, of anybody that didn't look or act exactly like us. Before this time in our history everybody of the universe lived together in peace. Was it perfect, no? But we were at peace. Now the outlying districts are in ruins, there are groups of people fighting, and the rest of us live in fear of the Planetary Government. Of the rule that tells us that to fit in that to belong, we must be like everyone else. We must behave like everybody else, if not we are punished or exiled.

The PG also doesn't believe in any other viewpoint contrary to their own belief system. they believe the earth's natural resources will be around forever, that nothing is wrong with our planet. They scoff at any scientist who says anything to the contrary and suddenly those who opposed the PG disappear. I know this better than anyone else... this happened to my very own parents and it is a day I will never forget.

CHAPTER
ONE

WILLOW

I am running through the tall yellow sunflowers. The morning sun shines brightly through the giant flowers in the fields and warms my face. Running back toward the farmhouse, I smell smoke. It burns my lungs, and at once the bile swirls in my stomach as dread and helplessness wash over me. Hearing the piercing screams of my parents ringing in the air, I know something is wrong. I know it, but suddenly my feet will not move. I am paralyzed, in the midst of the sunflowers, unable to help my parents as flames engulf our farmhouse. I hear the buzz of the military drones fly over me in the smoky sky, I drop to the ground, and bury myself deep in the damp soil and leaves to camouflage my body. "They" have found us. I stay hidden for what seems likes hours, and I slowly walk toward the farmhouse, my small body quivering as I stare at the horrific sight. Our lovely home is a smoldering pile of black ash. I scream out for my mom and dad, as tears are rushing down my face.

I suddenly feel something hitting my head, and waking up I realize it's my roommate's pillow.

"Sorry, am I dreaming again?" Wiping my tears and feeling rather exposed, I mutter and shake my head as I try to get my bearings.

"More like screaming again. You need help, like serious mental help," screams Dara. Dara is my mean-tempered roommate. She is from the mining colony on Hugo 521 and has little time for social niceties.

"I'm sorry, I had the dream about my family again."

"Cry me a river, Willow. We all know your perfect life ended when you were five years old, and you were brought to this hellhole by your horrible grandmother."

"Oh shut up Dara, you know Willow saw her parents die, and she still feels responsible for their death."

I wince when Tina says I saw my parents die and feel guilty. I know she is trying to stick up for me, but she said it so abruptly that it was almost cruel.

Nevertheless, Tina is most like me, born on Earth and brought to the Planetary Government Boarding School for Girls. Tina hates tension and confrontation, which is pretty much the norm in our dorm room these days.

Dara gets out of her bed and stands in front of Tina, so their noses are touching. "I can't wait to graduate this month and get away from you bitches. I will not miss you at all. Tina, I am so tired of you sticking up for Willow. She needs to learn what it is like out there. It's not all flowers and sunshine."

With all the yelling in the room, our fourth roommate wakes up.

"Why don't you all shut up so I can get some sleep, I have a final tomorrow," complains Saundra, the Casson in the group. The planet Casson has the most military bases in the quadrant. The boys on Casson were bred to be soldiers for the PG, and the girls were abandoned, left on the streets to fend for themselves. Some girls were lucky enough to be rounded up and brought to schools like this one. Saundra is harsh and bitter, but thankfully she keeps to herself.

"I know the world is not all flowers and sunshine, Dara," I mutter under my breath hoping she didn't hear me so she would not lash out again. *As I look at Dara, I see vicious green vines wrapping around her neck squeezing the life out of her until there is no breath left in her limp body. The vines drop her to the ground with a sickening thud. As the rest of us watch in absolute silence, I find it hard to be remorseful, as it is finally my moment of vindication against Dara.* I shake my head and see Dara standing in the same

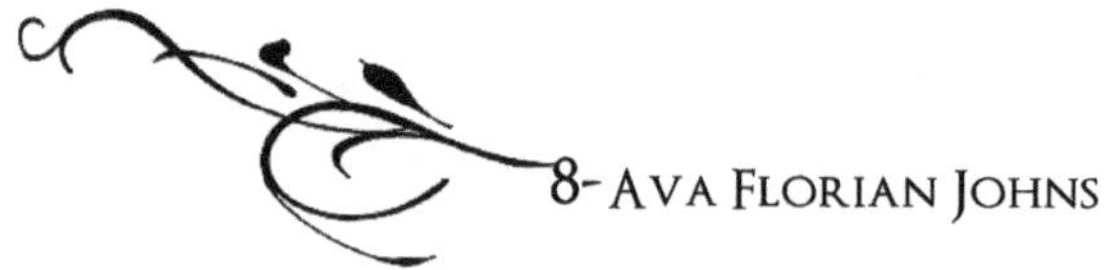

place as she was before, still battling with Tina. I suspect I am slowly and unequivocally losing my mind.

Although Dara thinks of me as child-like, I do fully understand the current state of our world, and it is not ideal. Earth is the controlling planet in the ruling body called the Planetary Government. We have a new Supreme Chancellor who rules centered upon the belief that humans versus other people of alien or non-human backgrounds are superior in every way. Therefore, he believes humans should politically and economically govern non-humanoid people. I remember a time when the ruling government of Earth welcomed people from all the planets. I wish it were still like this.

I like thinking there is a world where people can celebrate their differences, life is jubilant, and sunshine is abundant. I sit on my bed for a moment feeling thrilled to be thinking about the perfect place and wondering if I will ever be lucky enough to be a part of something so ideal. I shake my head to snap out of my daydream. I'd better get back to my reality and the harsh, sterile environment of our boarding school and my offensive roommates.

All the girls at our boarding school, including my roommates, are required to wear the same ugly gray plaid school uniform, but the four of us couldn't look more different. Dara is a real beauty, tall with black hair, dark eyes, and a gorgeous face – too bad she has a ruthless personality. Dara calls me a fairy or pixie, because of my platinum blonde spiky short hair, my tiny frame, and typically sunny disposition (when I am not around her, that is). Dara is almost a foot taller than I am, and she uses her height to her advantage to make me feel small. Tina is very dull looking compared to Dara, but I consider her somewhat pretty, with medium length light brown hair, freckles on her little nose, and hazel eyes. Tina is very wholesome looking and the nicest one in the bunch. Then there is Saundra, who barely speaks a word unless she is agitated. Saundra has short dark brown hair and brooding dark brown eyes that never smile. And I know why. She had a horrific life before she

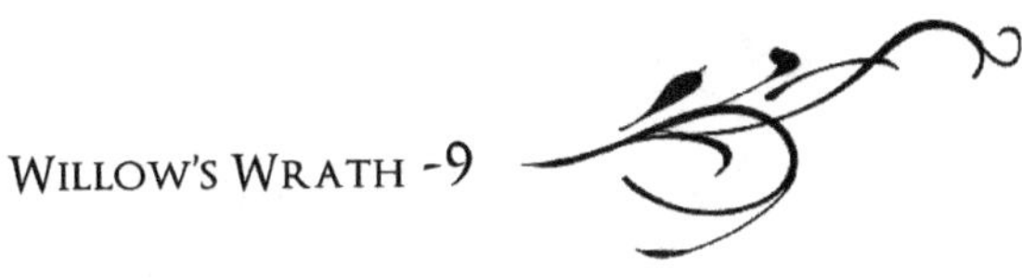

came to the school. Dara calls our boarding school a hellhole, but it's nothing compared to where Saundra originally came from. Casson is the worst type of hell in the universe.

I wish it could be different between the four of us, but sadly, we never bonded, like other girls our age. By this point in our school career, we should be the best of friends, but we are not. I have never felt a part of anything since my parents died on that summer day twelve years ago.

♦♦♦♦♦

Unfortunately, I have a meeting first thing this morning with the very dreadful Headmistress Yvonne, who has been in charge of our all-girls school on the space station for a little over a year. The headmistress is a revolting woman in her early fifties with a huge blonde wig. She wears too much makeup and dresses like she is going to a party instead of to work at a school. When Headmistress Yvonne arrived a year ago, all the privileges we enjoyed were immediately revoked, like the freedom to roam the space station, meet new people, and hang out in the common areas. It was about the same time my roommates, and I started fighting with each other. We had nowhere to go but our room.

When I look at the headmistress, I see tree branches and vines coming through the wall from behind her head. There is a look of surprise and agony on her face as the branches wrap around her arms and legs, threatening to separate them from her torso. The thick green vines pull her limbs in opposite directions I can hear the sounds of her ripping cartilage...

"Willow, are you paying attention?"

I put my head in my hands to block out the images. I have to figure out what is happening to me. These horrible visions are occurring more often, and they are becoming more violent every day.

She repeats the question, louder this time. "Willow Marie Martin, are you paying attention? You need to decide what you are going to

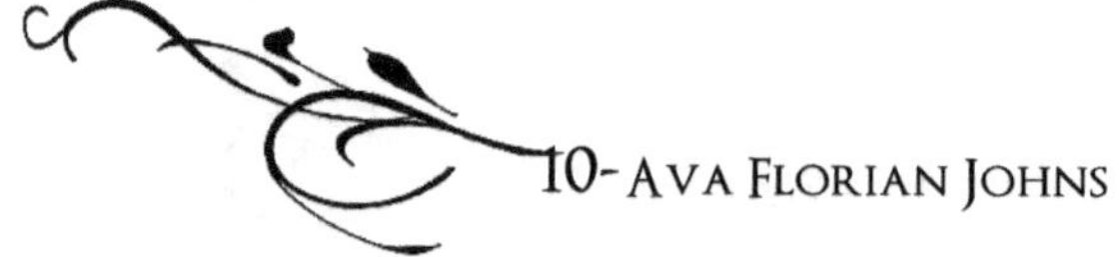

do when you leave here next month." Headmistress gives me an impatient look and taps her two-inch blue nails on her new mahogany desk. "You are the only graduating senior who has not chosen a job with the PG. You should be thankful you have this option."

"I don't want any of those jobs. All those jobs are in the cities, or on the space stations. I want to live in a vast open space again and feel the sun on my face."

"Willow, you know these are the only jobs available to girls without families. They are good steady jobs, much better than you deserve."

"No offense, Headmistress Yvonne, but I know I can do more than work in a kitchen or a factory. I believe I can do more than these menial jobs, I can feel it."

Headmistress Yvonne shoves the paper in my face and snorts. "You cannot do more than this, nor do you deserve more than this, you are lucky to get anything. These are the positions that are open to you. Pick one NOW!"

As she says her final words, I stand up and run toward the door, knocking over the massive nude statue she keeps in the center of the room, causing it to crash to the floor. I can hear her screaming at me as I run down the hallway, sobbing. After the disastrous meeting with the headmistress, there is only one place I want to go. I head to my private sanctuary, the arboretum. It is the only place on the space station I feel I belong. I walk in and sit down on my favorite bench in the center of the room. It's the best vantage point to see everything. I have spent many hours here, talking to the plants. The plants are my friends. When I am lonely they comfort me, when I am sad, they make me happy. They also remind me of my parents and the farm, especially the sunflowers. It is the only connection I have left. They used to make me unhappy, but now they give me comfort.

♦♦♦♦♦

I hear the door open and see my botany teacher strolling in. Dr. Carol Carver looks around at the flowers, then tosses a quizzical look at me. All of the flowers around me are closed or are in a wilted state. She has often mentioned how the plants seem to take on the mood I am in when I visit them. If I am happy, they are in full bloom. When I am miserable, they are wilted and forlorn too.

"What's up buttercup?"

"Funny, Dr. Carver. What makes you think something is wrong?" I say sarcastically looking around at the wilted flowers.

"Well, I know you had a meeting with Headmistress Yvonne, and I guess by your mood the meeting didn't go as well as you hoped."

"It didn't. Headmistress wouldn't even listen to me. She told me the only jobs available for girls without families are the ones on the list. I informed her I am meant for something bigger than this, but she didn't care. She wants me to pick a menial job with the PG and leave her space station. I don't have a choice. I will have to pick one, so I can go."

"Willow, what if I told you there is another choice?" She whispers this last statement and looks around the room. We were the only two in the arboretum, yet she sat for a moment without saying a word. "I have a plan."

♦♦♦♦♦

Feeling dizzy as I often do as I walk through the much too narrow corridor back to my dorm room, I think about the cryptic conversation I had in the arboretum with Dr. Carver, who left before telling me her "plan." She quietly stood up left the room. I called after her, but she ignored me. That is Dr. Carver for you. She is an odd duck, but she has been like a mother to me. A friend. A confidant. I believe she is the only person in the world who understands me, and she is the one person on this station I will genuinely miss.

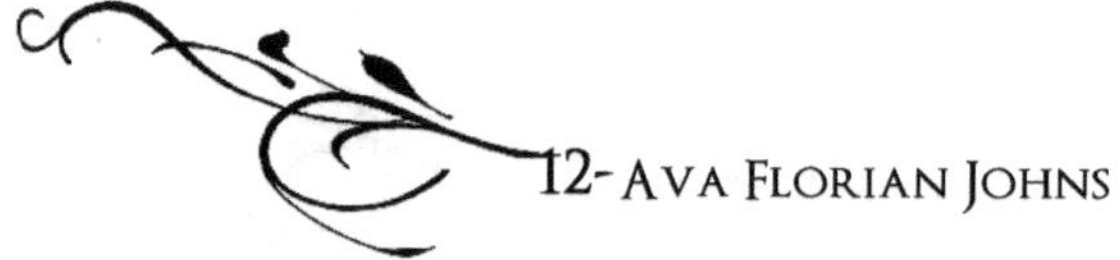

12- Ava Florian Johns

Dr. Carver teaches my favorite class, botany. Although she's a good teacher, she is a little strange, always managing to get more lipstick on her teeth than her lips; her short brown hair is frizzy and unmanageable, she wears mismatched socks and is continually pushing her oversized glasses up her nose. The best thing about her though is she never worries about rules or regulations, and she is the only person on the space station who is not afraid of Headmistress Yvonne.

I have been helping Dr. Carver with the arboretum as her assistant for the last six years. I handle the plants from the time they are seeds. The plants need more care and monitoring because of the disadvantage of gravity's absence on the space station. The plants need enough oxygen, carbon dioxide, humidity, light and temperature control, and gravity to be sustainable. So being on the space station has its challenges when running an arboretum.

I walk down the long, dreary, gray corridor toward my living quarters. I reach the door of my room and hear the sound of breaking glass coming from inside. Dara is at it again, screaming at the top of her lungs at Tina. Poor Tina. My hand trembles as I reach for the doorknob, I bite my lip and tighten my fingers around the cold knob. I am stalling, not wanting to go in, but knowing I have to save Tina from Dara's wrath. After all, Tina did stick up for me yesterday.

"Hello ladies, how are things going?"

"Oh shut up Willow, I am so not in the mood for your crap." Dara violently stomps around the room and bolts past me, walks out into the hallway and slams the door so hard I can feel the vibrations through the soles of my shoes.

"Good riddance," Tina mumbles under her breath.

"Why is she so upset? I haven't seen her this mad since she failed her history final."

"She didn't get the job she wanted, so she decided to take it out on your poor plant and me," Tina points to the shattered pot and mangled plant on the floor.

"Oh, poor thing." I pick up the plant and gently set it in a mug. Once I touch the plant, it springs back to life, and the bloom is bigger than ever. I think Tina pretends not to notice the flower looks better now than before the accident, with only a simple touch from my hands. I know it's against the rules to have flowers in our dorm room, but I don't care. It is the one thing that makes me happy. And I need something to make me happy.

Our room is cylinder-shaped not even ten feet long and ten feet wide, with gray metallic walls with four thin mattresses, double stacked, two on each side of the room, coming out of walls held up by chains. We have a simple black chest to keep our clothes in, and no personal items of any type are allowed. Not that any of us have much, nevertheless, it would be nice to have some color in the room: a throw pillow, a quilt, a photo, something.

The space station décor isn't much better than our room, with its bare corridors and colorless classrooms. Even after twelve years I have the feeling of being trapped as if the walls are closing in on me. Before my Grandma dropped me off here, I spent all my time outside on Earth. Now all that is outside for me is the enormous black vacuum of space.

Tina did notice my trick with the plant. "You are so good with plants, how do you do that?"

"I'm not sure, I have always been good with plants."

The plant makes me remember the time on the farm, feeling the sun on my face and the wind in my hair like it was yesterday. Tina is great. She knows when to leave me alone and let me zone out in my thoughts. I will miss her in a way, too. We were never the best of friends, but we took care of each other when it came to Dara.

♦♦♦♦♦

Dara is back about an hour later, still in a rotten mood. I pretend to be asleep on my cot. My trick doesn't work, and she pulls a strand

of my spiky platinum blonde hair and screams in my face "Headmistress Yvonne wants to see you now. Have fun!"

I head out the door, and down the long corridor. The place is pretty deserted at this time of night, as it has to be after ten p.m. There are other people on the space station beside the students at the boarding school. Many travelers from all over the galaxy visit our space station. They used to let us meet the visitors in the common areas of the station, but now we are relegated to the boarding school area only. We are permanently banned from the rest of the space station unless we have class business elsewhere. The rule changed when Headmistress Yvonne came about a year ago. She didn't like the freedom it afforded us because a couple of the girls left the boarding school for romantic adventures on freighters and other ships flying to all quadrants of the galaxy.

I think back to the time I had met someone, his name was Stephen. Stephen was so handsome, more gorgeous than any other boy I had ever met. I knew we were in love. For four magical weeks, he captivated me with talk of his remarkable adventures. It turned out Stephen was a con and a scoundrel. He had had no adventures at all. He was on the run and had stolen valuable cargo from a Zelkovian freighter to pay his way off the station. He got caught and was banned from the space station forever. And that was the end of our romance.

I reach Headmistress Yvonne's office, take a deep breath and walk in. She is sitting behind her desk with a smug look on her overly made-up face. "You will be transported to another facility immediately." She pretends to study the papers in front of her and adds, "That will be all."

"What facility? I thought I would start working when I graduate. I still have time to pick a job and graduation isn't for another month." I held onto the wall to steady myself. This place is hell most of the time, but it had been my home for twelve years.

"You will not be graduating. You will move to a clinical study facility on Earth. Your orders came in today. Pack your stuff. You

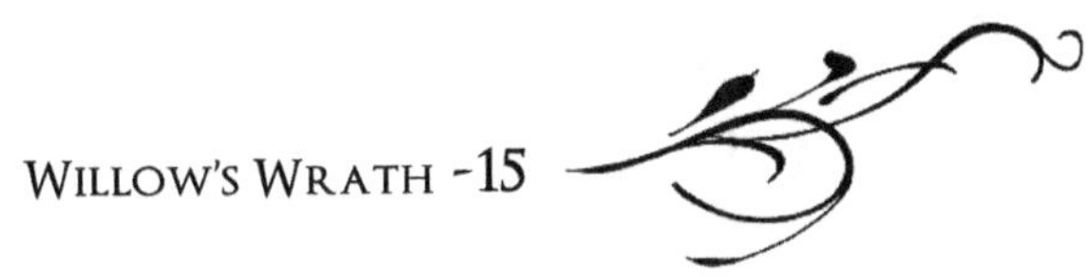

will be leaving for the first transport tomorrow morning." Her impatience with me is growing with every word she spits out of her unpleasant mouth. She tries dismissing me again, but I won't leave.

The branches and vines come out of the ceiling this time, wrapping around her scrawny neck with alarming swiftness, lifting her out of her chair and dangling her by her neck, her feet are kicking in the air trying to gain traction, trying to reach the floor to no avail. The vines are strangling her and all I hear is a faint gurgling noise, then silence.

I shake my head to rid myself of the horrendous image so I can continue my argument with the headmistress. A thought crosses my mind that I should tell someone about the imagery I have seen lately, but that is not my primary concern right now.

"Headmistress Yvonne, please tell me why I won't be graduating and why I am leaving so soon. Please, you owe me that much." My voice came out as a whisper, "Please."

"Willow, I don't owe you anything. You have been the bane of my existence since I arrived at this school and I am glad to see you go. You have always acted like you were better than everyone else, and people hate you for it. Do you know how many times your roommates tried to have you removed from their quarters? A lot. Now, get out of my office. You will be given instructions tomorrow morning." She is so mad at me her voice is coming out as a high pitched shriek.

I stand there for a moment letting the words sink in. How many times have I wished to leave this place? Too many to count. I should be happy I am finally getting out of here, but I have so many questions that the headmistress won't answer, like what are they going to do to me?

I finally gather my wits and leave Headmistress Yvonne's office without another glance from her. She doesn't care about me, about any of us. It's only a job for her.

I know it's late, but I need to see Dr. Carver to say goodbye and to thank her for her support and friendship for all these years. She isn't

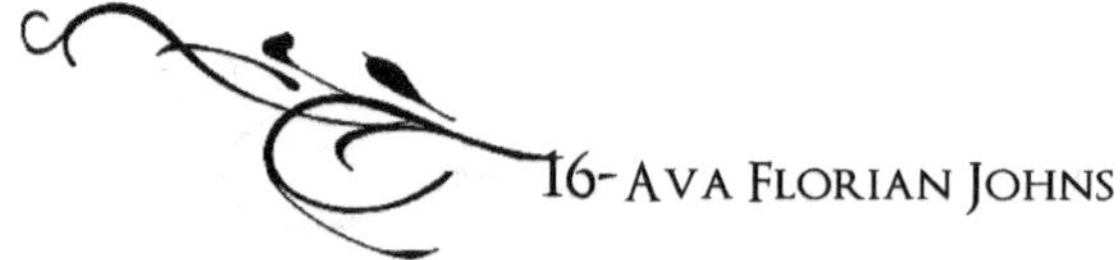

in her quarters, so I look in the next logical place, and I am right, she is in the arboretum. When I walk in, she doesn't look at all surprised to see me. In fact, it seems like she is expecting me. I stand in the doorway for a moment and start to sob. She comes over immediately and dries my tears with her scarf. "Honey, don't cry, you will be okay. It is all part of my master plan. You will be out of here and away from nasty Headmistress Yvonne. You are right. You do not belong in one of the awful PG positions. You are so special, more than you even know."

"What do you mean special? Headmistress Yvonne said I am the bane of her existence."

"Don't listen to that old bat. You are incredible. You have powers you haven't yet discovered. You know it deep down inside, so release them, and good things will happen to you, I promise."

Dr. Carver has a way with words. I laugh as she says "old bat," but pause when she says I have powers. What powers? I am good with plants, but what else do I have? I don't dare to ask her.

"I will miss you so much."

"Willow, I know you will see me again. I guarantee it," she says while hugging me hard. "Now I want you to do something for me. Come over here and make these flowers bloom, they are all wilted."

I walk over to the bright pink Gerber Daisies and wave my hand over the top of them. They all open as if by magic. I have done it before many times on my own, but with someone watching me, I am a little nervous. I walk to each flower bed and my hand shakes a bit as I wave it over the top of the flowers, and they all come to life again. They are beautiful. I know I will miss this place more than anything else.

I say my final goodbyes to Dr. Carver and walk back to my dorm room. I am sure my roommates will be devastated I am leaving. Not.

I get to my room, and all my roommates are asleep. Well, it is after midnight, and I know I am leaving in the morning. I keep thinking about the clinical research facility I will be moving to tomorrow. I will never sleep in this bed again, or hear Dara yell at Tina, or visit the arboretum. I finally doze off.

♦♦♦♦♦

My mom is humming as she pulls my long strands of blonde hair through her tiny fingers, it's a song she used to sing to me every night. The birds in the meadow, fire is coming. She stops brushing my hair, looks directly into my eyes and says, "You have special powers my darling, and you must use them for good. Please remember this."

I wake up wishing I had another minute with my mom. I realize my roommates are already up and dressed.

"Well, nice of you to wake up sleeping beauty. You better get a move on, you don't want to miss your transport. I would say I will miss you, but I won't," Dara snarled.

"What do you mean? Are you leaving, Willow? Before graduation?" Tina acts genuinely sad to see me go. Then I remember Tina will be on her own with Dara.

"I am going to miss you, Willow." Tina comes over and hugs me. "Good luck, I know you will be great."

What a strange thing to say to me. Frankly, I am a little paranoid. I feel like everyone knows where I am going except for me. What does Tina mean, I know you will be great, great at what?

I say goodbye to all the girls, and Tina hugs me again. Saundra grunts and Dara snarls. That's okay. I am out of here. I start getting excited to be leaving. I pack up the few things I own, throw my bag over my shoulder, and head to the arboretum.

♦♦♦♦♦

I walk in through the main door as I expect Dr. Carver is waiting for me on my favorite bench. Saying our last goodbyes is the hardest thing I have ever had to do. She assures me she will see me again,

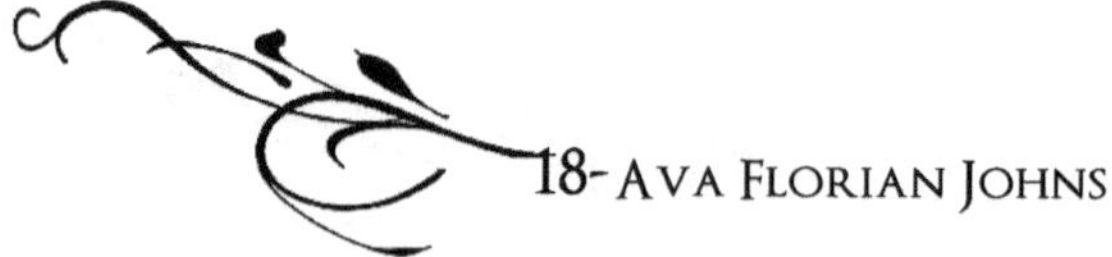

but I wish I knew that for sure. She offers to take me to the transport, but I decide I don't need a long goodbye.

♦♦♦♦♦

So far today I have been on a transport, a plane, a bus, a train, and finally, we make it to the research facility, and it is literally out in the middle of nowhere. There is security everywhere, but not military. They don't wear the insignia of the PG, and instead, it says APA on the patches on their blue jumpsuits. I am exhausted and anxious. My butt is sore, my legs are numb, and to make things worse, the guy seated next to me fell asleep on me and drooled all over my shoulder. Besides the drooling guy, there are about twenty other kids on the trip with me, and they don't seem to know what is going on either. I would say they range from ages six to twenty.

A young girl is sitting in the back of the bus. She is probably around ten years old, with her long auburn hair in pigtails and bright green eyes. Once the bus stops moving, I look back, and she is refusing to get off. Her chaperone is gently trying to persuade to get off the bus, but she is not moving. I realize the girl has a cognitive disability. I am not sure what the name of the disability is, I never had the opportunity to be around people like her before. The horrible Supreme Chancellor has rules about people with disabilities using government-funded facilities, like the boarding school.

Everyone has gotten off the bus, except for me, the chaperone, and the young girl. She has now flopped out of her seat onto the ground and is sitting on the dirty floor of the bus. Her chaperone is at her wit's end and looks to me with pleading eyes. Well, I suppose I can give it a shot, it can't hurt anything.

I make my way to the back of the bus to meet the girl and see what I can do.

"Hello there, my name is Willow, what's yours?"

She looks up and me and sticks her tongue out.

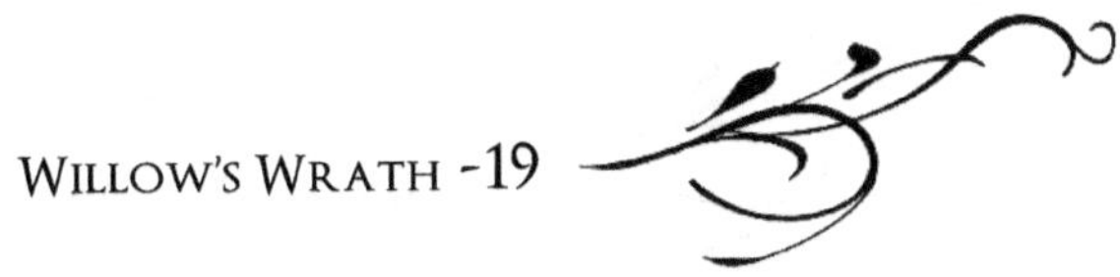

I snort laugh. Both the young girl and the chaperone laugh at my snort.

"Yoo-uu lau-ugh fuu-nny." She says every word very slow and deliberately, to make sure I understand her.

"Lizzy, that's not very nice." The chaperone reprimands her.

"It's okay. I do laugh funny don't I? My mom used to laugh the same way. My dad used to say we both laughed funny."

"Where's yoo-uur mom noo-ow?" She was still speaking slowly, but because I could understand her, she started talking faster.

I wasn't sure how to answer her question. Do I tell this young girl that my mom is dead? Do I just say that she is gone? The look on my face must have said it all.

"Don't be saa-aad Willow. My mom-my is goo-ne too. They tell me she is in a bet-ter plaaa-ce."

"Thank you, Lizzy, I think my mom is in a better place too. How about we get you off this dirty floor now and go inside. What do you say Lizzy?"

"Okay Will-oow, if you will walk with me?" Now that she knew I could understand her she spoke faster.

"Sure thing."

The three of us get ready to disembark from the bus. Lizzy's chaperone thanks me as we grab all of Lizzy's belongings. She explains to me that Lizzy has Down syndrome and that she has an extraordinary power. Lizzy grows impatient with our conversation and escorts us off the bus and down the stairs.

Lizzy grabs my hand as we go to stand by everyone else and wait for our next set of instructions.

♦♦♦♦♦

I want to make a good impression, but I'm not sure who I am meeting or how I am supposed to impress them. A middle-aged man comes out to greet us. As he walks closer to me, he looks like he wore his clothes to bed and just rolled out. He greets us with a

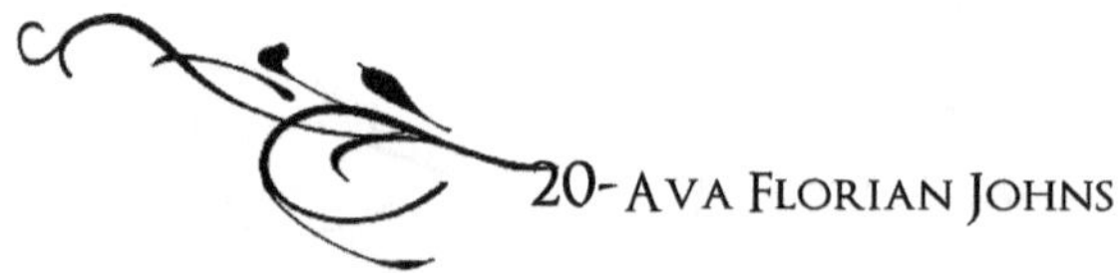

sarcastic grin and wave. "Welcome to The APA Annex, your new home, if you pass the test," he announces chuckling to himself. "Follow me." We follow him into the enormous industrial-style building. The hallways are all brightly painted in a multitude of colors, blue, green, and yellow, with bright orange floors. The look is entirely different from the cold, sterile environment of the space station and the endless metallic gray corridors.

When we reach a large room, we are told to split into two groups. I know that Lizzy will have a hard time if I leave, she has had my hand in a death grip since we stepped off the bus. Her chaperone is still following behind us. The young kids are told to go with Ashley, who looks like a camp counselor, with her long blonde hair pulled into a ponytail, worn jeans and a t-shirt with a logo that reads Omega Team.

"Lizzy, you need to go with your group now, and I will need to go with mine."

"Nooooo Will-oow. You stay with me."

She was making a scene, and I was not sure how to handle it. Ashley starts walking toward us.

"You must be Lizzy, I have heard so much about you. I can't wait to see you fly."

Lizzy takes up a position directly behind me and is peeking at Ashley from around my back. The older group has stopped in the hall and is waiting for me to finish up with my new friend. I hope this doesn't affect my standing here negatively, I'm just trying to help.

"I didn't know you could fly Lizzy, that is so cool. You will need to show me sometime. But right now, I need to go with the older group, and you need to stay with Ashley."

"Lizzy, you will get to see Willow at dinner tonight and for all the meals here at the Annex. I promise you will get to see a lot of her. Is it okay if she goes with her team now?"

Lizzy releases my hand a bit and moves in front of me. She reaches up and brings my head down, so her green eyes are looking into mine.

"Will-oow, promise me that you will see me tonight. PROMISE."

"I promise, Lizzy."

"Okay, you can go." And she gives me a big hug.

"See you later, Lizzy."

I head in the direction of the older group, led by the disheveled middle-aged man we met outside. He told us to call him Director Jackson. What he explains to us is today will be our orientation day. We will get our rooms and see the rest of the Annex. We are to stay together in a group for the tour and dinner, but we will have some free time to be on our own later tonight.

I look at the group, sizing up the rest of the people, and they don't look like they have special powers. But in all fairness, neither do I, and I doubt I have any skills at all. I wonder again why we are all here. I heard a couple of the boys talking on the bus about how their parents didn't know how to handle their unique gifts anymore and sent them away to this place. They were speculating that the people in this facility would help them improve their special powers and that they would become superheroes and save the universe. No one is quite sure if the APA is part of the government or apart of a new underground rebel movement. More and more there were reports of protests and violence in the streets as the PG enforced stricter and stricter rules on the people of Earth.

We stop walking and come to the area with dorm rooms. A young woman in her mid-twenties stands by with a clipboard. Director Jackson positions himself in the middle of the hall and makes an announcement. "All right, listen up! I am your lead instructor for this three-month training exercise. I'm sure you all have a lot of questions, and I will give you a chance to ask them after I get you your gear and we show you to your rooms. Beth will take the young ladies, and I will take the men. Each of you, please take the backpack with your name on it and follow either Beth or me to your room."

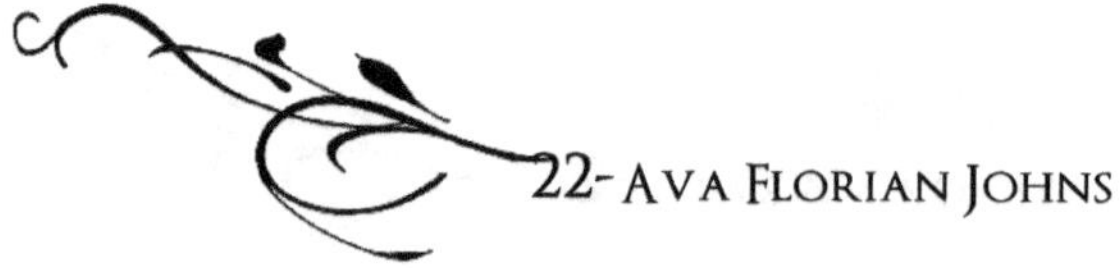

Beth stops in the hallway, looks at her list one more time, and takes the lanyards and keycards from her backpack. "These are your room keys, and they also open the doors to the sections in the Annex where you will have access. Each of you has unique power skills which we will help you to develop. You will be allowed to use several sections of the building to accommodate your specific skills. When I call your name, please come forward, take your key, and go to your room. We will meet back here in five minutes."

"Willow Martin," Beth calls my name first. I take my keycard and head to the room. I feel all eyes on me as I walk down the hallway. They are probably wondering what can I possibly do that is special. I am so nervous about all the people looking at me, I don't even realize I am heading to a room of my own. It has been so long since I have had a place all to myself. The last time was in the farmhouse twelve years ago. I open the door, and my room is beautiful. There is a digital screen on one entire wall which I can set for any scenery I want. I immediately pick farmlands, which makes me feel at home. The walls are a soft yellow, and there is a beautiful colorful quilt on the bed. I already like it here a lot. I know the annex is going to be my new home.

✦✦✦✦✦

After we are assigned our dorm rooms, we head to the large area again. We are to demonstrate our powers for all to see. I am incredibly nervous since I am not sure what my abilities are. All of us are in the order in which we are to demonstrate, and I am given number ten out of ten. Crap. I will have to wait until everyone else finishes their demonstrations and I am growing more anxious by the moment.

Director Jackson, Ashley, and Beth are sitting at a long table in the front of the room. There is a large balcony section in the room, which has two-way glass. I know someone is watching from above.

I can feel it. I try to shake off the nervousness and concentrate on the other members of my new team.

Director Jackson explains we are now part of a super-secret elite group called the Omega Team. We will be working on our skills at the Annex, and after three months we will be assigned a position with the APA. This information is all he will tell us until each of us complete our demonstrations.

♦♦♦♦♦

"We are going to announce each of you one at a time to come up and demonstrate your power. Please come to the center of the room when we call your name. We have arranged items to be brought in for you to perform your unique ability. First one up, Mr. Todd Jacob Anderson, age eighteen, Planet of Origin: Earth."

I watch as Todd walks past me and stands at center stage. I noticed him on the bus. He has a beautiful smile and is very pleasant looking. However, he now seems as nervous as I feel. He stands in the center of the room as Director Jackson and the others wait for him to begin his demonstration. "Should I start?" Todd asked nervously. "Yes, please begin when you are ready," Director Jackson responds.

Todd turns around and runs full speed to the back of the room. He jumps nine feet up on the wall and proceeds to scale the surface all the way to the ceiling. Todd hangs from the beams for a moment, then continues to scale back down the wall as quickly as he went up. He is spectacular. "How does he do that?" whispers the boy sitting next to me. "I'm not sure, but I've never seen anything like it," I answer in a whisper.

"My name is Christopher James. And you are?"

He extends his hand, and I shake it, "Willow Martin."

Director Jackson has a folder for each one of us, with information regarding our unique gifts. He asks Todd a couple of questions. Todd explains he has scales on his hands and feet similar to a gecko,

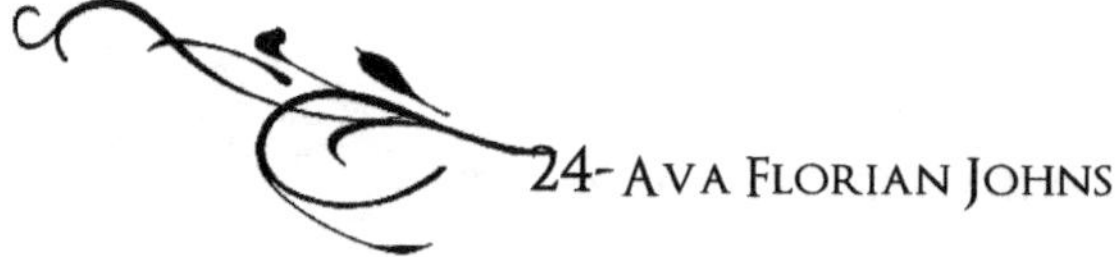

which help him climb the wall like a reptile. He was born with the power and got into some trouble at his last school because of it. His parents were not sure what to do with him, so they sent him to this facility.

Beth stands to announce the next participant. "The second person to give a presentation is Megan Sansone. She is nineteen and from the Hugo 521 Mining Colony." Wow, I thought, Megan is from Hugo, like my roommate Dara at the PG School for Girls. I should have noticed she looks a lot like Dara, dark hair, dark eyes, but Megan seemed to have a more pleasant disposition. Maybe her friendly nature is what threw me. Megan went to the center of the room where Todd stood moments before. She smiles, looks around the room at all of us, and then completely disappears. We all gasp and wait for her to reappear. I am so jealous, her power is invisibility, how cool is she?

"Next in line, Christopher James, age nineteen from planet Earth. Welcome Christopher, we are bringing in something in which you will need to demonstrate your power. You may start when you are ready." As Beth finishes her statement, a team of workers in blue APA jumpers enters the room with a large metal box. Director Jackson warns everyone to stay in their seats. The team of judges at the front of the room put protective gear on their bodies and faces. I wonder how dangerous his power is and if I should have been sitting so close to him or even shook his hand. He seems to sense my discomfort, looks at me and smiles. "My power is called poison generation. I can create a poisonous substance with my saliva." He leans down toward the box and spits directly in the large metal container. The metal immediately starts to disintegrate. "Wow, what a shame. I was thinking about kissing him later." Megan laughs at her own joke.

"Number four in our lineup is Jacqueline Meyers, age eighteen and her planet of origin is the Zelkova. Special note, she likes to be called Jax," Beth announces as Jax sits down at the judge's table directly across from Ashley. I notice she has not said one word all day. I am very curious about her and have felt her presence all day. Nothing bad, more of a feeling of her presence I seem to get when she is in my vicinity. Director Jackson addresses us. "Jax was born mute, she can hear, but not speak. Jax is a mind-reader, and she has the power to receive and transmit information with only her brain." Ashley adds, "When Jax connects with another person they don't have to use verbal cues or words. She can speak to the person telepathically."

The workers in the APA blue jumpsuits come in again and hook up two computers. They place one in front of Ashley, and one in front of Jax. Ashley looks at an image on the screen, and Jax answers with the same picture from her computer. So far, she has gotten thirty out of thirty correct. I am starting to feel discouraged. Another incredible ability and we are not even halfway through our group. My power is going to look lame compared to a gecko, a telepath, an invisible girl, and a boy who spits poison.

I'm impressed by what I see so far, and the judges look like they are excited as well. The next person up is Donna from the planet Eryngium. She is gorgeous with long dark brown hair and beautiful brown skin. She emanates confidence from every pore of her being. Donna saunters into the center of the room without a shred of nervousness. "Hello all, my name is Donna, and I am going to transport you." Director Jackson nods his approval to continue and instantly I am sitting in the middle of the jungle. A Brown Capuchin Monkey stares at me from a couple of feet away. I put out my hand to touch him and feel his soft fur. The imagery is so real that I can feel the humidity in the air, my sweat beading on my skin, and I can hear the noises of the animals in the jungle. It's miraculous. We find out from Director Jackson that Donna can convert physical matter into thought waves and trap them in peoples' minds, putting the subject under the power of Donna's imagination. She can also do the opposite and collect images from peoples' minds and use the thoughts against them. I made a mental note to stay on Donna's good side.

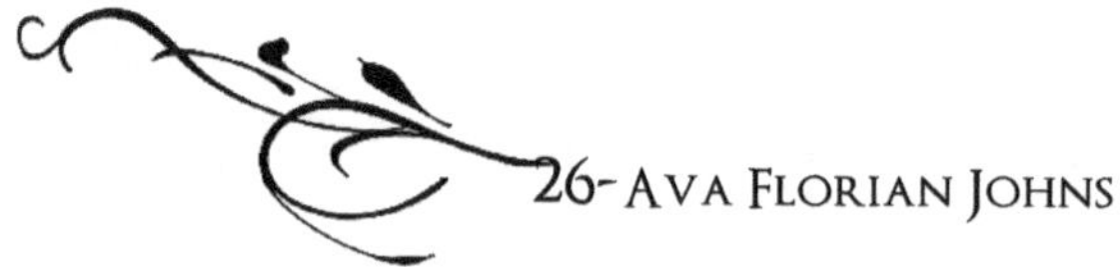

Director Jackson announces the next person like a game show host. "The sixth contestant on our amazing show is Caroline Wagner. She goes by the name Cobalt, and she is from the third planet in the Zea Mays system and loves taking long walks on the beach." Cobalt stands in front of me, "Will you be my assistant?" I am uncertain what to say, and I am a little apprehensive because I'm not sure what her special power is, but I nod yes. I don't want to appear awkward on my first day, and I want to make connections with people. Good ones this time, and not the horrible relationships I had with my roommates at the boarding school.

I get up from my seat and follow Cobalt across the room. "Please relax and clear your mind." I close my eyes, and when I hear a gulp from the audience, I realize Cobalt has me suspended six feet in the air. I did not even feel anything happening. I am now lying parallel to the ground, floating above the room. It is a surreal experience. I feel weightless, relaxed, and completely calm. All the anxiety and nervousness I felt before this moment has melted away. I wonder if she felt my tension and wanted to help. Maybe all my uneasiness is making her edgy. Either way, I thank her for picking me.

"The next person is Dharma, no last name listed, and we're not sure where she is from or how old she is because there is no known record of her birth. Here is Dharma..." Ashley stumbles through the introduction, not quite sure what to say. Apparently, there is very little information regarding Dharma's life. Nevertheless, you can tell she is unique by looking at her.

Yes, she is an extraordinary person indeed. She doesn't speak, and I'm not sure if she can or just chooses not to. Dharma stands up from her chair and leaps across the six rows of seats in front of her. By the time she clears the last row of seats, she is a stunning mountain lion. Her paws hit the floor with a thud. One person in the back of the room screams and the others are too shocked to speak. She prances around the center stage and ends up directly in front of me. I reach out and pet her fur, not afraid of her transformation. I think whatever Cobalt did to calm me is still working. I should have her suspend me in the thin air every day.

Two more participants to go, then me. Next is Maddox from Muscari. She is the most unique person I have ever seen, with chocolate skin, burgundy hair, and purple eyes. She easily stands over six feet tall. Maddox can manifest wings which grow and are attached to her body allowing flight. She bows her head and extends her arms. Her wings appear and they are a multifaceted brown, with purple and burgundy feathers, to match her hair. Magnificent. Maddox is truly a majestic creature. "Next time can we have you demonstrate your powers outside so we can see you fly?" Director Jackson looks very impressed, and I don't blame him. Maddox just nods in agreement and returns to her seat.

Next up Sophia. Sophia's gifts are also surprising. She is the smallest person in the room, even shorter than I am, and her power is supernatural strength. Director Jackson tells us to follow him outside. Sophia proceeds to pick up a car, then a jeep, a bus, then all of them together. She is stronger than any person I have ever seen! I am hoping she will lift a few more things so I can stall with my demonstration, but no such luck. I am up next.

"Okay everyone, follow us to the arboretum." Beth walks over to me after her announcement. "Willow, relax, you will be wonderful."

"Before Willow starts her demonstration I would like to introduce another member of our Annex teaching staff. Welcome aboard Dr. Carver." I can't believe my eyes. I run as fast as I can to Dr. Carver and fling my arms around her. "I am so glad you are here." I sniff, noticing the entire class is watching our exchange.

"Willow, I promised you would see me again and here I am. Now get over there and show them what you can do." I start walking around the flowers, and as I walk by the flower buds visibly perk up and turn to face the direction I am walking. At first, all I do is place my hand gingerly over the plants and flowers, getting to know them. I stroll around the entire room, and as I do, I hear whispers in the class. I imagine they are talking about how lame my talent is.

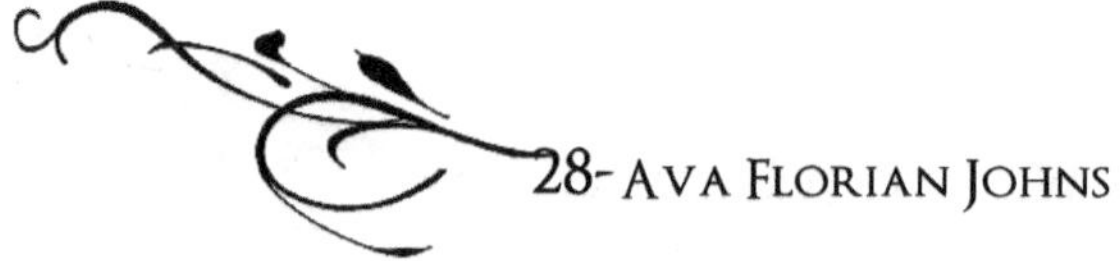

I decide I will let loose and see what I can do. I raise both of my arms in a grand gesture, sweeping them toward the sky. The flowers and plants start growing taller and taller, twisting around and around each other, up and up, rising hundreds of feet tall in mere seconds. I stop them when they hit the domed roof of the arboretum.

"Wow," I hear one of the girls say. I smile and direct the plants back down to their normal size with a just sweep of my hand. I look at Dr. Carver, and she beams at me, addressing the class for the first time. "Willow has what we call Botanical Communication, or Botonopathy. With her mind, she can communicate with plants and flowers. We have only begun to see the real potential of her powers."

"Thank you, Dr. Carver. Staff and participants, please follow me to the dining hall." Director Jackson starts walking toward the exit. I stay behind with Dr. Carver and ask her the question I had been dying to ask. "How did you know about my powers?"

"Willow, I was assigned to watch you for all these years, to make sure no one harmed you, and let your skills progress naturally. Quite simply, I was hired to make sure the PG never got their hands on you. Now, let's go eat."

"Let's go eat! Are you kidding me? You drop this bomb on me, and you want me to eat?" I am hysterical.

"Come on Willow, we will have plenty of time to talk later. I'm hungry, so let's go." Dr. Carver chuckles as she leaves the arboretum. I follow her because I have no idea where the dining hall is, and to be honest, I'm hungry too.

♦♦♦♦♦

"Willow, where are you from?" Todd asks politely. He sits across from me, and I can tell he has been gathering up his nerve for quite a while to ask me a question. "I was born on Earth, but I have lived in the Division 19 Space Station and attended the PG Boarding School for Girls for the last twelve years. I was brought there after my parents died." Great going Willow, pleasant dinner conversation. What a dork I am. I can't believe I blurted out to someone I met today that my parents died.

"I'm so sorry for your loss, Willow."

"It's okay Todd, I regret that I blurted it out. This food reminds me of what we used to eat on the farm, and I guess it brought the memories back to me."

I realize the whole table is quiet, silently listening to our conversation. Why am I such a dork? I'm trying to make a good impression on these people, not blurt everything out about my life all on the first day.

Director Jackson finally breaks the awkward silence. "Okay people, this is what is going to happen tomorrow. You will wake at seven a.m., get ready and meet here in the dining hall at eight for breakfast. Classes start at nine sharp. All of you will take the same basic classes, such as math, history of the universe, and government. You will also have private time throughout the day to be with one of the instructors to work on controlling and honing your specific powers. The rest of the time we will work on conditioning, mental fortitude, and drills. We will eat breakfast, lunch, and dinner as a team. Dr. Carver, Beth, and I will be your instructors. Ashley will be working with the younger kids. You will have a couple of hours each night to relax and get to know each other. You will be working together for the next few months, so the better you get along, the easier your time here will be. You can leave the dining hall when you are finished eating. Lights out at eleven p.m., no exceptions."

I walk over to the other side of the dining hall to say hi to Lizzy. She runs over to me with her hands outstretched to give me a big hug. She is wearing a long red cape.

"WILLOW!"

"Hello Lizzy, how are you?"

"Look at my new red cape. It is for flying."

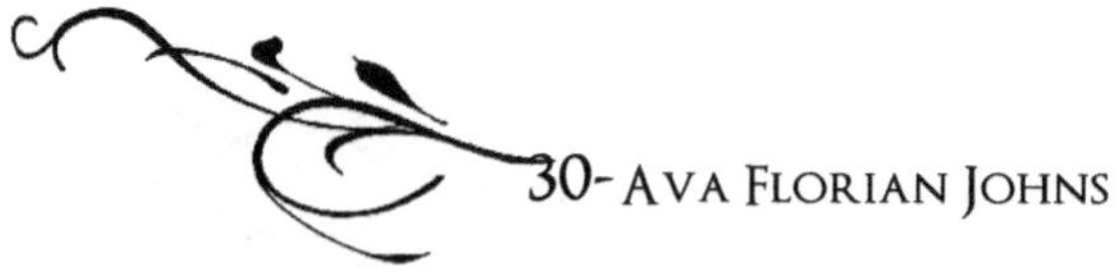

"Wow, that is amazing. I love it. I am so glad to see you, but I have to talk to one of my teachers now. I will see you tomorrow, okay Lizzy?"

"Noooooo Willow, that wasn't long enough."

I knew she would want me to stay longer, but I knew I had to find Dr. Carver.

"I promise I will see you tomorrow Lizzy."

"No."

And she plopped to the ground. I look over to Lizzy's chaperone, and she nods her head in understanding and comes over to help.

I start to back away and realize while all this was going on Dr. Carver left the dining hall.

I stop and think for a moment, where would she go? The arboretum, of course, our special place, and it is the one place she knows I will find her.

Sure enough, Dr. Carver is hovering around the petunias. The pink ones are her favorite. I stand directly behind her and will the pink petunias to grow tall. Not as tall as they did in my demonstration, but so they will be close to her face. She turns around and smiles. "I love petunias, but I guess you didn't come here to make my favorite flower grow, did you?"

"Dr. Carver, I would like some answers. Will you please tell me now?" I want her to disclose the information about my past, my life, and why I have the power to make things grow.

"Well you better sit down, it's a long story. Okay, let's get started. Your parents were Jeffrey and Maria Washburn. You were born Willow Marie Washburn, not Willow Marie Martin. Martin is the name we gave you when you came to the boarding school. Your parents were both scientists working for the PG. They were developing chemicals to enhance natural abilities in humans. Your father found out the government was using their research to build biochemical weapons, and that is when your parents reached out to the APA for help."

My head is spinning and I am hyperventilating. As much as I wanted to hear it, I don't know if I can handle the truth about my life.

"Willow, if this is too much for you, we can take it slow. We have a lot of time to go through everything. Please don't feel like you have to hear all of this in one night."

"No," I lie, "I am fine, please continue Dr. Carver."

"So, your parents started working for the APA a couple of years before you were born. They loved working for the APA and specialized in the field of Omnilingualism, specifically Botanical Communication, the power to communicate with plant life, and plant manipulation. They had a break-through right before they died. The information leaked from someone in the APA to one of the directors in the PG."

"My parents worked for this facility? Why didn't you tell me before I came here?" I am dumbfounded that Dr. Carver withheld this information from me. What possible reason would there be for deceiving me? I feel the bile in the back of my throat threatening to spray out my mouth. I calm myself with deep breaths.

"Willow, you have to understand, we didn't know who we could trust. If anyone found out who you were, you would not have been safe. We feared you could have been captured or worse."

"What is the *or worse?*"

"You would have been executed."

"Why would I be executed? For what my parents did? I was a child, only five years old."

"Willow, please calm down and listen to the rest of the story, then I will answer your questions, I promise. Will you do that for me please?"

"Yes, I will listen, Dr. Carver, I am sorry for interrupting, but, this is all so overwhelming."

"I understand dear. So where was I in the story? Oh yes, your parents were living on the farm with you. At this point, they were hiding from both the operatives at the PG and the APA. They knew

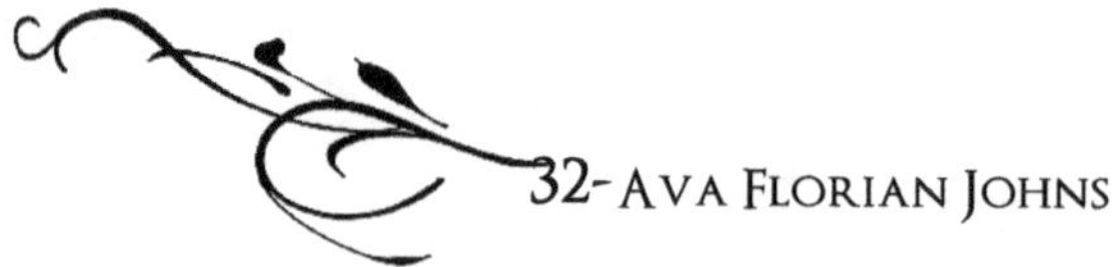

they had to lay low to get their work done. They understood it was too important not to finish. They had developed a chemical to enhance natural abilities in humans, and it worked. They used it on themselves, and it was a huge success. Your dad knew the PG would never stop looking for them, so they had to inject the chemical into someone else. Someone the government didn't know existed. That someone is you, Willow."

The sweat is pouring off my forehead into my eyes, I am light headed, and suddenly the room spins and goes black.

When I awake, Dr. Carver is holding me, gently touching my hair, making soft noises of assurance. "It will be okay Willow, I promise."

I can feel the anger well up inside me, my blood boiling, and my pulse quickening, I can hear my heart pounding in my chest. "I wish I could believe you, but it seems my whole life is made up of lies. My name isn't even what I thought it was. Continue with the story NOW! I need to know everything." I look around the arboretum, and the plants have grown at least twenty feet and are standing at attention, ready for battle. I try to calm myself so the plants will relax, but it is not working. I am too angry with Dr. Carver for her betrayal.

Dr. Carver has not started speaking again, so I will the plants to move closer to her. She notices they are about to touch her leg, and she looks terrified and continues her story.

"Your parents injected you with the serum because they were sure the government didn't know of your existence. They needed to make sure the serum didn't end up in the wrong hands. I am the only one who knew you were born and where you were living. I became your protector. Your grandmother was contacted about your parents' passing and followed orders to get you to the boarding school. You should know she didn't want to hand you over to me. She wanted to raise you on her own, but it was far too dangerous."

She pauses, making sure I am still okay. I nod my head for her to continue.

"I am sorry to say your grandmother passed away a couple of years ago, Willow, and I want you to know she was very proud of you."

I start sobbing, my heart breaking for a woman I didn't even know.

"Buttercup, I am so sorry for everything that has happened to you."

"Don't call me that!" The plants grow taller and threaten Dr. Carver – they move within an inch of her neck and it takes all my power to will the plants away from her.

Dr. Carver looks hurt and frightened by my outburst, but she straightens up and continues the story. "The day your parents died, you were playing outside in the sunflower field you had created. I believe when the drones attacked the farmhouse the sunflowers protected you from the PG's detection system. You were found covered in mud and leaves after the fire. The neighbor called your grandmother, and then I was alerted. I left the APA Annex and headed to the PG School for girls as your instructor. For the last twelve years, I have protected and loved you."

By this point, I am sobbing so hard my back and shoulders hurt. I am shaking uncontrollably, my mind in a fog. How can my life be made up of so many lies?

"Let's get you to your room. That is enough for today, and I can answer any questions you have tomorrow."

I let her lead me out of the arboretum and to my dorm room. I doubt I would have made it on my own.

I crawl into my bed and awake at seven a.m. when the announcement comes over the speakers. "Rise and shine everyone. You have one hour to get ready and meet in the dining hall. Welcome to your first day at the APA Annex," Director Jackson's jovial voice booms over the loudspeaker. He is way too happy for this early in the morning.

Remarkably, I slept through the night, with no disturbing dreams or horrible thoughts from the day before. I think I was so mentally

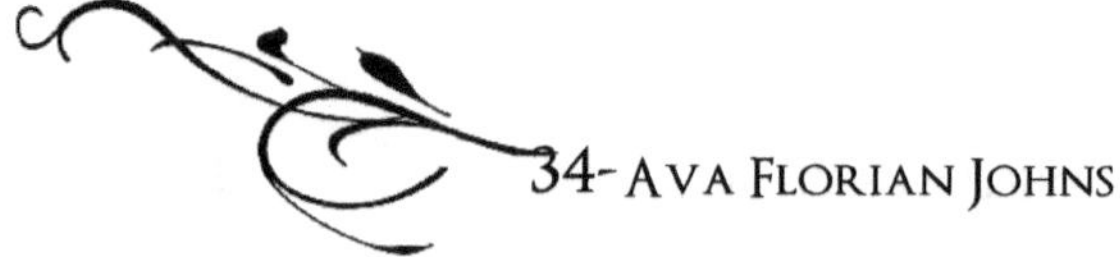

exhausted I just shut down. I shower and put on my new orange Omega Team jumpsuit. I shake out my wet hair and look in the mirror, murmuring "Good enough, I have more important issues to worry about than my looks."

♦♦♦♦♦

The dining hall is as boisterous as it was for dinner the night before. I take my food and walk over to the table. Cobalt and Todd make room for me between them. "Sit here Willow," Todd says as he slides closer to Christopher. Christopher looks a little annoyed, but I don't want to read anything into it. I sit down and search the table for Dr. Carver, but she isn't there.

I am about to ask where she is when Director Jackson speaks. "The other staff members are getting ready for your first day of classes. Dr. Carver will teach math this semester and science next semester. Beth will teach history for the entire three months, and I will teach your government class. Willow, Cobalt, Dharma, and Maddox will have Dr. Carver as their power instructor. Todd, Christopher, and Sophia will be with me, and the rest of you will have Beth. No more announcements today, enjoy your breakfast."

I knew I would be with Dr. Carver. It's only logical since she teaches botany. But after yesterday, I'm not sure if I can trust her anymore. She kept something from me, the most significant thing, my identity, for all these years. She says it is to protect me, but who would come after me? I don't believe the situation is quite as dire as she makes it out to be.

To take my mind off my issues with Dr. Carver, I ask Cobalt a question. "Why did you pick me to be your assistant yesterday?"

She laughs "You were THE most stressed out person in the room. You were a perfect subject for my demonstration. Everyone could feel the anxiety emanating from your little body. I figured if I made you relax they would know how good I am."

The rest of the participants laugh in agreement. Usually, I would get defensive about everyone laughing at me, but this time I know the team isn't mocking me. I have to remind myself these people are not like Dara and Saundra, my old roommates.

♦♦♦♦♦

We finish breakfast and head to our first class. Dr. Carver is at the front of the room using her whiteboard. She is a bit old school and doesn't care for the computer boards. I can tell the rest of the class is surprised by her out-dated teaching methods.

"Hello class, welcome to advanced calculus. This week I will be assessing your levels, so we don't go too fast or too slow for anyone. In front of you is a test packet. Please open it and begin to fill out the answers, making sure you show your work. The class moans in unison. "All right, I know it's not super fun, but I have to figure out how much you know. Advanced calculus is a six-week class. Then we will switch to science, botany to be exact. Some of the younger participants from the other Omega Team may be joining us after their testing is complete, and I expect you to be good role models. Now no more bellyaching, start the test!"

I chuckle to myself. Dr. Carver is the same odd person she was on the space station. I have to come to terms with the fact she is not deceiving me to be malicious; she is trying to protect me. Dr. Carver merely is one of the pawns in this game like I am. It may take me a while to forgive her, but I have to. She is all I have left.

I finish the test and wait patiently for the next set of instructions. Dr. Carver comes over and grabs my test, and pats me on the arm. I know she feels terrible, but I am not quite ready to forgive her yet. When everyone completes their test, we shuffle to our next class, the history of the universe. Yuck. I hate history. All those dates and facts, no matter how hard I study the information, it never stays in my brain. Beth is at the front of the room with the computer board, at least she is one teacher who is in this century.

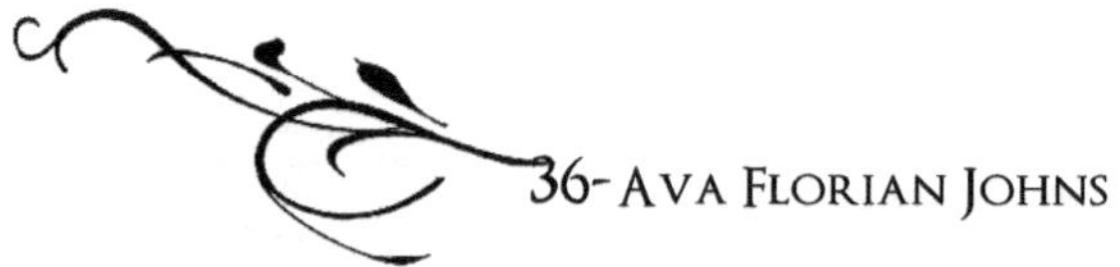

36- Ava Florian Johns

"Hello all, please take a seat. As you know, I am Beth and will be teaching the history of the universe. I know dates and facts aren't fun, so instead, I will bring history to life." Beth pushed a button, and as soon as the word "life" leaves Beth's mouth the room filled with holograms of people from all different times and places in the universe. I can see that the participants are visibly impressed by Beth's teaching method. "We will use the holograms in the classroom, the Omni-theater, and in the holo-rooms on level three of this Annex. You will be able to sign out the holo-rooms at any time during your study hours. I hope you enjoy this class."

"The first thing we are going to talk about is how history affects you. You may have been taught in the past to memorize a bunch of dates, events, places, and people. Then you were told to regurgitate them onto a sheet of paper in some semblance of order. Not in this class—there are no written tests. The most important thing to me is that you understand the people of this universe, by their history, what they have fought for, and continue to fight for to make our lives better. If you know the people of a planet, you then will be able to comprehend your similarities and differences. You will be able to work together to achieve remarkable things! You may ask why we need to study other cultures. Well, some of you will have the opportunity to work with people from other places, in other galaxies around the whole universe. I will tell you more about the work available to you as the course progresses. Now I will start the lesson. This is your class, so please ask me questions at any time."

This class sounds great. I may like history after all.

♦♦♦♦♦

The pace is fast here, and my head is spinning a bit. I am now in Director Jackson's class.

"Hello everyone, I hope your classes have been fascinating up to this point because now we get into the dry stuff. Government. I will try to make it as exciting as I can, but no promises. First, I will make

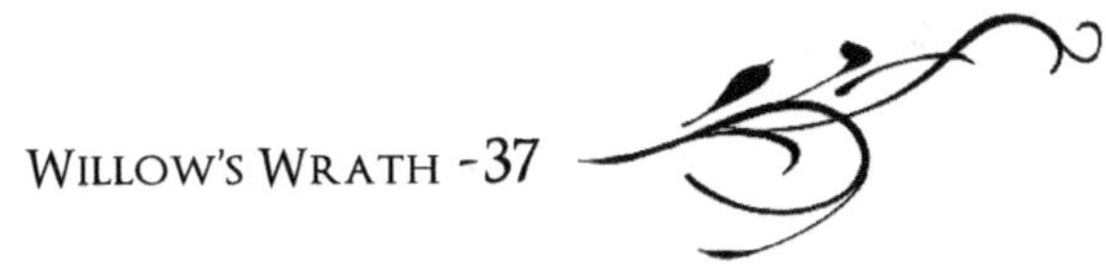

announcements. Please take the tablet with your name on it, and pass the rest to the other participants. Each of you will have an electronic tablet which will keep your schedule. You can take notes on the tablet, and communicate with others in the Annex. Please let me demonstrate."

Just as he said that my tablet buzzed in my hands, I touched the green button, and his face appeared on my screen. Cool. We never had technology like this at the boarding school. We were lucky to have pencils.

"Hey Willow, how are you doing?"

"I am fine, Director Jackson, how are you doing?"

"I am great. And that is all there is to it. All of your names are programmed into each other's tablet. All you have to do is touch the name of the person you want to call. The staff is also on your tablet, so if you need us all you have to do is call. Okay, now for your schedule. Please tap the icon on your tablet which says *schedule*. Is everyone in the right spot?"

I open the schedule, and this list pops up:

Daily Schedule: Willow Martin
7:00 a.m. - wake up
8:00 a.m. - breakfast with The Omega Team
9:00 a.m. - math with Dr. Carver
10:00 a.m. - history with Beth
11:00 a.m. - government with Director Jackson
12:00 p.m. - lunch with the Omega Team
1:00 p.m. - team conditioning - staff
2:00 p.m. - mental fortitude - staff
3:00 p.m. - drills - staff
4:00 p.m. - group meeting with power instructor
5:00 p.m. - breakout with power instructor
6:00 p.m. - dinner with the Omega Team
7:00 p.m. - study and free time
11:00 p.m. - lights out

Director Jackson is right, the government class curriculum is very dry subject matter. He tries to make it fun in his weird way. Director Jackson and Dr. Carver are very similar. I wonder if they knew each other before Dr. Carver started working at the boarding school.

After government class, we all head over to the dining hall. I purposely sit next to Jax. I am intrigued by her and want to see if I can learn to communicate with her. Her back is to me when I approach the table with my food, but she seems to sense me and turns around. She motions for me to sit next to her.

Everyone at the table is talking about the classes so far, how hard they are, how weird Dr. Carver is, and how dorky Director Jackson acts. The teachers are not with us today, so the participants feel okay talking about them. I listen, aware Christopher is staring at me from across the table. He acts anxious when I am around, maybe he is attracted to me.

"So what's up with Dr. Carver? You knew her from the space station, right?" Megan leans in from the opposite side of the table.

"Yes, I knew her from before I came here. She was one of the teachers at the PG School for Girls. I have known her since I was five years old, and she was my botany teacher for several years." I didn't want to tell them the whole sordid story. I hadn't asked Dr. Carver if I could tell anyone about my past. I make a mental note to ask her later.

We realize it is almost one o'clock and we need to head to conditioning, a class to get us physically fit. My build may be slender and petite, but I find I am completely out of shape. We run around the track, lift weights, and throw around a medicine ball. I am the slowest, weakest, and most out of shape person in the room. Maddox, Sophia, Donna, Jax and I throw the ball for a while. It gives us a chance to talk about our lives before the APA scooped us up and brought us to the Annex.

It's great getting to know them better, and for the first time in my life, I feel like I belong.

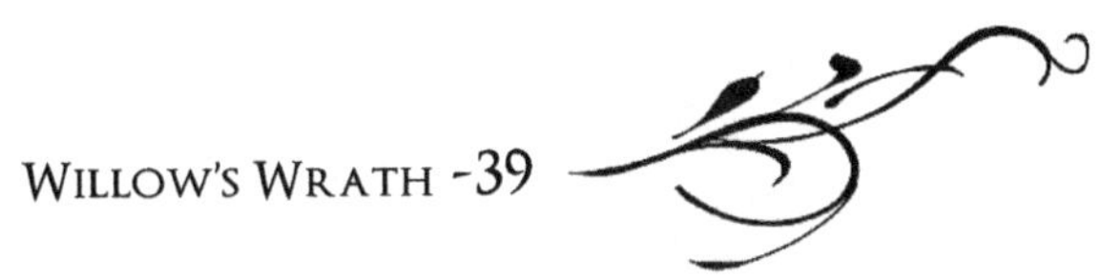

Next, we go to mental fortitude class which is a bunch of mind games, riddles, and puzzles. Then we go to drill which is military-type training. I certainly need to get in better shape if I am going to keep up with the rest of the class. I am dreading the four o'clock meeting with Dr. Carver. I haven't seen her since math class this morning, and I am not in the mood to discuss my situation in front of the others.

♦♦♦♦♦

Cobalt, Dharma, Maddox, and I head toward the power practice to meet up with Dr. Carver. She sent us a message for us to meet her outside for class. I love to be outside, and the quad seems like a perfect place to meet. However, I soon figure out why the four of us are practicing our power outside. We would destroy the building if we were inside.

"In this class, we will talk about your specific power, and research to find out as much about your ability as possible. You will practice, practice, practice, and practice some more. If you need something to help you, you simply ask, and we will get it for you. Do you understand?" We all nod in agreement and get started.

"Willow, you are up first. I want you to take this acorn and grow an oak tree."

"What? I have never done anything that big before."

"Oh, yes you have, you used to grow entire fields of crops. You can do this Willow. I know you can."

I take the tiny acorn from her hand, roll it over and over in my hands trying to get the feel of it. I want to understand where it comes from and connect with it. I set the acorn down on a mound of dirt, cover it gently, making sure I have enough room to for the roots to grow.

"Please stand back and give me some space."

Everyone does as I ask and steps back. I bring my hands together over the mound of dirt with the acorn in it and lift my arms up in a

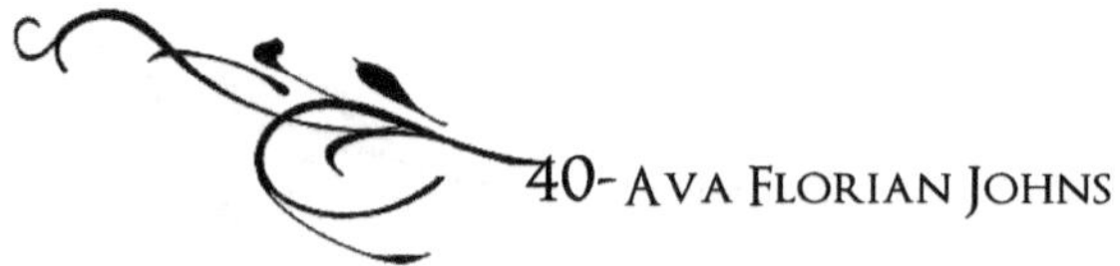

sweeping motion. I do this a few more times and see the acorn sprout. All the while I am communicating with the acorn in my mind, willing it to grow and seeing the finished product in my head. First, it is a little twiggy tree, but then it flourishes into a majestic tree, with strong roots, and fantastic thick green foliage.

Cobalt, Dharma, and Maddox look stunned, Dr. Carver claps and hollers. "I told you, you could do it, Buttercup. You are marvelous!"

I walk over to the others and fall to the ground. I don't know how I ever created full fields of crops when I was five and now one tree completely wipes me out. I sit down on the grass and wait for the next participant to practice their power. Next up is Maddox. I am excited to see what she can do and how far and fast she can fly with her magnificent wings.

"Maddox, please extend your wings when you are ready, and if you are so inclined, I think we would all love to see you fly." Dr. Carver claps her hands together like an excited little girl.

Maddox stands in the center of the yard and generates her wings. She spreads them out to show her full span, spins around for us to see, and flies into the air like a rocket. I have tears in my eyes watching her fly through the perfect, cloudless blue sky. I have never seen or met anyone like her in all my life. Maddox makes one more full circle in the air and lands right in front of us. We erupt with cheers. She smiles and takes a seat next to me.

As Maddox lands, I see my friend Lizzy soaring over the tops of the trees, peering down at me. "Hi, Will-oow! See me flying WOOOO!"

"I see you, Lizzy, you are amazing."

"I know I am Will-oow."

Everyone on the ground laughs at Lizzy's self-confident statement. I wish I were as half as confident as she is in my abilities.

Next up is Dharma. I am so impressed with her changing into a mountain lion yesterday. I can't wait to see what she does today. "Okay Dharma, please shape-shift into whatever you would like. If you take requests, I would love to see a panther."

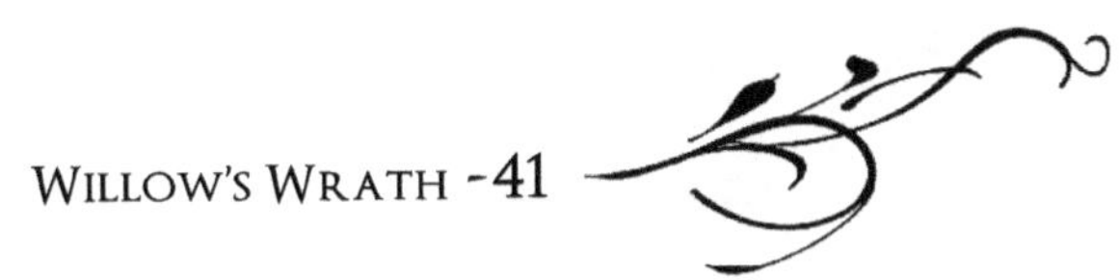

"Okay Dr. Carver, a panther it is." And in an instant, Dharma is a beautiful panther. She is black, sleek, with beautiful golden eyes. "Incredible" is all I can say.

Dr. Carver claps like a little girl. I can tell she enjoys this part of her job here at the Annex with the Omega Team. It makes me wonder how miserable it must have been for her on the space station, teaching those horrible kids at the boarding school. I didn't think about how hard it was for her to give up her entire life to protect me. I am not her biological child, and she certainly doesn't owe me anything. I wonder if I am the reason she never got married and never had any children of her own. Yesterday when she was telling me about my past, all I could think of is how it affected me and how I felt. Never once did I think of what it did to her life. What she gave up for me. For twelve years, she put her life on hold, thinking of only me, and how do I repay her? By giving her the cold shoulder, by not forgiving her immediately, and by being a brat.

I walk over to her and give Dr. Carver a big hug. "I should have thanked you yesterday for protecting me for all these years, for your support, and most of all for your love."

"You are welcome, my dear Buttercup."

"Okay Miss Cobalt, you are up. Show us what you got," Dr. Carver says, backing up to give her space. "Here we go." Cobalt proceeds to suspend Dharma, Dr. Carver, Maddox, and me, plus a couple of huge decorative boulders scattered about the quad, about six feet in the air. "Okay, show-off, you can let us down now, gently please," Maddox screamed from her suspended position.

"Thank you for sharing your powers with me. Now we are going to the computer lab. I want you to pull up every bit of information on your specific powers. You have full access to the APA and PG databases." We all follow Dr. Carver to the computer lab. I wonder what information I will have access to.

Dr. Carver can tell what I'm thinking. "Willow, you have access to everything, including your parents' case files and research notes."

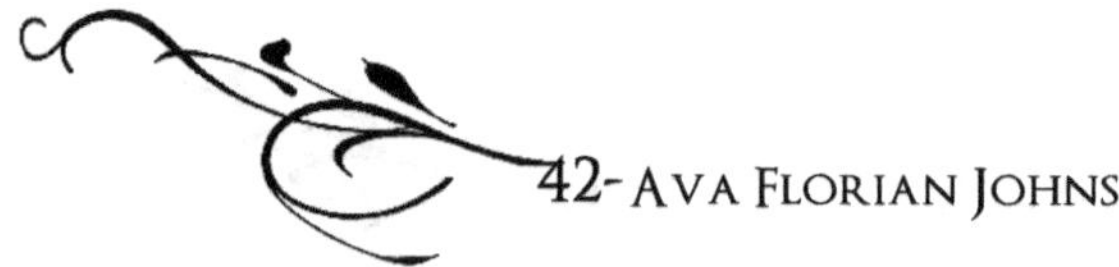

42- Ava Florian Johns

I give Dr. Carver an affirming nod, afraid to open my mouth. I am so excited to find out more about my parents. I have tried searching databases for them several times but was searching for Jeffrey and Marie Martin, instead of our real last name Washburn.

We have about an hour left before we have to get to the dining hall. I start digging into everything I can find on Omnilingualism, Botanical communication, and botanopathy.

♦♦♦♦♦

I go straight to my room after dinner. I want to collect my thoughts, organize my room, and go to bed early. Suddenly, there is a knock on my door. I am surprised to see Dr. Carver holding an old jewelry box. "Hello Dr. Carver, what brings you by so late?"

"Sorry to bother you dear, but I want to give you this, it belonged to your Mother."

I let Dr. Carver in and motion for her to sit on the bed with me. I take the beautiful gold leafed antique jewelry box out of her hands and hold it for a moment. I am hesitant to open the box. "Oh," is all I can get out of my mouth before I start to sob. "It's my hairbrush. The one, my mom, used to brush my hair when I was little." The music box starts to play, and it's the song my mom used to sing to me when she brushed my hair. The song is about the birds in the meadows. In the very bottom of the box are a few crinkled up photographs. One is of mom and me in front of our Christmas tree, and another is a picture of the three of us in the meadow by our farmhouse. I remember the day vividly. I wanted to run through the fields, but they wanted me to sit still for the picture. So they let me blow the tops off the dandelions as a treat for staying still. I hadn't thought about who is taking the picture. "Dr. Carver, were you there that day? Did you take this photo?"

"Yes, I was Buttercup. I was there many times."

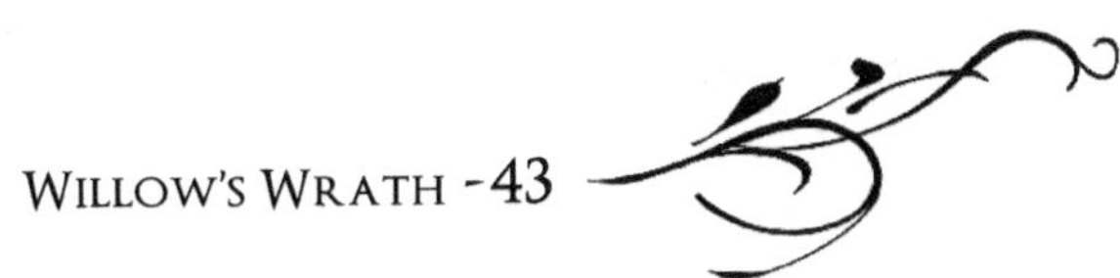

I sit and cry for my dead parents while Dr. Carver holds me. "I miss them too Willow, so much."

♦♦♦♦♦

Over the next two weeks, we start to gain momentum in the program. We go from classes to conditioning, to power training, and never skip a beat. We have all bonded, and I have never felt closer to anyone. Not even my parents. The people at the Annex are my family now. The only person I am still awkward around is Christopher. I hear he tried to bribe Dr. Carver to let him switch to my power training group. Maybe I am paranoid, but I know there is some reason he wants to be near me, and I no longer think he is attracted to me. I believe he is spying on me. Often, I turn around, and he is right behind me, and it happens everywhere. I tell Dr. Carver my concerns, but she just says he passed all the background checks and had the highest security clearance like the rest of us. I know something is up with Christopher, I just can't figure out what it is. If he likes me, he has a funny way of showing it.

♦♦♦♦♦

In class the next day, Beth gives us information about the work assignments which are available to us when we graduate from the program.

- A commissioned rank on the Starship Armargosa
- Special Operations
- APA Annex - Research and Development

The most sought-after position is on the Starship Armargosa. There will be four individuals chosen out of the ten participants for a three-year mission in space. Everyone wants the job on the Starship Armargosa, everyone except for me.

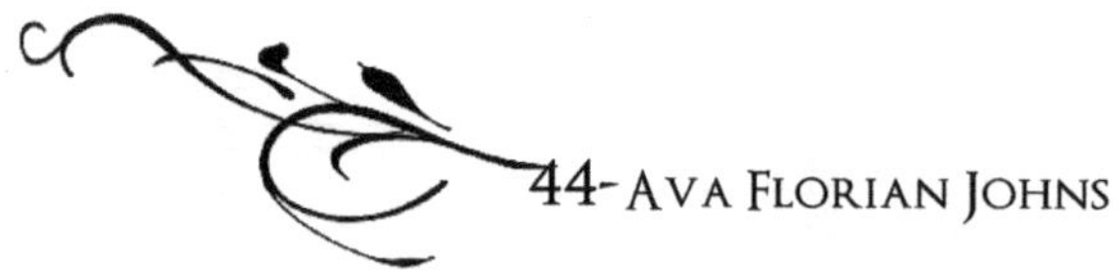

I am hoping to get research and development and stay at the Annex with Dr. Carver and my plants.

The Captain and the Commander of the Starship Armargosa are showing up today to see who qualified for the super-secret mission. I have little interest in their visit until I see the Commander. He is the most handsome man I have ever seen. All the girls at lunch are asking if I saw him. They are gorgeous, so I have been told about a thousand times. It is all anyone can talk about at lunch.

Donna explains that the Captain is Captain Chris Holloway. He is over six feet tall with light brown hair and blue eyes, and a good share of boy-next-door good looks. He is only twenty-four years old, the youngest captain in the fleet. The Commander is Commander Dalton James Alexander. He is six foot two with dark hair, and dark eyes, very mysterious. He is the youngest commander in the fleet. Rumor has it they both came from the same PG boot camp on Casson.

"I think the Commander is yummier than the Captain, you know, in a bad boy way." Donna stretches out the words baaa-aad boy and winks at me.

"Oh, I will take either one of them, they are both H-O-T, hot," Maddox says, fanning herself.

"Willow, have you ever had a boyfriend?" Megan asks, joining the conversation.

Everyone turns to stare at me, even Christopher and Todd, who had so far stayed out of the conversation.

"Yes, I did, for a short time on the space station. Stephen was one of the visitors who came in on a freighter. He ended up being a thief and was banned from the station. I never saw him again."

"That's so sad, Willow." Sophia looks genuinely sad for me.

The conversation then turns to who we think will be picked for the operation aboard the Starship Armargosa. No one knows, and all we know at this point is that it is a three-year mission to find a suitable planet for colonization. When we come across people of other worlds, we are to engage them diplomatically. The APA is looking for new allies as well as a new planet. They want to establish a base for the APA in a different world, so we will be stronger for the time when the Alliance will rule again.

♦♦♦♦♦

I go about my day, working with Dr. Carver in the botany lab. I am trying to perfect my growing of edible food. I have mastered plants and flowers, but am having trouble with some of the vegetables. They are not looking like they're supposed to look. I need to focus. Instead, all I can think about is the Commander.

DALTON

Walking around the Annex is a bit unnerving. First, the colors of the hallways and floors are giving me a headache. Hasn't anyone heard of neutral colored paint? Not this blue, green, yellow, orange, rainbow shit. Those colors belong outside. How is anyone expected to concentrate on anything serious? I can't even think. I rub my temples as I walk down the long corridor and into the conference room. Second, why is everyone so happy all the time? Don't they ever have a bad day here? I have only been here once before, but it's the same experience. I swear they pump hallucinogens through the air ducts. If one more person welcomes me to the Annex, I will scream. And finally, I am not entirely convinced we should be going on this mission in the first place. I can't believe we have to watch these science experiment freaks and find some who are suitable for a military assignment – no way. If I were the Captain instead of the Commander, I would tell them all to go to hell.

I informed Captain Holloway several times we do not need civilians on a military operation. I am not paid to babysit, but Captain Holloway insists this is not a military mission. Apparently, we are supposed to be an undertaking of peace to find a suitable planet for colonization, separate from the rule of the PG. The PG has eyes and ears everywhere. I don't think we are going to get very far without a military battle. If they find us, they will kill us. There is no way to make it sound better than it is. I am fine working with

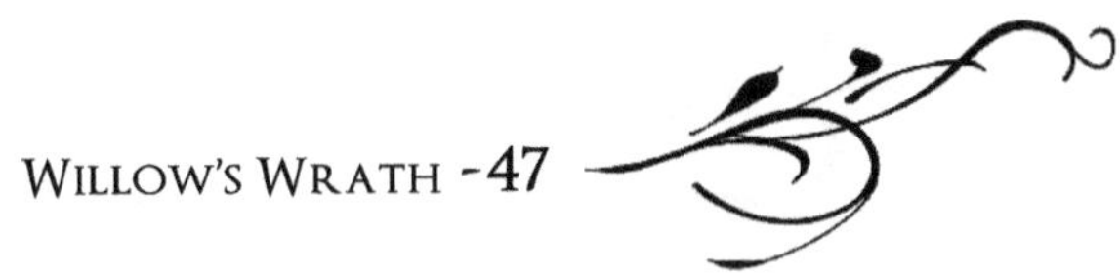

and reporting to Captain Holloway, we have known each other since Junior Bootcamp on our home planet of Casson. Captain Chris Holloway recommended me to be a commissioned officer with the APA, and now I am his second in command of the Starship Armargosa.

"I will make this debriefing as quick as possible. Commander Dalton Alexander, you remember Director Scott Jackson, Executor of the Annex."

"Yes, nice to see you again Director."

"Commander." Director Jackson gives a polite wave. "Welcome to the Alien Planetary Alliance Annex."

I have to bite the inside of my lip to keep from screaming.

"Director Jackson, please fill Commander Alexander in on what powers your participants have and how you have trained them for our particular objective. Once we go through the profile of each of the ten members of the Omega Team, we will then observe them for the next few weeks and consider their value for our mission. Director, please start when you are ready."

"First of all, there are twenty participants in total, ten of whom are under seventeen years old. We have decided to keep the younger group for another term so they won't be ready for five more months. The first Omega Team will be ready in two months. The members are very talented individuals indeed." I highly doubt it, but decide to keep a somewhat open mind.

Director Jackson fumbles with the projector, then brings up the first profile. The girl looks about twelve years old. There is no way she is going on the mission with us.

"This is Sophia. She is eighteen years old and from planet Earth. She is five feet tall and weighs a mere 100 pounds, but don't let her small stature fool you. Her special power is she has super physical strength. Here is a short video demonstration."

I watch with disbelief as this little red-haired girl picks up a bus with one hand and a jeep with the other, it must be a video trick.

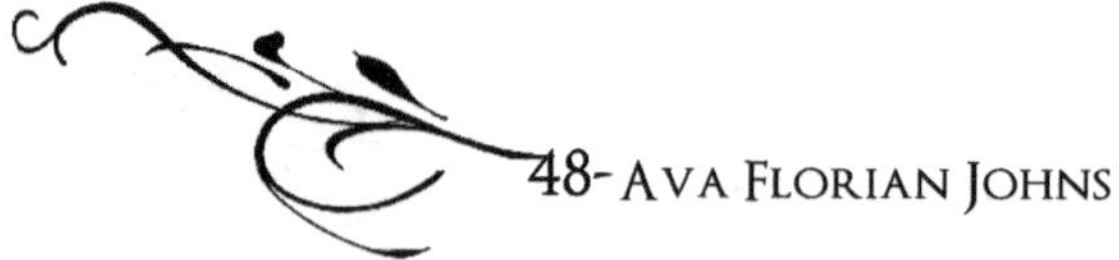

"I assure you it is no trick." Director Jackson says as he pulls up the next profile.

I swear I didn't say it out loud, although I do think it is a trick.

"Next up is Maddox. She is from the planet Muscari and is over six feet tall. She can manifest wings and fly." Director Jackson showed a video of a young woman generating wings and flying through the air. She made one big loop and landed gracefully. I am having a hard time believing this. I guess I will be witnessing it firsthand for the next few weeks. I dread staying here any longer than I have to, but if some of these people are going to be on our ship, I need to know what they can do.

"The next person I will show you is Donna, she is proficient in mind transportation and what that means is she can transport you into any setting she wishes. She can transport people with her mind and make them see something which is not there. It is, of course, difficult to show this on video, so you will need to see her in person. She is quite remarkable. Donna is from Eryngium and is twenty years old."

Again, I'm having a tough time believing most of the stuff but I will get to see it myself in the coming weeks, and hopefully, they are as astounding as Director Jackson thinks they are.

Director Jackson proceeds to fumble with the equipment one more time. This guy is annoying and acts completely inept. You would think he would have the skill to run a simple projector considering he is the director of a massive facility. Director Jackson finally got the slide to work, and my breath catches in my throat. Staring at me from the screen is the most stunning woman I have ever seen. She has platinum blonde hair and large piercing blue eyes. It is weird, but I feel like her eyes are looking deep within me.

"This is Willow Marie Martin, and she is from Earth. I find her to be one of the most interesting participants on the Omega Team. She has a unique special power, Botanopathy, which means she can communicate with plants and make them grow. We hope with continued training she will be able to control other things like the

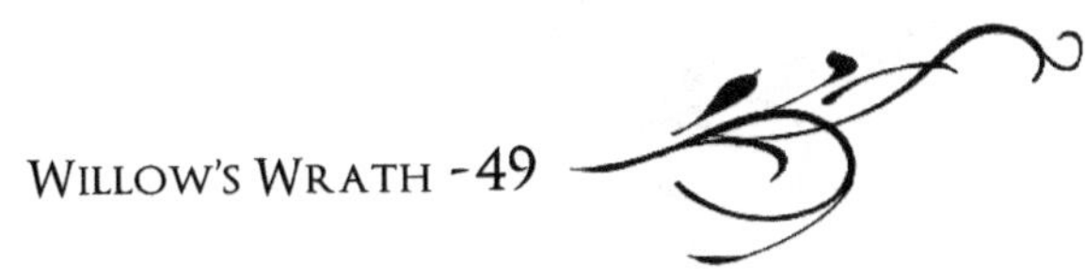

weather and planetary conditions. Her parents were both scientists with the APA, but they were killed in 2070. Willow witnessed the event and has never forgiven herself for not being able to save them. She was only five years old."

Jackson pauses and looks very sad. I wonder if he knew Willow's parents.

"As I said, Willow can communicate with plants to make them grow. She is capable of creating crops of corn, grain, and potatoes. She created an oak tree in our quad from a tiny acorn. She is one of the most talented participants I have ever seen, and I think she would be perfect for your mission."

I haven't even met her yet, and I know she will be trouble for me.

Director Jackson finally got Willow's video to work. The footage shows Willow with her arms outstretched over a small mound of dirt where she had placed a tiny acorn. As Willow gestures with her arms in a broad sweeping motion, s a beautiful full-grown oak tree emerges standing over twenty-five feet tall. Willow looks delicate and angelic, but I can tell that she has an incredible strength which I have not seen in many people I have known.

Director Jackson continues with the next person. However, my thoughts remain on Willow. I am hoping she won't be as amazing as I think she is. Director Jackson breaks into my thoughts, and says "She is amazing." I swear this guy can read my mind.

"The next person is Jacqueline Myers. Jax is unique indeed. She was born a mute, but she can connect with others telepathically. The one person Jax has made a connection with is Willow. They can communicate non-verbally. We think it is because of Willow's ability to contact plants telepathically, and she can talk this way with Jax, as well."

"How does Jax communicate with people who are not telepathic?" Captain Holloway asks. I am wondering the same thing myself.

"Jax can use sign language and her electronic tablet to communicate with others. I will show you the video of her first

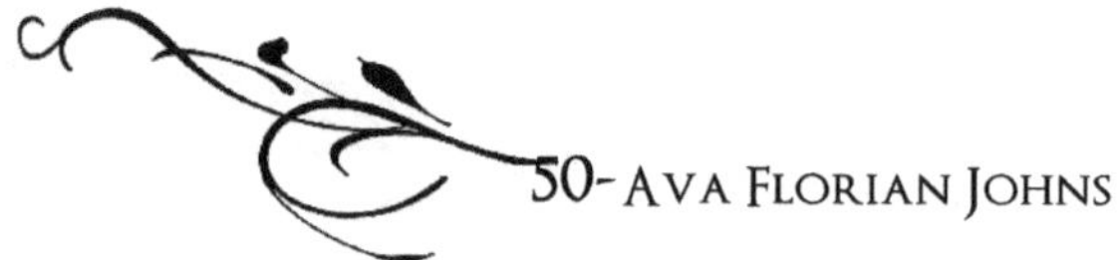

demonstration with our staff member Ashley. Jax is another participant who you need to see in person to get the full effect. I would recommend if you take Willow on the assignment, you could take Jax as well. She would be an asset to you, meeting people from different planets. Once properly trained she will be able to read minds which could come in very handy."

"Next up is Cobalt. Her real name is Caroline Wagner. She's eighteen years old, and she specializes in telekinesis. Telekinesis is the ability to manipulate and control objects with the mind. She is most recently from the third planet in the Zea Mays System."

"With four members left to go, next up is Dharma. She is a shape-shifter. We have no idea where she's from or how old she is. There is no known record of her at all anywhere. Dharma can shape-shift or transform from a human being into an animal, or another person. I've seen her turn into a mountain lion, a black panther, a man, a child, a baby, and even a penguin. She is another Omega Team participant who would be very useful on your Starship."

I am getting antsy for Director Jackson to finish his presentation.

Next is Todd Anderson from the planet Earth. He can scale walls, due to the fact he is part reptilian. But, he looks humanoid. Here's a video of him climbing the wall, hanging from the ceiling, and scaling back down again.

Even I have to admit the last one is quite cool. What I wouldn't have given to be able to climb walls when I was younger.

"All right, next up Christopher James. He is a poison generator, which means he can generate, create, emit, or otherwise produce a poisonous substance and inflict pain or death on his victim."

Director Jackson is saying less and less about the participants as the time goes on. Either he is getting tired of speaking, or he has already talked about the ones he wants us to pick, or he is reading my thoughts and knows I am no longer paying attention.

"The last participant on the Omega Team is Megan Sansone. She was born on Planet Hugo 521, the mining colony, and her power is invisibility. Here is a video of her demonstration and her practice sessions with her teacher."

Again, I find her power to be very surprising. What I wouldn't have given to be invisible when my father was angry. He hated that my mother encouraged me to be something other than a killing machine and she ended up dying fighting for me. She wanted me to be more than a soldier for the PG. My mom wanted me to create and build something with my hands, so she taught me to construct birdhouses and small wooden structures when I was young. She encouraged creativity, and soon I was building bigger and bigger houses. My father found out and killed her in front of me, not only to get rid of her but to teach me a lesson. He went to prison for a short time, but he was let out because of what she was showing me. It is against our ways on Casson to do anything other than to fight for the PG.

I went on to enlist in the military air force which included training for space flight. I was top of my class until one day....

My thoughts shattered when Captain Holloway stands up. Director Jackson is already out the door. What did I miss?

"Jackson is going to give us the full tour of the Annex."

"Then what? What's the plan?"

"Tomorrow we will watch the candidates demonstrate their special powers. After the demonstrations, we will interview each of them over the next three days. By the end of the week, I want our list cut from ten to six candidates."

"Why are we moving so fast? Don't they have two more months of training?"

As we walk down the corridor, the Captain explains, "Director Jackson thinks there may be a security threat. We may need to move fast." He whispers this last part. "The Director is not sure who to trust here. He knows there has been information leaked to the PG. Let's talk about it in a more secure location."

Well, this day is getting more interesting by the moment.

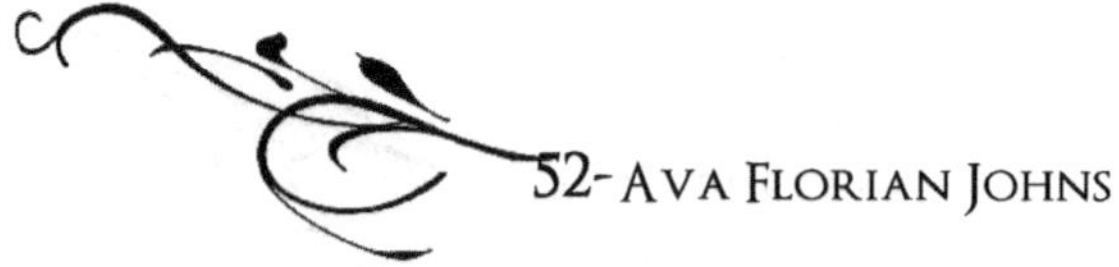

♦♦♦♦♦

Director Jackson gave us the tour of the Annex. I had seen most of it when I was here before. I wonder why the PG didn't blow it up from the sky. I found out today there is a very sophisticated cloaking device which lets the Annex remain unseen from an aerial view. Which would make sense why it is so "cloak and dagger" to get into the facility. Nobody knows where they're going and where they end up.

Today, we are watching the participants demonstrate their unique abilities. We discussed their skills on the slides with Director Jackson, but nothing prepared me for viewing them in person. They are something else. I am still apprehensive about taking civilians with us on the Starship Armargosa. Captain Holloway has given me this assignment, this incredible opportunity to be a commander, his second in command, and I don't want to let him down. I am responsible for every person on the ship. I need to make sure they understand what can happen when we are in battle, and I am confident there will be a battle.

♦♦♦♦♦

We have been at the APA Annex for three days now, and I have seen everyone demonstrate their power multiple times. I have watched their power practices, I have seen what they can do and talked to their instructors about what they can't do yet, but are expected to do by the end of their training. I have a recommendation for the top six out of ten for Captain Holloway, and Willow is not one of them. I don't think she has the stamina, the strength, or the personality to be aboard a Starship for three years. I also found out Willow requested to remain on the planet stationed at the Annex. She would rather garden than go on a mission, and she told us she hates space. She is not what I would consider a prime candidate for one who operates in outer space.

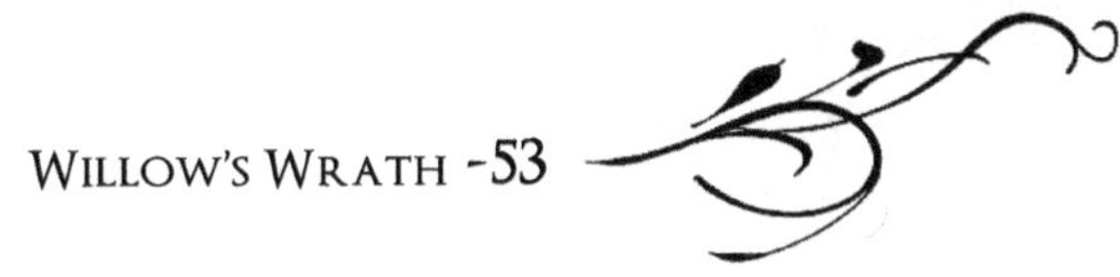

I also can't help but wonder if my decision is based on the fact when I'm around her I am extremely agitated, even for me. I'm very irritated and angered by these feelings. I've never had this response to anyone before, and I wonder what her power is over me. She is everything I am not. She is light, innocence, promise, and I am dark, brooding, and cynical.

I have to say I'm not very nice to her. I'm hoping my horrible disposition will scare her away. She looks at me as if she sees through me which is frightening for someone like me. I've done awful things in my lifetime, and I don't want to bring that into her life. I know she would be a great asset for the mission, but I can't imagine the next three years on the ship with her.

Well, today is the day Captain Holloway wants to talk about who we are choosing for the three-year mission. The six people I've narrowed it down to are Jax, Cobalt, Megan, Sophia, Maddox, and Donna. The Captain and I are going to meet first without Director Jackson, and then we'll pull him in for the remainder of the meeting. I think our top priority is to make sure the candidates we choose are combat-ready. We also need to discuss with Director Jackson what the threat is and what the validity of the danger is. The Captain and I have been here for a few days now, and have not seen anything out of the ordinary as far as security matters are concerned.

"Okay Commander Alexander, are you ready to discuss the candidates?"

"Yes, Captain."

"Should we adjourn to a conference room?"

"I hope this is a good idea, having any participants of the Omega Team on our assignment."

"Why do you not think it's a good idea? Let's hear your concerns one more time before we pick the candidates."

"I think it's tremendously dangerous for civilians to go into space. They are not soldiers."

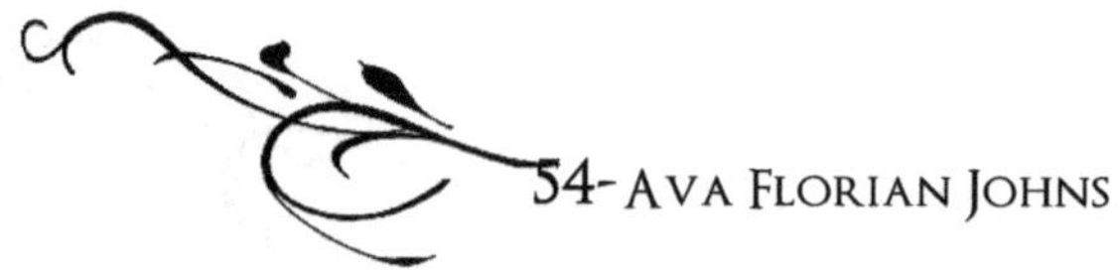

"You forget this is not a military mission—this is an undertaking of peace. We are to scout out suitable planets for colonization."

"Don't you think once the PG finds out what we're doing, they will come after us?"

"I believe that it is a risk, but I believe it's a risk we have to take."

"All I'm saying is the candidates need to train in military maneuvers and basic training. Right now, they have nothing but their superpowers. And how is Willow supposed to defend herself when all she can do is grow plants. I feel responsible for the candidates, and that will put me in a dangerous and potentially vulnerable position."

"Dalton, are we talking about the candidates or are we talking about Willow?"

"Why do you say it that way Captain?"

"Because I've seen the way you look at her Dalton, you can't deny you're attracted to her."

"That is not entirely true Captain. I promise you I will not let this interfere with our assignment. Whoever we choose to be the candidates for the three-year mission, I promise I will treat them as professionally as possible. It will be a strictly working relationship with all of them."

"Dalton, I am not judging you, I am asking you if your hesitation to bring anyone aboard is your attraction to Willow."

"Captain, personally I wouldn't pick Willow for this assignment, regardless of my feelings for her. She is not one of the people on my list. Yes, I can see how planting crops would be ideal for coloni-zation, but I don't think we're there yet. She should go in the second wave of ships when we have already found a suitable planet."

I write the names down as my choices for the six candidates for the operation, and I pass the sheet to Captain Holloway. He makes a face like he smells something bad, so I know he doesn't agree with my choices and I know why.

"Thank you for your list, Commander Alexander. We will now bring in Director Jackson and see what he thinks."

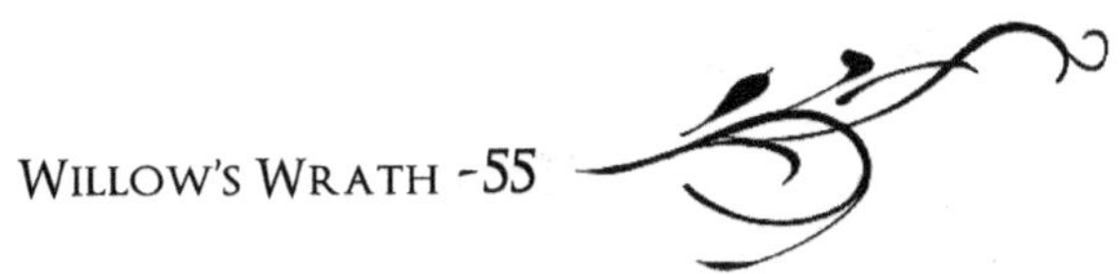

"Captain Holloway, may I see the people you've chosen?"

"Why don't we wait until Director Jackson gets here, then we will discuss it and come up with our top six together? I want you to know I do understand your concerns. I promise we will start training them for the mission as soon as we narrow our list to six candidates. I want the list by the end of this meeting today. We have to be ready to leave within two weeks."

"But Captain Holloway, they haven't finished their training yet. How are we supposed to help them with their powers when they are on the Starship?"

"The ship has holo-rooms, so we will be able to simulate practice conditions. Most of the candidates are in good shape to go, so there isn't much more they need to train. I think most of what they need is more power practice. They've had a month of conditioning, and we should be able to get them up to speed by the time we need to leave."

"Captain, can I ask why we are planning on leaving so soon and exactly what the threat is?"

"We will discuss the threat with Director Jackson."

The Captain pushes a button on the control panel and announces over the loudspeaker. "Director Jackson to the conference room."

I sit and silently stew. I know what is about to happen. Willow is going to get picked for this assignment. She does fit what we need for the future, but I don't want her anywhere near this operation. I feel so protective regarding her, more than I have felt toward any other person, other than my mom. I hope this feeling goes away and soon.

I remember the first time I saw Willow. I walked past the lab, and she was growing her flowers. She was working with Dr. Carver, and Dr. Carver seemed amusingly irritated. Willow couldn't seem to focus on the task at hand. She started growing her plants, and they took over, knocked over their pots and made a big dirt mess everywhere. I would have liked to say Willow got flustered because she saw me, but I don't think that was the case. I had slipped by the

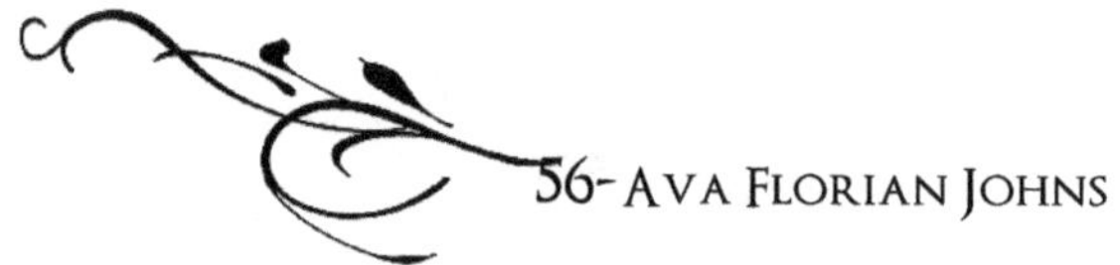

window before she saw me watching her. The one thing I remember thinking about the encounter is the photo of her didn't do her eyes justice. They are beautiful.

It is unlike me to obsess about a woman, and, to me, Willow seems like such a girl, instead of a woman. The differences between the two of us are staggering. She is happy; I am not. She is light, and I am dark. Nonetheless, she pulls me in as no one has ever done before.

So I guessed it right. The six candidates selected are Cobalt, Dharma, Christopher, Jax, Sophia, and of course no surprise, Willow.

After the selection meeting with the Director and the Captain, I walk around the Annex alone. I need to clear my head. I sit in the quad for a while when I notice Willow in the distance. She is concocting one of her plants in the yard. I watch her as she raises the seedling out of the ground, gesturing wildly with her hands toward the sky. When she stops, there is a ten-foot-tall sunflower. She is amazingly talented, and even I have to agree grudgingly.

I walk over to her. She still doesn't see me, and as she is raising her hands upward, she hits me square in the jaw.

"Wow, what a great hit, Willow. Didn't know you had it in you."

"I am so sorry Commander Alexander, I didn't see you. Are you okay?"

Well, at least I know she can protect herself if she needs to. She has a great right cross.

"Is there something I can do for you?" She asks tentatively.

"No, I thought I'd come over and see what you were doing. I see you are making sunflowers."

"I'm practicing my crops. I want to make a crop of sunflowers. I haven't gotten the balance quite right yet. The plants do well for a while, but then some of them die."

"I want to let you know you are one of the top six chosen to go on the three-year assignment with us. I have to ask, is this something you want to do?"

I look at her curiously to see her expression. I can tell I make her nervous, and she starts to stammer.

"I want to. I mean, I know I would be able to help. But do you not think I'm qualified?"

"It's not that. I can't imagine you would care for a military mission."

She is standing so close I can see specks of silver in her indigo eyes.

"I didn't think the mission is expected to be military. Captain Holloway indicated it's more a peaceful mission of exploration."

"Well, that is what they're saying, but once the PG finds out what we're doing, I don't think it will be very peaceful. I want to make sure you're okay with it."

"I will be okay, I promise. I'll tell you if I'm not."

I back up a step, Willow's proximity is making me jumpy.

"I also thought you put in a request to stay here with Dr. Carver and continue your research and power practice."

"I did at first, but now I'm excited about the prospect of colonization. You could use my ability on a mission like this. I am tired of playing it safe—I want to live my life... finally."

I stare at her for a moment. Not sure what to say, I curtly blurt out, "Okay. I get it Willow. Combat training starts tomorrow."

"Aren't we already doing conditioning, skills, and mental fortitude for the mission?"

"That's nothing compared to what you will be doing. I need to make sure you are ready for a potential combat situation. Truthfully, I don't think you belong on this mission, and I think you should reconsider, so you don't hurt yourself or someone else."

I turn and walk away so I can't see the hurt look on her face.

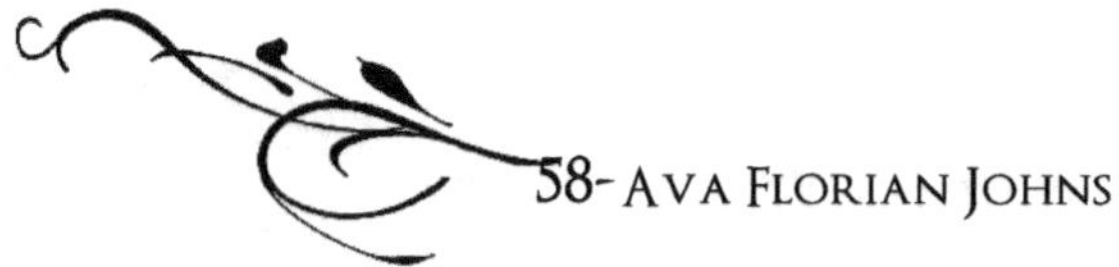

CHAPTER
THREE

WILLOW

What an ass! I can't believe he said that to me. I have just as much right to be on the mission as anyone else. I wish I would have knocked him out when I hit him in the face.

I can feel the bile in my throat threatening to come out my mouth. The anger is welling up inside me, and the sunflower in front of me has doubled in size.

The sunflower swiveled and ate the commander in one gulp, spitting his shoe out on the ground in front of me.

I turn around suddenly because I feel someone watching me. Christopher is directly behind me. He is everywhere.

"What's up, Willow?"

"What do you need Christopher?" I am so not in the mood for him.

"I saw Commander Alexander talking to you. What were you discussing?"

I know it is none of his business, but I decide to answer him anyway. He will find out soon enough.

"We were talking about the combat training taking place tomorrow."

"Yes, I heard you were one of the six chosen for the Starship Armargosa Mission. Willow, do you think you're up for it? You don't seem like starship material."

He is the second person today who has questioned my readiness for this mission. Frankly, I am getting a little tired of it.

"Christopher, I am perfectly capable of handling this mission. I work harder than anyone in conditioning and skills training. I have improved more than anyone here, and I deserve a chance."

"I hope you're right. Well, good luck." He gave me a half-hearted wave and sauntered away.

After my less than stellar conversations with both Dalton and Christopher, I decide to treat myself and sit in the arboretum for a while. I walk through the plants and flowers, feeling at home, and wonder how I am going to leave them for three years. I probably shouldn't pack my bags yet. I am only one of the six, not one of the final four.

However it turns out, Starship Armargosa Mission or not, I am grateful for this opportunity to be part of the Omega Team. I have such an overwhelming sense of belonging here, and I have never felt like this before. The Omega Team is my family. I love them all, even Christopher. Nevertheless, I have to move on. I have to experience what life has to offer. I told Headmistress Yvonne I believe I can be more than this, so I will.

♦♦♦♦♦

"Escaping to the arboretum again, Willow?" Dr. Carver says as she walks through the sliding doors.

"How can you tell I'm hiding out?"

"Because I know you Willow, better than you know yourself, I think. What's wrong?"

"Nothing's wrong. I got picked as one of the top six candidates for Starship Armargosa Mission."

"Well okay, but I thought you were going to stay here at Annex to work on your power. I thought you wanted to continue your parents' work on research and development?" Dr. Carver got a weird look on

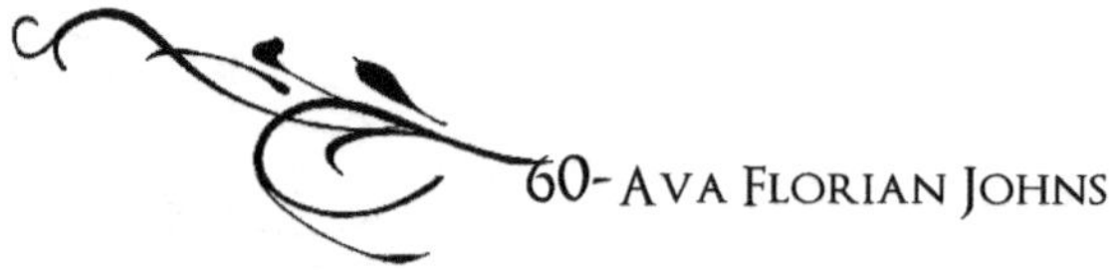

her face and continued. "I didn't realize you would run off at the first opportunity and frankly, the mission doesn't suit you."

"Seriously, not you too, Dr. Carver? I'm tired of people thinking I can't do this. I want to start living my life. I want to take risks, and more importantly, I want to do something that means something. I want my life to matter. Of course, I want to continue what my parents wanted for the project, but I can still do that on the Starship Armargosa Mission. Even more so, because I will be helping real people."

Dr. Carver looked hurt. "Willow, it's not that I don't think you can't do it, I think you can, but I think your talents will go to waste on a Starship. I believe you need to stay here and practice your skills. Plus, I would miss you terribly if you go."

Well, there's a guilt trip for you.

"Dr. Carver please don't make me feel guilty. I want to do this. No one thinks I can, not you, not Christopher, not Commander Alexander, nobody thinks I can do this, but I DO. I believe this is the right thing for me. I'm going to start combat training tomorrow, and I know I will be picked for this mission. If I don't get selected for the assignment, I will stay and hone my skills, but until we find out, I am going to try my hardest."

"Okay Willow, but I think you're wasting your time."

"Dr. Carver, I need you to understand no matter what happens, I appreciate what you've done for me, but I have to live my own life. I can't keep doing what everybody expects me to do. Lastly, I feel like I can do something incredible with my life and I feel like everyone's trying to stop me."

I am so angry with Dr. Carver for not being supportive of my decision. I know why she wants me to stay at the Annex. Nonetheless, this is what I want to do. I don't want to play it safe anymore. I want to be able to take risks and live my life. I'm not the shy quiet person from the boarding school who never spoke up because she was afraid of what Dara or Saundra thought.

I left Dr. Carver in the arboretum and went to the next place I feel safest, which is the lab.

I keep working on the shapes of my fruits and vegetables. Although some of them are kind of funny looking, I am getting better. I look up and see Director Jackson walking toward me.

"Director Jackson, what can I do for you?

"I was looking for you, Willow."

"Is something wrong?"

"No, no, nothing's wrong. I want to make sure you're okay with the combat training for tomorrow."

"Yes sir, I'm fine. I am very excited to find out I am one of the final six. Although, I am a little upset about everyone's reaction to my getting picked. Commander Alexander, Christopher, and even Dr. Carver are questioning my ability to serve on the Starship Mission."

"The important thing is what you think, Willow. And for what it is worth I believe they are wrong. You are ready."

"Thank you, Director. I want to do this, to go on the mission. I think it will be a challenge, but I also believe it will be an adventure. If I don't try my hardest, I will regret it for the rest of my life."

"Just out of curiosity, what did Christopher say to you?"

"Well as you probably know I have reported his weird behavior to Dr. Carver. I feel like he is stalking me. Every time I turn around, there he is. In the computer lab, in the science lab, out in the quad, everywhere. Today, Christopher saw me speaking with Commander Alexander and was very negative. He doesn't think I have it in me to complete the combat training."

"Do you think he likes you? Boys do act weird when they like a girl."

"I did at first, but he is not very kind to me. It seems more like he is spying on me. He's always asking me a million questions and wants to know what I am working on all the time. I reported it to Dr. Carver several times, but she doesn't see an issue. She said he has the highest security clearance and his background checks were excellent."

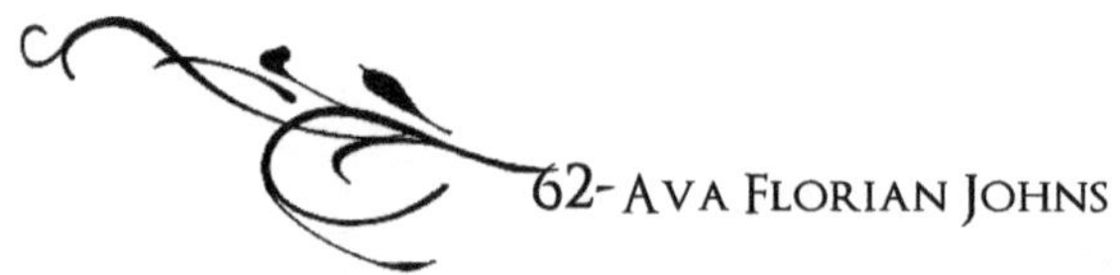

"That's very interesting Willow, I will check into that for you."

"Have you noticed anything else strange?"

"No, but I am surprised Dr. Carver was not very supportive when I told her about being in the top six for the starship mission. I thought she would be excited for me or at least proud of me for getting this far. She wants me to stay here with her and continue the research my parents didn't get to finish."

"Interesting," was all the Director said.

♦♦♦♦♦

We worked in combat training for the next week. I am sore, but I think I am doing pretty well. Christopher is a pain in the butt, and he put me down at every turn. I refuse to let him get to me. Other people are impressed with the work I am doing in combat training. I am surprised, but even Commander Alexander seems impressed with me. I have never worked so hard for anything in my life. Dr. Carver is still upset with me. She told me several times not to try for one of the four spots on the mission because I am wasting my time. Dr. Carver says that it is what is best for me, but I believe she's only thinking of herself. I know she's raised me since I was five but she should be okay with this, considering it's what I want more than anything.

She thinks part of it has to do with my infatuation with Commander Alexander. That is not the case. I mean obviously he is gorgeous, and of course hot, but he is also an ass. And I know he doesn't want me along on the mission. Commander Alexander is not what is driving my need to be chosen. I want to prove everyone wrong. I want people to know I'm more than what they think I am. Especially Dr. Carver.

The schedule is rigorous. Each day I have breakfast, lunch, and dinner with my team, and I go to my classes. I do all my conditioning, skills, mental fortitude training, power practice, and combat training. By the end of the day, I am thoroughly exhausted.

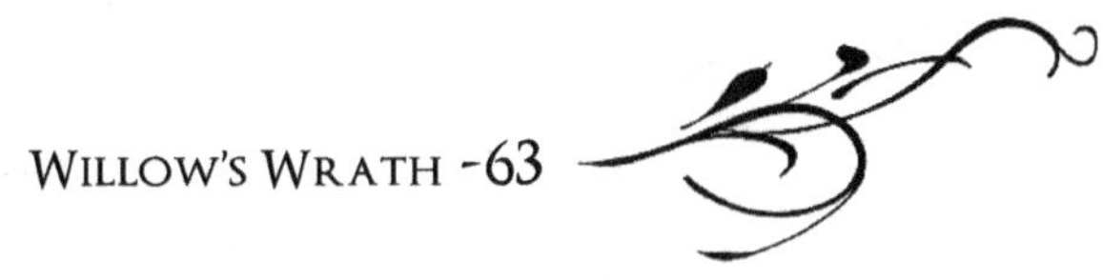

Combat training is the hardest for me. It consists of us learning how to shoot and fight hand-to-hand. The gun doesn't bother me as much as I thought it would. But the hand-to-hand combat is challenging.

Today, Commander Alexander asks us to take the class outside. It's a little late at night, but we can still see. He thinks it would be beneficial to practice the hand-to-hand combat in the quad.

"Come on Willow, let's go!" Commander Alexander barked. "What's the holdup, Martin?" He calls me by my last name when he is upset or irritated with me, which is all the time. I swear this guy is never happy.

"Coming, Commander Alexander."

"All right, Willow and Christopher you are up first. Hand to hand combat, start now."

Seriously? He is going to make me fight Christopher. Christopher's twice as big as I am and he doesn't like me at all, so I know he won't take it easy on me.

Christopher immediately lunges then stops right in front of me and tackles me to the ground—brutally.

"See Willow; it'd be better if you stayed here. You won't be able to handle it on the starship mission. You should stay here and tend to your little garden." I can feel the pain moving through my body, my legs and arms are heavy, they surely will be sore and bruised tomorrow.

I am getting angry. I can feel the rage welling up inside me. The trees behind me lean forward, their branches multiply and reach out toward Christopher and grab him. The vines around the trees stretch out to latch onto Christopher's legs, and arms and they powerfully pull him from me. I can't believe what I am seeing and neither can the rest of the class. Christopher starts screaming.

I am in a fog, and I'm not sure what to do to help. In fact, I'm not sure that I want to help – Christopher deserves it for the way he's been treating me. My anger has not yet receded, and I can feel the

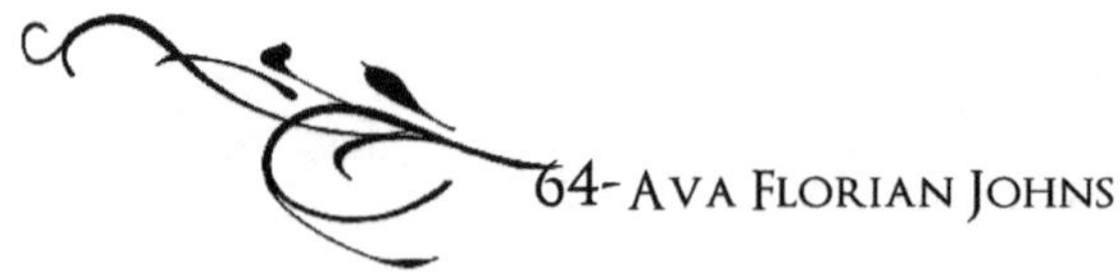

vomit rise in my throat. Christopher is still screaming bloody murder. I think he is more scared than hurt, as he is hanging from the branches of the trees as the vines and branches wrap around his legs, arms, and torso.

In my mind, I see him ripped limb from limb by the branches. The vines are wrapping around his neck and draining the life from his body.

"Willow, please stop what you're doing. Let Christopher down," Commander Alexander says, but with an amused smile on his face.

I breathe deeply trying to calm myself and communicate telepathically to the trees to let Christopher down. I neglect to say gently, and they drop him from about six feet in the air. He lands on the ground with a thud. I sense I am in trouble.

Out of the corner of my eye, I can see Commander Alexander and Captain Holloway grin at each other. Maybe I won't be in trouble after all.

"This round goes to Willow," Commander Alexander announces.

Christopher explodes, "You bitch. It isn't fair. That isn't hand-to-hand combat; she had help. If I spit poison at her will, I win?"

"Christopher, that's enough," Captain Holloway said. "You are dismissed - all of you," he points his finger at Christopher. "We will pick this up again tomorrow."

CHAPTER
FOUR
DALTON

I am so proud of Willow. I watch her walk to her room. I am about to go after her to make sure she is okay when Director Jackson steps up to the Captain and me. He looks worried and is apparently upset. He needs us to come to a secure room as soon as possible.

We go into one of the smaller conference rooms, where he tells us he intercepted a signal piggybacked on a data feed. It is a message to a high ranking Director in the PG.

"Commander Alexander, Captain Holloway, I've some alarming news. I now know the information leak is from Christopher James to his father in the PG. I apologize because we did not connect the fact they are related. We missed it in our vetting process. They have different last names and no known contact. Christopher James is the PG Director Amundson's son. I believe Christopher is a plant here to gather data on the mission. Your mission. I think he's trying to sabotage Willow to make sure he's one of the four chosen. We need him removed from this facility immediately!"

The Captain and I locate Christopher James swiftly and remove him from the facility. He is in a holding cell at another APA base, where he is to await trial. Christopher denies the whole time he had any involvement in a plot against Willow or leaking information to the PG. Unfortunately, he isn't the only one suspected of doing

something wrong. Director Jackson knows there is another hole in the organization. He can't prove it yet, but he is getting close.

Director Jackson explains to us he is aware that Willow is in danger. He didn't realize how much or why. That's why he kept pushing us to pick her for the three-year mission on the starship so that she would be away from the threat. However, it looks like it's going to come to a head tonight. We are going to have to figure out who the other leak is and fast. Director Jackson indicates he would have to get Willow and the others out of the APA Annex. It's too dangerous for them now, after discovering the PG knew everything about their plans through Christopher.

None of them knew how high the corruption went up in the APA hierarchy, or how many people at the APA facility are affected. The Director has been doing this all on his own, watching people, researching, and finding out who the leak is. I'm glad he finally came to us for help.

"Captain, Commander, I could use your help on this one. I know Christopher did not act alone. He didn't have the security clearance to send those messages. He had some help higher up."

The Director pauses and looks around the room and then continues with his narrative.

"I think I know who is helping Christopher."

He went on and explained who it is, and how he knows who it is, but he has one more thing to check. He is aware that someone is sending messages other than Christopher through a secure network. He wants to catch them red-handed.

As Director Jackson tells us all this information, my head is spinning. Knowing Willow is in danger is more than I can take. I leave the room and run down the hallway.

I knock on her door. She opens it on the second knock and looks surprised to see me.

"Commander, do you need something?"

She is all ready for bed and is trying to wrap her robe around her more, to cover up her PJs.

"I wanted to make sure you were in for the night."

"Of course, where else would I be?"

"Willow, listen very carefully. I need you to lock the door and not open it for anyone but me. Do you understand? Not the Director, not Dr. Carver, not any of your friends. No one. Do I make myself clear?"

"I understand, Commander," she said.

"Good. I'll be back for you soon, I promise."

CHAPTER
FIVE
WILLOW

I quickly dress. Two minutes later there is knocking at my door. I pretend to be asleep. It is Dr. Carver. I wonder how the Commander knew she would come.

"Willow let me in, you're in danger." Dr. Carver pleads. If you don't let me in, I will use my keycard to open your door."

I tried contacting Jax telepathically. We had only been able to connect in the same room, but it's worth a try. After I didn't feel a connection, I decide to use my tablet to contact Jax. I turn the video screen on so she can see my face and whisper: "I'm in trouble, get help."

I left the video screen on and went to the door.

"Willow honey, open the door. I know you're in there."

"Dr. Carver, Commander Alexander told me not to open the door for anyone."

"He's the one you should be afraid of harming you. Open the door, Willow. I've given up everything to protect you. Trust me. Open the door now."

"Dr. Carver, let's wait until the Commander gets back, then I will open the door for both of you. And then we can get this all cleared up."

I know my tablet is still on and I know Jax can see and hear what is going on. She will get help if I need it. I don't know who to trust—

Dr. Carver, whom I have known my entire life, or a man I met a couple of weeks ago.

I know Commander Alexander would not make this up. There is no reason for it. Dr. Carver has been acting strange, ever since I told her I wanted to go on the starship mission.

She starts to pound on the door. I know she is going to come in any moment and Dalton still isn't back. I hope Jax gets help.

"I am coming in Willow," Dr. Carver sounds pissed. "I gave you a chance to do this the easy way."

Dr. Carver bursts through the door takes me by my arms and pulls me into the hallway. Unfortunately, no one is in the hall this time of night. I keep yelling for her to stop, I try pushing her down, but she is much stronger than she looks. There were no plants around so I couldn't get them to help me this time. I try all the hand-to-hand combat maneuvers I learned, but she is too powerful for me to overcome.

She keeps telling me to trust her, but there is such an odd look on her face. She doesn't act as flummoxed or foolish as usual, and she looks highly agitated. I can't figure out where she is taking me. We are going deeper and deeper into the Annex, into elevators, hallways, and more elevators. We go through a door on the lower level that says "Transport Vehicles."

"Get in Willow." She points to a large truck.

I refuse. "Dr. Carver, you have to tell me what's going on."

"No, actually I don't. Get in the truck, now." Her voice reaches a high-pitched screech, "Now Willow!"

I stand my ground.

"Willow, I'm the only reason you are still alive. The PG would have killed you years ago. I begged them to keep you alive."

"Dr. Carver, I am not getting in the truck until you tell me what is going on and where we are going."

"Willow, I can't. You need to get in, now. I don't want to hurt you."

I am trying to stall as long as I can, hoping the Commander will find me soon.

"Willow if you get in, I will tell you what's going on. We have to leave now."

"Tell me first Dr. Carver."

She pulls the gun out of her jacket pocket.

"No. This is the last time I will tell you before I start shooting. Get in the truck now."

I get in the truck. I am still trying to figure out how to stop Dr. Carver. I know once we leave the Annex, Dalton will not be able to find me, ever.

As I am opening the truck door, I think about how surreal all of this is. Here is this woman who has raised me since I was five years old, kidnapping me in the middle of the night at gunpoint. She gets in and swears under her breath. Apparently, she doesn't have keys for the vehicle, so she ends up hot-wiring the truck. I was hoping if she didn't find keys it would delay us for a while, but she is very efficient at hot wiring. How does she even know how to hotwire a car? She isn't who I thought I she was. She starts the truck but has to get out to hit the door release for the large garage door.

"Stay in the truck, Willow."

I figure this is my last opportunity to do something to save myself from Dr. Carver. I can't wait for someone else to save me. I know if Jax understood what is going on she would get the Commander and the Captain. But they will have a hard time finding us because even I am not exactly sure where we are.

I am running out of time. I move over to the driver seat, having no clue what I am doing, put the truck in reverse, and hit the gas as hard as I can and spin backward. Dr. Carver is screaming at me and waving the gun over her head. I have to keep going long enough for someone to find me.

The Captain and Commander come bursting into the room with guns blazing, at the same moment I crash the truck into other vehicles, hitting my head on the steering wheel—hard. There is blood everywhere. Correction, my blood is everywhere.

Captain Holloway confronts Dr. Carver and sends Commander Alexander to help me.

I look up from the driver's seat of the truck to see Dr. Carver turn the gun on herself.

By this point, the blood is running down my face and into my eyes. I hear Captain Holloway scream, "You're not getting away that easy," and shoots the gun from her hand. It lands on the floor with a clank.

Meanwhile, Commander Alexander is trying to get me out from under the steering wheel. The back of the truck is smashed, and my legs are wedged solidly underneath the dashboard. I am sure I am about to lose consciousness, and the last thing I remember is seeing the worry on Dalton's face.

CHAPTER

SIX

DALTON

I can't believe how close I was to losing Willow. She was smart to make contact with Jax before Dr. Carver grabbed her. Now I may have a chance to save her.

Director Jackson figured everything out just a bit too late. We were in the briefing when Jax came running in. It seems Dr. Carver used to work with Willow's parents, Jeffrey and Marie Washburn. She was always jealous of their success and pretended to be friends with them to gain their confidence. Dr. Carver ended up working in the lab and helped them develop the serum at the PG, then continued to collaborate with them at the APA. Dr. Carver was always working for the PG. She was and is a double agent.

Willow's parents wanted to enhance human characteristics with the serum, but the PG discovered another use for it. The PG can use it to destroy the entire human race. When Willow's parents found out it was Dr. Carver who deceived them, it was too late. They did the only thing they could do—they injected the serum into Willow so it would be safe and so Willow could protect herself.

They knew the plants would protect her. The plan was to have Grandma take care of Willow if something happened to them. Dr. Carver contacted Willow's grandmother and convinced her this was the only way to keep her safe. The Grandma thought Dr. Carver was Jeffrey and Marie's friend and never suspected she was the double agent who had Jeffrey and Marie killed.

So, Willow went to live at the boarding school with Dr. Carver. Dr. Carver gained her trust and intended to exploit her powers. She wanted Willow to continue the research her parents didn't finish. Dr. Carver couldn't decipher the research notes on the serum but had high hopes Willow would be able to do so given time. Then, Dr. Carver, Headmistress Yvonne, and Director Amundson carefully orchestrated Willow's move to the Annex. The plan was years in the making.

Dr. Carver was going to convince Willow to finish the study knowing she had means to do so. She had all the research notes from her parents at the APA and all the facilities and backing. Dr. Carver believed she would train her in power practice, and get her to crack the code on the serum to create more. All she would have to do then was to move Willow to another location, telling her they were part of APA, and letting Willow believe she was doing something right in her parents' name. Her plan would have worked if it wasn't for the Commander and the Captain showing up at the APA earlier than expected. If Willow hadn't been interested in the Starship mission, Dr. Carver would not have had to rush the plan. She would have had months, if not a year to finish the research.

Dr. Carver had gained Willow's trust so wholly she had no doubt her plan would have worked. She dedicated her life to this. She needed Willow to be mature enough to understand the information in her parents' notes and for her powers to develop and grow. The PG was not very patient, but she convinced them her plan would work.

The Director found out the only reason her plan didn't work was because of the piggyback signal Christopher had sent to his father, which alerted them to Dr. Carver's transmissions to the PG.

I am so thankful Willow is still alive. If anything had happened to her, I would have felt responsible for not getting there sooner. It is fortunate that Willow had the foresight to communicate with Jax. Jax immediately contacted us, but it was too late. Dr. Carver had already gotten to Willow and moved her to the basement of the

facility. Willow was also smart not to let Dr. Carver take her out of the Annex. She knew once they left, it would have been tough to find her.

I ran as fast as I could to the point of having no air left in my lungs and got to Willow. She was bleeding profusely out of a large gash in her head where she hit the steering wheel. I moved her out of the vehicle, held her in my arms and laid her gently on the floor. I started to get the bleeding under control. Director Jackson called for an emergency medical technician to help us out. I was able to get the bleeding under control before the Emergency Medical Techs arrived.

♦♦♦♦♦

The EMTs took Willow to the Infirmary. The doctors didn't think she would have any permanent damage besides a big goose egg on her head and a nice scar where they had to stitch her up.

I will never forget the look in her eyes when she figured out the woman she had trusted and looked up to for years deceived her. Those beautiful eyes were swimming with tears. She knew Dr. Carver had betrayed her. I wonder if I went through the same thing if I could learn to trust again. Her eyes flutter open, and a breath of relief fills my lungs.

"Hey Willow, how are you doing?"

She looks at me and starts to sob.

"Willow, I'm so sorry about Dr. Carver."

"Why are you sorry? You saved my life. I still can't believe she could do this to me," Willow said, sobbing into her hands.

"Willow, you saved yourself. You alerted Jax to your situation. We know Dr. Carver used her keycard to get into your room. I should never have left you. I don't know why I didn't think she would use any means necessary to get to you. She has had this planned for years."

"What will happen to Dr. Carver?"

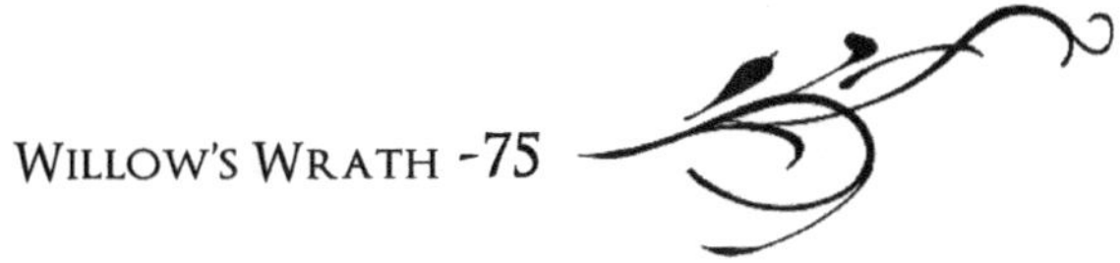

"I can't believe you're worried about what will happen to her."
She looks at me to continue.

"Fine. Dr. Carver is in an APA holding cell until her trial. We still have to figure out how much damage she has caused. The deception goes up higher than Dr. Carver in the APA. It goes all the way to the Director level. I guess Director Jackson has a lot more on her. He's been watching her for years. There is much more information we found out."

"Will you tell me the whole story?"

"Yes, when you're feeling better, I promise."

♦♦♦♦♦

The Omega Team is briefed the following morning by Captain Holloway and Director Jackson. We fill them in on what is going on and what will need to happen moving forward. We decide it is too dangerous to stay at the Annex any longer. My team would be rolling out today as soon as Willow is feeling well enough to travel.

Willow, Jax, Cobalt, and Dharma will be a part of the Starship Armargosa mission, and the rest of the Omega Team will be in the special ops unit. None of them will remain at the Annex—it was deemed too dangerous. Everybody is okay with their assignments, and the four girls are thrilled to be staying together. However, Willow floated in and out of consciousness for the next 24 hours, so we weren't able to leave as planned.

CHAPTER
SEVEN

WILLOW

I feel like my head is splitting open. What happened to me? I open my eyes, vaguely remembering the horrors of the night before. I wonder how long I have been sleeping. Dalton is holding my hand and has his head on my bed. He must have stayed the whole night. I know by the way he acted the night before that he feels responsible for what happened to me. I know if I had left the facility with Dr. Carver, Dalton would have had a hard time finding me.

I squeeze his hand, and his eyes fly open.

"Hey there, how are you feeling?"

"Much better thank you, Dalton, may I call you Dalton?"

"When we're alone you may but not when we are in front of the crew. Do you remember what happened?"

"For the most part, but you should fill me in."

"You've been sleeping on and off for about 24 hours. We are still planning on leaving later today if you're up to it."

"I'm so happy to be a part of this mission. I can't thank you enough."

"It isn't me; it's you. You impressed everyone, in particular with the last trick with Christopher, and the trees. It showed us you could protect yourself. You were also incredible in the situation with Dr. Carver. You thought on your feet, and you saved yourself. On a mission of this magnitude, it's important you can think defensively, and that you can protect yourself. Because, as you saw tonight, I can't always be there to keep you safe."

Dalton moves closer to me, and I know he is about to kiss me. Just then Director Jackson walks in.

"Hey, how are you, Willow?" He roars.

"I have a little bit of a headache, but I am okay," I say softly to set the tone.

"Oh sorry, I'll be quieter. I'm so glad you're okay. I wish I would have figured out what Dr. Carver was doing before this situation got so out of control."

"Me, too. I can't believe Dr. Carver was capable of all of this."

"She's had an agenda for a long time, actually, since before you were born. She's always wanted to create this weapon, but she never had the ingenuity or the intelligence to do it on her own. She studied your parents' research material, and she didn't quite understand it. She figured once she had you here with all research information available you would be able to figure it out together. That was her plan all along. Willow, if there is anything I can do for you, please let me know."

"I actually would like a glass of water and maybe something to eat."

"Will do Willow."

CHAPTER
EIGHT
DALTON

Wow, that was a close call, if Director Jackson hadn't walked in, I would have kissed Willow, and most likely I wouldn't have stopped there. I'm not sure what comes over me when I'm with her, but I have to get a handle on it, or it will be difficult to be on the Starship with her for the next three years. We will have to go on missions together, we will see each other every day, so I have to be able to control myself around her. She is not someone who would ever be happy with me. I'm not nearly good enough for her.

I make sure Willow is stable and go to find Captain Holloway to give him the situation report.

"Captain Holloway, may I speak with you for a moment?"

"Yes Commander, walk with me," the Captain motions for me to follow him down the corridor.

"I want to let you know Willow is in stable condition. All she has now is a slight headache, which I'm figuring she'll have for a while. She loves the scar, and she thinks it will make her look tougher."

The Captain laughs, "Well at least her sense of humor is back."

"She should be ready to ship out later this evening. Where are we going, Captain?"

"We're heading to the shipyard to check out the Armargosa. I want you to recheck the crew to make sure the PG hasn't infiltrated anyone else in the APA. I hope Christopher and Dr. Carver were the only double agents, but we can't be a hundred percent sure. Go to the computer lab and rerun every background check on every member of our crew, Omega Team included. I want checks run on their family, their friends, everyone. We need to make sure we're clean before we leave the dock. Understood?"

"Yes, Captain."

I run to the computer lab and complete background checks on every single member of our two hundred fifty-person crew. It is a daunting task, but one I know is entirely necessary. I want to make sure this mission goes off without a hitch. Just getting out of here is proving to be more complicated than I would have thought. We haven't even started yet, and we have had two security breaches and one major accident.

CHAPTER
NINE

WILLOW

I can't believe Director Jackson walked in right when Dalton was about to kiss me. I can still feel his breath on my face and the excitement in my stomach. I know he thinks he shouldn't get involved with me, and he's telling himself he doesn't want to. Nonetheless, I know it's right. I know Dalton is the one for me.

We are heading out on the mission later tonight, and I couldn't be more excited to have three of my best friends with me. Even though I've only known them a month, I feel like I've known them for my entire life.

I can't wait to go on adventures with them. I know it's not all going to be fun. It's going to be hard work. I know the conditions aren't going to be exactly ideal, either, but I know I can do this. I know I can make a difference and I can't wait to start living my life. I do love it here at the Annex, but I could never be happy here again after what Dr. Carver did to me. It would be a reminder of how she deceived me for all these years. I would never feel safe or secure here again, so it's a good thing I'm traveling light-years away. I know how critical this mission is to the people under the rule of the PG.

CHAPTER
TEN
DALTON

I head to the infirmary to check on Willow. I peek in her room, and she looks so much better than she did when I saw her a couple of hours ago. Someone brought her the uniform for the ship. The Omega Team will be wearing a black jumpsuit, so it isn't precisely the uniform I wear, but they will blend in, and I have to admit she looks great.

"Hey Willow, you look way better than the last time I saw you."

"Well thank you for noticing Commander Alexander, I do feel better and look at this cool uniform. I love it. I am honored and very pleased to be going on this mission, and I do appreciate the opportunity you have given me. You will never know how much. Thank you again."

I am not exactly sure how to respond to her statement, I already told her that it was her that got her the spot on the mission, not me. I say, "I am glad you're feeling better. We will be leaving in two hours, so grab what you need from your room, personal items, and meet me in the conference room. I'm going to call Jax to walk with you. I'm still not completely sure Christopher and Dr. Carver are the only two double agents. Director Jackson agrees with me and is continuing to look for any other traitors known to the APA. I know he will flush them out, but in the meantime, don't be alone."

"Well, Commander, you act like you almost care."

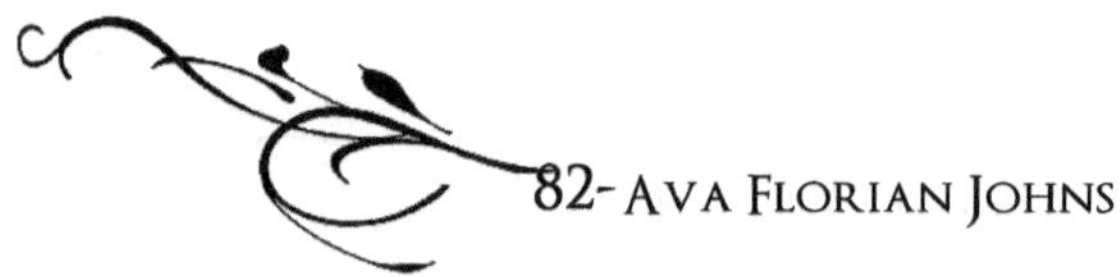

"I do care, Willow, I care about your well-being." I lean forward toward her face, "You're part of my crew now."

She looks disappointed for a second until I gently touch my lips to hers. I knew I made a grave mistake. It was the gentlest of touches but packed with so much meaning. It is hard to express in mere words, how incredibly relieved I am that she is alive. When she moves her body toward me just slightly, it completely breaks my resolve to keep the moment light. I deepen the kiss. It is like an out-of-body experience, I can't explain it. I have no thought in my head but her taste. She leans flush against my body, and I lose my mind. I pick her up and lean her against the wall, and now we move together in unison. Our bodies are swaying as one—trying to get closer together. I know it is crazy, but I swear I can hear her thoughts.

I listen to a noise coming from the hallway—someone is coming in the room. I set Willow on the ground and back away. In a flash, I see the look of disappointment in her beautiful blue eyes. And an instant later a nurse walks in to do one final check on her vitals before she can be released. "Okay Willow, time to take your blood pressure." Willow snorts.

CHAPTER ELEVEN

WILLOW

"I think my blood pressure may be a little high. It has been an exciting couple of days." I wink at Dalton when the nurse isn't looking.

He has a look of surprise on his face. I guess he thought I wouldn't be as cheeky as I am. The kiss was mind-blowing. I swear I can hear what he was thinking which made the experience that much more intense.

The nurse finishes taking my vitals—as expected; my blood pressure is a bit high, go figure.

As soon as the nurse leaves, Dalton says, "Let's go to your room, we can pick up your stuff, then we can walk to the conference room together. I would feel better if you were not out of my sight."

"I like the sound of that." I love to see the look of surprise that crosses Dalton's face.

We walk through the corridors. People have heard about my brush with death, so they all stop to make sure I am okay. I can tell Dalton is getting annoyed. It's taking forever to get to my room. At this rate, we will be late for the meeting.

"Willow has to go now," Dalton says as he drags me through the last part of the corridor to my room, past a bunch of well-wishers.

"Finally," Dalton says curtly.

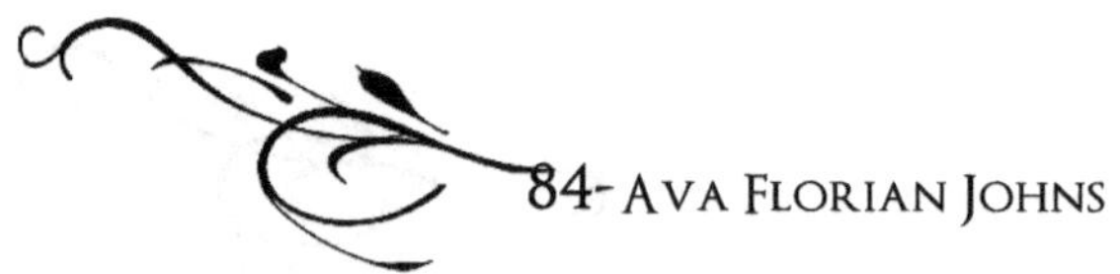

I laugh. Somehow the kiss gave me confidence, and I can feel it coursing through my blood. It isn't like me, but it feels good.

We stand at my doorway looking in my room in disbelief. Someone has destroyed my dorm room. My pillow is cut open, and there are feathers everywhere. "Stand back Willow." Dalton makes me wait in the hallway while he polices the room. He grabs his gun out of the holster and walks around the area, in the bathroom, and even looks in the closet. He gets on the communications device and alerts the Captain. "Captain, Willow's room has been ransacked. It seems like it happened a while ago, at least 24 hours."

"How did you know when it happened Dalton?"

"The plant is completely dried up. It didn't happen recently; it is at least a day old."

"Oh, poor thing," I coo as I pick up the plant and put it in a cup.

"You are worried about the plant?"

"Well, I wasn't here, so I'm not worried about myself. And you said the intruder is gone, so that's good, right? I don't feel like I am in danger."

"Can you tell if anything is missing?"

"No. I don't have anything. Nothing worth stealing."

"Are you sure?"

"Oh, wait. The jewelry box Dr. Carver gave me from my parents, which contained a couple of pictures and a brush. I don't think it's worth much; it just has sentimental value."

"Where is it?"

"I put it in my suitcase and put it under my bed. I already packed for the mission. I thought if I had a positive attitude I would be sure to get picked for it."

"See if it is still under the bed."

"Here it is," I pull the suitcase out from under the bed and open it up. In the center of the bag is the jewelry box, undisturbed.

"This must have been what they were looking for in my room. I don't have anything else."

"There must be more to the jewelry box than you think. Somehow, I don't believe the people who broke in were after just this. Could there be something else in it, something you don't know about?"

"What's going on?" The Captain asks as he walks in the room.

"Captain, the area is secured. The only thing we can think of that someone would want is the jewelry box Dr. Carver gave Willow."

"I don't have anything else, Captain."

"How is it that the intruder didn't find it?"

"I was an optimist and already had packed it for the mission. It was in the suitcase under my bed."

"Understood."

"Commander, let's get her and her belongings out of here, we will sort all this out later."

"Since everything else I own is shredded, I guess this is it. I have the shirt on my back and the bag with my jewelry box in it."

"We will give you everything you need aboard the starship. You don't have to worry about a thing," the Captain says as he turns and walks out the door.

"Sir, we need to leave as soon as possible. I am still concerned about Willow's safety."

"Yes, Commander, I can see that,"

"Okay Willow, let's get going,"

I turn to look at my room one more time. Who would do this? For my hairbrush and a box. I would have to look at it later to see if there is anything else hidden in the jewelry box. Right now, I want to concentrate on the fantastic adventure I am about to have. I walk down the corridor with the Commander and Captain flanking me. I think it is a little ridiculous to have this much security, but they want to be sure I make it to the meeting, then to the starship.

"Can I say goodbye to Lizzy and the others?" I ask tentatively, but I already know the answer is probably no.

"I don't think it is a good idea, Willow. I don't want to put you in any more danger than you already are."

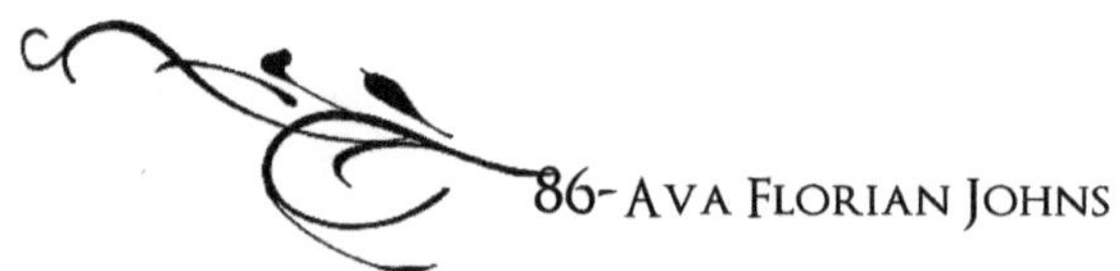

"I agree with the Captain, Willow. I'm sorry, but I don't think it is a good idea to parade you around the Annex."

"Maybe the Director could bring them to me to say goodbye. It would be Lizzy, Todd, Meagan, Donna, Sophia, and Maddox."

"I will think about it."

"Captain, I believe that it is an unnecessary risk. We almost lost her once."

"Okay, okay, it's fine. I won't say goodbye. Maybe I can use my tablet to communicate with the team. Would that be okay? They wouldn't have to know where I am."

"Ok, Willow, that you can do."

I will feel much better to know I can say goodbye to my friends. I hope I will see them again.

♦♦♦♦♦

We go to the conference room, and everyone is there. The Director, Jax, Cobalt, Dharma. The Captain and Commander continue to flank me as we sit down. I hope they lighten up once we are aboard the starship. I have no idea what to expect once we're on the mission. I'm afraid they will have a hard time running the ship if they are always worried about my safety.

I hope the person who trashed my room will not be aboard the starship. It might have been Christopher before they apprehended him, but he was already gone before Dr. Carver came to my room. Well, it's a mystery because it had to be someone else. It looks like the Director is correct that there is someone else in the Annex who is working with Dr. Carver and Christopher. I hope they figure out who it is and soon.

Captain Holloway begins, "As you know, the four of you will be leaving for the mission aboard the starship. We will not be able to finish your training at the Annex. I want to say a few things before we are aboard. You will be each assigned an officer and position on the starship. You will be an integral part of the crew, and you will follow the rules, like the other members of my team. You are not any more special than any other member of my crew. I need you to understand this before we go aboard."

We all nod in the Captain's direction. I can't imagine any of us causing problems, but frankly, I don't know the rest of the group very well. I knew Dr. Carver for twelve years, and I most certainly wasn't an excellent judge of character with her. I have only known Jax, Cobalt, and Dharma a month at most. I like to think I have gotten to know them, but I no longer trust my judgment.

"Here are your assignments. Willow, you will work with the science officer, Lieutenant Noah Williams. Jax, you will report to the communications officer, Lieutenant Astrid Allium. Cobalt you will be working engineering, with Chief Engineer Lieutenant Luke Cameron. Dharma, you will report to the head of security, Lieutenant Commander Lor Kal."

He pauses to see if we have questions, and when no one says anything, the Captain continues his briefing.

"We paired you up with the most relevant departments to highlight your unique gifts. That doesn't mean they won't change once we are aboard. You will each be given shifts in the departments I have assigned. The position is a full-time job, plus some. You will each take shifts like any other member of the crew. You will be assigned special projects to work on and be called upon to go on away missions. You will train with your commanding officers. If you have any questions, ask me now."

"Do we get to meet our commanding officers before boarding the ship?" Cobalt asked.

"You will meet them on the ship before we take off. We don't want to stay at the Annex any longer than necessary. Willow still may be at risk. Any other questions? Okay, if there are no other matters, grab your gear and follow Commander Alexander to the ship."

We say goodbye to Director Jackson, grab our bags and follow Dalton to the ship. I still have my tablet in my hand and motion for him to see if it was okay to say goodbye to Lizzy and the others.

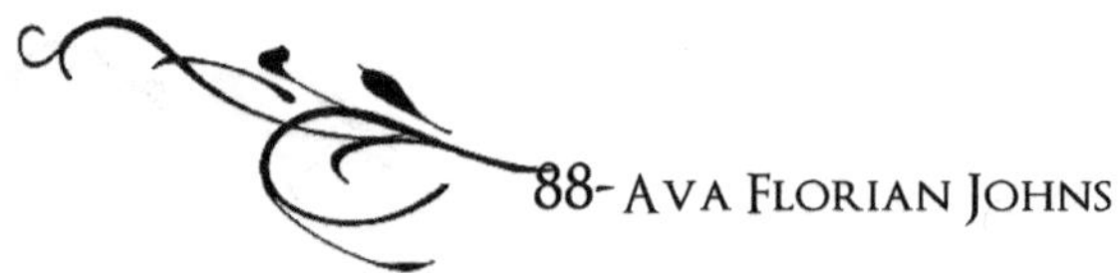

"Willow I don't think it's a good idea. They will understand."
"Okay, I will send them a message once we are sure I am safe."
"That is a much better idea. Now get aboard."
"Yes, sir." I wink at him as I walk up the ramp to my new home.

CHAPTER
TWELVE
DALTON

I worry that we left without figuring out who trashed Willow's room. One of the Omega Team members could be the culprit. I don't think so, but then again you never know. I would have never thought Dr. Carver was capable of everything she did. I also wouldn't have guessed the clean-cut Christopher would be a traitor, but I have been wrong before.

Once on board, I have the Omega Team go to their assigned rooms. For the time being, they are going to share quarters. Willow and Jax in one room and Cobalt and Dharma in another. I inform them to report to the bridge at 2300 hours, and they look a little confused by the military lingo. They have to get used to military time if they are going to function here.

I feel better now that I am on the bridge. The Captain and I go through the checklists with all department heads, and we are ready to go.

We perform one final security sweep and find nothing.

"Okay Captain, security check clear, all department heads checking in, and we are ready to shove off," I said, so glad to be on a mission and away from the Annex.

"All right, Commander. Let's get out of here. Ensign set coordinates 02-50-78-978 to the Oleander Cluster."

I still worry about Willow being aboard the ship for three years. I am sure she will be okay, but I just feel so over-protective of her now

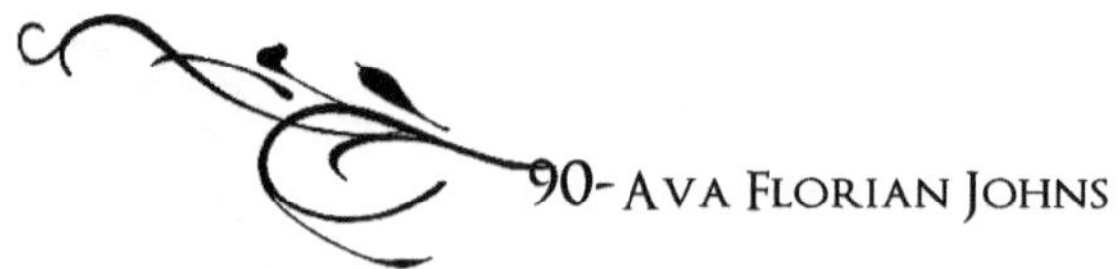

that I figure it is better to have her close to me. I would be a nervous wreck if she were still in the Annex.

The meeting of the officers and Omega Team is going to commence in a couple of minutes, so I sent the ensign down to escort the team to the conference room. The department heads, Lieutenant Williams, Lieutenant Allium, Lieutenant Cameron, and Lieutenant Commander Kal are all in attendance when the Captain and I walk in. The Omega Team isn't here yet.

"You all have been chosen to be the commanding officers of some remarkable individuals. You have seen what they can do on videos, but to see them in person is quite astounding. You will be working with all of them closely. If you sense anything out of the ordinary or have any concerns, you need to contact Commander Alexander at once. Do you understand?"

"Yes sir," they all answer in unison.

"Welcome Omega Team. These are the heads of departments on the ship. Willow, this is Science Officer Lieutenant Noah Williams."

"Hello Lieutenant Williams, I look forward to working with you," Willow says.

"Jax, your commanding officer for this mission, is Communications Officer Lieutenant Astrid Allium."

"Hello Jax, I am very pleased to meet you," Lieutenant Allium greets Jax.

Jax signs a word of greeting and sits next to the Lieutenant.

The Captain continues reading the assignments, "Cobalt you are assigned to engineering. You will be reporting to Chief Engineer, Lieutenant Luke Cameron."

I can tell Cobalt is excited, I know she will fit in exceptionally well in the Engineering Department.

"And last but not least, Dharma, you will be working with the head of security, Lieutenant Commander Kal." The Captain motions for Dharma to sit next to the formidable Lieutenant Commander."

"I will give you all some time to meet and take a tour of your respective areas. We will also arrange for a tour of the whole ship.

Today is orientation and tomorrow you start your shifts. We move fast here, so try to keep up. Any questions?"

"Captain, what exactly is our purpose here?" Cobalt asks.

"We will be discussing the goals at the staff meeting tomorrow. However, I would like to say this is the most critical operation I have ever been on and I am incredibly honored to be leading this objective. I have two hundred fifty souls on this ship counting on me, and I won't let them down."

Cobalt nodded in understanding.

"Everyone dismissed."

The Omega Team went with their prospective leaders and the Captain, and I stayed back to discuss the operation in a bit more detail.

"Commander, you are in charge of the Omega Team. Please let me know if there are any concerns about placement or skill set. We are heading into uncharted territory, and I want to make sure I can rely on all two hundred fifty people aboard this vessel. I know you had concerns regarding the Omega Team's readiness, but I have to say I am impressed by their skill-set and think they will be a great asset to our mission. I wouldn't have allowed them on the ship if I thought otherwise."

"I agree, Captain. I also believe they have amazing abilities and feel more comfortable now that we have paired them each with a commanding officer. They are in good hands, and I am confident the departments we chose will be a good fit for them. I still have some reservations about having them along on away missions, but if we can continue to train them on the ship, I will feel better."

"They will have training time worked into their daily schedule. If you think any one of the team needs more time in combat training, let me know. We can work it into the schedule."

"Captain, thank you again for the opportunity to serve with you on this critical mission. I won't let you down."

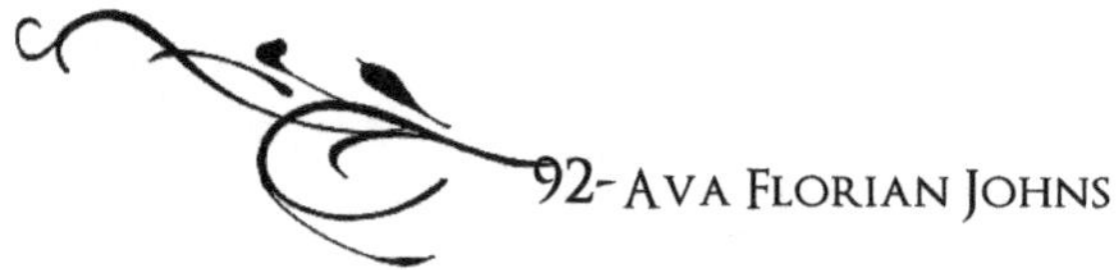

Chapter Thirteen

Willow

I have to admit I am glad that we are not reporting directly to Commander Alexander, it is a bit easier for me. I don't know what my relationship with Dalton means at this point, not having to report to him is one less thing for me to worry about on this mission. With one kiss, I have more confidence than I have ever had in my life. I feel like he transferred some of his self-confidence and arrogance to me and he has plenty to spare. I know it shouldn't be possible, but we felt so connected, it was an incredible experience.

Now it is time to focus. I walk to the science lab with Lieutenant Williams. "Willow, I have to say I was very reluctant to believe the stories about your powers. But after seeing the videos and reading your research notes, I think your ability is what this mission needs. The things you can do with plants and crops specifically will help a lot of people, and that is what this mission is about."

"Thank you, Lieutenant. I will do everything I can to help."

"The first thing I want you to do is to demonstrate your powers for me, and this is the best place to do that." He stopped, and we were standing in front of the arboretum.

My face lights up, and he smiles.

"I thought this would be one of the first places you would want to see. Let's go in and take a look around."

I walk in, and there are plants and flowers everywhere. They have corn, grain, potatoes and other vegetables for me to practice my skill.

"Wow, this place is fantastic."

I wave my palms over the plants and flowers as I walk in, and in typical fashion, they respond to a touch of my hand. I walk around to all of them saying hello, and getting to know them. I can hear positive sounds coming from the Lieutenant. I know he approves of what he is seeing, and although he saw my videos, he still didn't quite believe everything I can do. Now he does.

I have a surge of confidence and show him some of what I can do. I think this is an excellent way to impress my new boss.

I stand in the center of the room and will the plants and flowers to grow as high as they can go. The plants respond to my command and react amazingly well. They grow and spin around each other putting on a show. I tell them I want to impress my commanding officer and they understand. When I finish the growing process, I look at Lieutenant Williams face. He appears both dumbfounded and delighted at the same time.

"What do you think?" I ask, feeling pretty damn confident.

"I am astonished at your ability Willow. I see why Commander Alexander speaks so highly of your skills. I have never seen anything like it in all my years, and I am twice as old as everyone on this ship, so that is a lot of years."

"Thank you, Lieutenant Williams. I know how important this mission is, and want to do everything I can to help."

"Can you tell me what you say to them to make them grow?"

I snort laugh, then feel a little embarrassed.

The lieutenant chuckles, so I continue.

"I told the plants I wanted to impress you because you are my new boss and I wanted to make a good impression. When I first walked around them, I was getting to know them. Like saying hello. Every place I have been, plants and flowers have been my best friends. And I don't doubt it will be the same way here."

"Great, now can you get them to go back to their normal size?"

"Of course, would you like me to do that now?"

"Yes, please. I want to take you to the Science Department, introduce you to the crew, and talk more about how it is you do what you do. I understand you have had some issues with the sustainability of the plants and crops you work with?"

"Yes, I have. I was starting to figure it out when we had to leave the Annex. I have the research notes from my parents and will continue to work on them while I practice my skill."

I walk around the room, telepathically thanking the plants for helping me today and letting them know Lieutenant Williams is impressed with them. I wave my hand at them and will them to go back to their standard size. They respond within seconds and are back to the same size as when we walked in the arboretum.

"Wow. Your power is certainly astonishing."

♦♦♦♦♦

"Okay everyone, please gather around. I want you to meet an exceptional individual. I would like to introduce you to Willow, who will be working with us on this mission. She has an extraordinary power with plants, and you will get to see the demonstration tomorrow. I can assure you it is amazing."

I am slightly embarrassed by the Lieutenant's introduction, but I want to remain confident. I know I can do this—it is what I am born to do.

The lieutenant continues with individual introductions. I learn the Science Department has fifty-three people on staff. It is great to know that science is an integral part of this mission.

The lieutenant shows me where I will be working. My station is small but suitable for what I have to do. The rest of my power practice will take place at the arboretum.

Lieutenant Williams gives me my schedule for the week. It certainly is full, but then again, I didn't expect this to be easy, and

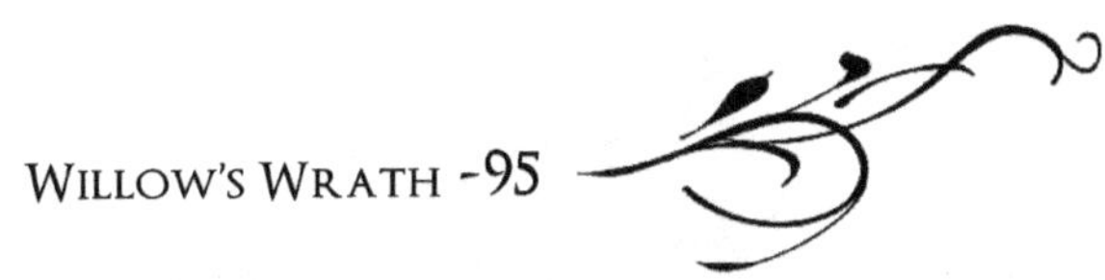

I'm glad I'll keep busy. It'll take my mind off what happened with Dr. Carver. Just thinking about it makes me sad. I loved Dr. Carver like a mother. She is the only one I trusted for a long time, and she betrayed me. My instinct tells me not to trust again, but common sense tells me I have to. I have to believe in this crew, I have to have faith in the Omega Team, and I have to count on myself, more than I ever have before.

I notice on my schedule they also slated time for me to work with Jax. We are already getting so good at being able to read each other's minds, we can speak to each other at the dinner table, and no one knows what we are doing.

Lieutenant Williams finishes my tour in the Science Department. Then he assigns an ensign to take me around the ship. I thought we were going to do this as a group, but I'm glad I'm getting the tour now. I would hate to get lost later because it would be embarrassing.

"Ensign Johnson, will you please take Willow on a tour of this vessel?"

"Yes, sir."

I can tell people respect Lieutenant Williams, and this helps me in giving him my trust.

"So Ensign Johnson, where do you come from?" I ask as we start our tour.

"I am from Casson ma'am."

"How did you get selected for this mission?"

"I knew Commander Alexander from basic training, and he recommended me for the position, ma'am."

"Have you known Commander Alexander for a long time?"

"Yes, ma'am we grew up together."

"What was Commander Alexander like as a child?"

"I don't understand the question, ma'am."

"I mean what was he like growing up?"

"Pretty much the same, ma'am."

"The same as he is now?"

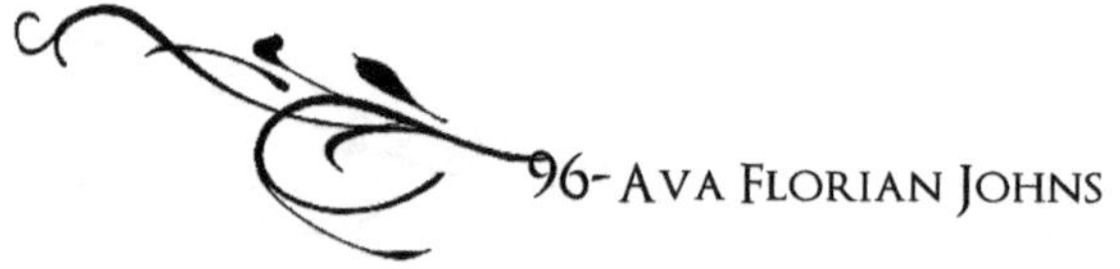

"Ma'am, on Casson we start training military when we are still in diapers. We don't have a childhood, not like most people do. We are prepared to protect individuals at a very young age. That is all we are expected to do. There is no room for anything else." He looks embarrassed that he shared so much information and immediately stopped talking.

"I understand. Thank you, ensign."

We continue on the rest of the tour in silence. I know I overstepped my bounds and didn't want to put the Ensign in an awkward position again.

I am interested to find out what Dalton was like as a child. I guess that explains a lot about him. He never had a childhood. Not like most people have. Not like I had for five short years. I also had to grow up quickly, so that is something Dalton and I have in common.

I know there's something else that happened to Dalton when he was young. Something which defines the man he is today. Something which keeps him guarded. I hope I have the opportunity to ask him and find out more about this man who is turning my life upside down.

My thoughts are on Dalton for the rest of the tour. I vaguely hear what the Ensign says about different departments. It doesn't interest me much, but I need to focus if I am going to do well here. The Captain is right that they move fast, and I need to keep up.

The Ensign returns me to the Science Department, where Lieutenant Williams is waiting for me.

"Willow, now we are going to go through some of the research you have been working on at the Annex and what you still need to do. I need to know what your obstacles are and we will find a way to overcome them." He pauses and gestures around the room. "I think you will find state-of-the-art equipment. You will have access to everything in this room and if there's something you need, just ask me for it."

"Thank you, Lieutenant, that is very kind. I am excited to get started."

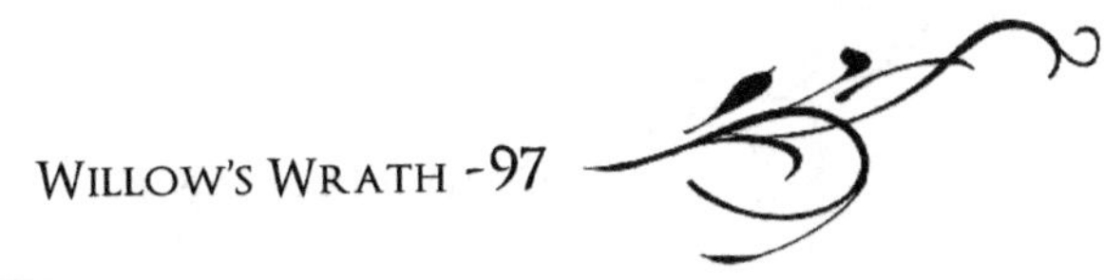

"As you saw in the arboretum today, I have a special knack for plants and flowers. I can get them to do whatever I want them to. I communicate with them telepathically. The one trouble I have is with my crops. They do fine when I'm around. Unfortunately, if I'm not, they cannot sustain themselves. I have gone through all my parents' research notes and have found nothing to indicate they had any problems with this at all. I must be missing something."

"Willow, let's go through everything with the members of the department. One thing we are good at is working together. They may see something you have not been able to see. More sets of eyes is always a good thing." He moves to the center of the room, "All right, everyone gather up again. We're going to go through all of Willow's videos and the research notes from Jeffrey and Marie Washburn. Our problem to solve is once the crops grow, they are not self-sustainable. They seem to need Willow to take care of them consistently. We need to find a way for her to produce crops and be able to leave them on their own."

"I have looked through my parents' research notes several times, I've tried creating crops of potatoes, grains, corn, and sunflowers, and every time I don't pay attention to them they die. Here is a video of me creating a sunflower crop at the Annex. You can see they're doing great immediately after creation. Here is one week after conception, and here is two weeks after creation. They have all died. Even though others cared for them—they fed, watered, and talked to the plants, they still didn't survive."

"That is interesting. Willow, do you have any thoughts on why this is happening?"

"No, unfortunately, I don't, Lieutenant Williams. I am curious, however, to know how the sunflowers are doing that I created the day my parents died. That was twelve years ago. But there might have been something my parents did when I created them. It may have been something small which I didn't notice or understand. I feel like I'm missing something."

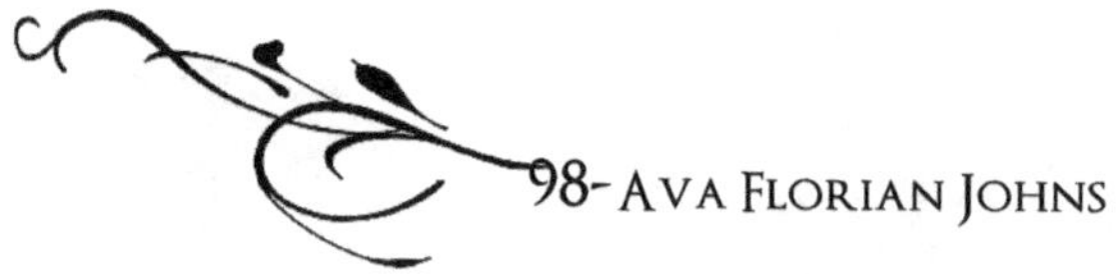

I am getting frustrated talking about it. I should be nervous about fifty people here listening to me, but I'm not. I want to figure this out, and I know I can't do it on my own. I decide at that point that I am going to look at the jewelry box a little closer when I get back to my room. Maybe there is a clue I missed. I didn't mention it to the lieutenant yet because I figure it could be nothing. Still, in the back of my head, I wonder why someone would destroy my room on the Annex for an old jewelry box.

I met with the scientists in the department for a few more hours. They are undoubtedly brilliant and have some great ideas for sustainability of my crops. The best part is I think some of their ideas will work. I am in my work area when Lieutenant Williams comes back.

"Willow, you can go back to your room now. You have a big day tomorrow. Why don't you try and get some shut-eye and I will see you in the morning. Please report to the bridge at 0700 hours."

"I don't mean to ask a stupid question, but is that at seven in the morning?"

"Yes, Willow it is," he said chuckling. "I have a chart for you to explain the military hours, so it makes sense to you. I know it's confusing at first. I made a cheat sheet for each of the members of your team."

STANDARD	24-HOUR	STANDARD	24-HOUR
12 MIDNIGHT	2400	12 NOON	1200
12:01 AM	0001	12:01 PM	1201
12:15 AM	0015	12:15 PM	1215
12:30 AM	0030	12:30 PM	1230
12:45 AM	0045	12:45 PM	1245
1:00 AM	0100	1:00 PM	1300
2:00 AM	0200	2:00 PM	1400
3:00 AM	0300	3:00 PM	1500
4:00 AM	0400	4:00 PM	1600
5:00 AM	0500	5:00 PM	1700
6:00 AM	0600	6:00 PM	1800
7:00 AM	0700	7:00 PM	1900
8:00 AM	0800	8:00 PM	2000
9:00 AM	0900	9:00 PM	2100
10:00 AM	1000	10:00 PM	2200
11:00 AM	1100	11:00 PM	2300

"Thank you, Lieutenant, I appreciate you making us feel at home."

"No problem, Willow, do you need an escort back to your room?"

"No, I think I can figure it out, thank you."

"Have a good night."

"You too, Lieutenant Williams. I know it will be a pleasure working with you."

CHAPTER
FOURTEEN
DALTON

"Captain, are you sure?"

"Yes Dalton, I'm positive it was Director Jackson who trashed Willow's room. Did you think I would give up the search? I've been pouring over hours of video looking for the person who went into her room. There was only one, and that was Director Jackson. I couldn't board this ship not knowing if we were carrying a traitor aboard. Now I know."

"But why would he do that? What was he looking for?"

"Well, I think we should ask him. We are still in communication range. We can have a video call with him now. I have the proof, and he can't deny it."

"Let's get him on the communication device now."

Director Jackson's face appears as large as life on our screen.

"Captain and Commander, great to see you so soon. How's everything going? How is Willow?"

"That's what we want to talk to you about, Director Jackson." The Captain says in a serious tone. "I looked through hundreds of hours of video surveillance of Willow's room, and you were the only one to enter it. "Do you care to explain yourself, Director Jackson?"

"Captain, I knew you would find out it was me, I wasn't trying to hide it."

"Tell us, what were you looking for Director, were you looking for the jewelry box?"

"No, I wasn't looking for anything. I just wanted you to take Willow and get off this planet. I wanted you to have a sense of urgency to leave. I still think she's in danger, but she would be in more danger here. I trust you, and the Commander can protect her better than I can."

"Director, why do you think she's still in danger?" I ask as my concern for Willow grows with every word the Director is saying.

"Commander Alexander, I worked with Willow's parents very closely. I know what they created, and I know Willow has way more power than she realizes. I want to make sure that you are adequately protecting Willow, as I can't protect her here."

"What kind of powers, Director?" I ask.

"Let's just say it is much more than growing plants. When Willow realizes her full power, Willow will be able to... If the PG were to get a hold of her...."

There is a loud crack, static, and then blackness. The connection is lost.

"Director are you there? Director, what happened?" The Captain screams at the screen.

"Captain, is something wrong at the Annex?" I could feel in my gut that something terrible has happened. It's like they're no longer there.

"Let's not panic Commander. Let's figure out the situation. Scan the area of the Annex and see if you see a problem."

"I don't see anything on the scan, Captain." Of course, with their cloaking device, nobody can see the Annex. Nevertheless, I don't see anything peculiar about it either. If someone attacked them, I would see other vehicles, an explosion or something, but I don't see anything out of the ordinary. I have to remember that an air strike wouldn't work on the Annex. "I guess it's just a bad connection."

"Let's try again later, okay Commander? Please check on the Omega one team to make sure they are in their quarters and remind them to report to the bridge at 0700 hours tomorrow morning. That will be all."

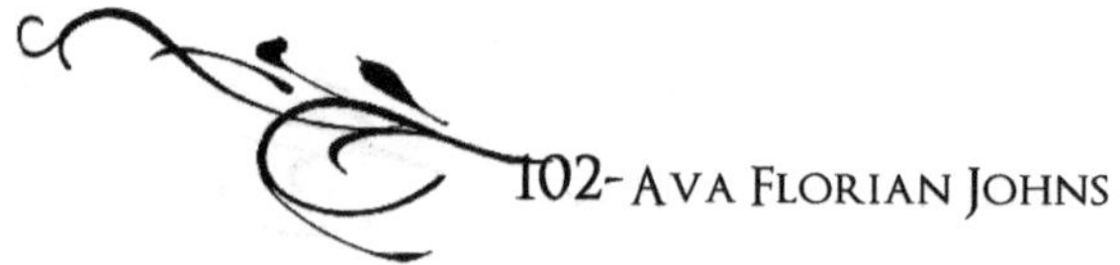

"Thank you, Captain."

I go to Willow's room first to see if she and Jax are in for the night. I knock on the door and Jax answers. She looks like she's already been sleeping.

"I'm here to check in on both of you. Is Willow here?"

Jax shakes her head no. She goes into the room to get her tablet, and types out that Willow hasn't yet returned.

My blood boils instantly. Where could Willow be? Just at that moment, she turns the corner into the corridor.

"I'm right here, Commander. I was working in the science lab."

Jax retreats into the room to let us have privacy and shuts the door behind her.

"Commander, I'm fine. You have to stop reacting like this. I am perfectly safe aboard the ship."

"We don't know that for sure."

"But you have to trust I can take care of myself. I can't have you freaking out every time I'm not where you think I am. I was working with Lieutenant Williams. He asked if I needed an escort to my room and I told him no. I got a little turned around in the corridors, but I made it here all on my own. You have to trust me, Dalton."

"I do trust you, Willow. It's other people I don't trust. There has been a new development. We know now who destroyed your room at the Annex. The Captain and I will brief you on it in the morning. Now get some sleep and report to me on the bridge at 0700 hours."

I stomp down the hall very agitated with Willow, and with myself as well, for losing my temper so quickly.

I knock on Cobalt and Dharma's door. They open it a crack.

"Yes, Commander."

"Are you both in for the night?"

"Yes sir, we were both sleeping."

"Report to the bridge at 0700 hours. See you then."

I continue this stomp back to my room. In the mood I'm in right now, I'll never be able to get to sleep.

CHAPTER

FIFTEEN

WILLOW

I love it on the ship, mostly. The only thing I don't like is Dalton's overprotective nature. I know he feels responsible for me, but he makes me feel like a child. I should cut him some slack however because he knows something I don't. He knows who trashed my room at the Annex and there might be more to the story.

Nonetheless, he has to lighten up. There are other people on the ship who are also concerned for my well-being. He is not the only one now. And he's going to have to trust me. I know I've gotten in trouble before and truth-be-told, my judgment isn't always great. But in all fairness, I did know there was something up with Christopher right away, so he has to give me credit for that one. Dr. Carver ... Well, that's another story.

I open the door and walk into my room.

"I am so sorry, Jax, I didn't know how long I'd stay in the lab. I am finding out so many interesting things by talking to the other scientists that I've never considered before. I think they have a way to sustain my crops, and I just got so excited I lost track of time."

She connected with me telepathically. "It's okay Willow, sleep is highly overrated."

We laugh.

♦♦♦♦♦

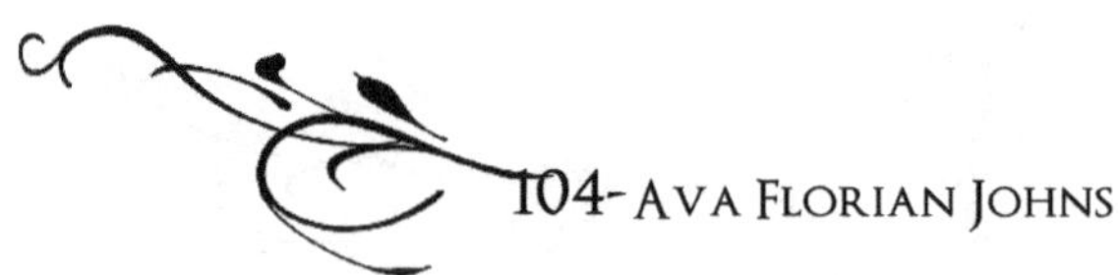

My mother is brushing my long blonde hair, and singing her favorite song about the bird in the meadow. The fire is coming. She stops and takes my face in her hands, caressing me gently. Oh, Willow, I wish I could explain all of this to you, but you are too young. I hope someday you understand we did this to protect you because we love you more than anything. More than our own lives. I want you to understand the power you have, but you will figure it out when the time is right. Please remember Willow, how special you are, please remember.

I wake up when the alarm goes off. I wish I could have had two more minutes with my mom. I think she is trying to tell me something. I think rather than these being dreams; they are memories. I have to check out the hairbrush. There has to be something with the hairbrush.

"Jax, are you up?" I think this statement, instead of saying it out loud.

"Yes, Willow. You had a dream about your mom."

"Yes, I did. How did you know?"

"I could see some of it in your head. But it was fuzzy—like a dream or like a memory."

"Yes, I was thinking the same thing. It seems more like something that already happened than a dream."

"Why don't you get ready first and then we can walk to the bridge together."

While Jax goes to the bathroom, I pull my suitcase out from under my bed. I take the jewelry case out and look at it carefully, turning it upside down, inside up over and over. I push on all the hinges and the wooden slabs on the top, the bottom, and the sides. I don't see anything unusual, but I think there may be a secret compartment.

I then start looking at the hairbrush. I turn it over and over in my hands, trying to feel something from it. I hope maybe some memories will flood back, but they don't. I turn the hairbrush on end looking closely at the handle, and I finally discover a loose piece.

Rather than open it now, I put it back in the jewelry box and decide to bring it with me to the meeting today. I want the Commander, the Captain, and Lieutenant Williams to take a look at it with me. I don't want to damage anything opening the compartment on my own.

Jax comes out of the bathroom. "You found something," she thought.

"I did. I found a loose piece on my hairbrush. I'm going to bring it to the meeting today. I don't want to do anything to damage it, but I'm not sure what it is," sending a thought back to Jax. I sit on my bed thinking for a moment.

"Hey, get ready and let's go, or we will be late." Jax urges me.

We have a food dispenser in the room, so we grab something light for breakfast and head out. My sense of direction is dismal, so I rely on Jax to get us to the bridge. Cobalt and Dharma are already there.

I decide I'll tell them about the hairbrush right away.

"Captain and Commander, before we get started I found something this morning. I looked at the jewelry box Dr. Carver gave me. As you know, it was my mom's. The only things in the jewelry box were two old photos and a hairbrush. I was looking at the hairbrush this morning and found a loose piece on the handle of it. I didn't mess with it. Instead, I put it back in the jewelry box and brought it here."

"Let's take a look at it in the conference room. Commander, please get Lieutenant Williams immediately."

"Will do Captain."

We all move into the conference room adjacent to the bridge.

When the Captain and Commander left the bridge, two other officers immediately took over. You can tell this ship is run like a well-oiled machine. They seem to anticipate each other's movements, which would come in handy if the Commander is correct in his assessment that the PG would immediately come after us. I hope it isn't the case, but I would trust the crew.

I take the brush out of the jewelry box and hand it to the Captain.

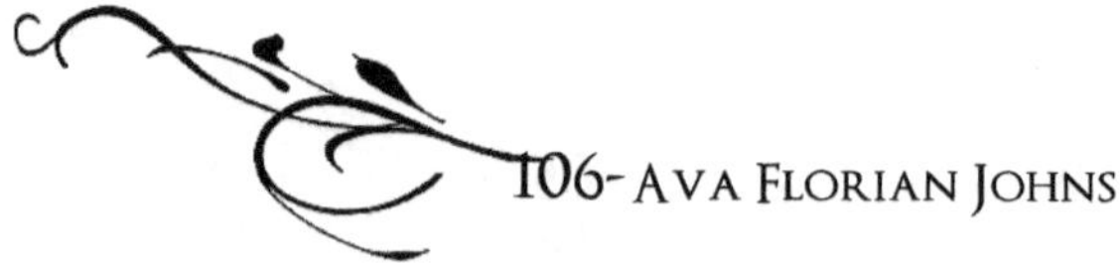

"Sir, here is the free point in the base of the handle of the brush. As I said, I didn't move it or mess with it at all. I wanted to make sure it stayed intact."

"Thank you, Willow. Let's take a look at what we have here."

Just as he is about to pull a piece out of the hairbrush, the Lieutenant walks in.

"What do we have here Willow?"

"Lieutenant, this is the hairbrush my mother used on my hair when I was a child. This morning I discovered a loose piece at the base of the handle."

The Captain hands the hairbrush to the Lieutenant.

"Lieutenant, are you able to remove the piece without damaging it?"

The Lieutenant nods his head as he takes a small tool out of his pocket and carefully removes the piece wedged in the hairbrush handle. He holds it up for all to see. It is a little disc, no doubt containing information regarding the serum.

"I think your mother is trying to tell you something, Willow," the Lieutenant says. "Let's get it back to the lab and see what we have."

"First, we need to discuss something," the Captain says. "It came to our attention that Director Jackson is the one who upended Willow's room before we left the Annex." The Captain pauses while looking at the surprised expressions around the table.

"Why would he do that?" I say.

"He stated that he did it to create a sense of urgency to get us out of the Annex. He said he was thinking of your safety. The Director was in the middle of explaining it when we lost the communication signal. We're not sure what happened there or if the Annex is still safe. We haven't been able to reach anyone at the APA since then, but we will keep attempting to reach the Annex. In the meantime, you will all report to your department heads for your daily assignments. Willow and Lieutenant Williams, please go to the lab and report back when you find out anything regarding the information on the disc. You have your assignments. Do well, dismissed."

I glance across the table at Dalton. I can tell he is still concerned about me. I wish I could reassure him everything is going to be okay. I'm not sure how to do that though. I have to prove to him I can take care of myself.

♦♦♦♦♦

After the meeting, I follow Lieutenant Williams to the lab. There, we work for hours. We report back to the Captain every hour regarding our progress. Dalton, I mean Commander Alexander, came to the lab several times. The disc contains my parents' research notes—notes that are not in the APA database or the PG database. They are documents written in my mother's handwriting. Looking at it makes me feel like I am seeing a part of my mom that I didn't know existed.

We also found photos on the disc, pictures of the farm and my mom and dad together. Some of the images were the ones the Dr. Carver said she took. It was the day she was on the farm when I didn't want to sit still for the family photo.

The notes also indicate there is another serum. This one is for the plants once they've grown. The calculation is not with the notes. It has to be encoded somewhere else on the disc. Or somewhere else entirely. I'm getting frustrated. I know my parents are trying to tell me something, but I don't know what it is. I need to take a break.

"Lieutenant Williams, can I take a break for a moment, please. I need to clear my head."

"Yes, of course, Willow, take as long as you need."

I head to the arboretum. I know this is the one place I can relax. I make it there with only one wrong turn this time. Feeling proud of myself, I saunter in the arboretum. No one else is here. I am entirely alone, and I like it that way. I need the time to think through all the

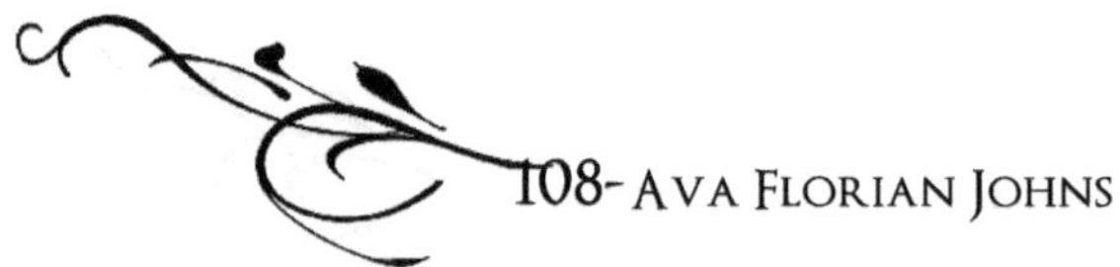

information I have been reading today. I walk over to the plants and hold my hand out over the top of them.

"Hello everyone," I say out loud. "It's great to see you again."

If others were here and saw me with the plants, they would think I'm crazy.

I walk around all of the plants, as they spring to attention. They are waiting for a command from me. "Not today guys," I tell them telepathically. I just wanted to come and visit.

People ask me if the plants talk back. I tell them it doesn't matter if they don't respond in the traditional sense. I know they understand me and I know when something's wrong with them. That's what bothers me when I create a crop, and it doesn't make it. I feel like it's like a child dying.

I sit on the bench for a long time, hoping if I sit here long enough I will figure something out. I will understand where my mom put the code in the other serum.

"Think Willow," I say out loud.

"Talking to yourself now huh?" says Dalton as he walks in the arboretum.

"Yep, I'm going crazy already. I can't figure out what my mom is trying to tell me. I know there's another serum. The Lieutenant and I figured that much out, but we can't find out what's in the other serum. I know there's code, but I don't know where it is. And I'm getting frustrated with myself because I can't figure this out."

"Willow, it's only been a day, give yourself a break. It may take longer than this. You have a whole department of people willing to help you, and they are competent. They're the best in the APA. Please let them help you, and don't feel you have to do this on your own. That's the great thing about being on a Starship as part of a crew. Everyone has your back."

"Thank you, Dalton."

He is sitting next to me now on the bench. I lean my head against his shoulder. He stiffens up a bit, then relaxes into me.

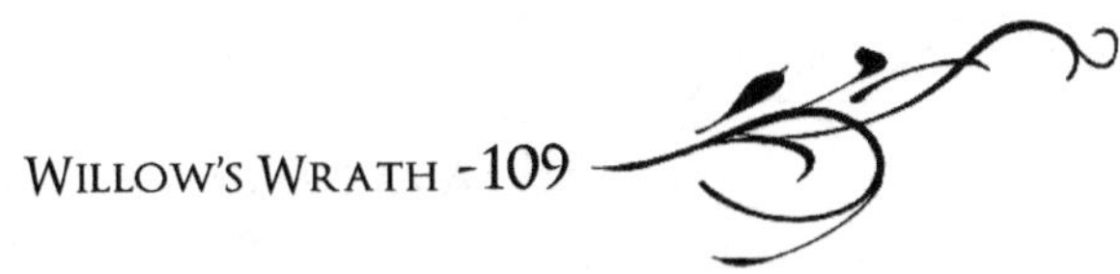

I know he's worried about the rest of the crew seeing us together. But no one else is here, and I need a shoulder, if only for a moment.

"Thank you, Dalton," I whisper as I get up and walk out the door.

✦✦✦✦✦

Later that night I am still working in the lab. I haven't eaten lunch or dinner, and I haven't gotten up from my seat for hours. My last break was the few minutes I spent in the arboretum. Dalton comes by and grabs my arm, and pulls me from the computer. "Come on; we're going to eat now."

We do have food dispensers in our rooms, but there is also a dining hall in the common area of the ship. I haven't been there yet, but I know the other members of the Omega Team were going to go tonight.

"We're going to the dining hall and get a bite to eat. Your friends are already there and told me to come and get you, drag you by your hair if I had to. Come on Willow; you have to take care of yourself."

"I was hoping I could figure out the disc."

We walk to the dining hall in silence.

There is something so comfortable about us walking together. Just like at the arboretum with my head resting on his shoulder, I felt safe. It felt comfortable. I no longer feel awkward around him. I feel confident. I feel beautiful, and he makes me feel that way.

We get to the dining hall. He walks me over to my friends and excuses himself to sit with the officers.

"That is a handsome escort you have there," Cobalt says.

"Yes, he is, isn't he?" I agree. "Thank you for sending him to get me."

"Oh, we didn't send him, he volunteered. I think he has a little crush on you Willow," Dharma says knowingly.

"I believe it's more than a little crush," Cobalt adds. "He looks like he would jump in front of a bullet for you."

"I wouldn't go that far ladies," I say laughing.

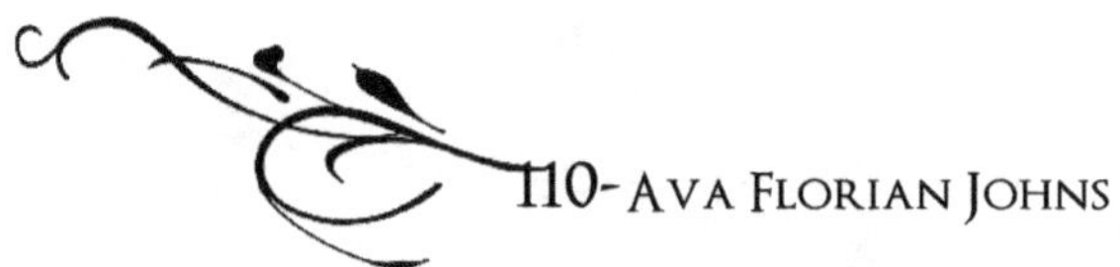

We have a great dinner together, then walk to our rooms. I love being silly with the girls. Laughing. Talking. It reminds me of the Annex, and I suddenly realize I hadn't said goodbye to the rest of the Omega Team and especially my dear friend Lizzy.

I know I have to ask permission to use the communications system on the ship. I walk over to the officer's table. "Commander Alexander, may I speak with you for a moment, please?"

"Yes, Willow, go ahead."

"May I contact the other members of the Omega Team at the Annex? May I use the communications system to do it?"

"Willow, we've been trying all day to reach Director Jackson. It's like they are not there. I can't explain it. You can try, but I don't think you will get through. I fear something has happened at the Annex."

"May I try to personally contact Beth or Ashley to see if I can get through on our tablets?"

"Go ahead and try, if you get through please let me know immediately."

"I will, thank you."

I run to my room, grab my tablet and try to reach Beth at the Annex. Dalton is right. It's like they are not there at all. I am getting nothing. I try Ashley, Todd, and Megan as well. It's like no one is even there.

♦♦♦♦♦

I am in a deep sleep when the alarms go off. I know this is the general quarter warning, and this is serious—"all hands to battle stations." Even in a sleepy state, I know what this means. The PG has found us.

CHAPTER
SIXTEEN
DALTON

Shit, the general quarter alarm is sounding. I grab my uniform and get dressed as I am running down the hallway to get to the bridge. The Captain is already there.

"What's going on Captain?"

"You were right Commander; the PG is coming for us. We intercepted a transmission from their flagship. They are two light-years away and closing in on our position. It's like they know exactly where we are heading."

"What are your orders Captain?"

"We don't have the power to outrun them. We do have one option, but it is risky. There is a relatively stable wormhole nestled within a trinary star system about a light year away. If we move now, we can beat the PG to it. The PG sensors will not be able to pick us up once we are in the wormhole."

"That seems like a risky maneuver. We don't know where we will end up. Can one of the Omega Team members help us out? How about Cobalt? She can manipulate and control objects with her mind. Could she move the PG's ship in the other direction?"

"That is an interesting concept. Ensign Radke, please get the Omega Team, double time."

"Yes, sir."

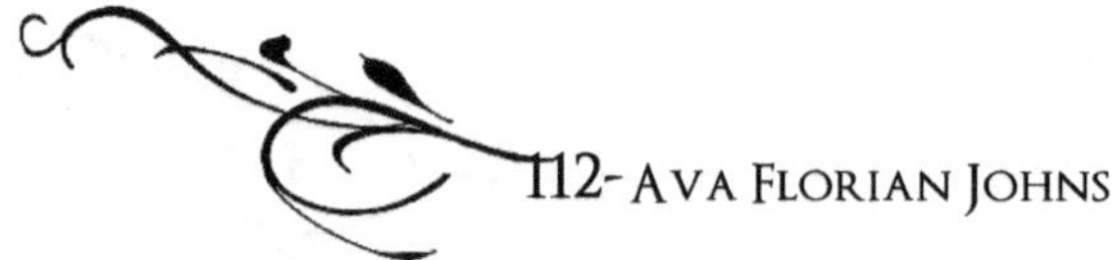

"We will continue to travel in the direction of the wormhole, top speed. We will consult with Cobalt to see if she can divert their ship before it gets to us. I don't know the depth of her powers. Kal, what is the time of the PG ships intercept?"

"Forty-eight minutes sir," Kal responds.

"Helm, what is the time to the wormhole?"

"Thirty-six minutes, sir."

"Commander, we have thirty-six minutes to determine if Cobalt can move the PG ship."

The Omega Team must have run from their quarters. They made it to the bridge in record time. I am glad they are taking the security of this ship seriously.

"Omega Team, this is the situation. The PG has located our ship and is on an intercept course. They will be here in under forty-eight minutes. Their ship is much faster than ours, so we can't outrun them. The only option we have to is to go through a relatively stable wormhole and hope for the best. The wormhole is approximately thirty-six minutes away. Commander Alexander has an interesting idea which concerns your team. Commander, please explain."

"Cobalt, would you be able to move the PG ship out of the way? Send them in an entirely different direction?"

"Commander, I have never moved anything that large before, or anything that is moving that fast. I can certainly try. But if I were you I would keep traveling toward the wormhole as a back-up."

Cobalt has incredible powers, but she is right, I have never seen her move something this large before. The other members of the team give her encouragement, then back up, and let her do her thing. When Cobalt does her telekinesis, it looks like she has a wind machine blowing in her hair. She closes her eyes, puts her arms at her side, her palms out, concentrating as hard as she can on moving or stopping an object. Her long red hair blows backward creating waves of movement. It is quite fascinating to watch her.

She is concentrating so hard; she almost loses her balance. The Omega Team runs up to stabilize her and continues to help her maintain her focus and balance.

It is great to see them work together—they are a real team. It makes me think I was wrong about bringing the Omega Team onboard, although I wish the team were not in the imminent danger we are all in now. I wish I had been wrong about that too.

I know Cobalt is working as hard as she can. She says she has to locate the other ship in her mind's eye, and it is too far away. If it were closer to our proximity, she would probably have a higher rate of success. Although if they were closer to our vicinity, they would blow us out of the sky.

Our time is ticking down. I know we have to do something soon, or we will be destroyed. Our ship is no match for the flagship of the PG. Although our ship is an excellent maneuvering ship, and we may be able to out-maneuver them, there is no way we could outrun or outshoot the PG ship.

"Kal, what is the time of the PG ships intercept now?" the Captain asks.

"Eighteen minutes sir and closing in fast," Kal responds.

"Helm, what is the time to the wormhole?"

"Less than five minutes, sir."

"Omega Team, any progress?" The Captain asks hopefully.

"No sir, they would have to be closer to us for my telekinesis to work." Cobalt looks defeated.

"Helm, point us toward the wormhole at maximum speed," the Captain orders.

"Yes, sir."

I hope this works. The problem with wormholes is we could end up anywhere, or worse; it could destroy us. If we end up in a different quadrant of space, we may never make it back to Earth in our lifetime. It is one of the risks we know can happen when enduring space travel, but we don't like to think about it.

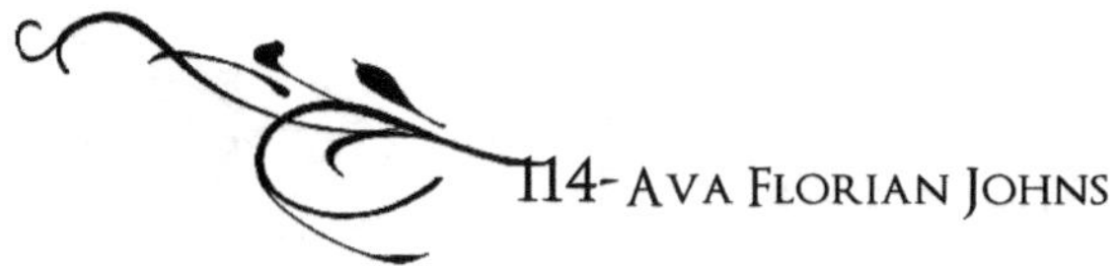

"Omega Team, strap in, this may get bumpy," I point to some empty chairs on the bridge.

We get closer and closer to the wormhole. We all turn toward the Captain when he starts his announcement to the crew.

"Crew of the Starship Armargosa, this is the Captain speaking. The flagship of the PG Armada is closing in on our position. We can't outrun or outgun them, but we can out-maneuver them. We are about to head our ship directly into a wormhole. All hands brace for impact."

"Captain, enemy ship closing in quickly."

"Wormhole on the main viewer," the Captain orders.

Our first look at the wormhole is spectacular. It is directly ahead. The scientist says it is only visible every two hundred thirty-three minutes, so we have to time our entry correctly.

"Enter now!" the Captain's voice booms. "If we don't make it through immediately, it will close up on us, and we will have to wait another two hundred thirty-three minutes. We won't make it that long in a firefight with the PG ship!"

I can hear the gasps of the Omega Team and the bridge crew. The view is fantastic. I have certainly never seen anything like it. It's breathtaking with vibrant and magnificent colors. It looks like we can see the other side of the universe.

As we start our ascent into the wormhole, I can feel the tension of the crew rising. The science officer, Lieutenant Noah Williams, is announcing the readings from the wormhole as we continue our trip inside. He is indicating the wormhole is stable enough for us to enter. As soon as he says this, we enter the wormhole. The master alarms go off with ear-splitting shrieks, and the entire ship starts violently shaking. It feels like the ship will break apart around us.

"How much longer until we are through the wormhole?"

"Three minutes, Captain."

"Will the ship hold together that long?"

"Yes sir, Captain, she will hold together," answers Lieutenant Cameron.

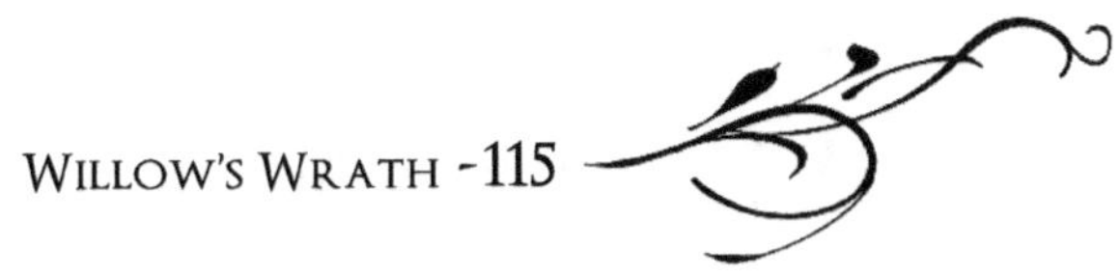

"Another ninety seconds and we will be out of here," Lieutenant Williams states.

We hold our breath for another ninety seconds and desperately hope the ship will stay together. Abruptly, we shoot out of the wormhole with high power. The view is unbelievably gorgeous, with pink and blue sky and bright stars all around us. Now to determine where we are.

"Where are we, helmsman?" the Captain asks.

"We are at coordinates 08-90-55-62. We have traveled to the other end of the quadrant from where we started out."

"How soon can we get back to Earth?"

"I would estimate at least five years, Captain," Lieutenant Williams states.

"I concur, Captain," answers Lieutenant Cameron.

"Understood Lieutenant Cameron, please dispatch an engineering crew immediately to check for damage to the ship. Have them run diagnostics on the central computer and shields."

"Yes, Captain."

We will need to figure out how to get back sooner. This mission is too critical not to do everything we can to get back quicker. I can tell the Omega Team is severely shaken as they are not used to this kind of stress. Fortunately, I have faced this type of pressure several times in my military career.

"Commanding officers and Omega Team, to the conference room. We need to devise a plan."

We all follow the Captain to the conference room and as soon as the door slides shut he addresses us.

"We are in an unexpected situation. We need to work the problem and not let our emotions get in the way. Our mission has not changed in any way. We still need to find a planet to colonize for the APA. We are going to start from this end of the galaxy and work our way back. We will search and barter for supplies on the way. We will ration our supplies, and find allies to work with."

"Are you worried about the PG finding us out here?" Cobalt asks.

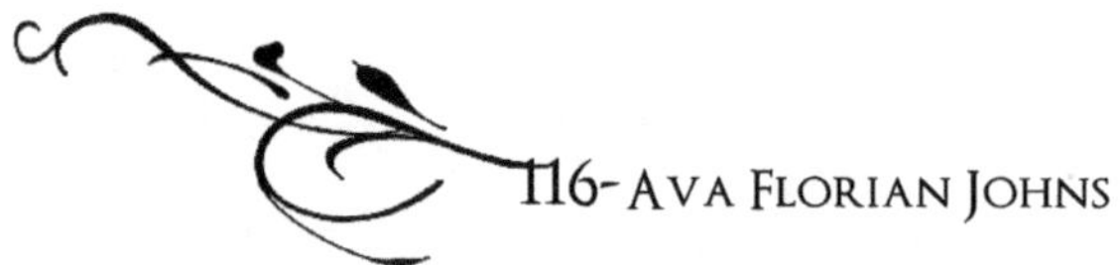

"The end of the wormhole shifts positions, so I am not concerned about the PG starship being able to get us anytime soon. I doubt they even followed us through. They may think we broke up on impact in the wormhole. I want the Science Team to do extensive research on any methods they can find to get back. Another wormhole, an anomaly, anything. Work with the Engineering Department to come up with viable solutions and get them to me within the next twenty-four hours. Do well, everyone dismissed."

Everyone else left the room, but I stayed behind to see what else I could do. I hate feeling this helpless. It reminds me of when my father used to beat my mother. I felt weak and alone. I couldn't defend or protect her, and I believe she ended up losing her life because of me. I am not going to let that happen to this group. I need to protect my crew, the Omega Team, and Willow.

"Captain, what do you think of our situation?"

"Well, it seems dire, but I know we have a good crew. We also have superhumans on board. I think we need to utilize the skills of the Omega Team at every opportunity. Start working with them and the department heads to see what they can do to help with the supplies, to make our energy last longer, anything that will prolong the life of this ship."

"Will do, Captain. You made a tough decision today. It was the right one. You saved the lives of two hundred fifty souls. I am very proud to be your second in command."

"Thank you, Dalton, I appreciate it."

I walk out of the conference room trying to think of a plan to extend the life of what we have on board. We will need fuel for the engines, food for the crew, and of course other living supplies. We can ration the three years of supplies into four years, but probably not five. Without delay, I contact the department heads and schedule a meeting. When we have a plan, we'll get the Omega Team on board. Having Willow on the ship certainly makes getting food easier. With her power over plants, she can create the food we will need to survive. We brought everything she would need to build crops on the new colony, and she can use them here first.

✦✦✦✦✦

"As you know our mission has suffered a little setback. Instead of having the directive to look for a suitable planet for colonization we will be in areas of space we haven't been before. We will need to rely on our intuition and skill to get us back to our space and meet our objectives. I know all of you are up for the challenge. The first thing I learned about space travel is something will always go wrong, then something else, and it continues. We need to come up with a plan from every department. The Commanding Officers and Omega Team members will give us their suggestions. We will not leave this room until we formulate a plan for the Captain. He made a tough decision today, but one that saved the lives of every person on this ship. I have pledged to assist him until my dying breath, and I know you all feel the same way."

All the commanders nodded their heads in affirmation. I am glad to see their loyalty; now our mission has extra challenges.

"First up the Communications Team. Lieutenant Allium and Jax, please share with us your thoughts on the current situation."

Astrid stood up to speak for the Communications Team. "Thank you, Commander Alexander. Jax and I have been working on how to expand our communications system so we can improve communication at a further bandwidth. We want to get a message to the APA military group to advise them of our current status. Jax and I will have a test ready by 2200 hours today."

"Good. If you need any other resources, please let me know. Do you have any other suggestions or thoughts?"

Jax is tapping at her tablet like a crazy person. Trying to get her thoughts out so Lieutenant Allium can read them out loud. Jax thrusts the tablet in the Lieutenant's hands.

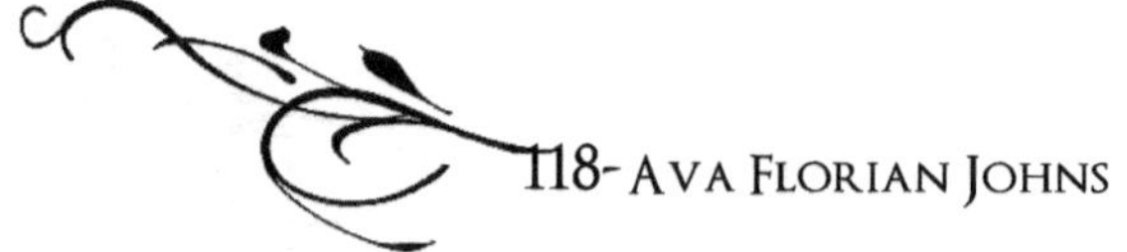

118- Ava Florian Johns

"Jax obviously has an idea. 'What if we sent out a signal to our allies and other APA ships alerting them to our presence in this sector? We know some people in the APA and former partners of the PG are in hiding in the outer ring. We would have to code it, to keep our position a secret until we validate they are real allies."

The rest of the table agreed. It is an effective plan considering Jax has had no formal training in the area of communications.

"You will need some help with programming, and when do you think you could have it ready to test?" I ask.

"Give us a couple of days for that one. Jax and I will work on attempting communications with the APA. Then we will start working on the program for the message."

"All right, good job Communications Team. Next up, Security. Kal and Dharma."

The Lieutenant Commander stands. He is an incredible force of nature. Kal is almost seven feet tall. I feel dwarfed standing next to him, and I am over six feet tall. He has black skin, a bald head, and dark piercing eyes. He is incredibly intimidating if you don't know him. Everyone looks a little scared of him, everyone except Dharma. She is as relaxed as if she has known him her whole life. Although if I had Dharma's shapeshifting ability, I probably wouldn't be afraid of anyone either. If I considered Lor Kal a force of nature, I give Dharma the title amazingly fierce.

"Commander, I would caution sending out any messages into space. There could be hostile enemies out there waiting for someone like us. They could steal our technology and our ship and most likely leave us for dead. I would like to work with the Communications Team to come up with a safe way to find allies. I think it's a good idea, but we need to be careful. Dharma and I also want to continue combat training drills for everyone. Mandatory. We will set up a daily schedule. When we go on away missions, I want everyone prepared for the worst. We have no idea what we'll find out there. We could find an enemy far worse than the PG."

Kal sits down.

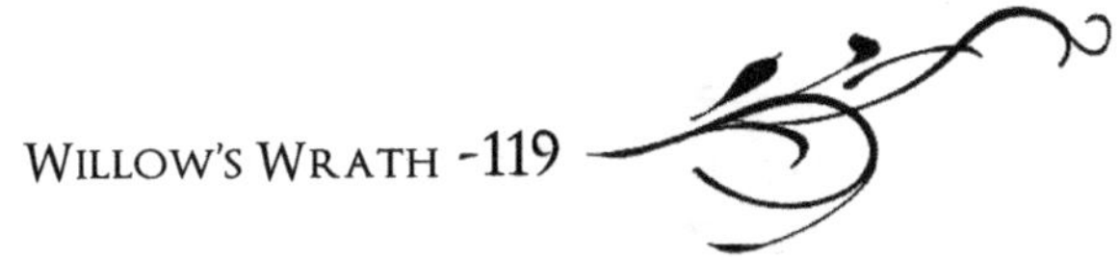

"Dharma do you have anything to add?" I ask. I'm curious to see what she thinks about the situation.

"Thank you, Commander. The other thing the Lieutenant Commander and I discussed is getting an inventory of our weapons. We need to prepare for any contingency because we don't know if we're in hostile territory or not. And it's best to be equipped. We should also look at what we have to make weapons."

"Thank you, Security Team. I will expect an inventory of the weapons systems by 1900 hours tonight."

"Next up Science Department. Science Officer Williams will you please start?"

"Yes, Commander. The good news is we have Willow on board, so we don't have to worry as much about rationing our food supply. She will be able to create crops in the arboretum, and we have everything necessary for her to do so. We can also build another greenhouse in one of the cargo bays. That way we will have our resources doubled. We can get started on that today. Another idea is to come up with an alternate fuel source. We would need to research and develop something in the lab. My team can start working on it today, and we will have a full plan for you tomorrow at 0800 hours."

"Very good Lieutenant. Willow, do you have anything to add?"

"I thought if there are planets in the vicinity we could go to find alternate food sources. Possibly some birds or animals for protein and raise them on the ship. We could section off part of the cargo bay from the greenhouse to accommodate them. The other thing is looking for other types of fruits and vegetables on other planets. This way we could find suitable planets for colonization, and at the same time restock our supplies."

"Good, Willow, you and Lieutenant Williams get a plan together."

"Last but not least, Lieutenant Cameron and Cobalt. Cameron, please share your suggestions."

"I would like to say something first," Cobalt interjects.

"Yes, Cobalt go ahead."

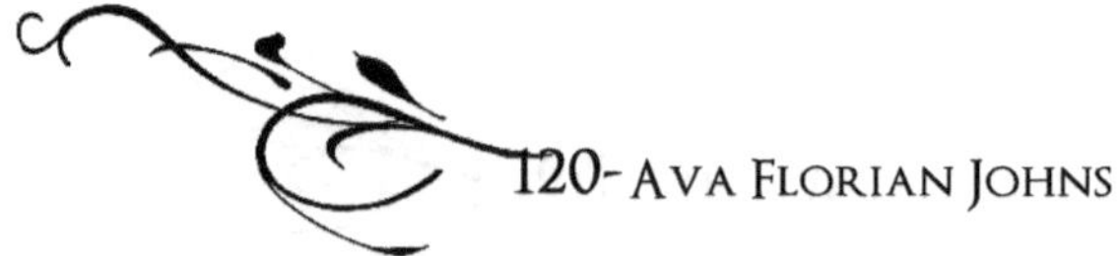

"I want to apologize for earlier today. I wish I could have helped us, but I couldn't. And now we're so far from home I feel it is my fault."

"No, Cobalt it isn't your fault. This is not something we had a contingency plan for. It is something which happens in space travel," I say, trying to reassure her. "I assure you we will be okay. We will continue our mission as planned. We asked you to do something you have never done before. We do not blame you, do not blame yourself, and that's an order. We need you, and we need everyone to focus on a plan."

"Thank you, Commander."

Now that Cobalt stopped apologizing. Lieutenant Cameron stands up.

"The Science Department already mentioned fuel. That is my biggest concern right now. I want to ensure we have the power to get back. There are some modifications we can make to the engines to save power, and we will conserve as much as we can. I would suggest rationing out food dispensers. We can use the food Willow grows, and we can use the dining hall for our meals. I believe if we do that we can stretch the power we have to last the five years."

"Thank you, Cameron. Does anyone have anything else to add?" I say, looking around the room. "I want updates on all your tests as soon as possible. If you need anything else to do, your jobs ask for it. If there's nothing else, do well, everyone dismissed." I stand as everyone leaves the room.

I feel good about the suggestions the team has. There are some possible ideas. I know Cobalt feels terrible, but she will have to get over it and move on. We need to work the problem, not make it worse.

CHAPTER
SEVENTEEN
WILLOW

I can tell Cobalt is having a difficult time. I hang back and walk with her to the Engineering Department. I look to Lieutenant Williams, and he understands I need to comfort my friend.

"Cobalt, it isn't your fault. It is not something you remotely thought you would ever have to do. You never practiced your power on something so large. It would have been a fluke if you had been able to move the ship." I rub her shoulders. "We will be all right."

"I know Willow. I just feel terrible. I promise I'll get over it, but I wish I would have been able to help."

"You will help Cobalt. Please put this behind you."

"Thank you Willow; you are a good friend."

I walk back to the Science Department. I didn't get lost this time which is a big win for me.

"All right Willow, let's get to work. Would you like to head to the arboretum first or check out the cargo bay space for the new greenhouse?"

"Let's go to the arboretum first. I can start working on the corn, potatoes, and grain. Lieutenant, what do you think we should grow in the greenhouse?"

"Let's take a look at our inventory before we go to the arboretum. We have seeds and starter plants in the cargo bays."

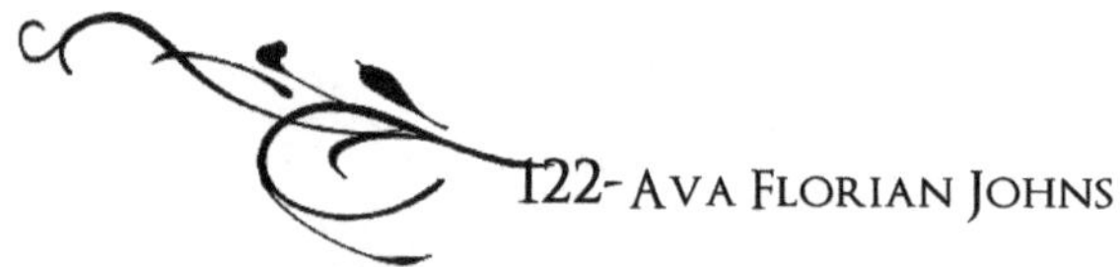

"We will see what we have and then make an educated decision. My thoughts would be cucumbers, green beans, pumpkins, and fruits. You are right about adding protein to our diets. Although we probably have enough protein powder to last a lifetime."

"Gross," I shiver and make a face. "We can do better than that."

"All right let's get to work."

We head to the cargo bay to get an inventory of our seeds and starter plants. Everything is still in the boxes. We pull everything out to categorize and count them. I write everything down so we can have them included in our report to the Commander.

I can feel the Commander's anxiety radiating from him. He looks cool on the outside, but inside he is concerned. I know he's putting an awful lot of pressure on himself to make sure we are okay. He is right the Captain saved our lives today. We need to help him and get ourselves out of this.

I keep reminding myself it could have been a lot worse. We could be eighty years away from home instead of only five. I have heard of this happening before about ships being lost for years or never being heard from again.

There are wormholes and anomalies all over this sector. If we can communicate with the APA-military I know, we'll be in good shape. They will be able to guide us home, but right now we have to help ourselves.

◆◆◆◆◆

We finish in the cargo bay and go the arboretum to get started planting. I'm still having trouble with potatoes. They are turning into lumpy brown balls instead of decent potatoes. I'm still not sure what I am doing wrong. I finish up with the corn and the grain. Those crops turned out well. We head back to the lab to research my parents' notes on the potatoes. Remembering I have another place to look as well, I take out the disc from the hairbrush.

I find out from looking at the research notes that my parents also had issues with the potatoes. It turns out you need to go slower with those. You can't grow them and harvest them in only one day. After figuring this out, I go back to the arboretum and fix the potatoes.

Just as I am leaving Dalton walks in.

"Hello, Commander."

"You can call me Dalton, Willow. As long as we're alone."

"Hello, Dalton. Should I ask how you're doing? I know it's been a very stressful day." I try to keep the mood light.

"Well, that's an understatement. But as I said before it's the way space travel goes."

I'm glad to see he still has his confidence and somewhat cocky attitude, but I am not sure if it's entirely real or if it's a facade. I think he is trying to appear more confident than he feels. I can't explain it, but I can feel it. It is like we are still connected. Sometimes I think I can hear his thoughts. Crazy, right?

"Everything will be okay Willow, you'll see. Things will work out. We have to work together to figure it out."

"I came to the arboretum for a status update. Where's Lieutenant Williams?"

"He's in the lab finishing up the information on the disc. We found some useful information in my parents' documentation."

"Interesting, continue," Dalton looks intrigued.

"You know how I've been having trouble with the potatoes. They all turn into big lumpy brown balls. Well, I figured out why. It turns out you have to go slow with potatoes, and you can't grow them all in one day. I know it's not a big thing, but I'm glad we found the disc to help us. It also makes me feel more connected to my parents."

"I see the corn, grain, and potatoes in the arboretum. What are you planting in the greenhouse?"

"Lieutenant Williams and I finished the inventory in the cargo bay. We have green beans, cucumbers, snap peas, carrots, and some variations of squash. It should be enough for us to get started. We

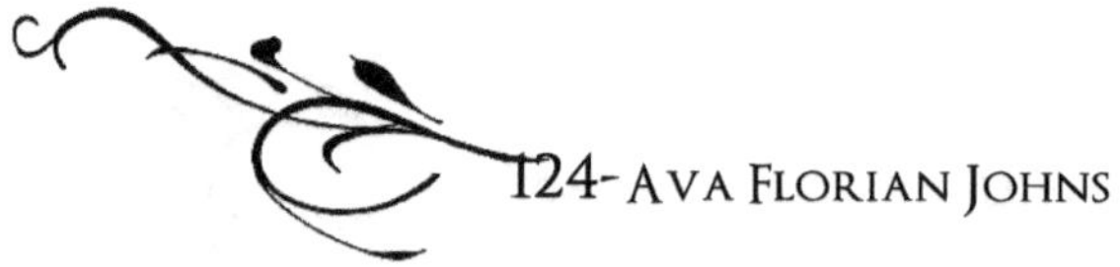

124- Ava Florian Johns

will continue to save seeds and starter plants so we won't run out of food. Our biggest issue is we may run out of space on the ship."

"Well, that's great news. I came from the Communication team, and things are not going as well there. They were not able to contact the APA military base. They'll continue to try, but it doesn't look good."

"Shoot, I was hoping it would work. So, do you want to sit down with me on the bench for a minute? I bet you have not taken a break all day."

"You are right; I haven't."

We sit down on the bench, and. I lean in and put my head on his shoulder. I feel better having this little bit of contact with him. This time he doesn't stiffen up or pull away from me. Instead, he turns and faces me, and kisses me ever so gently. It's a simple brush of the lips.

"I was wrong about you coming on the ship. You have been a tremendous asset. And somehow I feel better when you're around me. I feel more grounded and a lot calmer. Thank you for that."

Even a slight touch of his lips to mine is enough to make my insides slushy. He has such a commanding presence but is so gentle when he wants to be.

He puts his arms around me and holds me close for a couple of minutes. But it feels like an eternity.

He gives me one quick kiss and off he goes. "I have to get back to work now."

"Will I see you later Dalton?"

"Chances are yes, it's not a very big ship. I'll check on you tonight, but don't work too late."

"I won't, I promise."

✦✦✦✦✦

I walk back to the science lab feeling revived. It's amazing what one little kiss does.

Lieutenant Williams is waiting for my return to the science lab. "Time to get started on the greenhouse plans. I want you to indicate where you want the plants to go and how much room you need. We'll work with the designers and architects to build the greenhouse, and we'll probably need engineering as well."

I nod in agreement.

"Do you think any of the members of the Omega Team could help us out with building the greenhouse?" the Lieutenant asks.

"Yes, I'm sure they would. Cobalt would be a great help. She can move the heavier pieces for us with her power. The other two could help with grunt work and move other stuff around. I'm sure they wouldn't mind helping out."

♦♦♦♦♦

Our plans for the greenhouse are due at 0800 hours tomorrow. I need to make sure I finish them tonight. We also need to give our idea for the greenhouse to Commander Alexander for the Captain. I want to ensure yields on the crops are calculated correctly, so I check them three times. I then have two other members of the department recheck them.

Time is passing, and I know if I don't get out of here soon Dalton will come and drag me out again. I am halfway down the hallway from the science lab and run into Dalton.

"Of course, you're just leaving."

"Yep, I figured you were on your way to drag me out again."

"I'm worried about your well-being. This job can consume you, believe me I know. That's all I used to think about."

"And what do you think about now?"

"I believe you know," he says, winking at me.

This moment is the most playful I have ever seen him.

"You want to take a little walk before you turn in?"

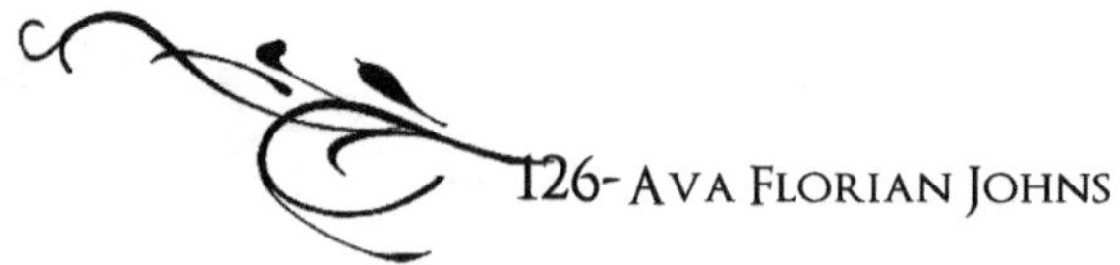

"Yes, that would be great," I respond. "I've been sitting at the computer so long I'm a little sore. Then I have combat training tomorrow with Dharma—ouch."

"You should be lucky you don't have it with Kal. He's tough even on me."

"He looks harsh all the time, and I'm surprised Dharma is not afraid of him. But, she seems to get along well with him."

We walk around one whole deck and then end up back at the science lab. Neither one of us is ready to say goodnight.

"Dalton, would you like to go to the arboretum again?"

"Maybe we should say goodnight."

I try to hide the disappointment on my face.

I thought he had opened up more, but I guess I am wrong.

"I will walk you to your room," he says. "At least I know that way you're going to get there."

"You are funny."

"All right let's go."

We head to my room. When we get to my door, he kisses me gently on the forehead. "Goodnight Willow."

"Goodnight Dalton."

DALTON

Why do I keep kissing her? I am an idiot, that's why. I can't help myself. When I am around her, I lose control. It nearly broke my heart to see her so sad tonight, but I have to stop. I can't let people on the starship know I have a relationship with her. I'm not sure if it is a relationship, but it's something. I should never have kissed her back at the Annex.

Ever since that one mind-numbing kiss, I feel so connected to her. I can't stop thinking about it. I have to focus. I have to be aware of everything else that is going on, on the ship. I know the crew is feeling stressed. I need to make sure everyone remains focused and works the problem. The focus needs to start with me. I need to set the example.

♦♦♦♦♦

Instead of going to my quarters, I stop at the Captain's room. I knock.

"Come in."

"Captain, before I hit the rack I wanted to see if you need anything else from me tonight."

"No Commander, good job today. You kept it cool, and you kept everyone on track. Focused. We got a lot accomplished today and

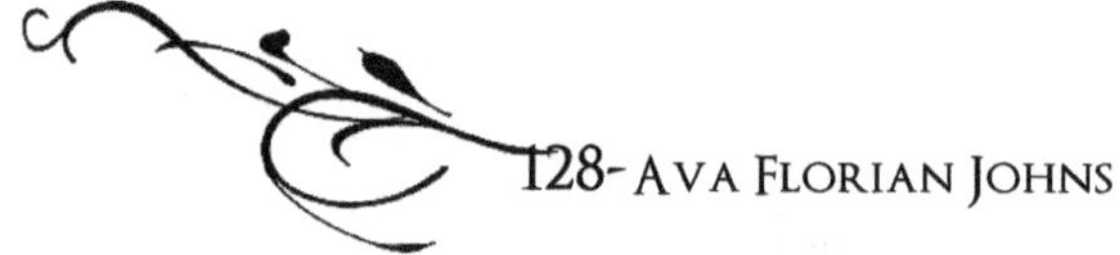

got some great ideas from the teams. I know they couldn't have done it without you."

"Thank you, Captain, I appreciate the compliment."

"Goodnight Commander, see you tomorrow."

♦♦♦♦♦

I find myself walking past Willow's room. I stop and am about to knock, but change my mind. How would it look if the Commander is knocking on a team member's door so late in the evening? What is wrong with me? Why can't I stay away from her? I hardly know her, and I am acting like a damn fool.

WILLOW

I hear beeping in the middle of the night. It is coming from under my bed. I try to be as quiet as possible so as not to wake Jax, and I start pulling out my suitcase from under the bed. The only thing that could be beeping would be my tablet.

I pull it out and turn it on. My heart sinks when I realize there is a message from the Annex. The Omega Team at the Annex is trying to contact me. I take the tablet into the bathroom and start playing the message. It's a video from Megan and Todd. It came in right before we entered the wormhole and directly after I tried to contact them for the last time.

Todd and Megan seem panicked. They are both talking over each other. Then Todd takes over.

"Willow. We were hoping to reach you in person. Something's happened here at the Annex. We've been taken over by the Planetary Government. Beth and Ashley suspected something was going on with Director Jackson, so they had Megan use her power of invisibility to spy on him. Megan was in his office when the Supreme Chancellor from the PG walked in. She overheard Director Jackson saying he killed Dr. Carver and Christopher. They knew his real identity, and he couldn't afford to keep them around any longer. Megan recorded part of the conversation. We want you to see this, please help us."

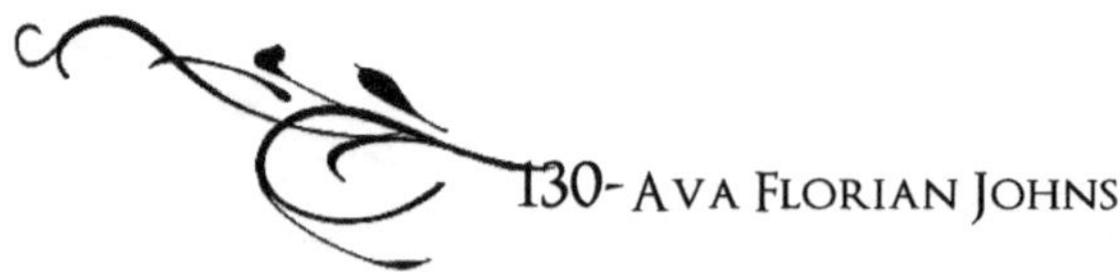

Todd started the recording.

You can see that Megan is at a weird angle because she is trying to keep the tablet out of sight. The Supreme Chancellor and Director Jackson come on the screen.

"Supreme Chancellor, welcome to the APA Annex. We are happy to have you."

"Brother, it's good to see you. I've missed you since you came out here to this hellhole."

Brother? What does he mean brother? The Director is brothers with the evilest man in the world, the Supreme Chancellor. I can see how wicked the director looks. He isn't his usual silly self. I still can't believe Todd and Megan said he killed Dr. Carver and Christopher. What reason would he have to do that?

"Scott, where are Dr. Carver and Christopher? The Director is looking for his son and hasn't been able to get ahold of either of them."

"They were both taken care of."

"What do you mean 'taken care of'?"

"I had to kill them because they both knew too much, and besides, Dr. Carver was getting soft. She had an emotional connection to Willow, and she was more interested in the science than she was in our weapon. She was a fool. Willow could have been so much more. Even Dr. Carver has no idea of the power she possesses.

And Christopher was a huge liability. He knew my real identity. You understand why now, don't you, brother?" He laughs maniacally. "So what happened to the ship? Did you blow it out of the sky?"

"No the flagship of the PG armada is on course for an intercept with the APA Starship. But don't worry Brother, we gave them faulty information the fools are headed right into an unstable wormhole. It doesn't matter if we blow them up or not, they will get torn apart by the wormhole. The wormhole will do our work for us."

"I hope you're right for your sake." He laughs again, "Just kidding, brother."

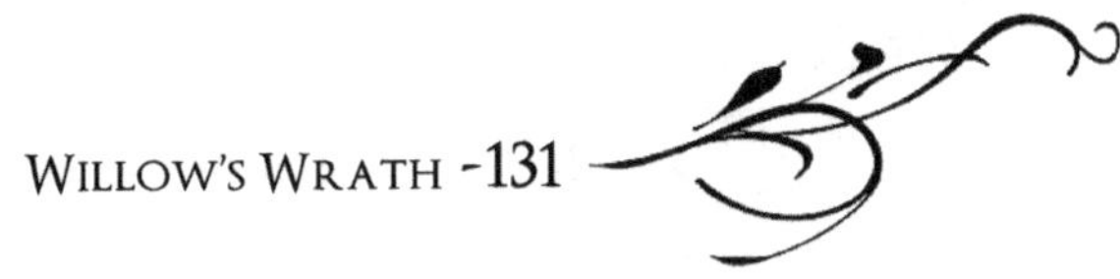

At this point in the recording, the tablet beeps. Both the Supreme Chancellor and Director Jackson turn and look directly at Megan. They apparently can't see her, but they know she is there.

"Megan, I know it's you. Come out!" Director Jackson screams.

That is the end of the video. Todd turned his tablet back on Megan and himself.

"Don't worry Willow; I am fine. By the time they came after me, I was well on my way down the hallway. We got the Omega Team out of the Annex with help from Beth and Ashley, including the younger team members as well, your friend Lizzy made it out, too. We are all safe, but we're unsure of what to do and would like some help. We don't know who we can trust. We can't trust the PG, and we can't trust the APA. We are now hiding out in an abandoned building trying to take care of the kids. Everyone's pretty shaken up. The PG took over the Annex."

Todd chimes in, "We're not sure where to go. Willow, please let us know that you are okay. There is a message from Dr. Carver you have to see; I can't explain it to you now, we don't have time."

The screen went black, and that is the end of the message. I have to get this to the Commander and Captain immediately.

I walk out of the bathroom and gently wake Jax up. "Jax I need to talk to you. It's important," I say, wiping my tears from my cheeks.

Telepathically, she asks what is wrong. My mind is a jumble, but I try to piece together the last images I saw. Jax looks shocked. We leave the room still in our pajamas and run down the hallway to Dharma and Cobalt's room. We knock several times before they open the door.

"Willow it better be important." Dharma snarls.

"We have something to show you."

We grab Dharma and Cobalt and continue running down the hallway. We knock on the Commander's door.

"I bet if you say it's you Willow, he will open the door in a jiffy," Cobalt says.

I give her a dirty look.

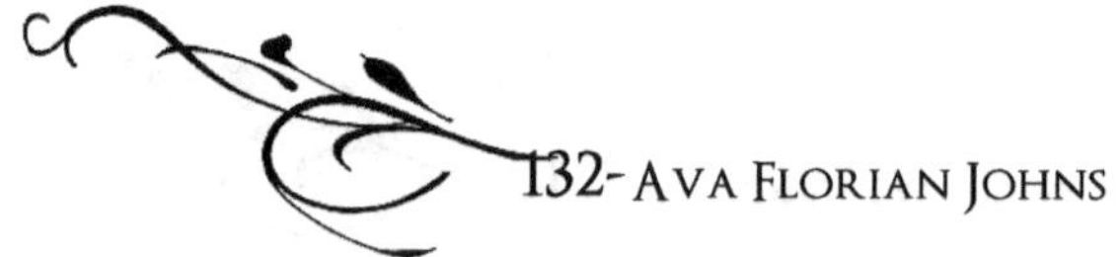

It took only a second for the Commander to answer.

He has thrown on a pair of pants but doesn't have a shirt on.

"What's wrong?"

"Can we come in?"

"Yeah sure." He moves aside and lets us in.

"What's wrong ladies?"

"I need to show you something. It's a message I received from Todd and Megan from the Annex. They sent it right before we went in the wormhole. I feel so sorry that I didn't see it until now."

"It's okay Willow, play the message."

I start up the message. Dharma and Cobalt gasp over the part about Director Jackson and his brother the Supreme Chancellor. I realize then that I haven't explained to them what happened. We watch to the end of the video, and nobody speaks for a moment.

"Well let's go wake up Captain Holloway. He is going to want to see this."

Commander Alexander put a shirt on. What a pity, I thought. We head out to the next room.

We all get to Captain Holloway's door, and Dalton knocks.

"Captain Holloway, its Commander Alexander and the Omega Team. We have some urgent news from the Annex. Please open the door."

We don't hear anything.

"Chris, it's Dalton," Dalton says, knocking again.

"I don't think he's in there," Dharma states.

We all turn and head to the bridge.

Sure enough, Captain Holloway is sitting in this chair on the bridge.

The girls finally realize they are in their pajamas. Captain Holloway's seems to notice as well and has a bemused look on his face.

"Captain Holloway we need to see you immediately."

"Let's go in the conference room."

"What's this all about?" He says when we get in the meeting room.

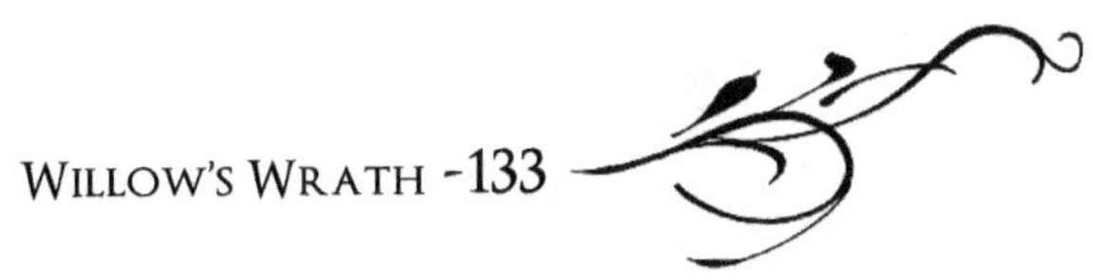

"Willow, please show him the video."

I put the screen in front of the Captain.

He doesn't say a word, but the look on his face says everything. Now I understand why communications aren't getting through to the Annex. I didn't realize the gravity of the situation until now. I'm glad the Omega Team is safe for now, but I'm not sure how we can help them from here.

"Commander, please wake up the head of the departments. Tell them there's an emergency meeting in five minutes. Omega Team, go get some clothes on."

"Thank you, sir," we all say in unison.

The Commander gets up from the table and goes to communicate with the department heads. The Captain put his face in his hands looking discouraged.

CHAPTER
TWENTY
DALTON

Well, this is a new predicament. The mission, the APA, Director Jackson. I can't believe all this happened and it's only been forty-eight hours since we left Earth.

We need to work on our problem here, and now we're worried about the people in the Annex. I can't believe the deception went as high as the Director, and that he's related to the Supreme Chancellor. He sure had me fooled. He acts like such a bumbling idiot, so utterly incompetent, I would never have expected him to do something like this. I knew there was something I didn't like about him. He made me uneasy because he always seemed to know what I was thinking.

"I got a hold of all the department heads; they are on their way."

"Thank you. What do you think of the newest development Commander?"

"Frankly I'm shocked. Director Jackson is an idiot. I never thought he'd be capable of something like this. And how did he hide the fact for all these years that he is the Supreme Chancellor's brother? He's been working with the APA for at least fifteen years."

"What do you think our next move should be?"

"We have to do everything we can to try to communicate with the Omega Team on Earth. They are our best chance of finding out what's going on. We were also unable to get hold of the APA-military. I wonder if it is also taken over by the PG."

"I know we have other APA cells on Earth and throughout the Galaxy. Maybe we try contacting one of the smaller bases? Maybe one closer to our present location?"

"Sounds like a good plan."

"Let's get engineering and the Communications Team on it immediately."

"Maybe the teams will have some other ideas as well. We have to be able to boost our signal strength to communicate further. Maybe we can piggyback on another signal. Or maybe we can find an ally here with the technology to help us."

At that moment, the teams walk in.

The Captain plays the video for the department heads.

Everyone in the room falls silent. The Captain waits a moment before beginning.

"Willow received this message shortly before we entered the wormhole. She discovered it tonight. I need ideas, now. We need to figure out how to communicate with the Omega Team. Do whatever we need to do to piggyback a signal on another transmission, or find somebody with the technology to help us get a message through to them. Any ideas?"

Cameron speaks first. "The Engineering Department will search for other transmissions leaving this area. We will let the Communications Team know. We should be able to find something to help us. What's the closest inhabited planet from here?"

Captain Holloway answers, "That is what I was doing when the Omega Team came in with the video. The nearest planet is Artona in the Selinon sector. It has one billion inhabitants, but we don't know much about them. We have never traveled out this far before, so we don't have a lot of information, and we don't know if it is up-to-date."

Lieutenant Cameron speaks again. "My suggestion would be finding out as much as we can about these people. We'll see what kind of technology they have and see if they're sending deep-space transmissions out. Maybe they can help us."

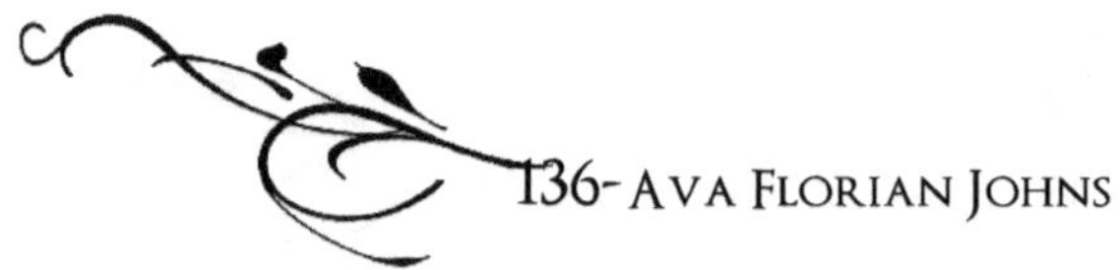

"All right. I think our first task is to assemble an away team. Commander Alexander, please pick your team members. I want two teams."

"Captain, we will go down armed, won't we?" The security officer asks.

"Yes, Lieutenant Commander, we will go down armed, and I do want a mix of the crew with the Omega Team. Omega Team, you will be armed as well. I will not risk any of you on this mission. Commander, please take Kal in the first team to secure the landing site."

"Yes, sir. I will assemble my away teams and have the information to you within the hour."

"Thank you, Commander, do well, everyone dismissed."

As we all walk out the door, the Captain puts his head in his hands again.

CHAPTER
TWENTY-ONE
WILLOW

I walk back to my room with the others but decide I need a moment to myself, so I head to the arboretum. It seems like it is one thing after another on this ship. I get used to one disaster, and then there is another. I am not complaining. I feel like I matter here. People listen to me, and I know I make a difference.

I haven't let myself think about the Director killing Dr. Carver and Christopher because I didn't want to cry in front of the others. As soon as I get to the arboretum I let the tears flow for Christopher, but more for Dr. Carver. She may have been working for the other side, but she raised me. She was kind to me at the boarding school when nobody else was. She believed in me and supported me my whole life. All the way up to trying to kidnap me and make me build a weapon of mass destruction for the PG. So the last part is bad, but everything else was good, even if she had evil intentions.

I wonder what Dr. Carver told them about me? I don't know if I would trust anything she would say at this point, but still, what would she gain by lying? And what did Director Jackson mean the power I possess? It is enough to drive me crazy, and I realize I am devastated by her deception and her death, but I still miss her.

I am a terrible judge of character on two counts. How could I miss that Dr. Carver lied to me for all these years and how could I miss that Director Jackson is such an evil man? I feel stupid, but I

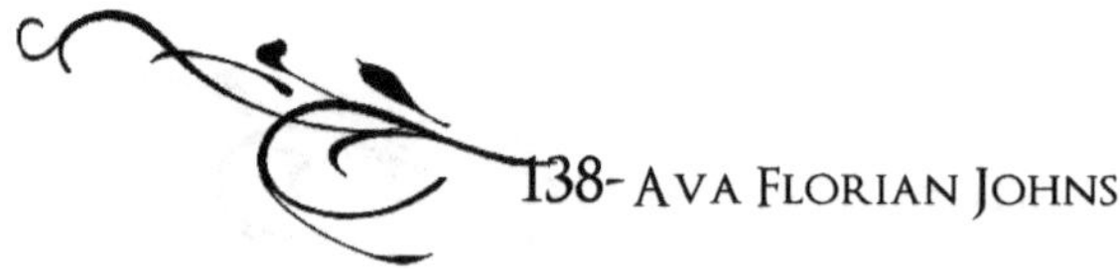

remember everyone else was taken in by his act, too. He acted so incompetent that people didn't see who he truly is. A madman.

I am face-to-face with Director Jackson. The wind is wiping the branches upward, and I will them to grow high into the sky. He calls out to me, "You don't scare me, Willow, you are no match for me. You have no idea what I am capable of, my dear; your powers are no match for mine." He brings his arms up over his head and hurls pure energy

I cry my last tears and head to the lab.

♦♦♦♦♦

"Where have you been Willow, we have been worried sick."

"Sorry Lieutenant, I needed a moment to myself."

"Understood. Next time tell someone where you are going, clear?"

"Crystal."

"All right, let's get to work. Do you have any ideas to help the communication situation? "How can we communicate with the Omega Team on Earth to get a status report?"

"Other than the plans we already have in place? I can't think of anything. I wish our telepathy stretched farther than it does."

"Let's think about this. We have two people who specialize in telepathy. We should be able to do something with all the brain power on this ship."

"Senior Officers and Omega Team to the conference room stat," the announcement booms over the speakers.

"I guess they picked an away team. Let's go, Willow."

♦♦♦♦♦

All of us file into the conference room once again. Commander Alexander stands at the front of the room getting ready to run the meeting.

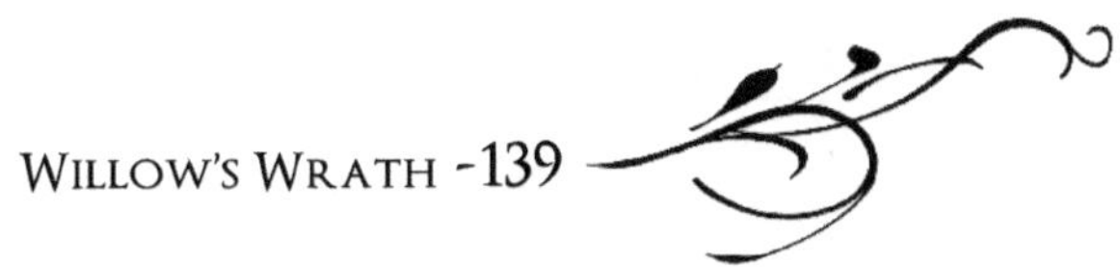

CHAPTER TWENTY-TWO
DALTON

"Everyone take your seats. The first away team will be taking a shuttlecraft down to the surface of the planet Artona in two hours. The second unit will leave one hour after the first. The first group will consist of myself, Lieutenant Allium, Lieutenant Commander Kal, and Willow.

I can see Willow exhale a breath she has been holding. I knew she wanted to go on the mission and there is no way she is going to go without me. She has to be in the first group so I can make sure I am there to protect her.

"The second team will include Lieutenant Williams, Lieutenant Cameron, Cobalt, and Dharma. Jax, you will stay on board with the Captain and attempt to maintain a telepathic connection with Willow. Any questions?"

No one speaks.

"If there are no questions, you are dismissed."

♦♦♦♦♦

The first away team assembles in Shuttle Bay two. After loading our cargo, we take our seats in the shuttle and are soon in high orbit around the planet stationed between two of their moons. We try sending a message to the inhabitants of the planet Artona, to no avail. We also try scanning the world, but cannot get a good reading due to the magnetic interference. I hope they are friendlies.

I am piloting the first shuttlecraft to the surface. Lieutenant Cameron is piloting the second craft. I hope we find a suitable place for landing. The one I am flying is the bigger of the two shuttlecrafts, so I need to make sure I have room to land.

"Shuttlecraft one to the Starship Armargosa, permission to take off."

"Permission granted, Commander."

The shuttle bay doors open, and I start the engine. There could be a hostile boarding party waiting for us when we land, or there could be nothing for all we know. The information on this planet is decades old and isn't very reliable.

I pilot the craft looking for a suitable landing area. The flight isn't bad until the last couple of minutes. It is turbulent. Willow has a brave face, but she is probably scared out of her mind. The Lieutenant Commander and the Lieutenant are used to this kind of trip, so they both look calm.

I stabilize the ship before landing in spite of the turbulence. We get to a good spot, and I set the craft down gently. It is a textbook landing if I do say so myself. I love to pilot the shuttle. I feel both free and in control at the same time. There's no other feeling like it.

The Lieutenant Commander is on high alert. The second we touchdown, he is on his feet, gun in hand.

"Okay Kal, secure the perimeter."

The Lieutenant Commander and I get out of the shuttle and survey the surrounding area, but the planet looks desolate. There isn't much vegetation, and we don't see any inhabitants. No life signs of any kind are registering on this side of the planet, but the current scans indicate there is a colony on the other side. I wish we had known this before I landed the shuttle. Our scanners were ineffective because of the planet's magnetic qualities. The best thing to do now is to get back in the shuttle and fly to the other side of this world.

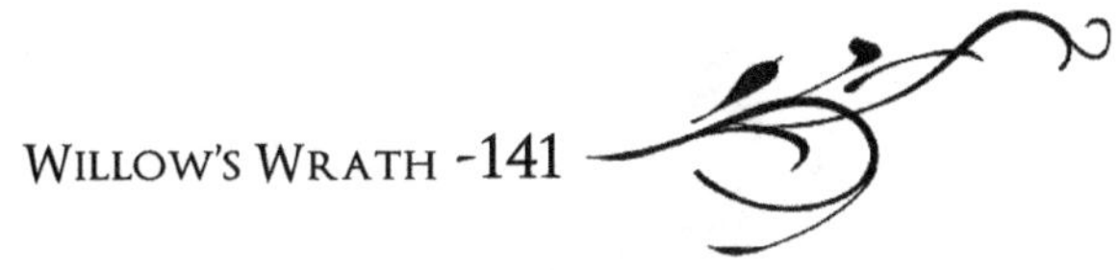

"Lieutenant Commander, let's go back to the shuttle."

"Yes, sir."

We board the shuttlecraft again and explain the situation to our team.

"We're taking another flight toward the settlement, which we didn't know is on the other side of this planet. Everyone strap in for take-off."

I maneuver the shuttle, and again it is a smooth flight. I find a landing space outside of what looks like a village. It is far enough away so the population can't see us. I want to make sure we have enough cover to hide the spacecraft in case the inhabitants are hostile.

We do the same procedure as we did before, and I secure the shuttlecraft. Lieutenant Commander takes point in securing our location, and I follow until he gives me the all clear. We board the shuttle again to tell Willow and the Lieutenant to get ready for a hike into the village.

My team's safety is important to me. I'm very proud of Willow for being calm under pressure. I know she's freaking out on the inside because I can feel it. We still seem to have this weird connection. I can't explain it.

We go over the hill, and we see the structure. No people yet. I'm wondering if they know we're coming and could be waiting to ambush us. The Lieutenant Commander is still on high alert. I can feel the intense energy radiating from him. I would worry about this with most people, but he thrives under pressure.

The four of us walk into the center of the town, or what looks like the heart of the city. We still haven't seen a single life-form.

Do I call out? Do I say hello? I'm not entirely sure what to do.

The decision has been taken away from me when one of the inhabitants suddenly walks right up to Willow. He doesn't say anything to her. He just stares into her eyes. She doesn't see him, and before I can say anything, he reaches out and touches her hair.

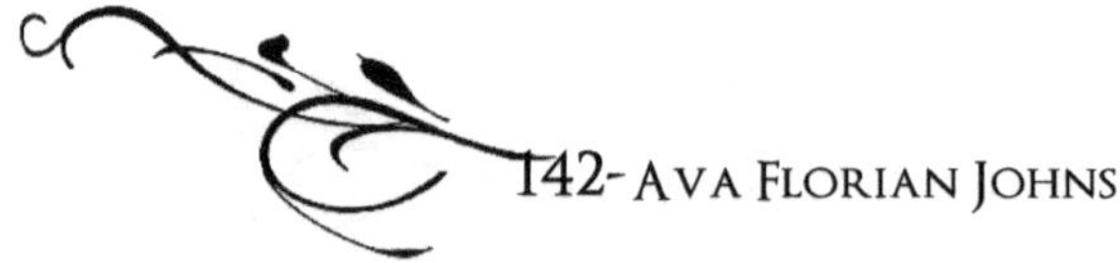

Within a nanosecond Kal is between the inhabitant and Willow, gun drawn.

"Everyone must remain calm. Remember we are guests on their planet. Kal put your sidearm away."

The Lieutenant Commander does as asked, but stays in the same position between the citizen and Willow, widening his stance and is poised for battle.

The inhabitant is watching the situation unfold with amusement on his face. He is a tall man, over six feet, in his early fifties, with gaunt features, and a pale complexion. To say he is skinny is an understatement. I have seen many malnourished people, and he is the worst I have ever seen.

I walk forward with my hand extended in greeting to the man. I step in front of Kal, much to his dismay. The man stares at my hand, then looks into my eyes. In one look, I feel the devastation he feels. He reaches out and grabs my hand, and holds on to it for a long while. It is almost like he is gathering information from me by holding my hand. It is the strangest experience. Not bad, or good, just peculiar.

Kal is bristling with negative energy. He doesn't like the man touching me at all. I can tell he is very uneasy about the entire situation. The resident gives me a half smile and releases my hand. At this point, the Lieutenant Commander relaxes a bit. The man motions for me to follow him into a building. Although I am hesitant, I don't sense any danger, and I consider myself a pretty good judge of character.

I instruct Lieutenant Allium stay with Willow outside the door. I know if something bad happens they will contact the other shuttle immediately. Again, I don't get any negative vibes from this man. I hope I am correct in my assessment.

We follow the man through the doorway and down a dimly lit hallway. At the end of the hall, there is a door with a crack of light beneath it. I still don't hear any sounds. I only hear the whistling wind outside. The man has not uttered one word, not even a sound since we have been here.

When we get to the door, he turns the knob and opens it slowly. He gestures with his hands to other individuals in the room. The room is full of men and women who look like he does, undernourished and emaciated. One of the other men in the room stands up, and his body is skeletal, skin and bone. When he grabs my hand, I can feel his thoughts, but I can't read them. It isn't like we are speaking telepathically, but I can see visions of what happened to this planet. I see the world as it was in the past, luxurious, breathtaking, and full of vegetation and life. Now, the planet is a barren desert, void of any life, except for these malnourished occupants. Something horrendous happened here. I don't know if it was an invasion or if a plague devastated their world.

The only thing I understand is that it wasn't always like this.

I tell them what we are looking for and who we are. I know by looking around at the barren topography that the residents will not be able to help us in the way we had initially thought. At this point, I am hoping we can help them.

I ask the Lieutenant Commander to bring Willow in the room. I believe if anyone can communicate with these people and empathize with them it will be her. She has such an authentic way of interacting with people and plants. She seems to have unconditional love for everyone. Even after Dr. Carver almost killed her, she's still protective of the woman.

Willow comes into the room with us. I asked Kal to wait outside with Allium. He looks hesitant to follow my order, but he does it none the less.

"Willow, will you please try to communicate with them telepathically? I can see images when they hold my hand. I think you may have a better chance at figuring out how to talk with them than I can. I believe they are not going to be able to help us with our communication issues. But I'm hoping we will be able to help them with their food issues.

She walks over to the man who had the first contact with us and reaches for his hand. She's impressive; she shows no fear. They seem to have an instant communications link. It makes her even more stunning, more attractive than I once thought. She has a fearless side to her that I don't believe she knows she has. I have a terrible habit of underestimating her. She seems to surprise me every day.

Willow and the man hold hands for quite a few minutes. I am getting a little edgy, but I know they mean no harm to us.

Willow takes a deep breath, then looks at me and nods her head. I follow her down the hallway and back outside where the others are waiting.

The other away team arrives, and they are discussing what we discovered. Willow remains silent through this conversation.

"What is going on Willow? Are you okay?" I ask her, feeling very concerned.

"I am attempting to communicate with Jax, to let her know what is going on, but I can't reach her."

It's okay Willow; we will go back to the ship and give the Captain a full report.

"Teams, move out," I order.

"Wait. Can we tell the Artonians when we will be back?" Willow asks.

"Willow, we don't yet know if we are going to be back. It depends on what the Captain says."

"We can't leave them like this. We have to help them."

"It is his decision, not ours. We will make our case, then let him decide."

"I can't believe you are okay with leaving them. There is a reason why we came here."

"Willow, board the shuttle now, and that is an order."

I can tell she is pissed, but she listens to me and boards the shuttle. The second team stays longer to survey the devastated landscape of the planet.

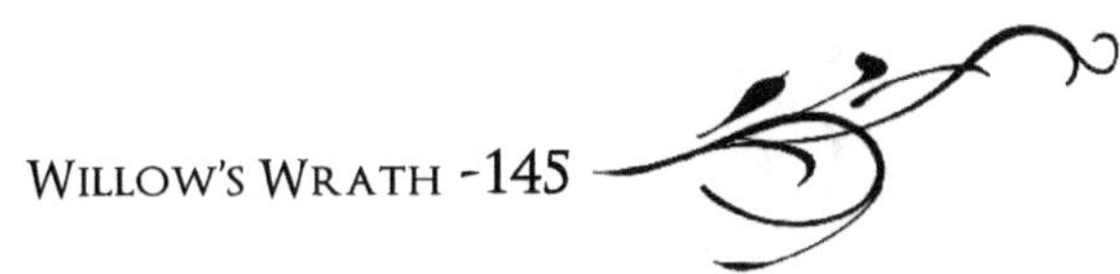

The four of us on the first team board our shuttle and take off to rendezvous with the ship. Willow spends the entire trip back to the vessel explaining what she learned from the inhabitants and what happened to their planet. She is trying to convince me to return to their world. The Captain is in the shuttle bay when we return.

"Report, Commander."

"Yes sir, the planet is completely devastated. It looks like a major catastrophe happened years ago. There is no vegetation, no cities, and no technology. The inhabitants are emaciated and living in horrible conditions. They either have no verbal communication skills, or they choose not to use them."

Willow interjected, "Sir, they need our help. Their once great world is now in ruins. The people are destitute, and they have tried everything. We are their last hope."

"How do you know if they can't verbally communicate?"

"Sir, Willow spoke with them telepathically, as did I, well, to an extent. But Willow gathered more information. Willow explain what happened to their planet."

Even though Willow spoke when she technically wasn't supposed to, I let her speak her mind. I know the Captain will listen to her and make the best decision for everyone involved.

Willow looks grateful to get the opportunity to speak on behalf of the inhabitants of the planet. "Captain Holloway, The Artonian people once lived an idyllic life. They had more resources than they needed and traded them with nearby planets. Their world was rich technologically and culturally. They studied nearby worlds and enjoyed learning as much as they could. They formed an alliance with many worlds, but one such alliance was deadly, the Zorians. They thought it would be equitable for both parties, but the Zorians pillaged their land and took everything. The images the Artonians showed me were frightening. Horrific. I can't explain in mere words what the Zorians did to the Artonians."

Just then Jax comes in. She runs to Willow and hugs her hard.

I knew Jax had seen what Willow did and it was as bad as Willow indicated.

"Captain, I would like to request I take another team to the planet surface. The second team should be returning to the ship any moment. I would like to take Willow, Science Officer Williams, Jax, and Lieutenant Commander Kal. We will assess the situation, determine if there is anything we can do to help, and return to the ship with a plan. You can then review the plan and give your orders."

"Do you think we can help them, Commander?"

"Yes, sir, I believe we have to try. We were the ones who needed help, and we would have taken it from them. I think we owe them this much. At least to give it a shot. We have a remarkable crew with brilliant ideas, and I know we can come up with something that should help the Artonians. I just hope we are not too late."

"I agree, Commander. Reassemble your team as soon as the second shuttlecraft returns. Do well, Commander Alexander."

"Thank you, Sir." I turn to shake his outstretched hand and turn back to the away team.

"Here is the plan, Kal. You will be accompanying us back down to the planet's surface. Lieutenant Allium, you will remain on the ship. Please report back to your station. Thank you."

We wait in the shuttle bay for what seems like hours for the second team to return. After thirty minutes, I fear the worst. I go to the communications council. "Bridge, have you heard from the second away team? They haven't returned yet."

"No sir we have not," Ensign Johnson replies.

"Captain, we are going back down to the surface, something is wrong if they haven't yet returned."

"Yes, Commander Alexander, I agree. Proceed."

"Captain, are you getting any readings from the planet."

"The interference from the magnetic field is still too strong for our sensors to get an accurate reading. Do well Commander Alexander."

By the time we are all aboard the shuttle again, the second away team has been on the planet for over an hour.

Jax and Willow take seats in the back of the shuttle and strap in. Kal and I take our positions in the front, both seemingly poised for battle. I can feel the waves of anxiety flowing off Kal. I know he is expecting the worst like I am.

CHAPTER
TWENTY-THREE
WILLOW

I am in agony thinking about the fate of the other members of the away team. I want so much to be able to help the people of Artona, although I never considered the second away team would be in danger if we left them on the surface. Once again, I blindly trusted someone I hardly knew and could have put the entire mission at risk. I believed the Artonian people wouldn't harm the away team, but I felt telepathically they were hiding something from us. There is some part of their minds I am not able to reach, and now my crew is in danger because I trusted the wrong person... again.

Jax can hear my thoughts and is vehemently shaking her head no. Willow, this is not your fault, she signs to me.

"Yes, it is," I say out loud.

"What is going on back there?" Commander Alexander barks.

I can tell he is beyond stressed. He feels responsible for the members of the away team as well, and I know he is ready for battle.

"Nothing Commander Alexander," I say, giving Jax a silent signal not to bring this up again.

We get to the planet surface again and set down by the village. Commander Alexander and Lieutenant Commander Kal secure the area before they let us out of the shuttlecraft. It is much windier than the first time we visited. I can hardly stay on my feet. Dalton sees me struggling and comes over to assist me.

"Hold on to my hand; I will get you to the village. Kal, please help Jax."

We all walk in a single-file line toward the buildings in the village. I am holding on to Dalton's belt, Jax is holding on to mine and Kal is following up the rear. The wind is whipping at an alarming rate, I can't see more than a couple of inches in front of me, and when I open my eyes, they get covered with dirt in mere seconds.

We finally get to the door we had gone in before. Dalton and Kal have their guns drawn ready to protect us.

We are surprised at the scene which unfolds when we open the door to the room. The Artonians are administering first aid to our people. They are helping us!

My hand goes to my mouth to hide my surprise. The Commander and Lieutenant Commander look stunned and confused. They immediately holster their guns when they figure out what is happening.

"Situation report."

"Commander Alexander, we got caught in a vicious storm. It came up out of nowhere. Our sensors didn't detect it until it was right on top of us. We are fortunate that we were not in the shuttlecraft when it hit or we would not be here."

"How did you get out of the storm?" Dalton said.

"We were taking a beating. The flying debris and dirt blinded us, and the Artonians came out and retrieved us and have seen to our injuries. They saved our lives."

While this exchange is going on Jax and I are attending to Cobalt and Dharma. They are lying on the floor, both with minor injuries. A few bumps and scrapes, but nothing serious. I hug them both, then turn to the Artonian man I spoke with before. I reach out and grab his hand. "Thank you so much for saving my friends. I can't tell you what this means to me."

I say it out loud, and in my head, so he will understand. He smiles at me and motions for me to sit at the table. I hadn't seen it in the

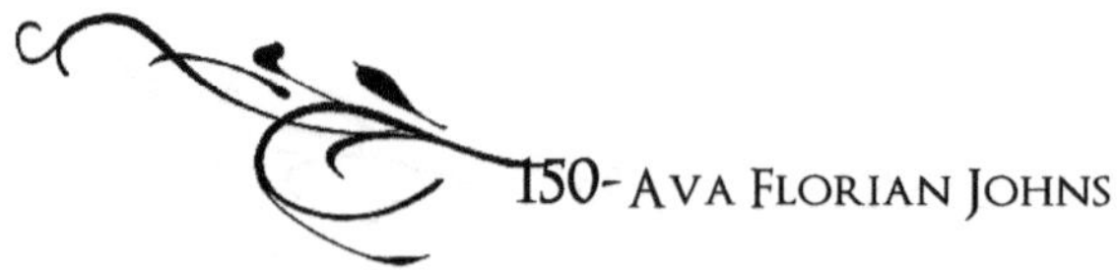

room before. All I noticed the first time I was in this place were all the emaciated bodies. It is a scene that I will remember forever.

I sit down next to the Artonian man. He grabs my hands and telepathically asks me to help his people. I can tell he is the leader and feels responsible for the conditions his planet and people face. He has a deep sorrow he didn't let me see before. Maybe that's what he is hiding.

"Is everyone okay? The Commander asks the crew.

"Yes, sir. Other than a few bumps and bruises I think we are all okay," Lieutenant Cameron answers.

"Good, here is the plan. Willow and Jax will communicate with the Artonians and find out what we can do to help. They obviously need food and water. This planet is the most barren planet I have ever seen. Lieutenant Williams, Lieutenant Cameron, I want you to survey the land with Kal and find out what you can about how much damage there is, and what we can do to repair it. I will stay here with the Omega Team and work with the Artonians on a plan. We need to report back to the Captain within the hour, or he will send another team down."

"Yes, sir." Everyone responds and starts working on their tasks. The Commander tries reaching the ship to no avail because the magnetic interference is still too high for a message to get through.

Jax and I communicate with the Artonians and discover their leader is a kind and gentle man, concerned only with the well-being of his people. Knowing they didn't have long to live, he had given up hope for his race. Then he saw our shuttle flying through the sky and had faith we were here to save them. We learn the Artonians are a race of technically savvy and courageous people. They are devoted to conquering sickness and death on their planet and came up with a way to extend the lives of their people. Through their incredible technical skills, their people thrived and lived on for hundreds of years. They no longer wished to travel into space but welcomed people of other races to their planet. They didn't believe in closing their borders for others in need of refuge.

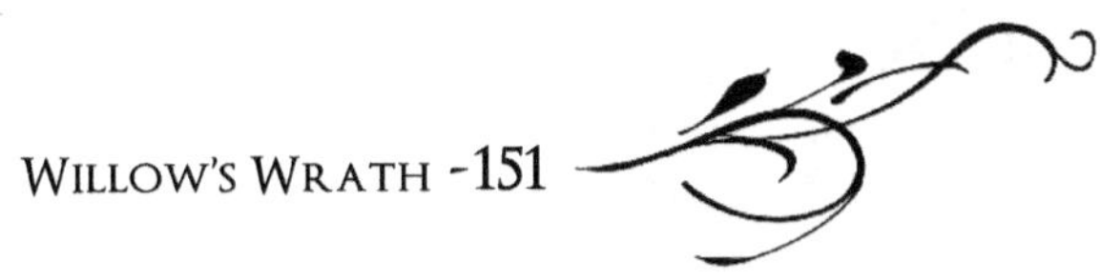

Then the Zorians arrived. At first, the Artonians thought the Zorians were comrades, wanting to advance their technology and scientific discoveries, but soon found they were only interested in draining the Artonian planet of its natural resources. They were also very interested in the technology to extend life, but the Zorians didn't understand how to use it. They took many of the Artonians back to their home planet to teach them how to use the technology. The others they killed, and there are only two-thousand Artonians left out of billions.

The leader of the Artonians pauses after telling his story. He can tell the story has made both of us sad. The Artonian leader looks at me and wipes the tears from my face. He tells me not to cry for them. He has faith in us that we will be able to assist them and deliver them from their hell.

Commander Alexander comes over to us, with concern in his eyes. I put up my hand to indicate we are okay.

I start to formulate a plan in my head. The dirt looks too far gone for me to plant anything in it, but I need Lieutenant Williams to give me a soil analysis before I make the final determination. I think we could use the serum to stabilize the plants, which could bring the soil on the planet back to being able to sustain plant life.

"All teams report back to the structure now." Commander Alexander booms over the communication device.

"What's going on?" I ask.

"I need one team to go back to the ship and get these people some food and water. We need to come up with a plan, but we also need to care for their immediate needs. I am disappointed that I didn't bring food down with us when we came back, but I was so worried about the second away team I didn't think of it."

"I know Commander Alexander; I didn't think of it either." I put my hand on his arm in a gesture of understanding. He shakes it off; aware others are watching.

"Sorry, sir." I stammer and head back toward Jax and the leader of the Artonians.

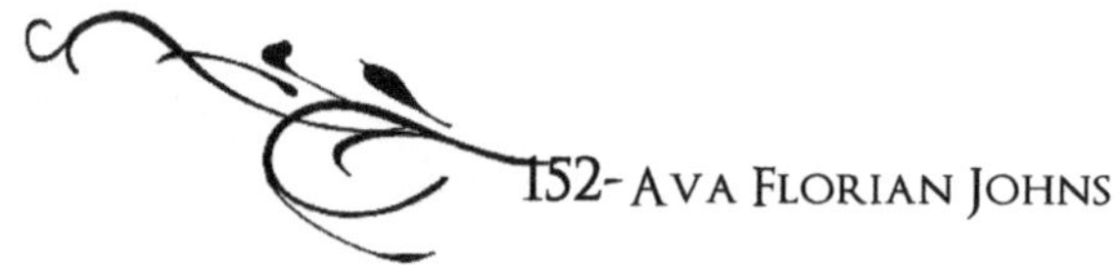

All the members of our crew and the Omega Team report back to the room. Dalton addresses them as they come in, asking for each commanding officer to report.

"Kal, situation report."

"Commander Alexander, the planet is secure. The second shuttle has suffered mild damage, but Lieutenant Cameron assures me it will be fixed before we return to the ship."

"Great, thank you Kal."

"I will need about two hours to fix the damage on the shuttlecraft. It is minor, but I want to run a diagnostic and make sure all the systems are operating at optimal efficiency."

"Thank you for the report, Lieutenant Cameron. Get started on the repairs immediately."

"Will do Commander Alexander."

"Commander Alexander, the wind has subsided. We should be able to get our shuttlecraft off the ground and through the atmosphere. Not having the proper equipment down here I can't predict when the storm will return. Willow, maybe you can ask the leader about the storm patterns so I can get a better idea of what we are working with down here," Science Officer Williams says.

"Yes, Lieutenant, right away."

I walk over to the leader and put my hand on his. I still can't connect with people without touching them, as Jax could.

I ask the leader about the storms. He says they are sporadic and hard to predict. Typically, there are eight to ten per day. They have already had four today, so they are due at least another four to six. He thinks it would be best if one of the shuttles goes back to the ship. He is concerned if the Captain sends down another shuttle to retrieve us, the shuttle may not be able to make it through the torturous winds.

"Commander Alexander, he thinks we should take the first shuttle out and rendezvous with the ship before they send another ship down. He is concerned they will get stuck in the storm. He said to expect another four to six storms today, like the one they already had.”

“Okay, I agree. I want one team to go back to the ship and grab supplies. Kal, Dharma, Cobalt, head back to the ship. I want enough food, water and blankets brought down for these people. Bring a food dispenser as well. Kal, please report to the Captain what we have discovered here and our immediate plan to help the inhabitants. Dismissed.”

Kal looks like he disagreed with Dalton’s orders, but he signals to Dharma and Cobalt to get aboard the shuttle double time. I know he wants to get the supplies and return here as soon as possible. I get the feeling Kal doesn’t yet trust the Artonians.

“Willow and Jax, find out if the Artonians have a power source for the food dispensers.”

“Yes, Commander Alexander.”

I turn to the leader. He understands what the Commander is saying and nods yes.

Looking at this room, which is the only place we have been on the planet, I find it hard to believe they have any power source which would work with our technology. But that reminds me that I don’t know much about their people, not nearly as much as I thought I did. I have to keep telling myself I knew Dr. Carver for more than twelve years and still didn’t know her. Hence the deception on her part. I am such a fool. I still miss her.

Jax looks over at me and shakes her head. She sends me a thought, “You can still miss her because she is still the woman who raised you. Don’t feel guilty or foolish for missing her. It is a natural response.”

“Thank you, Jax, I appreciate it,” I say telepathically back to her.

“Orders for the rest of you. Jax and Willow, continue to gather information from the Artonian leader. I want to know everything about their planet. Document your findings for the Captain, so you don’t leave anything out. Williams, continue with the readings on

the surface. Document your plan to the Captain, including a detailed plan on how Willow will be able to help."

"Yes, sir. Could I ask that one of the Artonians go with me? I would like to go outside this area and see what is beyond the ridge."

"Jax, ask the Artonian leader if that would be possible."

Jax communicates with the Artonian leader and nods affirmation at the Commander.

One of the Artonians gets up from his seated position on the old worn wooden floor and follows Lieutenant Williams outside to survey the planet.

I am feeling excellent about what we are doing here. I know this isn't getting us closer to home or a way to communicate with Earth, but it is helping another race. And who knows how this might help us in the future. I smile at the Artonian leader, and he smiles back and grabs my hand. He tells me how grateful he is for our crew, and for me for our fearless devotion to helping them, people we don't even know.

I assure him we will do everything in our power to help them. I know we won't be able to fix all their problems, but at least we can help them with getting some food and water now.

I have a thought. The Artonians were administering first aid to our people who were hurt, but we never thought to ask what they need as far as medical attention. Jax nods at me for the thought and asks an Artonian man the question. She says they are doing fine, that food would help most of their issues, and they will let us know if they think of anything else.

There seems to be a lull in the action, so I stop to take a look around the room. The room is no bigger than the bridge on our ship. It is an old structure with a worn wooden floor. Because of the storms, the rooms are dusty and dirty. The room size is maybe twenty feet by twenty feet. There have to be more than two hundred Artonians in the chamber, most of them men, and all emaciated. I wonder where the rest of them are. I walk over to the leader as Jax pulls out her tablet. I hope she will be able to take notes on it and that the magnetic field of the planet won't interfere.

She turns the tablet on, and it comes to life.

I grab the hand of the leader and start to formulate my questions. "First off, what is your name?"

"I am referred to as Elder John. I am the oldest Artonian. The oldest is usually the wisest, although I feel I have let my people down on that one. I am the one who trusted the Zorians to work with us, not plunder and pillage our land and take our citizens. Billions have died because of me, and the rest of us are suffering because of my decisions."

The other men in the room look over at him when he says this. I can tell they don't agree with his statements and feel an overwhelming sense of loyalty toward Elder John.

"I hate to disagree with you Elder John, but I don't think your people see it that way. All I sense from them is extreme loyalty toward you. I don't sense any blame or malice for the deal you made with the Zorians. They did this to you. You didn't do anything wrong. You couldn't have known of their evil intent."

"But I knew what we had was extraordinary, and I didn't adequately protect it. I was too trusting. I believed everyone was honest. I never thought people had a devious or malicious streak. I should have at least been able to sense their intentions. I couldn't do that for my people. I believe I have let them down, and I have destroyed us."

"I know exactly how you feel. All my life I have wanted to fit in, so I trust anyone who comes along. The woman at the girl's school befriended me. She treated me like her child by nurturing and supporting me my whole life. In truth, she was a complete fraud. I didn't have the backbone to stand up to her or others, and I let them trample all over me. I am done being the weak one. I am done trusting anyone ever again."

"Oh, sweet Willow, don't do that. You need to trust again, to love.

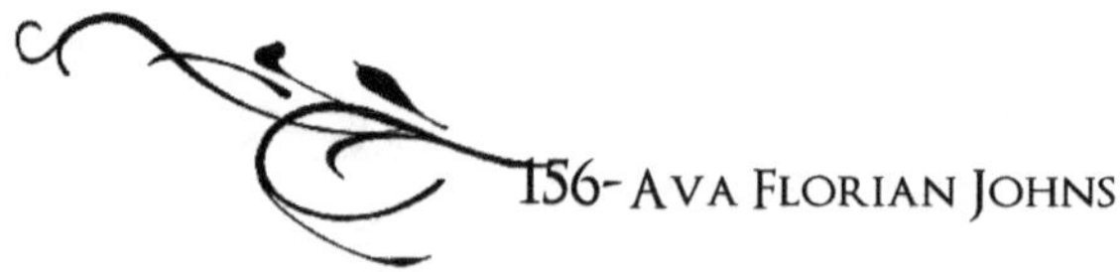

I was blind to the intentions of the Zorians, but I won't let that mistake happen again. I didn't listen to my heart then, but I will with you. You are a wondrous soul who needs to live life. Don't let one ruthless woman ruin you for love and life. I sense a certain Commander has a special place in your heart. Let him in. I promise you good will come from it."

I think about what Elder John has said. He is right. I can't close myself off because of one bad experience. Albeit, one incredibly unfortunate experience. He is also correct Dalton is gaining a very special place in my heart. There is only one other person I thought I loved. He turned out to be a conman. I didn't let myself know the person. In this case, I feel I am getting to know Dalton. I need to be open and explore the possibilities with him if he lets me.

Jax is on one side of the room talking to a several of the Artonians at the same time. My telepathy doesn't work that way. I can only connect with one person at a time, and I have to be holding their hand to make a telepathic connection. Not Jax, she can read the minds of numerous people at the same time. I don't know how she does it or how she ever shuts it off. It must be very noisy in her head.

I am sure she is asking some of the same questions I am about to ask Elder John, the leader of the Artonians, but it can't hurt to get multiple points of view. I pull out my tablet and type in my question. I turn to John and ask him where the rest of the people are. There were about two hundred Artonians shoved like sardines into this one room, but we haven't seen any other people at all. Not even walking around the square. We have only seen them in this place, except for Elder John.

"Elder John, you indicated there are two-thousand Artonians left on this planet, there are about two hundred here. Where are the rest of your people?"

"They are in other buildings like this one throughout the village. We don't want to all stay together in case a storm destroys one of the buildings. We want to make sure our race survives as long as we can."

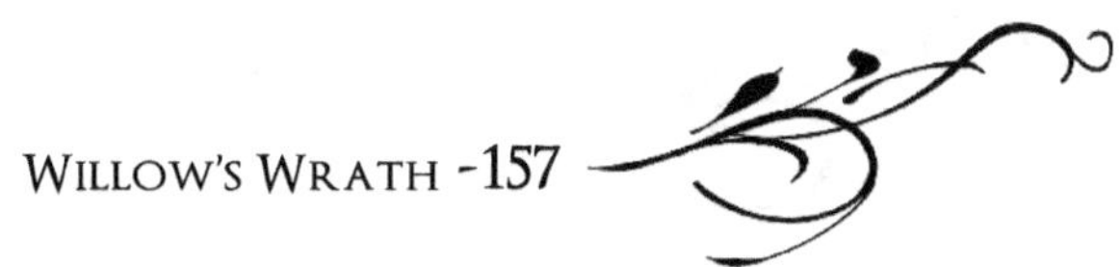

I typed his answer on the tablet, then again typed my question before I touched his hand to ask him telepathically.

"Why don't your people go outside? We have only seen you in the square. Do you all stay inside all the time?"

"There is nothing outside for them anymore. Most of us don't have the strength to walk, so we sit here and talk about our culture. We document our stories in the hope that one day someone will come upon our recordings and learn about how great we once were and how magical this place truly is. If we don't survive, I want you to have our documents. I want you to teach others about who we were and how we lived. We once had great cities and fields upon fields of food. We had an abundance of everything, which is why we left our borders open for others to share our bounty with us. I would say it is foolish, but I know I would repeat it, for it is the right thing to do."

I notice Dalton watching my exchange with Elder John with a look of pride on his face. He looks proud of me. I may be mistaken, maybe he is looking at Jax.

"No, Sweet Willow, he is looking at you," Elder John says.

I had forgotten he is still holding my hand and he can read my thoughts. Dalton is staring at me. I know he was hesitant to select me for this mission. But has made comments saying I am valuable to the crew. I hope he is seeing I am meant to be here on this mission, with him.

Lieutenant Williams and Lieutenant Cameron walk in with the Artonian who is showing Lieutenant Williams around.

"Commander Alexander, I have finished the repairs on the shuttlecraft. We are ready to go. Lieutenant Williams believes this would be the best time to leave. We don't want to risk getting caught in another one of their storms. I don't think the shuttle will hold up to another windstorm like the one we experienced before. Our readings show some of the winds got up to the speeds of tornados, with winds gusts up to 95 miles per hour."

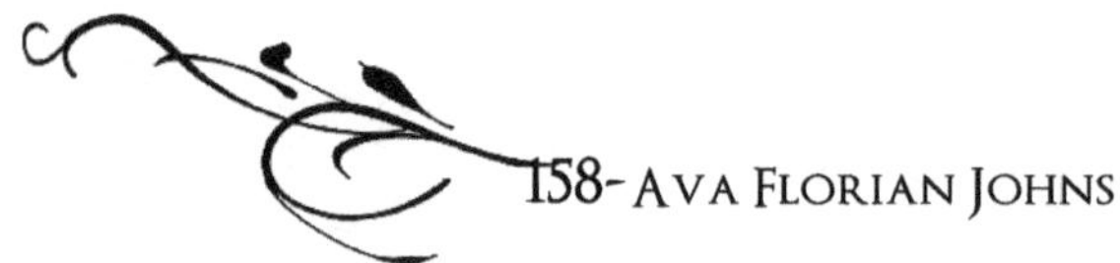

"I agree with the Lieutenant Cameron. I think this is the best time to rendezvous with the ship and give the Captain our plan. I have mine outlined, and I need to review it with Willow once aboard the shuttlecraft." Williams says.

"Where is the away team with the supplies and food dispenser?"

"The other away team arrived with everything for the Artonians a few minutes ago, and are headed back to the ship. We can get the food moved safely inside the building before we take off. I will hook the dispenser up on our next trip down," Lieutenant Cameron states.

"Willow and Jax, please let the Artonians know we will be back and tell them the food is here. Explain we need to discuss the plans with the Captain."

I do as told and feel the disappointment running through Elder John's body. "I promise we will be back. Our captain is a decent person. He won't leave without trying to help you."

Elder John holds my hand a little longer and brings it to his face. "Goodbye, my sweet Willow."

♦♦♦♦♦

Aboard the ship, we meet with the Captain in the Bridge Conference Room.

"When I took this post as Captain of the Armargosa, I didn't think we would be spending so much time in this meeting room."

Everyone laughs.

"Commander Alexander, please report."

"You understand the situation the Artonians are facing. They are starving to death because there is no food and no means to plant any on their own. They have no technology to speak of, although they did indicate they have the power to run the food dispenser we brought down. I am hoping it will work. Our supplies will help them for the time being until we can figure out how to plant food that will

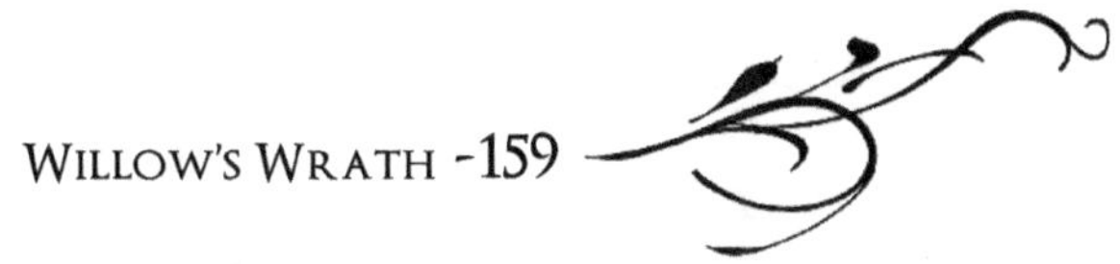

sustain them in the long run. Lieutenant Williams, report on your findings of the soil samples and the weather conditions."

"The land is barren. We are going to have to inject a serum to return some life to the ground. We have the formula for one, which I think will work. We have to run a few tests in the lab on the soil samples I brought up from the surface. I am hoping to have it completed tonight. Once we work on the soil, we will come up with a plan for planting. Willow, please elaborate."

"The problem is not only the soil but the winds and weather conditions they face. There is very little water on the planet. We would need to build a greenhouse which would withstand the wind and come up with an irrigation system to water the plants. Or, we use one of the structures that already exist. We could make some modifications and work Engineering's irrigation plan into the mix. What does engineering think?"

Lieutenant Cameron stands up. "I believe that it is a viable option. We know the buildings can withstand their weather conditions, so what we have to figure out is how to build an irrigation system which will work on the inside of the building. We have to build something that creates water. The plan is a challenge, but I think we can do it. I think by trying to help the Artonians, we are helping ourselves. These are all things we would have had to come up with for our own survival. Now we have to come up with them sooner."

"Good point, Lieutenant Cameron," the Captain says. "Cobalt, do you have anything to add from the engineering perspective?"

"I think it's a good plan. I'm excited to get started."

"Lieutenant Allium, any progress on trying to communicate with the APA Military bases?" the Captain asks sounding hopeful.

"No, sir. I have been trying different frequencies all day, with no luck. I need a stronger power source. Commander Alexander, you indicated they have a source of energy to run the food dispensers. Do they have anything else? Anything we can use to send a message?"

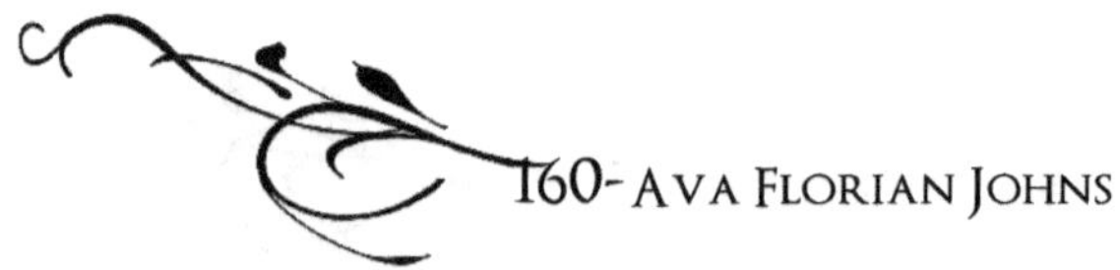

"I am not sure at this point. It will be the first thing we check on when we go back down to the surface."

"Good work. Everyone continue to work on your plans. I would like a status update at 1900 hours. Please reconvene in this room."

"When are we going back down to the planet?" I ask.

"When we have our plan hashed out. I don't want to give the Artonians false hope. I want to make sure we are ready with a viable plan."

I nod at the Captain with understanding and leave the room with the other commanding officers and Omega Team. Only Dalton stays behind to talk to the Captain. I hope Dalton doesn't think I am insubordinate or pushy by asking when we are going back down. I promised Elder John we will do everything in our power to try to help him and I am not going to back down on my promise. I am happy the supplies arrived before we left the planet. I am sure they will help the situation. I need to make sure I can create food to replace what we gave them. We still have to keep ourselves fed, too.

I never thought about my powers having limitations, like only being able to grow a certain amount of food. I blindly assume my ability will last forever. I should figure that out before I overextend myself.

♦♦♦♦♦

Lieutenant Williams and I work on the soil samples for the next couple of hours. We know we have to have our plan ready at 1900 hours, so we work as fast as we can, and I barely look up from my experiment. We found a variation of the serum we think can regenerate their land. We are going to move some dirt in one of their buildings and start testing it as soon as we go back down to the surface.

"All right Willow, please carry our soil samples and serum so we can demonstrate what we are proposing."

"Yes, sir."

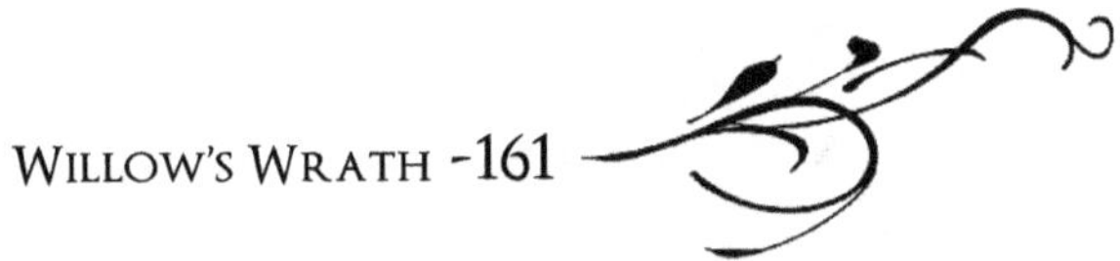

"You don't have to call me sir; you can call me Noah when it is the two of us."

"Thank you, Noah, I appreciate it." I think of Noah as a friend and a little bit of a father figure.

We gather all our supplies and the samples we will need to demonstrate what we are planning to do on the planet for our meeting.

All the department heads, Omega Team, and the Commander meet with the Captain again in the bridge conference room. I am excited to explain how we are going to help the Artonians. I want to go on this mission for precisely this reason—I want to be a part of something that is bigger than myself. I want to help others and do something worthwhile for humanity.

"Commander Alexander, please get us started."

"Communications department, you are up first. Lieutenant Allium and Jax, please report.

"We have attempted several different frequencies to no avail. We still cannot get a message out," Lieutenant Allium says.

"Do you think someone is blocking our transmissions? Who would have the capability to do that? The Artonians?" the Captain asks.

"Sir, the Artonians don't have the technology to block us," Cameron states.

"We don't know that for sure Lieutenant Cameron, we have not gotten a close look at any technology they may have. We are aware they have power because they have told us that, but we don't know from where. We don't really know them, not yet."

The Commander looks at me, knowing I am going to argue.

"Sir, I get no feeling of deceit on their part. I don't know why they would block our signal, they know we are trying to help them."

"Maybe they think we will leave if we can contact Earth. I don't know why, but I don't quite trust them yet," the Commander responds.

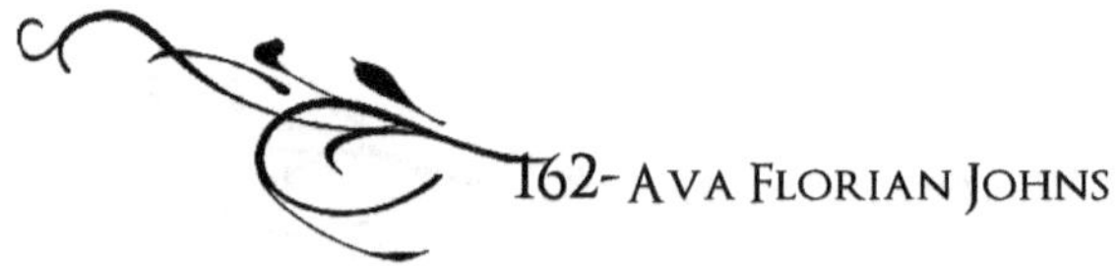

"Okay, so what should we do? Ask them more clearly?" I ask looking around the room. "Why don't we have Jax ask the Artonians? She has a great connection with them, and she may be able to feel something I can't."

"It could be someone else." Lieutenant Allium states. "It could be the PG for all we know. Can we run a test on the communications system to see if anything is blocking it from our end? Or see if we can tell where the block is coming from?"

"Lieutenant Cameron, please get your team on this as soon as possible."

"Yes, Captain."

"Anything else from the Communications Team?" the Commander asks.

"I think you should read Jax's report on the conversations she had with the Artonians. It's quite fascinating what these people were able to achieve in a short time. They have an amazing mental ability, and we could learn a lot from them. They once charted the stars and went on thousands of missions. Until they built their perfect world and never left it again," Lieutenant Allium says.

"The next team up is Security. Kal and Dharma, please give your report."

"Yes, Captain. I performed two complete security sweeps of the area around the village on the planet. I scanned nothing out of the ordinary, nor do I sense anything out of the ordinary. They don't appear to be a hostile race, but I still don't trust them a hundred percent. I want to be present for all away missions, to ensure the safety of the crew and the Omega Team."

"Yes, Kal, I would expect nothing less from you," the Commander responds.

I have to admit I do feel safer with him around. He is a force of nature.

"Engineering, anything to report?" the Commander turns and looks at Lieutenant Cameron.

"Yes, sir. We have the blueprint for an indoor drip watering system. We have figured out how to create and store the water, and here are the plans. It will take us a couple of days and a few crews, but we can get it up and running."

"Thank you, Lieutenant. The Science Team, please work with the engineers on this water system. Now, what have you found out about the soil?"

"Captain and Commander, Willow and I have produced a serum which will assist in reviving the land. Willow, please show them the demonstration."

I retrieve the box of soil we collected from the planet. "Here is the dirt we gathered from the surface of Artona. First, we will apply the serum like this. The good news is it doesn't take much to revive the soil to grow a plant. Here is a seed for a carrot plant." I plant the seed in the dirt and apply some water.

I then use my powers to grow the carrot plant. People in the room gasp. They have seen me do this several times before, but never with dirt that is this dry or lacking in nutrients, and never in subpar conditions like these. I reach over and pull the plant out of the box of dirt. The carrot is mature. They can harvest as soon as soon as I plant. I would like to do this first, then go slower with the crops we will keep.

"Very impressive Science Team, Willow, good work." The Captain says looking impressed. "What is the next course of action Commander?"

"The next away team to leave for the surface will be, Lieutenant Commander Kal, Willow, Lieutenant Williams and Lieutenant Cameron, and me. Everyone else will stay here and work on your department's plans. Away team meets in the shuttle bay at 2100 hours. Dismissed."

I am proud of myself, I am making an impact on the crew, and in particular on the inhabitants of this planet, but I feel tired.

"Willow why don't you go get some rest? You haven't slept in a while," Lieutenant Williams looks a little worried about me.

"Thank you; I think I will."

CHAPTER TWENTY-FOUR

DALTON

"I have to say I am very impressed with Willow's abilities, Commander Alexander."

"I am too, Captain. I am amazed at what she has accomplished in such a short time. If you don't need me for anything else, I will get some rest before the next away mission."

"Do well, dismissed Commander."

I leave the Captain and walk through the halls. We have only been on this mission for a couple of days, and the crew and the Omega Team are working together as if they have been doing this for years. They have an excellent flow in meetings and seem to get along personally. I am so glad this part of the mission is working out. If we didn't get along and we had this many problems, it would be tough to get anything done or have any hope of getting back to Earth.

I find myself in front of Willow's door again. I decide I don't care what anyone thinks. I had a rough day and need to talk to her for a moment. I need her strength and want to feel the connection we share. I also crave her in a way I have never desired anyone before. It is a surreal experience.

I knock on the door. Willow answers within a couple of seconds. She opens the door, and she is in her PJs.

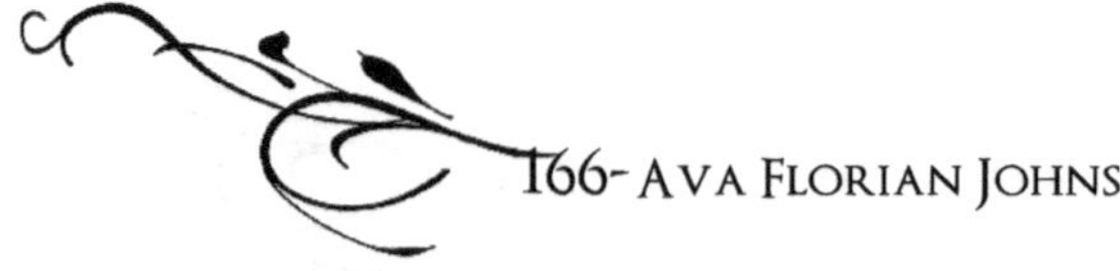

"Hello Commander Alexander, what a surprise to see you here. Please come in."

"I don't know if I should."

"Jax is in the Communications hub with Lieutenant Allium. I am alone. Please come in."

This time she gives me a little pout with her lower lip, and she is too cute to resist. I used to think she is naïve, but she surprises me every day. She is not as sweet and innocent as I once thought. She is a pretty big flirt, and she knows what to do to keep me interested. With most women, I have found the motions are contrite and practiced. With Willow, they are part of who she is. She doesn't practice anything. She is genuine in her very core.

I walk past her and into her room. The rooms have only two standard issue military cots, two office chairs, and two tiny desks. There are just two places to sit, either on her bed or the office chair. I pick the chair.

"Chicken." She says to me as she sits on her bed.

"What do you mean chicken?"

"You can sit over here; I promise I won't bite."

"I am not afraid of you biting."

"So why did you stop by?"

"I wanted to check on you. It has been a hectic few days. A lot of changes, a lot of danger, and a lot of hard work. I wanted to see how you were handling everything."

"I am doing quite well. I love that I am doing something that makes a difference. What we do here could help the Artonians survive, could help their entire race survive. I have never been a part of something like this."

"You impress the Captain."

"Just the Captain?"

I move over to sit next to her on her cot. I can't help it. I am breathing hard trying to control myself, but she has such a magnetic pull on me, I don't want to pretend I don't feel it. And I don't want to act like I don't want her.

When I sit next to her, my thigh touches her leg. I can feel the heat of her body through her pajama bottoms. I lean toward her and kiss her. Where our other kisses have been soft and gentle, this one is hard and passionate. Every ounce of feeling I have for her I pour into the kiss, so she knows how I feel. She doesn't pull back, she engages fully, sitting on my lap, pressing her body flush against mine. Straddling me, she wraps her legs around my waist, pushing against me as hard as she can. Her kisses are deep and full of meaning. I can feel her breathing growing ragged, and I have one brief moment of conscious thought that I better slow down before we take it too far.

"Willow, we should slow down a bit."

"Is that really what you want to do?"

"What if Jax comes back?"

"She is out for the night. You didn't answer my question."

"No, I don't want to stop, but this isn't the time. We leave for an away mission in one hour, and we need to be alert. I'm sorry, this is my fault. I just had to taste you. I missed you so much over the last couple of days."

She moves off my lap, still looking upset. "You are a very confusing man, Dalton Alexander."

"Am I?"

"Yes."

"Do you want me to leave?"

"No, I want you to stay."

"So tell me why I am confusing."

"You are so hot and cold. I want you to decide. Am I what you want?"

"I'm sorry Willow, I am a little out of my comfort zone with you. I have a connection with you I haven't felt before, and I am not sure what to do about it."

She pauses and thinks a moment, "Well, thank you for explaining. Come and lie next to me, you need a break too."

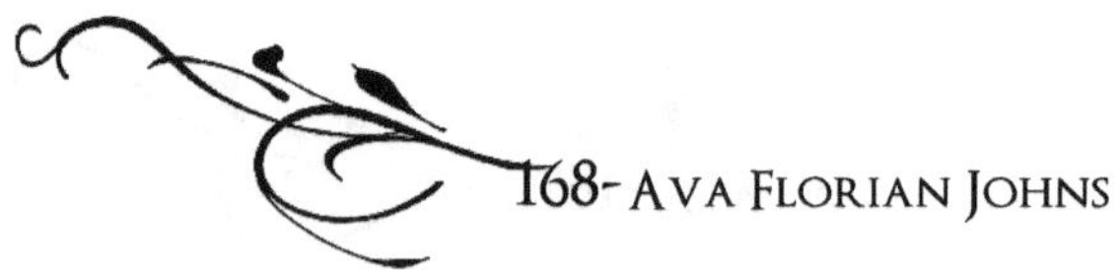

I set the alarm on my watch, so if we fall asleep, we won't be late for the away mission. I know I shouldn't be here, but I need this. I need this time for me. I could be checking and rechecking readings on the shuttlecraft, but everything will be okay. I am going to take this opportunity with Willow. I am going to enjoy something for once in my life and not feel guilty for having something I want. For having something which is good. For once I won't think Willow could do better than me. For once I am going to let myself enjoy her.

◆◆◆◆◆

My alarm rings. Willow's head is on my chest, and her body curled into mine. Willow is so sexy than other women without even trying. She is stunning to behold, and at this moment I realize I am falling for her.

◆◆◆◆◆

I head down the hallway to the shuttle bay. I leave her room first so she can get ready. Soon, Lieutenant Commander Kal, Willow, Lieutenant Williams, Lieutenant Cameron and I pile into the shuttlecraft one more time and head down to the surface.

CHAPTER
TWENTY-FIVE
WILLOW

I know I sometimes stun Dalton with my provocative behavior. It is scandalous, but it is thrilling for me. He isn't ready to commit yet, and he still thinks he is not good enough for me. I can hear his thoughts when he is kissing me.

The shuttlecraft bumps the air causing me to join reality again.

"Make sure your seatbelt is on tight, it is going to be a bumpy ride," the Commander says trying to maintain control of the aircraft.

I think I am going to puke. I am the only member of Omega Team and the only female on this mission, and I refuse on those facts alone to get sick. I won't have them thinking I am weak or fragile and can't handle a few bumps. Then the shuttle lurches forward and drops down. I bite the inside of my lip to keep from vomiting all over the shuttlecraft.

Commander Alexander finally lands the aircraft, but we can't get out yet. Not until the storm passes. The strange thing about this planet is none of our sensors work, so we sit in the shuttlecraft for a while. The commanding officers are all talking about the mission and the plan, while I quietly sit gathering my thoughts and my lunch.

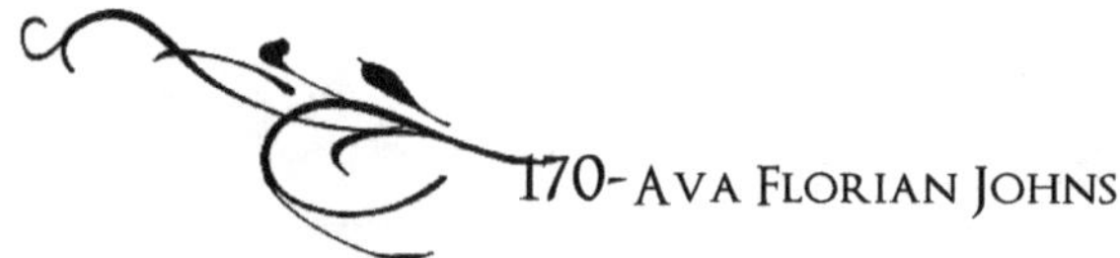

The storm passes, and we go outside. Dalton and Kal go out first, per usual and check the perimeter. Kal does one final security sweep before he will let me out of the shuttlecraft.

We start our walk to the village. Once again, there is not a soul in sight. We walk to the building, down the hallway, and into the room. I keep expecting we will find something horrible behind the door. I get a sense of horror when I touch the doorknob, but when we open it, it is the same scene as before. About two hundred people in long tan robes are sitting on the floor, like the monks in Earth's past. The Artonians are passing around and eating the food we have brought down for them.

I walk over to Elder John and hold out my hand.

"Hello my sweet Willow, how are you?"

"I am fine Elder John. I am so glad you are enjoying the food. I have to say you look much better than you did before."

"Please thank your Captain and crew for their generosity. I know it isn't easy to give us your supplies when you are so uncertain of your own future. Please know you will be okay. Your Captain and crew are strong. I promise you; I know you will make it back to your land, with new experiences and new knowledge to change the direction of your world."

"Thank you Elder John; you are a very kind man."

"Willow, are you ready to demonstrate your plan to the Artonians?" Lieutenant Williams asks.

I let go of Elder John's hand and grab my box of sample soil from the planet.

"Yes, sir I am ready now."

"If you speak verbally will they all understand you?" The Commander asks looking around the room.

Elder John nods yes, they will understand.

"This box contains a sample of topsoil from your planet. We have a serum which will regenerate the nutrients in the ground, so we will be able to plant crops for you to grow your food. We will talk about the logistics later. For now, I want you to watch when I add

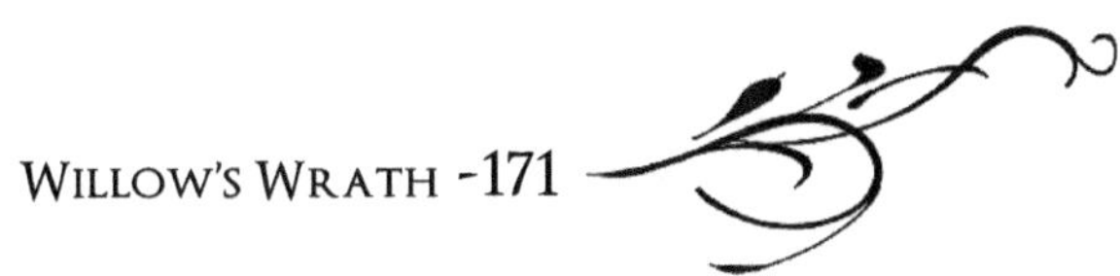

the serum to the soil. As you can see, there is a noticeable difference in the appearance of the earth. It looks richer and healthier. I now will make a mound of dirt, add carrot seeds, and some water. Now watch it grow."

I love to see the astonished expressions of the people looking at me grow plants from seeds to vegetables. I start with my hands on the mound of dirt and extend them in the air. The plant grows before their eyes. I get the impression some of them think it is witchcraft. Not Elder John. He is smiling the biggest smile I have ever seen. I pull out the carrot by the top and show them the finished product. They are all stunned.

Elder John comes over and grabs my hand. "My sweet Willow, you are amazing."

"Thank you Elder John."

"No wonder you thought you could help. You have a miraculous gift to share with the world. I am so impressed by you. You are the most genuine person I have ever met. There is no pretense with you, and you are who you are. I hope your Commander appreciates you."

"He will eventually. I hope he will."

"I know he will, my sweet Willow."

The others continue to stare until Elder John turns around and explains my power. I wish Jax would have come with us. I would have liked to know what he said to them to make them calm down. They seem a little anxious regarding my power. I will have to remember to explain it before I start next time. I guess I am the only one who has skills like this. I hope in the future there are more people like me. That is what my parents wanted as well, so we can repair our world and colonize others. Eventually, the serum is supposed to help me fix the damage humanoids have done to our societies. I had reached this possibility while reading their notes when we came to Artona. There will be many people like me fixing earth's issues.

Lieutenant Williams and Lieutenant Cameron explain the greenhouse portion of the plan to the Artonians and what we will

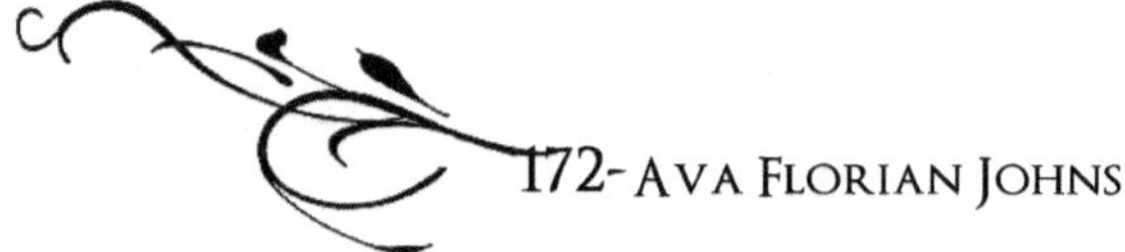

need from them. Elder John and a few of the others show them what they think is the most suitable building for the plants. It looks like it had once been an enormous dining hall. It has beautifully arched ceilings and a vast open space.

"This is perfect," I say to anyone who is listening. I am pleasantly surprised the Artonians have such an excellent place for us to start the process.

I can tell the Artonians are impressed with our plan. They seem grateful and excited at the same time. When we first arrived and saw the Artonians in the room, it felt like they were waiting to die. All sitting in the same place, not going outside, and I have learned they had been like this for so long they no longer had hope. When the Zorians first desecrated their planet, they had hoped they could fix it, but the Zorians caused too much damage. Once they took all the natural resources they could take, they released a plague on the land killing millions and millions of Artonians. Then the Zorians left the planet expecting all the others to die within a couple of months. That was years ago, and somehow they are still alive.

I am amazed by the will of the Artonians.

♦♦♦♦♦

For the next couple of days, the Starship Armargosa's Engineering and Science Departments work non-stop on the planet. I am so excited to be so critical to this mission I have named it 'planting day.' It is my special day. I know Dalton thinks it's silly, but he is humoring me nonetheless. The Omega Team and I work wherever we are needed. I have never been so exhausted and exhilarated at the same time.

DALTON

We have been working continuously on the planet for days. The departments have finally completed all of the building and testing. Elder John gave us a tour of the rest of the villages, and it is more of the same. The people are starving and needing help, unable to do anything on their own. I still have a feeling they are keeping something from us. Elder John seems to care for Willow, but the others look at her funny. I can't explain it, but I feel like something is going to go terribly wrong.

I decide to act on what I am sensing. I call an emergency security meeting. I ask Kal, Dharma, and Cobalt to join me in the conference room.

"I asked you here to assist me with an idea I have for security for Willow's 'planting day.' We are on track for her to start the day after tomorrow. I would like for the three of you to be the first line of security. I get a feeling from some of the Artonians that I don't like, and I feel that Willow is in danger."

At my use of the word "danger," Kal becomes more attentive.

"What danger do you foresee Commander Alexander?" Kal asks fist clenched.

"I don't know specifically, but I have a feeling in my gut something bad is going to happen. I don't entirely trust the Artonians. I think they are hiding their thoughts from Willow and

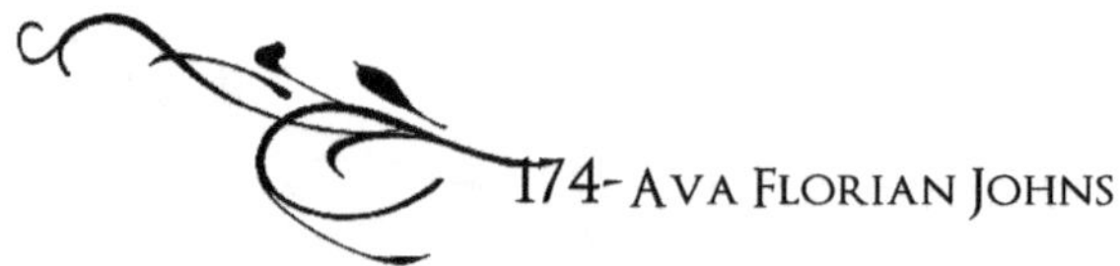

Jax. I can't explain it, and I am not physic, but it's my soldier's gut, telling me something bad is going to happen."

"What are your orders Commander Alexander?" Kal asks.

"Kal, Dharma, and Cobalt, I would like you to be in the greenhouse with Willow on her 'planting day.' I fear she won't be able to protect herself once she starts her process. We won't tell anyone you will be there, and that way if something does happen they will not know what to expect. I want you to protect her by any means necessary. Cobalt and Dharma, use your powers to protect Willow."

I know I am letting my personal feelings about Willow cloud my judgment, but I also know they are going to try something. Maybe Elder John is sending me a message. I don't know. All I know is she is in danger, and I am going to do everything I can to protect her.

Cobalt and Dharma leave the room and. Kal stays back to speak to me, and I know what is coming.

"Permission to speak freely?" Kal asks.

"Yes, of course."

"I don't understand. I thought you trusted the Artonians? What changed? Is this personal?" Kal asks in a very gruff manner.

I know he is worried about involving Dharma and Cobalt, the civilians.

"Kal, we have known each other for a long time. Have I ever put my personal feelings ahead of a mission?"

"No sir."

"This is something I sense deep in my gut. I feel like the Artonians are going to double-cross us somehow during Willow's 'planting day.' We made a promise we would help them. I know it's still the right thing to do. But I feel they are going to do something to Willow. I know you understand the soldier's gut."

"Yes, I do understand the gut, Commander Alexander, and I do agree with you. I am getting the feeling as well. I will also place guards around the outside of greenhouse for extra security."

"Thank you. I appreciate your candor and your support."

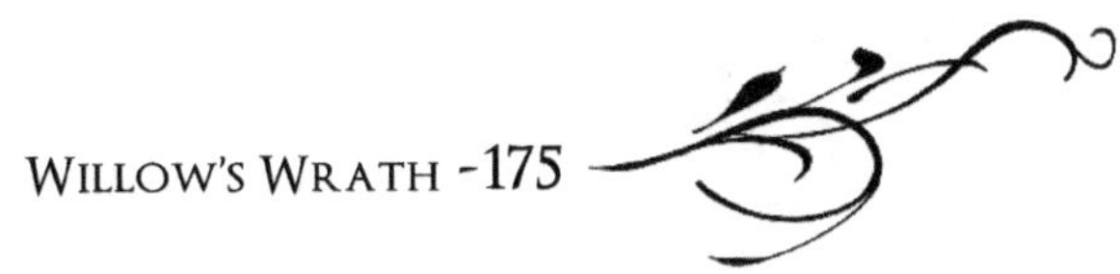

"No problem sir."

Kal leaves the room, but I continue to sit for a moment reflecting on the last couple of weeks. I can't believe how much has happened and how much we've been through in such a short time. I hope our plan works and the Artonians survive. But I will be happy when we're on our way back home.

I know Willow is in the arboretum practicing for 'planting day,' so I head to the arboretum. In my head, it is to check on her and the progress she is making with the plants, but I know in my heart that is not why I am going to see her.

When I get to the arboretum, I see she is in plant making mode. She doesn't hear me come in. This makes me feel good about my decision to add a security detail in the room with her when she is in the process of making the crops.

I sit down on the bench to watch her create her magic. She is so focused Willow doesn't see me until it is done. She had made a little field of corn. When she inspects the crops, she is delighted with her progress to tell by the look on her face.

"Good evening Willow."

She jumps about a mile in the air.

"Dalton, you scared the hell out of me. What are you doing in here?"

"I came to check on your progress to see how things are going."

"They are going well. I'm very pleased with my progress with the corn especially. Potatoes are still a little iffy. I still can't seem to get the shape right. But they taste okay."

"Well, I'm glad to see you're doing well." I step closer, reach out, and move two strands of hair off her forehead. I gently touch my lips to hers. I hear someone at the door. We hide behind the corn stalks because it would certainly look odd if we were caught kissing in the cornfields.

"Willow are you in here?" Lieutenant Williams calls from the doorway.

"Yes, sir I'm right here."

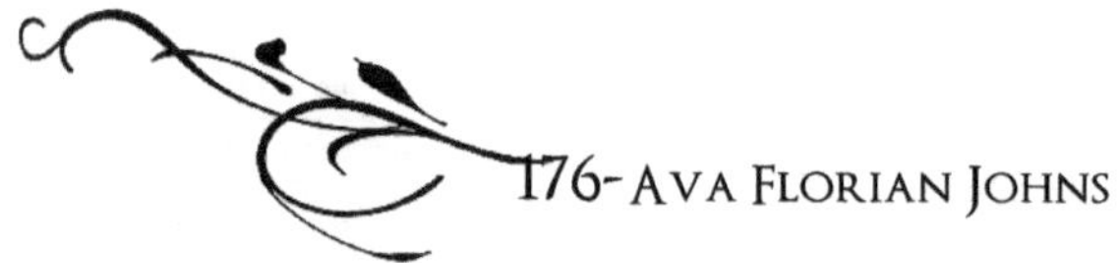

176- Ava Florian Johns

We step out from behind the rows of corn.

Williams gives me a funny look, but Willow handles it like a pro.

"Commander Alexander and I were inspecting the corn crops. I finished producing them a moment ago. How do they look Lieutenant?"

"I think they look great Willow. How are the potatoes coming along?"

"Not as great. They're still lumpy, but they taste okay."

"Willow, keep working on it. You have six hours to perfect your potato," he says chuckling.

"Thank you, Lieutenant, no pressure."

"Carry on. Goodnight Commander Alexander, Goodnight Willow."

After Williams leaves the arboretum, I decide to follow him out. No sense is putting myself through more torture. Willow is forbidden. I know that, so why do I put myself through this anguish.

CHAPTER
TWENTY-SEVEN
WILLOW

I am running through the tall yellow sunflowers. The morning sun shines brightly through the giant flowers in the fields, and it warms my face. Running back toward the farmhouse, I smell smoke. It burns my lungs, and I feel the dread wash over me. Hearing the piercing screams of my parents ringing in the air, I know something is horribly wrong. I know it, but my feet will not move. I am frozen in place in the midst of the sunflowers, unable to move, unable to help my parents as flames engulf our farmhouse. I see the military drones fly over me in the smoky sky and I drop to the ground and bury myself deep in the damp soil and leaves to camouflage my body. "They" have found them. I never did figure out who "they" were, but I heard my parents talking about "them" several times. I stay hidden for what seems like hours. Then I slowly walk toward the farmhouse. By this point, our lovely house is a smoldering pile of black ashes. I scream out for my mom and dad. Tears are rushing down my face. I'm awake and disoriented.

"Is something wrong, Willow?" I can hear Jax in my head communicating with me.

"I'm okay Jax, it's a nightmare."

"Oh, I don't think these are nightmares, I believe they're memories. I think your subconscious is trying to tell you something. What do you think the nightmare shows you?" Jax inquires.

"They usually tell me I'm in danger. You are right; I have to listen to them. Every time I have the dream I end up involved in a dangerous situation. Last time I almost lost my life. I didn't listen to it then but I will now. Thank you, Jax."

"I get a weird feel from the Artonians. I don't think they are a hundred percent honest with us. I feel like they're hiding something. It's not Elder John; it's some of the others. I don't want to mention it to the Commander because I'm afraid he will pull me from the mission."

"Willow, I think he already knows something's going on. There was a secret security meeting yesterday. He is going to have Kal, Dharma, and Cobalt in the room with you when you plant the crops. I know he feels something is wrong, and I strongly sense that from him. He is a man of action. He is not going to ignore his gut, and he created a plan to protect you. I am glad he did. I would hate for something bad to happen to you."

"Thank you for letting me know and for your support, Jax."

"It makes me feel better that he has a security plan for you. You better get ready and head out; it's 'planting day.'"

We get ready, leave our room, and head to the shuttle bay. Everyone is already waiting for us with the shuttle loaded.

"Hey, ready to go Willow?"

"I am ready Commander Alexander."

"All right, load up."

Everyone got in the shuttlecraft, and within minutes we are on the surface. I am so glad this ride was better than the last one. I would hate to vomit on 'planting day.'

Commander Alexander and Lieutenant Commander Kal have secured the area before the rest of us get out. Today, there will be two shuttlecrafts of supplies and crew coming to the surface.

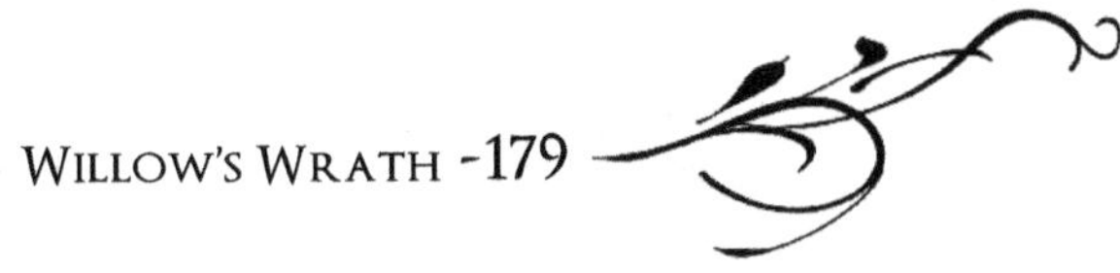

I am on the first one with Jax, Williams, the Commander, and of course Lieutenant Commander Kal. I think he has made it his mission to protect me.

I shouldn't complain if someone's going to protect me, and I'm glad it's him.

We get everything unloaded, and I prepare to start. Elder John has asked to see me before I begin. He walks over to me and gives me a big hug and takes my hand in his.

"Good morning my sweet Willow. It is so good to see you."

"Thank you, Elder John, it is great to see you too. I am going to miss you so much when I am gone."

"I am going to miss you as well, my sweet Willow. I have some gifts for you."

"No, Elder John I can't take anything from you."

"My sweet Willow for the gift you are giving us it is the least I can do. This disc contains historical documents and stories about my people. I want you to have it to teach your world about us. Maybe they can learn from our mistakes."

"Thank you, Elder John. I will cherish your stories." I have to gulp back tears.

"I have one more gift for your Commander. It is a map of this star system, which may help you get back to your land, my sweet Willow."

"Thank you so much. We will cherish these gifts."

Dalton walks up and stands behind me.

"Dalton, Elder John gave me this to give you. It is a map of this star system, and he believes it will help us get home."

"Thank you Elder John; we appreciate this."

Dalton puts his hand out to shake. Something passes through the handshake between the two men. I am not sure what it is, but it is evident Dalton got the message. He smiles and nods at Elder John. He takes the discs from my hand and continues his check on the other departments.

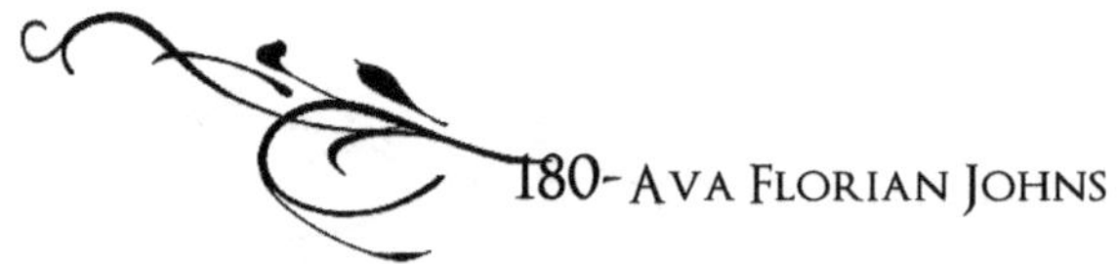

I hug Elder John again. "Not all of my people understand what a great gift you have given us. I want you to know that I do. Thank you so much my sweet Willow."

"Don't act like this is the last time you will see me. I will see you when I finish, won't I?"

"I don't think so. You will be leaving as soon as you complete your mission. It is safer this way. Goodbye, my sweet Willow."

"Goodbye Elder John."

Well, I am ready. The Commander is still running around like a chicken with his head cut off. Just thinking of the word chicken makes me remember when I called him a chicken in my room. I blush a little thinking about the kiss. It was so sultry and steamy. Yikes. I need to stop thinking about that and get to work.

"Is everyone ready?" Commander Alexander bellows.

"Yes, sir," we all said in unison.

"Are you ready, Willow?"

"Yes, Commander Alexander, I am ready."

"Okay commence project 'planting day,'" he says as seriously as he can muster.

I smile as I start producing the plants and within minutes I am completely in my zone.

CHAPTER
Twenty-eight
DALTON

I check with security one final time. Willow has started her process, and she figures it will take a few hours.

Kal has placed security officers around the entire perimeter of the building with orders to shoot if the situation warrants it. I don't want to hurt or kill these people, but I want to make sure the team is protected and err on the side of caution.

When I am confident the perimeter is secure, we position additional security inside the room. I also have Jax listening to their thoughts as much as she can so she can alert us to possible danger.

Willow is two hours into the process and hasn't yet taken a break. She looks exhausted. I hate to interrupt her but if she doesn't rest soon, I will. The plan is for her to stop every thirty minutes. I can tell something is different about her today. She isn't as giddy as I expected. She acts like she wants to get it over with and head back to the ship. I think that is why she is pushing herself so hard to get the job done.

She didn't complain at all about the extra security I set up. She must be feeling the threat as well.

I realize I have been staring at her for the last few minutes, so I quickly act like I am looking at something on my tablet.

At that moment, the alarms sound meaning that Jax is notifying us of a potential threat. A group of Artonians is coming our way. She says Elder John and a few others are blocking an angry mob from reaching the greenhouse.

"All right, everyone look alive. Kal, alert your Security Team now. Trouble is coming."

I run to Willow.

"There is danger. A group of Artonians is on their way, and they are not friendlies."

"What should I do? I need about another hour to finish."

"Keep going. We will hold the mob off as long as we can, and when we need to evacuate, I will get you. Do you understand?"

"Yes, I know. I promise I will go with you without argument."

"Thank you Willow."

I turn my attention back to the tablet.

The situation outside has escalated. The mob of angry Artonians has started fighting with Elder John and the others. Jax writes that she has never seen anything like it. The Artonians have morphed into monsters. They have shape-shifted to another being —a more vicious and horrifying being. Jax describes them as looking like zombie monsters from a horror movie.

Jax is in a position to record and send a video of the fight. She is right. It is like nothing I have ever seen before, and they are coming for Willow. I have to get her out of here.

"Kal, we are bugging out. NOW," I scream across the room.

Just as I get the words out of my mouth, Jax communicates that the monsters have slaughtered Elder John. The angry mob is headed straight for us.

"Kal incoming. Tell your security to shoot to kill. We need to get to the shuttles ASAP."

We left security by the shuttle as well, so they can't take our only means to get off this planet.

We are all poised at the entrance waiting for them to strike. We hear the guns go off outside. The only thing that is going through

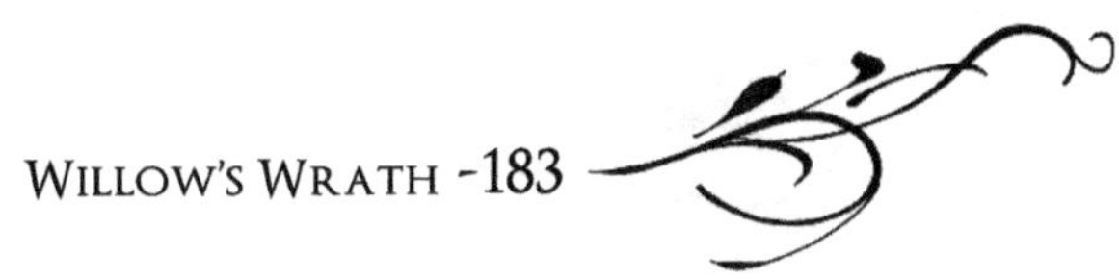

my head right now is that I hope no one from our crew will die on this mission.

The outer security perimeter holds for about fifteen minutes, but there are too many of the Artonian zombie monsters for our troops to fight on their own. They need backup. The monsters bust through the door and run right into Kal, Cobalt, and Dharma. Kal has a grenade launcher and starts blasting the monsters. Cobalt is flinging them out the door with her mind power. Some of the monsters she bashes against the wall several times rendering them unconscious. Dharma has changed into a strange beast, more terrifying than I have ever seen. Her reflexes are incredible, and she is going for the jugular. Cobalt and Dharma are amazing to watch, that is for sure.

I stand close to Willow. I have to give it to her; she is sure brave. Easily one of the most courageous people I have ever met. I have seen my share of battle, but this is the worst one yet. I have seen soldiers, big tough men, under heavy pressure, but here we have three of the bravest people I have ever encountered, and they look nothing like soldiers.

Kal, Cobalt, and Dharma are doing an excellent job of keeping the zombie monsters away from us. Willow turns her power on the last of the Artonians coming through the doorway. She has thick leafy vines coming at them and winding around their bodies to dangle them from the sky as she did to Christopher that day at the Annex. The vines and branches rip the zombie monsters in half throwing the pieces in the air, rendering the last of them useless. I grab Willow and the rest of the crew and head to the shuttles. I am glad I was paranoid and had a backup plan in place to protect her.

"Do we have everyone Kal?"

"Yes, sir everyone is accounted for."

I breathe a sigh of relief, then motion to Jax to tell Willow about the death of Elder John.

I know she has told her when Willow breaks down and cries. I know crying is not something she wants to do in front of the crew, but she can't help herself.

I hope the discs Elder John gave us explain what happened. And I hope what we did helps someone on the planet, and all the effort we put in is not going to go to waste.

I also hope Elder John explains the zombie monsters. Although they were scary creatures, they didn't have the military experience one would expect. They didn't fight very well or work together at all. I'm afraid if they had banded together, we would never have defeated them.

We are all back on board the starship. I am so proud of my crew and the Omega Team. We nearly got out without a scratch, although this will go down as the most peculiar battle in history.

CHAPTER
Twenty-nine
WILLOW

I was so happy and excited when I woke up this morning, thinking about the chance to save a planet. I am amazed to have had this opportunity. But after what happened today I am soured on *ever* helping anyone again. I see why Dalton is so cynical most of the time. He has seen his share of battles, and I know he has had his share of disappointments.

This time I didn't have to imagine the vines and branches strangling or ripping someone limb-from-limb, it was actually happening to those terrible morphed monsters. All I had to do was will it, and the plants did the work for me. They were my killing machine.

I have been crying for hours. Jax has come over to my cot countless times to comfort me, but I don't want pity. I am crying for Elder John, for Dr. Carver, and even for Christopher, who died way too soon. I want to mourn; I don't want to feel solace, not yet anyway. There is a knock at the door. I am in no condition to answer it; I am a slobbery mess. I guess it is Dharma and Cobalt again. They have been here twice already to check on me. They were amazing today. If I didn't know them, I would be scared. They kicked ass.

It isn't Cobalt and Dharma; it's the Commander and the Captain. As soon as I hear their voices, I run to the bathroom before they can see me.

"I will be out in a minute," I call through the door. "Make yourself comfortable."

Jax let them in, and they are talking in hushed tones. What are they saying? I can't hear through the door, so I quickly wash the boogers and tears off my face. I look marginally better.

"Sorry about that Captain, Commander," I nod in their direction. "What can I do for you?"

"We came to check on you. Is there anything you need?" The Captain says looking concerned.

"No, I am fine. I needed to get the tears out. I will be better tomorrow."

"I have no doubt. I do have something to show you. Would you rather meet tomorrow morning, or would you like to see it now? It is the disc that Elder John gave you. We want you to take a look at it."

"I would like to see it now. Please give me a minute to get dressed."

"Have your whole group meet us in the bridge conference room in ten minutes."

"Yes, we will. Thank you, Captain."

The Commander and Captain leave the room. I run to the bathroom again, and Jax goes to get Cobalt and Dharma. We all walk to the bridge together and enter the all too familiar conference room. The Captain is right; it feels like we are in here a lot. All of our commanding officers are in the room when we walk in. They stand as we enter, and applaud.

"We want to thank you for your service today. Each member of your Omega Team is spectacular. We couldn't have asked for a better team on the ground. Thank you!"

The Captain sits down and starts the meeting. My eyes fill with tears of pride for myself and admiration for my team.

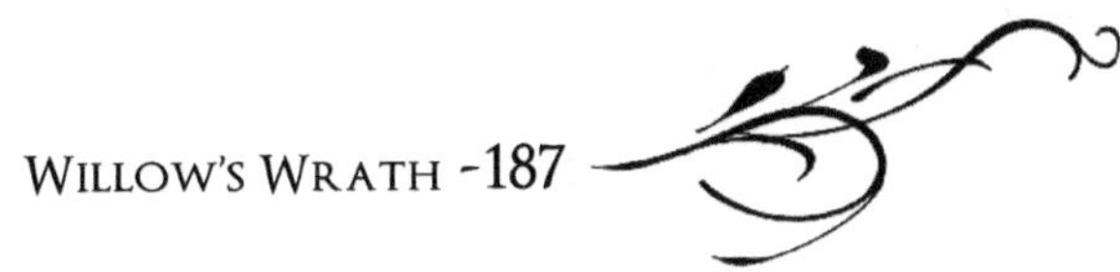

"First, I would like to preface this meeting by saying that without Willow we would not have gotten these discs. Elder John formed a unique bond with Willow and felt compelled to give her this information. It is so much more than we ever anticipated and it most likely is the information that will bring us home. First, we will view a message from Elder John."

Dalton starts the recording. Elder John's face fills the screen. Tears fill my eyes, and I immediately feel saddened by his death. He came to mean a great deal to me in a very short time.

He starts to speak, and we can hear his words. He has a device he hooked to his temple to his computer that will say the words as he is thinking them.

"Hello, my sweet Willow and the rest of the crew from the Starship Armargosa. I am so grateful for your assistance in trying to save my people. I'm afraid it was too late for some of us. We have morphed into these horrible creatures, and we no longer have the willpower to stop ourselves. The technology we used to prolong our lives has turned us into this."

He morphed into a zombie-like creature and then morphed back to himself.

"There is a group that will attack today. They want Willow. They don't want the greenhouse you so graciously gave us, this mob wants her power, and they won't stop until they get it. They believe if they steal her power for the rest of our people that we can repair our planet. I sincerely hope you all survive the attack and are seeing this message."

He paused for a moment to gather his thoughts, then continues.

"I tried to warn you the best I could. I sent as many messages telepathically to Commander Alexander as I could without being discovered by my people. I hope he received these messages and can save all of you and my sweet Willow. I am glad I had the opportunity to say goodbye to you and to give you this gift. It is the least I can do. Another bit of information is that we have been blocking your signal. You should be able to contact your homeworld now. We were

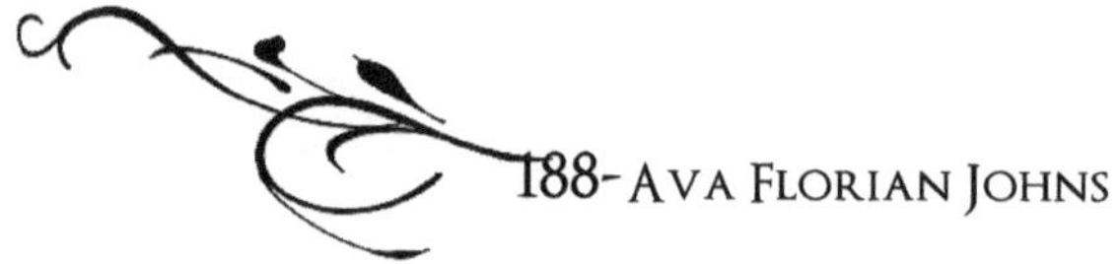

188- AVA FLORIAN JOHNS

afraid if you made contact you would leave. The first disc I gave you has all our technology and information regarding the plans for extending life. I also included the history of my planet and the wondrous things we once created."

I took a minute to look around the room. Everyone is listening intently. Dalton is staring directly at me. I am sure he is gauging my mood and how this is affecting me. I mouth to Dalton that I am fine and focus my attention back to the video.

"The second disc gives you an accurate map of the galaxy. I am very hopeful this will get you home. It was a pleasure meeting all of you. I wish you hope for the future. Goodbye my sweet Willow, goodbye."

The video ends, and everyone looks at me. I have tears streaming down my face. I loved Elder John. He was an amazing man and another person in my life I lost too soon.

I wipe my tears and indicate I am ready for the meeting to continue.

"Lieutenant Cameron. I want you and your team to study the maps and evaluate the other information on these discs. There are also schematics for a power source. Please review the schematics and assess its feasibility to connect to our ship's systems." The Captain pauses and looks around the room. "Thank you all for what you did today. I can't tell you how proud I am of all of you. You worked as a team, and that kind of teamwork is what we need to get us home. Now get some rest. Do well, dismissed."

We all walk toward the exit. "Jax, I am going to head to the arboretum for a while. I will see you in a few minutes."

I need a few moments alone. Everything that has happened in the last couple of weeks has been mind-boggling. I was a student at boarding school six weeks ago, and now I am fighting weird zombie-like creatures on a faraway planet. It is heady stuff.

I enter the arboretum and sit on my favorite bench. The flowers are happy to see me. I swear they know what is happening and feel worried for me. "Don't worry guys, I am fine," I say out loud. I close

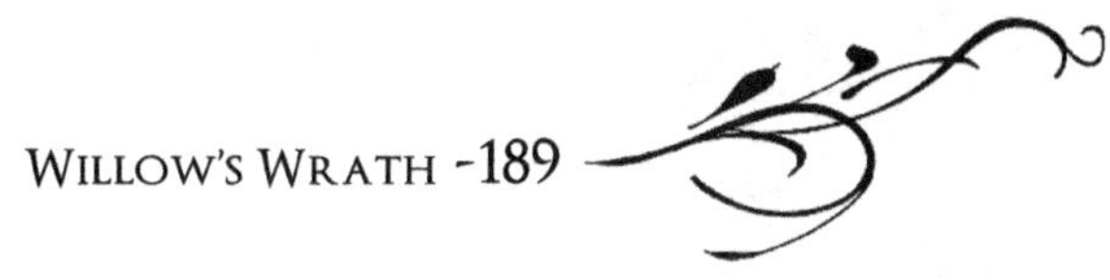

my eyes and think about Elder John. I feel like he is still with me. He had such a kind and calming soul. I will miss him.

I hear the door open. It is Dalton. I knew he would come here to check on me.

"Hello Willow."

"Hello Dalton, why are you here?"

"I want to check and see if you are okay."

"I am fine. I need a couple of minutes alone to clear my head before I go to sleep."

"I want to tell you how proud I am of you. You were amazing today."

"Thank you, Commander."

"It's Commander now is it?"

"Yes, I am too tired to play games tonight. You are not ready to commit. I get it that you have trust issues, but I can't do this anymore."

"Willow, I have a sordid past. I have had some shocking things happen to me, and I wasn't ready to share them. I think I am ready now. Because of you. Your trust in individuals, your faith in people, it astonishes me. It makes me realize how arrogant and cynical I have been my whole life. I don't want to be that way anymore."

"Can we pick this discussion up again tomorrow? I need to get some sleep."

"Yes of course. May I walk you back to your room?"

"Yes sir, you may."

"First a good night kiss."

He places his lips on mine, and I melt into him. I feel so brazen around him that I deepen the kiss. I throw my arms around him and move my body close to his. I don't know what comes over me, but I have never acted like this with another man before, I can't seem to get enough of him. He is everything I am not. He is dark, sullen, and brooding, but it has been so fun to try and crack his hard exterior.

I end the kiss this time.

"I think I'd better go to my room now."

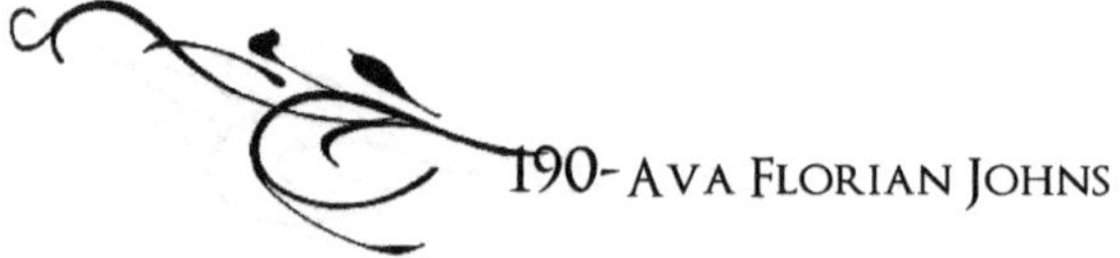

"Agreed. Let's go."

We walk hand in hand to my room. It surprises me that Dalton doesn't drop my hand when we get to the hallway. I thought we were forbidden to fraternize on the ship, but maybe it is Dalton's rule, and not the Captain's.

We get to my room, and he kisses me gently on the lips and forehead.

"Goodnight Willow, sweet dreams."

"Goodnight Dalton."

Dharma opens the door behind me, and I almost fall through the opening. "Wanted to be alone, huh. You don't look alone to me."

"Well, this is a good time for me to go. Goodnight ladies." Dalton calls through the doorway.

"Come in and tell us all the naughty details." Dharma grabs my arm and pulls me into the room.

"No naughty details to tell, ladies."

"Yeah right Willow, we see how you two look at each other. It's scandalous! Come on, tell us the tawdry tidbits." Cobalt says, and Jax nods her head in agreement.

They all sit on my bed staring up at me.

"Fine. The Commander followed me to the arboretum to see if I was okay."

"Boring!" Cobalt says dramatically.

"He kissed me. End of story. No more details."

"What kind of kiss? Was it a hot sinful kiss, or a sweet, gentle kiss?"

"Go away Dharma and take Cobalt with you."

"Fine, good luck sleeping tonight. I bet all you think of is Dalton's hot bod."

"Goodnight Dharma."

I throw a pillow at her on the way out the door. She throws it back laughing.

I appreciate the camaraderie I have with the members of the team. I feel like they are my sisters. I would do anything for them, and I know after today, they would do the same for me.

CHAPTER THIRTY
DALTON

I head to my room after dropping Willow off at her door. I can hear her roommates teasing her about me. I smile.

I stroll to the Captain's room before heading to my quarters. I know he will still be up. Probably reviewing the videos Elder John gave us.

I knock on the door, and he answers immediately. "Hey, Dalton come on in, I am going to get myself a drink. Would you like one?"

"Yes, thank you, Captain."

"At ease Commander, you can call me Chris when we are sharing a drink."

"Thanks, Chris. I need one."

"It has been a couple of wild weeks, hasn't it?"

"Yes, sir. I mean yes Chris, it certainly has."

We sit down on his couch.

"I have to tell you, I have been in a lot of battles but today was the weirdest one ever. The creatures the Artonians morphed into were a cross between a monster and a zombie. I may have nightmares for weeks," I say chuckling.

"I miss the days of away missions and battles now that I am stuck here on the ship. I guess I have to get used to the fact you are going to be the one having all the fun."

"I wouldn't exactly say today was fun. Freaky maybe, but not fun."

"Oh come on. It is like in the old days, come home from battle, get the girl. You can't deny something is going on between you and Willow. It is so obvious when you two are together. Don't bullshit me. And I would give you the speech about not becoming personally involved with the crew, but I am sure you have already given yourself the speech a million times."

I down my drink and Chris pours me another.

"Okay Dalton, I can see you are not ready to admit your feelings about Willow yet, and she is technically not part of the crew so I can't tell you not to fraternize. I promise I will stop busting your chops about her so we can talk about something else."

"Chris, I would rather talk about the zombie monsters."

He laughs.

It is so fun shooting the shit with another guy. I like Chris. He is a good man and a hell of a commanding officer. I couldn't ask for a better captain.

"As my captain, I want to tell you I am sorry for giving you such a hard time about bringing the Omega Team on this mission. I was wrong. It is not a babysitting mission. The Omega Team saved our asses today and at the same time did a great thing for a dying planet."

I pull out my tablet and show him a video of Cobalt, Dharma, and Kal kicking some ass.

"I didn't show you this before, Chris. How amazing is this?"

"Wow, it's like horror movies. Like a zombie apocalypse."

"I know, right? You should have been with us man; it's one for the books."

CHAPTER
THIRTY-ONE
WILLOW

I get ready for bed in my sexy military pajamas that are about three sizes too big for me. That's okay, at least they are comfortable. I have never been much of a fashion plate anyway.

I can't wait to go to sleep tonight. Before I know it, I am dreaming again.

I am running through the tall yellow sunflowers. The morning sun shines through the flowers in the fields, and it warms my face. Running back toward the farmhouse, I smell smoke and feel the dread wash over me. Hearing the piercing screams of my parents ringing in the air, I know something is horribly wrong. I know it, but my feet will not move. I am frozen in place in the midst of the sunflowers, unable to move, unable to help my parents as flames engulf our farmhouse. I see the military drones fly over me in the smoky sky, I drop to the ground, and bury myself deep in the soil and leaves to camouflage my body. "They" have found them. I never did figure out who "they" were, but heard my parents talking about them several times. I stay hidden for what seems likes hours and then I slowly walk toward the farmhouse. By this point, our lovely house is a smoldering pile of black ashes. I scream out for my mom and dad. Tears are rushing down my face. Elder John is standing in front of my burning farmhouse with his arms outstretched. I am no longer the five-year-old girl, but I am seeing myself as I am today.

He gives me a huge hug. "My sweet Willow, how I will miss you."

"I will miss you, too. So much."

"Willow, I want to thank you. You were so brave today. I am sorry for deceiving you. I want to make sure you know how grateful I am for you and your crew. Your greenhouse will help my people move on from this and start to rebuild their lives."

"But why did you have to die?"

"My sweet Willow. It was meant to be. I have lived many lifetimes, and it was time for me to move onto my next life. I promise you I will always be with you—always. Goodbye, my sweet Willow."

I wake up with tears on my face. It is only one o'clock in the morning. I know I won't be able to go back to sleep, so I sneak out of the room very quietly and head to the science lab. I forgot I am still in my pajamas, but I don't want to go back and wake Jax up to change.

The other people in the science lab don't give me a second glance. I go to my station and pull up my father's files. I want to feel closer to him today. I need some comfort in my very chaotic world. And I find it...I find a handwritten a note from my father.

The current condition of our world.

The PG tell us only what they want us to hear. They have known for over hundred years our planet is dying. They say everything is fine. They teach our school children recycling facilities are going to be enough to reverse the damage to our world, but it is not. We have to find a suitable planet to colonize on now. While we are building the new world, we can fix this one with the serum my wife, and I

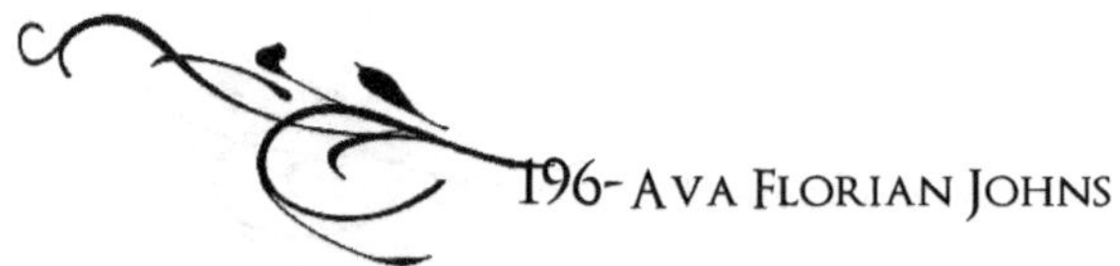

- Ava Florian Johns

developed. I hope we can convince them in time to save our race. If we wait much longer, there will not be a human race to save.

Jeffrey Washburn

I feel closer to him than ever. We are finally doing something to fix our situation, and his serum will be a reason for our success. I sincerely hope it is, so my parents' deaths were not in vain.

"Willow, what in the hell are you doing here—it is 0300 hours?" Lieutenant Williams says as he walks into the science lab.

"I couldn't sleep, so I am reviewing my father's journals. They are fascinating, and I lost track of time."

"You need to get some shut-eye. We have a staff meeting at 0900 hours. Please get some sleep. Dismissed."

"Yes, sir," I say a little sassy.

Williams laughs.

I take my time getting out of my chair.

"Now, Willow."

I walk back to my room finally feeling a little tired. I hope I can get some dreamless sleep.

I sneak back in without turning the light on so as not to wake Jax. Poor Jax —she drew the short straw when she got me as a roommate.

I hit my cot and fall into a deep sleep.

Our alarm rings at 0800 hours. We take turns with the shower, get dressed and head to the mess hall. Cobalt and Dharma are at a table, so we grab our food and join them.

"Hey ladies, how are you this morning? Dream about any hunky commanders, Willow?" Dharma says slyly.

"Nope," I say, feeling evasive.

"Where did you go last night?" Jax asks me telepathically?

"To the science lab." I mistakenly say out loud.

"What?" Cobalt asks.

"Jax asked me where I went last night. I had a nightmare and couldn't get back to sleep, so I headed to the science lab. I was there a couple of hours before Lieutenant Williams kicked me out."

"You went to the science lab in the middle of the night?" Dharma asks in a prodding manner.

"Yes, I had a nightmare and didn't want to wake Jax, so I went to read my parents' journal. I found some great information, and I can't wait to delve into it some more."

"You expect us to believe you have a hunky admirer and you were in the science lab?"

"Yep, because that is what happened." I turn and stick my tongue out at Dharma.

Kal walks over to our table just as I stuck my tongue out.

"All right Omega Team, time to go. You need to be on the bridge at 0900 hours," Kal barks.

"Yes, sir."

♦♦♦♦♦

"Good Morning Omega Team and Kal." We are the last ones in the room.

"Now we are out of Artona's orbit; we need a plan. Lieutenant Cameron, please give us a run-down on the maps we received from Elder John."

At the mention of Elder John's name I wince.

"Captain Holloway, the maps indicate galaxies, wormholes, anomalies, black holes, star systems, planets, nebulas, and milky ways. They are incredibly detailed, easily the most comprehensive maps I have ever seen." Lieutenant Cameron acts like an excited little boy with a new toy.

"The plan of action will be to head toward Earth. Along the way, we will scout a new world for colonization. The number one priority will be to establish communication with an APA military base in this sector. Communications Team, work on establishing contact. Elder

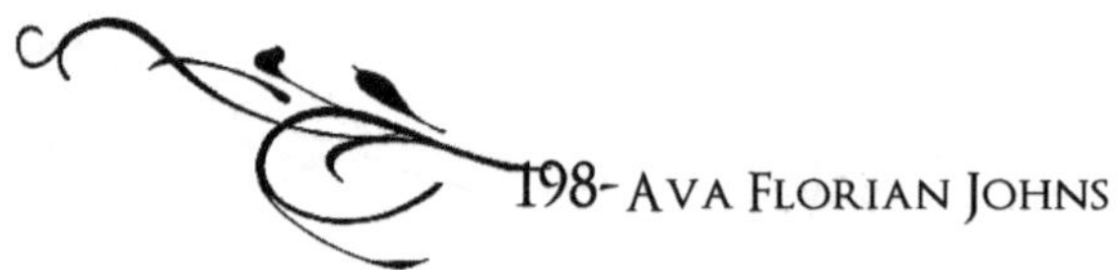

John confessed to blocking our signal, so I am confident it will now work." The Captain turns to Lieutenant Cameron and Cobalt, "Engineering, find the most stable wormhole and give the coordinates to Ensign Johnson as soon as possible. Science and Security Departments, please continue with what you were working on before our stop on Artona. Dharma and Kal, continue and schedule the combat training. Any questions?"

"Any new initiatives for the Science Department, now we know what Willow can do?" Lieutenant Williams asks.

"Keep studying the research documents and take a look at the information Elder John gave us. There is a lot of information regarding the life-extending technology they developed. Please forward updates to Commander Alexander by 1900 hours today. Do well. Dismissed."

We all file out of the room into the hallway. Lieutenant Williams and I walk to the Science Department together.

"Is there anything you are specifically curious about Willow, now you know more about what you can do?"

"I want to finish going through my parents' documents to see what they thought of the ecological condition of the Earth. I am also thinking about Dr. Carver's personal logs. Do you think I could get access to them?"

"I don't see why not, but why? What do you think you will find?"

"Well, she was a scientist too, and she spent a lot of time with my parents. She may have documented something they didn't, and she may have had a different perspective."

"Good thought. I will get you access immediately."

"Thank you, Lieutenant."

"What's wrong Willow? You seem off today."

"I am still concerned about the other members of the Omega Team, left on Earth. It has been such a chaotic few days for us; I forgot they still may be in danger. I have a really good friend named Lizzy that I left behind. She was in the younger group and may not understand why I can't communicate with her."

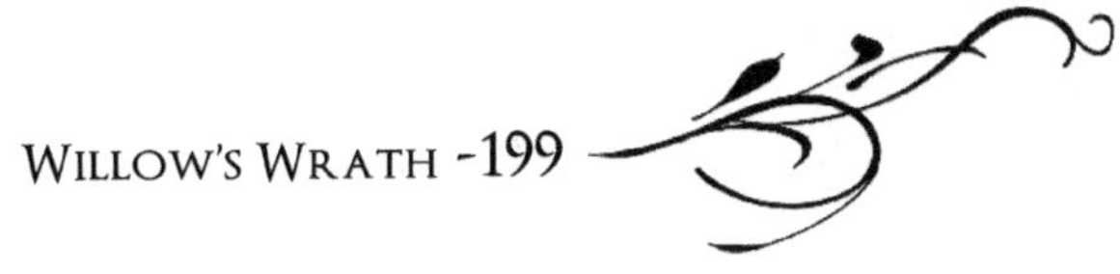

"I will send a message to Lieutenant Allium to reach out to them as well. We may be able to establish communications with them now."

"Thank you, Lieutenant Williams, I appreciate it."

I like Lieutenant Williams but am I once again trusting too quickly? I never thought there was a problem with that. I always considered trust an admirable trait, until I got burned, three times now. Three people, I have trusted have deceived me. Dr. Carver, Christopher, and Elder John, and now they are all gone. It is still so sad and still so raw.

CHAPTER

THIRTY-TWO

DALTON

I am sitting at my station on the bridge thinking about the last couple of weeks.

I hope we can get back to some normalcy aboard the ship. I can sense the anxiety of the crew. We need the team at the top of their game, not stressed and worried, although I can hardly blame them. It has been one thing after another on this mission. First, we are pursued by the PG through a wormhole which flings us on the other side of the quadrant, then we find out the director of the APA Annex is a traitor, and finally, we battle a race of zombie monsters. I chuckle to myself—it sounds like a plot for a terrible horror movie.

I hope nothing else happens for the next few months so we can be explorers and do what we are supposed to be doing out here, and that is finding a suitable planet for colonization.

"Captain on the bridge," Ensign Johnson announces.

"At ease."

"Commander, status."

"We are headed for the wormhole. Engineering feels it is the most stable one in our vicinity. Once we get closer to the wormhole, we will be able to get better readings. Cameron said this wormhole is marked on the map Elder John gave us. Cameron believes Elder John is giving us a path to follow because there is a clear delineation on the map. There is also a cluster of planets in the system that would be worth checking out."

"That is the best news we have had in a long time. How long before we are in the planetary system?"

"Three days, sir."

"Wonderful, carry on Commander, you have the bridge."

"Thank you, sir."

♦♦♦♦♦

Over the last three days, I have avoided Willow at all costs. I have worked and met with every other department on the ship, except for the Science Department. They were the only ones who were not working on something new so that I could avoid them, but as their commander, I should have at least checked in with them. I wanted a couple of days to sort through everything that has happened and yes, sort out my feelings for her. I feel like a little kid, worried about my feelings. I don't want to hurt her. She has had so many people in her life deceive her, I don't want to be another person who does that to her.

I always thought and still think to some degree I deserved what I got. I must have done something wrong that made a higher being give me the horrible life I have had. Seeing my mother murdered by my father haunts my dreams, but I do have to admit I have some good memories. My mom teaching me how to build things, reading me stories, and singing me to sleep. My grandfather, a dear man, would bring me to Earth a couple of weeks a year and walk me through his apple orchard. We would take care of the chickens and goats. He got great joy out of putting tiny baby eggs in my hands and watching my reaction. He was a farmer like Willow's parents and taught me the importance of building and growing something with your own hands, which is the polar opposite of what my Casson father believed. All he knew was how to destroy things and tear them down. He was a soldier after all.

I never understood why my mother married my father. They were literally from two different worlds. She was from Earth, born on a

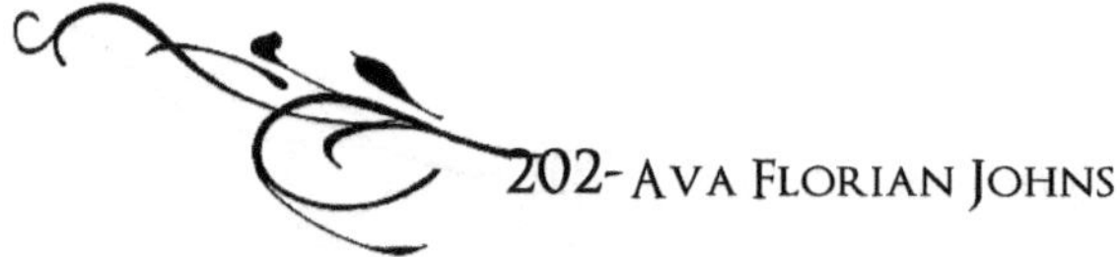

farm, a sweet soul. My dad was a killer, born and bred on the planet Casson. They had nothing in common and always fought about how to raise me. My father thought my mother was too soft with her style of upbringing. He was convinced I was going to grow up to be weak. My mom, of course, thought my father was too rigid, too strict, and too tyrannical. When he started beating me for misbehaving is when the real fighting between them started. That was when he turned on her. I still feel guilty for not being able to defend her, and she died at my father's hand.

I hadn't had contact with him since I left for junior boot camp when I was twelve, and that is okay with me. He is a miserable man who doesn't know how to do anything but kill. If I hadn't met Chris Holloway, I'm afraid I would have walked the same path as my father. I was angry over the death of my mother and more furious at myself for not stopping it.

Wow, not sure what spurred the walk down memory lane, but I need to snap out of it. We are coming up on the planetary system within the hour, and the Captain has called a staff meeting.

I walk into the room, still in a fog.

"Commander, will you please get started."

"Yes, sir." I shake my head trying to clear my thoughts and focus on the task at hand.

"This is a map of the system we are about to enter. We will be at this location within the hour." I point to a spot on the map. "This is the planet Aconite in the Kerberos system. As you can see by the map, there are hundreds of small planets in the area. We are going to select one a day to send a very small away team to investigate its suitability for a human colony. Engineering tells me there is an electrical current that runs through and around this area in space. It is called the Amugdalea Cluster. This area of space contains space debris, including false vacuum fluctuations, and metaphase radiation. We do know it has at least five habitable planets, one of which is the Aconite planet. The shuttlecraft will be outfitted to withstand the metaphase radiation. We want to keep the landing parties small until we have established the area is safe. The first team is Lieutenant Williams, Ensign Johnson, and me. Lieutenant Williams, meet me in the shuttle bay in one hour. Everyone else, your schedules were sent to your tablets. Review them and let me know if you have any questions."

I look over at Willow after I announce the away team. I can tell she is extremely disappointed she is not going on the mission. I can't handle putting her in harm's way again. The Captain is right. I am letting my feelings for her cloud my judgment. She should be going on the mission today, not Williams.

Willow leaves the room without a second glance my way.

"Commander, may I ask why I am going on this mission instead of Willow?"

There are three of us left in the room, Williams, the Captain, and me. The Captain looks curious about my choice as well.

"Permission to speak freely" Williams continues.

"Yes, Lieutenant, of course."

"Commander, this is why Willow is on this mission. She needs to be on the away teams. I looked at the schedule for the next few days, and you have not scheduled her for one away mission. Is there a reason? Has she done something wrong?"

I have to choose my words carefully, so I don't give away my real feelings about Willow. It is not very professional of me to not put her on an away team because I don't want her to get hurt. I am trying to protect her, but this is her job.

"No, Lieutenant, she hasn't done anything wrong. She handled herself quite well on Artona. My thought process is she will come in after we deem the planet suitable for colonization. Once the world is secured."

"Excuse me for being so blunt, but she can take care of herself. I know you don't want her to get hurt. I know you feel responsible for her, but you have given away missions to the other members of the Omega Team. You look like you are singling her out. Please

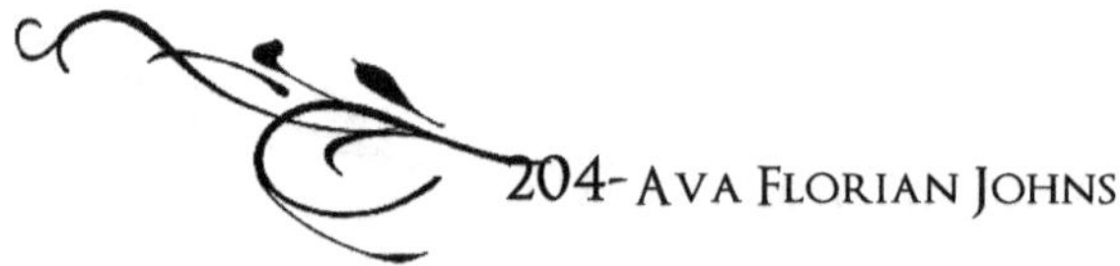

reconsider Commander Alexander. She is the one who should be going on the mission, not me.”

The Lieutenant gives me one final look and leaves the room.

“Dalton, let her go on the mission.”

“Captain, if something happens to her, I...”

“I know, I know you care for her, but you can’t treat her differently than the other team members. You have to let her do her job. We need her down on the planet. This mission is too important for our survival.”

“Okay, Captain, I will fix this.”

Only I don’t know how.

♦♦♦♦♦

“Willow, can I talk to you?”

I am in the science lab, and she is running in every direction to get away from me.

“I am a little busy here Commander.”

“You are going on the mission. Meet us in the shuttle bay at 0900 hours.”

She looks up, stunned.

“What?”

“You are going on the away mission. Get ready.”

“But why?”

“I was reminded you are capable of carrying out this mission, and you should be going instead of Williams. We need your expertise; you will need to determine if the ecosystem on the planet is capable of sustaining life.”

“Yes, sir Commander.” She says sarcastically.

Well, this sucks. Willow is still pissed at me for leaving her out. This will be a fun trip. I have a sick feeling in the pit of my stomach about this. I am not sure what could happen that is worse than zombie monsters, but I guess we will find out together.

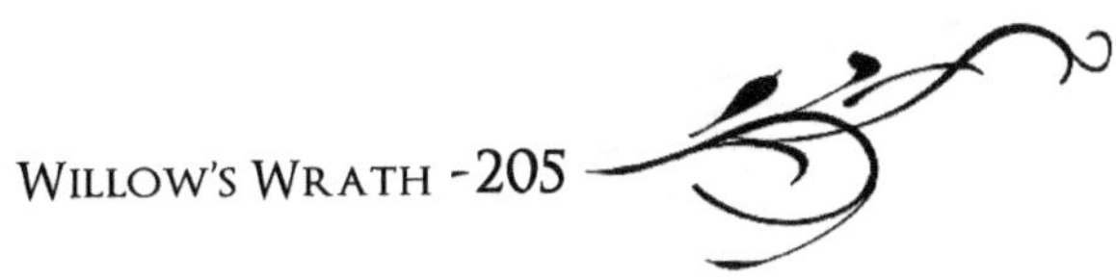

CHAPTER
THIRTY-THREE
WILLOW

I am excited about going on the away mission, but truthfully a bit apprehensive. Why didn't Dalton want me to go? Did I do something wrong on Artona? I need him to believe in me. More than as my commanding officer, but he is not there yet. I know he has a lot of trust issues, but so do I.

I tell Lieutenant Williams I am going on the away mission. He doesn't look surprised at all. I figure he is the one who said something to the Commander.

"Willow, before you leave I want to let you know that you have full access to Dr. Carver's notes and personal journals. Are you sure you want them? You may find out something that you don't want to know."

"Lieutenant Williams, at this point, I think I have found out everything bad I am going to find out about her. She pretended to be my parents' best friend, then had them killed. I am pretty sure that is the worst thing I will find out."

"Okay, Willow, you have full access."

"Thank you, Lieutenant; I will see you when I get back."

I head to my room to get a few things. I pack a light backpack with an extra shirt, jumpsuit, and some other little personal items, in case. You never know what the planet is going to be like and if I am going to need a change of clothes.

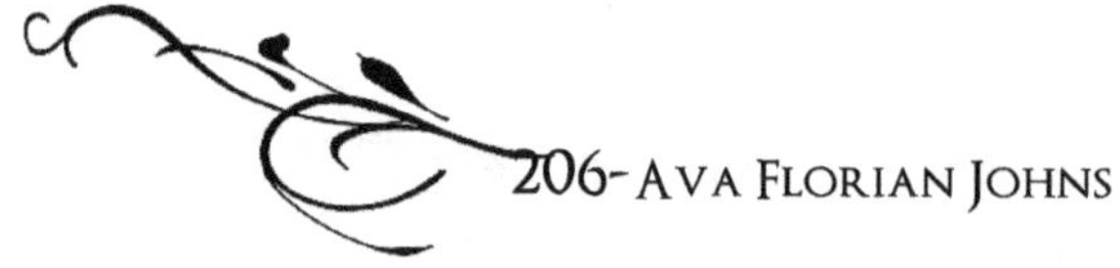

I would love to go through Dr. Carver's video journals now, but I know I don't have time. Instead, I go to find Jax, Dharma, and Cobalt to tell them I am leaving after all. They have already heard through the grapevine I am going. I swear the gossip moves faster on the starship than it did in the boarding school.

I am glad Ensign Ben Johnson is going on the mission. He has been coming to the arboretum the last couple of nights after his shifts. The first night he came in, I thought it was Dalton and was a little disappointed. I could sense Ensign Johnson, and Ben knew I was expecting someone else. It is nice getting to know others on the ship because most of the crew ignores the Omega Team. I think it's because they don't believe we trained enough to be on this mission. After Artona, they started opening up a little, hearing about our heroics.

I find out Ben is also a plant aficionado. He says the daisies remind him of his girlfriend because they are bright flowers and she is always happy, like the daisies. I can tell he is sad about being so far away from her. They knew this mission was scheduled to be for three years, and they wouldn't see each other, but they still wanted to make it work. They thought at least they could video conference. However, we are now expecting to be five years out, and because there is no communication yet, he doesn't know what she thinks. She could believe he is gone forever. If we can't get a communication through to the APA, they will probably think that we are all dead.

I hadn't thought of this because there is no one to care if I am gone or not. The team expected to be gone for three years, but they didn't expect this.

I finish saying my goodbyes and walk to the shuttle bay. They are finishing loading it for the mission. It looks like we are going away for a year with the amount of stuff we are bringing along.

"Why so much stuff?" I ask Ensign Johnson.

"We typically pack emergency rations on an away mission like food, and extra clothes. This time we are packing a bit more, such

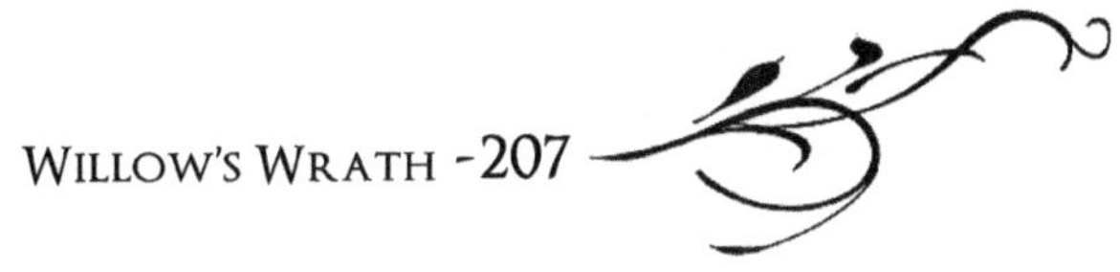

as a temporary housing unit, food dispenser, and an emergency generator. Our scanners are not working, so we can't tell if there are inhabitants on the planet. Commander Alexander wants to make sure we have something to give them if they need it or something to trade if we find something we need."

"Wow, it's a lot of stuff."

"Better safe than sorry."

"That is what my mom always said. Maybe we will find a new flower for the arboretum on the planet. I hope the inhabitants are friendly, so we can trade and find new things. They might have some fruits and vegetables we don't have."

"I forgot to tell you Willow; we also packed some seeds and small plants for you to see if they will grow in the climate of this planet."

"That is great, thank you, Ben," I say, feeling like I have made a good friend outside of the Omega Team.

"Are you guys ready to go?"

"Yes, sir." We both answer quickly.

"All aboard," the Commander barks.

This is not going to be a fun trip; he is in a terrible mood. We all climb in. Instead of the Commander piloting the shuttle, this time Ensign Johnson is going to take over.

"Ensign, ready to take off."

"Yes, sir."

"Shuttlecraft one ready for takeoff." Ensign Johnson tells the bridge.

"Dock doors opening, good luck away team. Our rendezvous point is 14-25-41-71 at 1400 hours. See you then. Do well," the Captain announces.

"All right Ensign, take us out."

"Yes, sir Commander."

"Ensign, be aware the metaphase radiation will cause some issues with the readouts on the control board."

"Yes, Commander. Here we go."

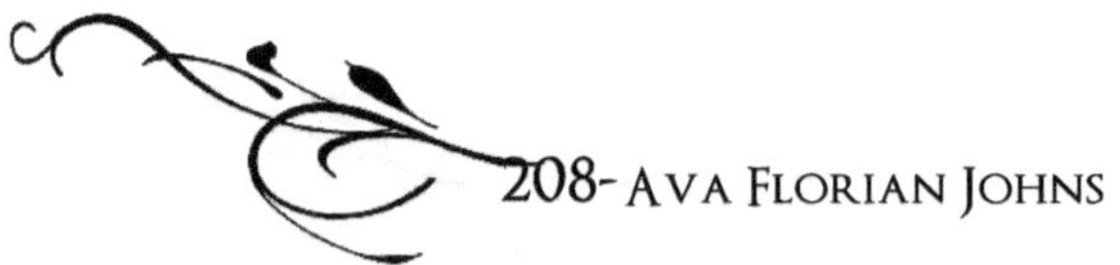

We shoot out of the shuttle bay doors. The first part of the trip is as smooth as glass. The second part is not. I am strapped tightly in my seat and still getting jostled. Judging by their conversation, there is space debris, including the remains of supernovae they didn't anticipate. I can tell Ben is having trouble piloting the shuttle, and he is losing control.

"Ensign, do you need me to take over?"

"No sir, I got it."

We swerve from side to side. I think I am going to vomit. The flight is a million times worse than our last trip to Artona, which was terrible.

"Commander, we are off our heading, of 55-88-97-63 by fourteen degrees. I am compensating for the drift."

"I am going to help you get it down. Keep it, steady ensign."

"Yes, sir, holding it steady."

Suddenly the shuttle hits a massive debris field. The shuttle lurches, and we are falling rapidly to the planet. Everything happened so fast, and without warning, I realize we are going down.

"Brace for impact," The Commander shouts.

I tuck my head down between my knees and throw my arms over my head.

Dalton and Ben try everything they can do to stabilize the ship.

"We are going down," Ben says.

"Impact in four, three, two, one."

Boom!

We hit the ground with such incredible force I don't think we can be in one piece. I was flung forward and hit my head on the seat in front of me. Blood is gushing out of a cut in my head. It is very reminiscent of the night Dr. Carver kidnapped me. Through the blood, I see Dalton and Ben have also flung forward.

The shuttle skids for a while before it stops. I lean back in my seat holding my hands on my head to keep the blood from spurting everywhere.

"Is everyone okay?" Dalton turns to look at me. He freaks out when he sees the blood coming from my head wound.

"I am fine, a little blood."

Smoke starts to fill the shuttle.

"Ensign Johnson are you okay? Ensign Johnson, Ben?"

Dalton puts his hands on Ben and turns his body toward him. When he lifts him back, we see the big open gash on his forehead. Dalton put his fingers on his neck, trying to get a pulse. I see the agonized look on his face when he realizes Ben is dead.

More and more smoke is filling the interior of the cabin.

"Willow, let's get out of here. Give me your hand."

I give him my bloody hand, and we exit the shuttlecraft. Dalton has to pry the door open for us to get out.

"What about Ben?"

"Ben is gone, we need to get out. There is nothing we can do to save him."

"I understand he is dead, but I hate leaving him in the shuttle. What if it explodes?"

"Let's get away from the shuttle and secure the area."

Dalton grabs his gun and walks around the shuttlecraft. There is smoke coming out of the engine area, but no fire. It doesn't look like it is going to explode, but it also doesn't look like we will be leaving anytime soon. And poor Ben. Tears start to fall. I try to wipe them off and end up making a big bloody mess across my face. The blood coming out of the gash on my forehead seems to have subsided a bit. I grab a towel out of my backpack and wipe the blood from my face.

Dalton is still securing the perimeter. I take my first look at the planet. It is beautiful. One of the prettiest places I have ever seen. It's lush and green and full of vegetation. It sounds like there are a few animals here as well. I can hear sounds of birds coming from the trees and listen to the rustling of small animals in the brush.

"Okay Willow, let's clean you up, and then we will attempt to establish communication with the ship."

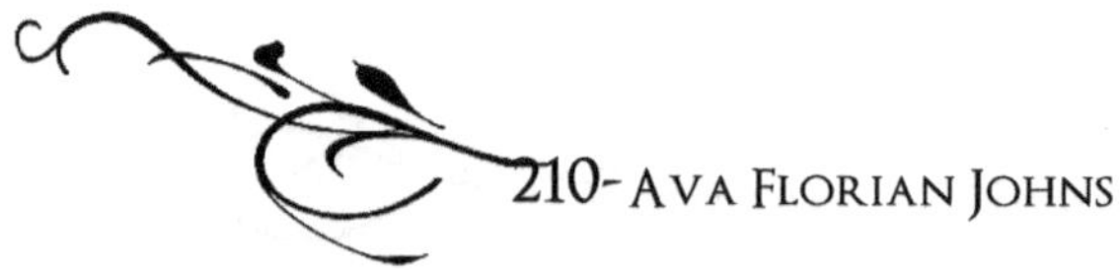

He takes the towel out of my hand and puts some water on it from a bottle he is carrying. He gently wipes the blood from my face and hair. As he cleans my face, he stares into my eyes. I can see and feel the guilt he is feeling for losing a crew member on his away team. He had the same look in his eyes the night I got hurt at the Annex.

"Let's get back to the shuttle and see if we can get the communications to work."

"Aren't you afraid it will blow up?"

"It's only smoke; it will be okay. We will grab what we need from the cabin of the shuttlecraft now. Then we can get the rest of the supplies out of the back after we try to communicate with the ship."

"Okay," I say, climbing into the shuttlecraft by Ben's body. I will never get used to seeing people die. I would make a terrible soldier. I am not ready for this part of an away mission, I just never thought something like this would happen to us.

"We will grab the communication devices and the map. We need to figure out where we are. Get everything you can carry out of this main area."

"Yes, Commander," I say on autopilot. I don't know how he can be so calm. I feel horrible about the death of a friend and uncertain about our present safety. We have no idea if anyone else is on this planet. If there are other people, what are they like?

I am amazed by Dalton's strength in this situation. I know it isn't easy for him, but he is doing it, trying to get us out of here.

"We need to set up a camp, a home base. What do you think about the spot right under the tree over there?"

"Looks good. I will carry everything over there."

I get everything under the tree. It is a perfect spot. The sun is shining, the birds singing, the flowers blooming, I would be enjoying myself if I hadn't lost a friend. I can't believe Ben is gone.

CHAPTER
THIRTY-FOUR
DALTON

I shouldn't have let Ensign Johnson pilot the ship. I know if I would have been flying, he would still be alive, and Willow wouldn't be hurt again—on my watch. I should have listened to my gut. I knew I shouldn't have brought Willow on this mission, but I let Williams and the Captain talk me into it. I need to trust my gut.

Okay, stop feeling sorry for yourself Dalton, and work the problem. I need to focus and get us out of this mess. We don't know where we are. I have no idea if we are on the planet Aconite we set out for, and I need to stop wallowing in self-pity and start putting together a plan.

First, I need to establish communications with the ship.

Second, I need to run a broader perimeter sweep to ensure our safety.

Third, I need to find out if there is humanoid life on this planet.

All right, good plan. Now is the time to focus. My insides are so jumbled, and I can't image what Willow is thinking. Well, I actually can, I can still feel things when she is around me. I can sense what she is feeling, and right now it is fear and sadness.

I sit down with the communication device.

"Starship Armargosa, this is shuttlecraft one, please respond. Starship Armargosa, this is shuttlecraft one, please answer." I repeat it twice, then wait for a response.

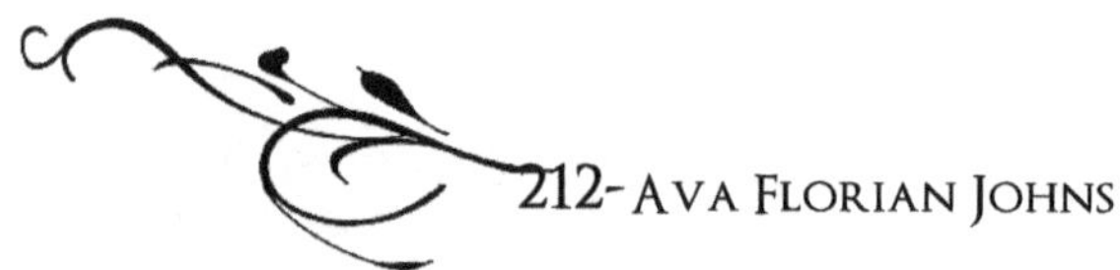

Nothing. Okay, one more time.

"Starship Armargosa, this is shuttlecraft one, please respond. Starship Armargosa, this is shuttlecraft one, please reply. We have crash landed on a planet in the Kerberos System. Not sure which one at present. One member of the team is down, and one member is injured. Please respond."

Shit, still nothing. I am about to throw the communication device on the ground but remember it is our only way off this rock.

Okay, on to part number two of my plan. I am going to secure a larger area of this planet, and see what is out there. I am not leaving Willow here by herself, and I am going to start listening to my gut.

"Come on Willow, let's go."

"Go where?"

"We are going to walk around and secure the perimeter, then set up camp."

"No luck with the communications?"

"No, no luck. I can't reach the Starship with all this interference."

"So they have no idea what happened to us, Commander?"

"They may, but I am not sure."

We walk in silence for a few minutes. Willow's courage in the face of danger is miraculous. It is more than I ever could have hoped. When I first met her, I thought she was a helpless little waif, but she is so much more than that. She is braver and stronger than most men I know.

"Do you hear something, Commander?"

"Yes, what do you think it is?"

Just then a bunny like-creature hopped out from under the brush.

"Oh, it's a bunny."

Willow reaches down for it. "Stop, Willow. You don't know what they are going to be like, remember the zombie monsters?"

She backs away from the bunny.

"I don't think this bunny is going to turn into a zombie monster, Commander."

"No, but I didn't think the Artonians would turn into zombie monsters either. Let's be careful, okay."

"Okay, Commander." She says in a mocking tone.

"And why do you end every sentence with Commander? We are alone Willow; you can call me Dalton."

"I figure you want me to be professional to get through this."

"I suppose you are right, but you can call me Dalton."

"Okay, sir."

I shake my head and chuckle. She is giving me the cold shoulder for ignoring her for the last three days and for not picking her for this away mission. Boy, she can hold a grudge.

"The perimeter looks secure. Let's go back to the shuttle, unload, and set up camp. Now we have seen a little bit more of the planet, do you think we picked a good spot?"

"Yes, but we will need to find drinkable water."

"Yes, I was thinking the same thing. Let's set up a camp and grab a scanner. We can explore the planet and find suitable drinking water. We should also calculate the time of the sunset. I don't want to be out here at night when we don't know what to expect."

"Don't you think they will find us before then?"

"I'm not sure. I will try to communicate with the ship when we are back at the site. We need to prepare for nightfall."

We get back to the camp and unload the supplies. We set up the temporary housing, and it is a little better than a tent. It has four plastic walls and two large slabs of plastic which come out of the walls that we can use as a bed. It also has an air mattress and folding chairs. All the comforts of home. As soon as we finish unloading, I walk over to the communications device and try again to reach the ship.

"Starship Armargosa, this is shuttlecraft one, please respond. I am Commander Dalton Alexander from the shuttlecraft one. Starship Armargosa, this is shuttlecraft one, please reply. We have crashed on a planet in the Kerberos System. Please send assistance."

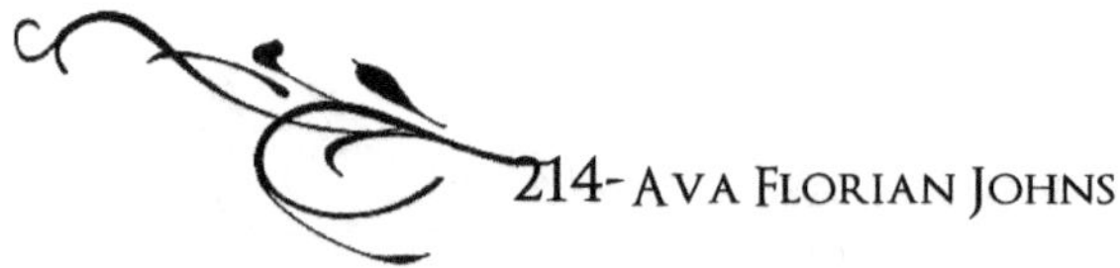

I wait for a couple of minutes and try again.

"Starship Armargosa, this is shuttlecraft one, please respond. Starship Armargosa, this is shuttlecraft one, please reply."

"Can you put it on an automatic message, which will keep trying to communicate with the ship?"

"Yes, it will take some programming, but I can do it. I will try one more time; then we can finish setting up camp. I would like to get the generator and the food dispenser set up, then we can head out and look for water."

"Starship Armargosa, this is shuttlecraft one, please respond. I am Commander Alexander. Please reply. Starship Armargosa, this is shuttlecraft one."

Still nothing.

Willow looks dejected that they don't answer. I am not sure how to comfort her when I don't feel reassured myself. We are in a scary situation, one member of the crew is dead, we are on an unknown planet in an unfamiliar system, and we have no idea if we are alone in the world or if there are others. If there are others, we don't know if they will welcome us, or try to eat us. And these are just some of our challenges.

We work together in silence. I didn't wish this for Willow, but I am glad it is her stuck here with me. She is a hard worker, and she doesn't complain. She listens to orders, well, for the most part, and she doesn't fill the silence with unnecessary chit-chat.

We finish setting up the camp. Willow is deep in thought, and I know she is thinking about Ben.

"What are we going to do with Ben's body? We can't leave him in the shuttlecraft. It's disrespectful." Willow says with tears running down her face.

"I already moved his body out of the pilot's seat. I put him in the back in a container used for situations like this. If we are rescued quickly, we will have a service for him on the ship. If not, we can bury him here and have a private service for him here."

I need to take her mind off Ben.

"Willow Let's go find some water."

I grab the empty containers to put water in when we find some. I need to be doing something to take my mind off losing Ben.

I suck at trying to give people comfort. I wish I were better at it for Willow's sake, but I am not. I never know what to say to make people feel better about a situation. That is why I am Commander and not the Captain of a ship.

I use the scanning device to find water, with no luck. None of our electronic equipment is going to work on this planet without a lot of modification.

"So this isn't going to work. Do you have any methods for finding water that doesn't require electronics?"

"We could use the old limb trick. My grandmother taught me when I was young."

Willow grabs a fallen limb from a tree. It is forked and has two smaller branches sticking out of the bigger one. Willow holds the bigger limb and points the other two at the ground. She explains the two smaller limbs will shake when we are close to water.

"If this doesn't work I can create a spiel out of something on the ship. We can insert it into a tree trunk and get water that way. I am hoping this limb trick will work. It should lead us to water."

Sure enough, the limb starts shaking. "Great job Willow, you found water, with a tree branch."

"It worked!"

I am stunned, She hugs me, and her body feels so amazing pressed up against mine, I realize at that moment how close I was to losing her today in the crash. I hold her for a second longer, enjoying the closeness.

She bounces up ahead of me finding a stream of water which opens up to a big lake.

"Wow, this is beautiful. Look at the waterfall and all the marvelous flowers," Willow says spinning around in a circle. She is right, it is incredible. I have definitely never seen a place like this. My world didn't look anything like this, Casson is all gray and black.

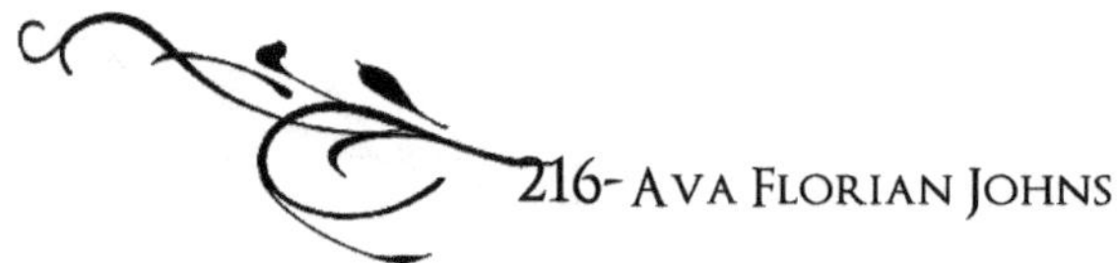

There is no vegetation to speak of, only row after row of barracks and military training facilities.

"We need to test the water to make sure it is potable. I have a kit along, here, fill this up."

She walks to the water's edge and fills up the container. She hands it back to me, and I add a chemical and shake the vial.

"Aren't you all sciency, Dalton?"

She smiles. It is the first time I've seen her smile since we have been on this planet.

"Not really, I guess you should be doing this; you're the science guru."

"No, its okay, it's good for you to venture out of your comfort zone."

"Thanks, I think. The water is fine."

I hold up the vial for her to inspect. The water is drinkable. Well, that is one good thing that happened today. There are other things we could do to make the water drinkable, but this makes it so much easier. If you were going to be trapped on a deserted planet, this one seems to be the one to be on. We have water, we have food, and besides that, the scenery is breathtaking.

We gather water in the jugs we brought and head back to the campsite.

"We need to determine what time nightfall will be. Can you do that while I attempt to contact the ship again?"

"Yes, no problem."

I walk over to the shuttle and grab the communication device again. I figure I will try to contact the ship one more time tonight, then work boosting the signal strength. I also want to put the message in an automatic loop and see if someone is out there. Maybe someone will get our message and send help. I need to figure out the best way to tell them where we are.

"Starship Armargosa, this is shuttlecraft one, please respond. Starship Armargosa, this is shuttlecraft one, please answer." I repeat it twice, then wait for a response.

I guess I can try to describe the planet and what I see in the sky. Maybe it will help someone locate us.

"Starship Armargosa, this is shuttlecraft one, please respond. Starship Armargosa, this is shuttlecraft one, please reply. I am Commander Dalton Alexander. My crew and I crashed on an unknown planet in the Kerberos System. The planet has three suns orbiting the Northern Polar Region. The sky is a purple hue. The planet is rich in vegetation. Two of us survived the crash. Please send assistance as soon as possible."

I copy the message and loop it. I set it up with an automatic feed, and have a feeling I will need to strengthen the bandwidth to get through the magnetic interference of the planet.

Now my primary goal is to make sure we are secure for tonight. Tomorrow we can come up with a game plan if we don't get rescued. First, I need to see if Willow can calculate the sunset.

"Willow, what time do you think sundown will be?"

"According to my calculations, sunrise will be at 2100 hours, give or take a little. It's harder to calculate with three suns, but I think I am pretty close."

"So we have a few more hours of sunlight. We were already supposed to have rendezvoused with the ship, so by this point, they know something happened to us. They would have started searching already. They won't be able to scan for us because our equipment doesn't work with this magnetic interference. They will have to explore planet by planet. There are at least a hundred planets in this system, so it could take a while for them to find us."

"What should we do?"

"I think we should explore the planet a little bit more. Find things we can use, like wood for a fire. We have no idea how cold it will get tonight. We can also look for food. We have some rations, but those will run out. Are you ready to explore our surroundings?"

"Yes, let me put my stuff away in my backpack."

We walk side by side for quite a while through the trees, and Willow finds some edible mushrooms on the forest floor. Again, I

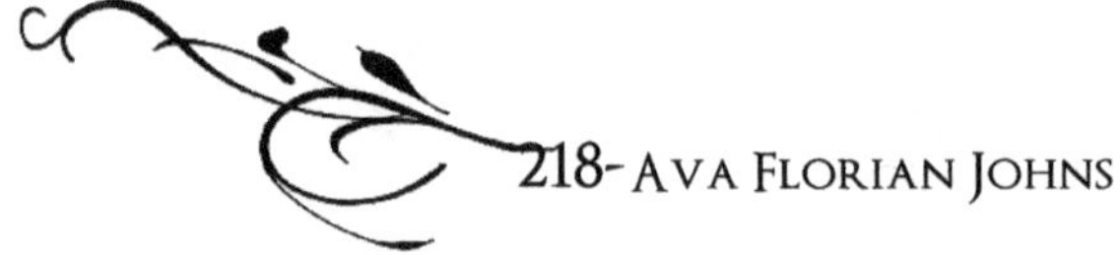

am thinking how great it is to be with her. She has excellent survival skills. She knows so much about plant life and can grow her own if we run out. I am glad we thought to bring seed and small plants for her to start a garden.

"Dalton, will you tell me one thing about yourself?"

"Where did that question come from?"

"It's just that we may not get out of here right away and I realize I don't know that much about you. You know a ton of stuff about me, but you never talk about yourself. Will you tell me?"

"You mean to tell me you didn't look up my profile when we were at the Annex?"

"Well, I might have, but it doesn't say anything about you. I want to know something no one knows."

"Okay, here is something no one knows. My mother was from Earth, and every year I would spend time with her and my grandfather on his farm."

"What is your favorite memory of your grandfather?"

"He had an apple orchard with apple trees as far as the eye could see. I loved walking down the rows and rows of trees. I would sit on his shoulders and pick the apples. I thought I was helping him harvest the apples. In reality, I think I ate more than I harvested."

"That's a great memory, Dalton."

"Yes, that was when my dad would still let me travel to Earth. After a while, I had to stay on Casson at the military training camps."

"Did you ever go back and see your grandfather when you were older?"

"No, I never got a chance to. I am not sure if he is still alive, but I would guess he is dead."

"We should look him up when we get back to the ship. What is his name?

"Edward Clinton. He was a great man and so different from my dad."

"Where is your dad? Do you have contact with him?"

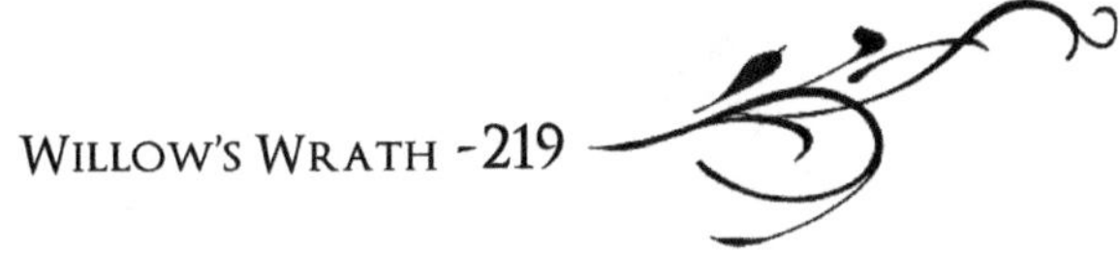

"Not sure. We haven't had contact since I left to fight for the junior boot camp. I'm certain he heard I washed out, and I am guessing he quit following my career."

"What about you? Do you have any family left?"

"I had a grandmother, but she died a couple of years ago."

"How did you find out?"

"Dr. Carver told me she is gone."

I could tell something suddenly dawned on Willow.

"What?"

"I wonder if my grandmother is still alive. I always accepted what Dr. Carver told me as the truth. She could have been lying, she lied about everything else."

"We will have to check when we get back to the ship."

"Good idea."

We walk for a while longer without saying anything.

"This is a beautiful planet. I wonder why no one lives on it. Do you think something could be wrong with it?"

"You could be right, or it could be uninhabited because it's hard to get to. Our shuttle got torn apart trying to land here. There are also many other planets. This one may be looked over. I guess this world is pretty small in comparison to others."

"It is breathtaking. I can't imagine anyone not wanting to live here. If it were easier to get to I would recommend it for colonization."

"I agree."

We walk around for about another hour and get back to the campsite around 1900 hours, two hours before sunset. I am so focused on a plan I didn't think about the fact Willow and I would be sharing quarters tonight, close quarters at that. Well, this should be fun.

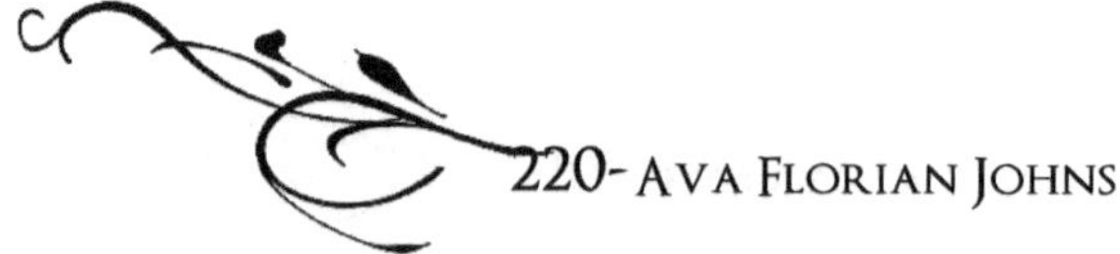

CHAPTER
THIRTY-FIVE
WILLOW

I am still so sad that Ben died. In such a short time he became one of my closest friends on the ship. He didn't deserve to die so young in life. I feel sorry for his girlfriend because they were planning on getting married when he got back. I decide since we have a couple of hours of sunlight left I am going to write Ben's girlfriend a letter. I have a paper journal in my backpack and a pen. As none of our electrical stuff will work here, I have to resort to the old-fashioned way.

Dalton goes into the shelter. It dawned on me as we were walking we would be sharing a room tonight. Maybe lots of nights. I have never slept in the same room with a man before. I hope I don't snore, or talk in my sleep. I know I have nightmares and I am sure to have one tonight, as this has been a nightmare-inducing day.

What will happen if they don't find us right away? What will happen with Dalton and me? I know he is attracted to me, but does he want to spend the rest of his life with me? He may not have a choice.

"What are you doing?"

"Writing Ben's girlfriend a letter."

"I didn't know he had a girlfriend."

"Yes, they were planning on getting married as soon as he returned from this mission in three years."

"How do you know so much about him?"

"He comes to the arboretum. He is or was a plant aficionado. He taught me things about some of the flowers in the arboretum. He was quite smart, and he liked science. He originally wanted to be part of the Science Department, but he was assigned to the bridge personnel instead."

"I didn't know that. I guess I don't know many personal things about the newer members of the crew."

"Have you worked with the commanding officers long?"

"Yes, I have known most of them for at least five years. I have known the Captain the longest."

I smile.

"What are you smiling about?"

"This is the most you have ever said to me. You have said more today than you have in all the other days combined."

"Is that so?"

"Yes, it is. I like it. I feel like I am learning something about you."

"I think I'm going to start a fire. All this sharing about me is making me uncomfortable. Be careful what you wish for Willow, you may learn things about me you don't like."

CHAPTER THIRTY-SIX
DALTON

I have always been uncomfortable sharing information about my life, but especially with Willow. I still think she is too good for me.

I think the more she finds out about me, the more she won't like me. Maybe it is a good thing. Perhaps if she weren't attracted to me, then I wouldn't be as attracted to her. Who am I kidding? I don't think anything would deter me from being attracted to her.

I grab some logs and head back to the campsite and start building a fire. Willow comes over to help.

"You don't have to help."

"That's okay; I want to. I want to keep busy."

I finish building a fire, and then she takes two chairs and sets them next to the fire. She also gets two glasses and fills them with water. She hands me one as she sits down.

"Thank you, Willow. Did you ever go camping with your parents, or were you too young?"

"I think we had fires similar to this one on the farm. We used to sing songs and roast marshmallows. I don't believe we technically camped, but we had bonfires on our land."

I can tell that she is thinking real hard about something. She pauses for a moment then asks.

"What now Dalton?"

"What do you mean?"

I'm not sure if she means about life in general or tonight. I don't know how I will control myself with her being in such close proximity. I don't have great control when we are on a ship with tons of people. How am I going to keep my hands off her when I know we are all alone? But, after all, no one from the ship would ever find out.

"I mean, what if they don't find us? What are we going to do?"

"You can't ever think that way. Captain Holloway will do everything in his power to find us. He would never leave a man or woman behind."

♦♦♦♦♦

She doesn't say anything for another ten minutes. I can tell she is thinking about something. I can almost hear her thoughts again. Abruptly, she says, "Dalton are you hungry? I haven't eaten for a while."

"Yes, I guess I am. I haven't thought about eating today."

"I will grab something from the rations, and I will figure out a plan for the food. I can start a garden and put together a plan for rationing out the balance of our shuttlecraft food. We also can use the backup generator, and the food dispenser, but we should probably save the generator for emergencies."

"Let's eat now and talk about the logistics tomorrow."

We eat our rations by the fire. They taste great, so I know I am hungry. Usually, I can't stand to eat the powdered crap, but everything tastes better outdoors by a fire. I get the communications device from the shuttlecraft and put out the fire.

I turn and look at Willow, and see that she is sound asleep in the chair.

"Willow, are you ready for bed?"

"Yes, sorry I fell asleep on you. I didn't realize how tired I was."

We walk into the unit together. It is a weird feeling, but oddly it feels right.

She flops on her cot. I had already blown up the air mattress and got her a pillow and blanket from the shuttlecraft.

"Thank you, Dalton. Goodnight."

"You are welcome, Willow. Goodnight."

She is asleep before I get my last words out.

I stay up for a while and watch her sleep. Willow is so beautiful, ethereal is the word that comes to mind when I think of her. She doesn't quite seem to fit into this world.

I turn the light off and crawl into bed. I make sure the door is locked so no one can come in. Well, it looks like bedtime with Willow isn't as awkward as I thought it would be.

WILLOW

I am running through the tall yellow sunflowers. The morning sun shines through the flowers in the fields, and it warms my face. Running back toward the farmhouse, I smell smoke and feel the dread wash over me. Hearing the piercing screams of my parents ringing in the air, I know something is horribly wrong. I know it, but my feet will not move. I am frozen in place in the midst of the sunflowers, unable to move, unable to help my parents as flames engulf our farmhouse. I see the military drones fly over me in the smoky sky. I drop to the ground, and bury myself deep in the soil and leaves to camouflage my body. "They" have found them. I never did figure out who "they" were, but I heard my parents talking about them several times. I stay hidden for what seems likes hours, and then I slowly walk toward the farmhouse. By this point, our lovely house is a smoldering pile of ashes. I scream out for my mom and dad. Tears are rushing down my face when Ben comes running up to me and scoops me into his arms.

"It's okay Willow. Shhhh, it's okay."

Only it isn't Ben's arms scooping me up; it's Dalton. And it isn't a dream.

He is sitting on my cot, cradling me in his arms, whispering soft words of reassurance in my hair. "It's okay Willow; I promise it will be all right."

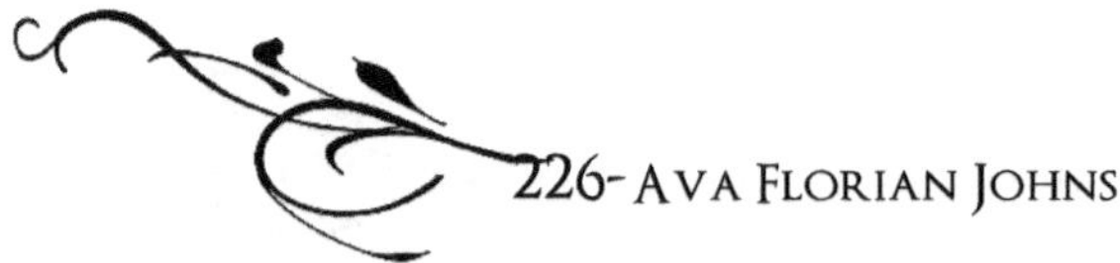

My face is wet with tears. Dalton gently wipes my tears away with his fingers. He tenderly kisses me on the forehead, then my cheek, and pretty soon my lips. The softest of touches, until I turn toward him, wrapping my arms around his neck and my legs around his waist. He doesn't have a shirt on, and the feel of his flesh is overwhelming. Then the soft kisses turn into something else. They are eager and passionate. I know he will put the brakes on, so I have to enjoy him while I have the chance. I push my body into his as close as I can get. I run my hands through his hair pulling him as close to me as I can get him.

"Willow."

"I know, slow-down."

"No, I hear a noise outside. I should go check it out."

"Why don't you stay in here?"

"What if there are people here? I should go see."

He grabs his jacket and his gun and walks out the door.

"Lock the door behind me, open it only for me."

"Okay. I will. Be careful Dalton."

"Will do."

I am scared for him. We have no idea what this planet is like, and we don't know if there are people on it or carnivorous animals.

He is gone for about ten minutes and comes back out of breath.

"What happened?"

"I ran around the entire perimeter, and there is nothing, not even a bunny."

"Maybe you heard things, like the wind or the rustling of the trees."

Maybe he is scared of what is happening between us and wanted a reason to stop it. That's what I think happened.

"That's not it."

"What's not it?"

"I didn't make-up hearing something outside, and I am not scared of what is happening between us."

"Dalton, I didn't say that out loud."

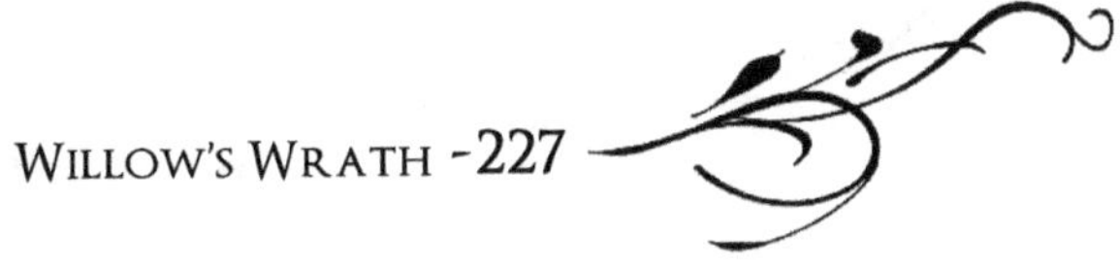

"I know you didn't. I have been able to read your thoughts since the Annex. Just vague images. At first, I thought I imagined it, but right now I heard your thoughts as clear as a bell."

"Are you telepathic?"

"Not that I know of."

"You may be. Elder John said he was sending you messages telepathically. And you must have received them because you added more security for my 'planting day.'"

"I have never been telepathic with anyone else."

"I have been able to read your thoughts too, but they have not been words. Just feelings."

"We should get some sleep. It's going to be a long day tomorrow."

"Okay. Goodnight Dalton."

"Goodnight Willow."

CHAPTER
THIRTY-EIGHT
DALTON

I can't be telepathic. I don't have any special powers. I am a soldier. This has been a devastating day with a twist of something wonderful, and her name is Willow. If we don't get saved tomorrow, I don't know what I will do. I do want to slow down with her. She is someone I could get lost in. I have never known another woman like her. All the other women in my life have been temporary. Not meant for the long haul. Willow is not like the others. She deserves happily ever after, and that is not what I can give her.

◆◆◆◆◆

I wake up at 0600 hours. It takes me a minute to realize where I am. I look across the room and see Willow, and she is still sleeping. I throw my shirt and jacket on and venture outside. I make sure I have my gun. I am not sure what I will find in our backyard this morning. I hope everything is where I left it last night. I am mainly worried about the shuttle. I don't know if there is any hope of fixing it, but we can still use the parts for other things to make it a little better here for both of us.

I step outside. The suns are coming up over the horizon. The sky is a mind-blowing hue of blues, pinks, and oranges. I stand in the doorway for a moment taking in the site. I must be getting soft, I have never stopped and stared at a sunrise before.

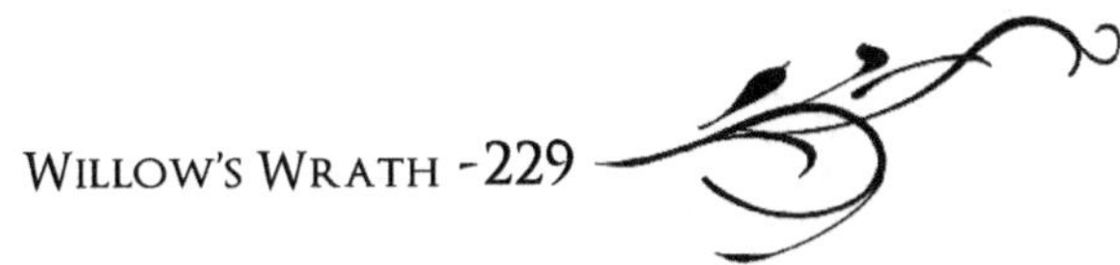

"Maybe you should," Willow says out loud.

"What?"

"Maybe you should stop and stare at sunrise more often."

"You read my mind."

"Yes. Our telepathic connection must be stronger here. Could it be because of our proximity or the atmospheric conditions on this planet?"

"I am not sure Willow, but it is weird."

I agree, she thinks.

♦♦♦♦♦

I inspect the shuttlecraft and our surrounding area. Everything looks good. Today we are going to take an inventory of everything we have and see what is on the planet we can use. We need to start planning for the future, but I also want to keep trying the communications device. I get Willow started on the inventory, and I start working on increasing the bandwidth.

I make a few adjustments to the communications device and then attempt to send a message.

"Starship Armargosa, this is Commander Dalton Alexander, from shuttlecraft one, Starship Armargosa, please respond. Starship Armargosa, this is shuttlecraft one, please answer." I repeat it twice, then wait for a response.

Again, nothing.

I keep trying. I am sure Willow is getting tired of me saying the same thing over and over. I am becoming obsessed with fixing the machine, even though I know there isn't much hope in getting through the atmospheric conditions.

Stop already.

I hear Willow's thoughts.

"I am sorry, Willow."

I had forgotten she is sitting across the yard from me. It has been hours since I started working on the contraption. I feel so

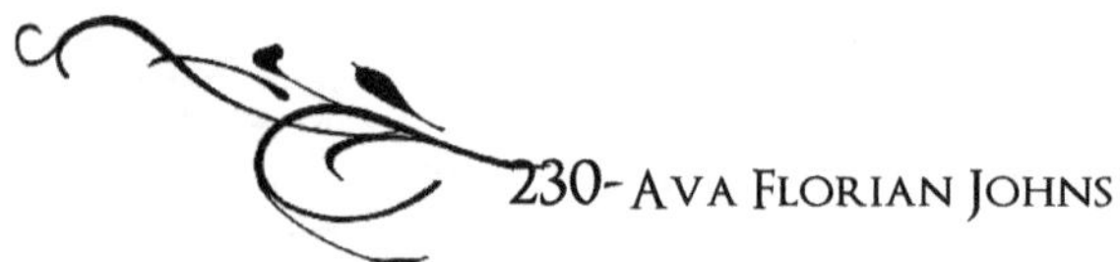

responsible for the death of Ensign Johnson, and I don't want to lose Willow too.

"You are not going to lose me, and it isn't your fault Ben died. Didn't they teach you that in military school? You are bound to lose some people under your command. You are working in a dangerous field, after all."

"Get out of my head, Willow."

"I'm trying, but it's hard to ignore when you are thinking the same thing over and over."

"Fine, I will stop. Where are you with the inventory?"

"It is done, organized, and cataloged."

"I think we should bury Ensign Johnson here on this planet. What do you think?"

"He would have liked it here. He would have loved the flowers."

I get a shovel out of the back of the shuttlecraft and start digging a grave. I have never done this before, and I didn't realize how difficult it would be actually to dig the grave. To think about the person going into the dirt, never to laugh or smile again. Never to marry his girlfriend.

I removed the container with his body from the shuttle and put it in the hole. When I have the container covered, Willow comes over and plants some flowers by the makeshift gravestone I made out of a large stone. She waves her hand over the flowers, and new ones sprout up the length of the grave, covering the upturned soil.

I watch the flowers pop up out of the ground, and suddenly realize she is crying, actually sobbing is a better description.

"He would have loved these flowers. They would remind him of his girlfriend. He always said she reminded him of a daisy because she is always happy."

The sky opens up, and it starts to rain. That's odd because it was completely sunny a minute ago. The rain came from nowhere.

"Let's go inside, okay?"

"You go ahead. Please give me another minute."

"Are you sure?"

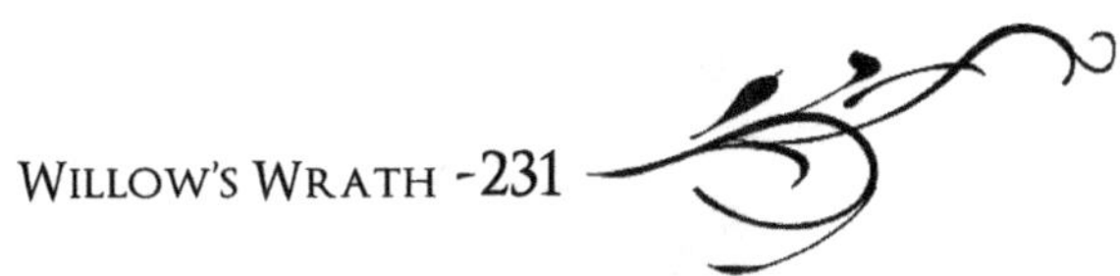

"Yes, please. I promise only one more minute."

I walk to our unit, still watching Willow from a distance. She is still crying, and it is still raining. I wonder if the two are connected.

CHAPTER
THIRTY-NINE
WILLOW

"Ensign Ben Johnson, you were a wonderful and kind person. I wrote a letter to your girlfriend telling her how you befriended me when others would not and how you spoke of her often. I told her you compared her to the daisies in the arboretum and how you talked about getting married when you returned. I hope I have the opportunity to send this message to her, or to meet her someday. I want her to know what a wonderful friend you were to me and how much I will miss you."

I stay by his gravesite sobbing into my already wet hands. The rain continues soaking my clothes to my skin. I sink to the ground crying even harder. Why is so much death around me? I sometimes wonder if people get close to me are they destined to die an early death? This happened to my parents, Dr. Carver, Christopher, Elder John, and now Ben. Will there be others? I can't bear to think of it.

A long while later I feel myself being moved. Dalton picks me up from the top of Ben's grave. I must have fallen asleep not long after Dalton left. It has stopped raining, but my clothes are wet and caked in mud.

"I am sorry I left you out there so long. I hope you don't get sick."

"I needed to be out there. To cry for everyone I have lost. I needed to get it out of my system. You can put me down now."

He has me in his arms again, taking care of me as always.

"I am going to go down to the lake and clean off."

"I will come with you; we don't know what types of animals are out there."

I want him to go with me. I don't want to be alone anymore. I need to feel the connection we have today. I feel when every person in my life who has died, a part of me has died with them.

"I am going to walk in the water with my clothes on, to clean them as well. Do you think it is safe?"

"I think so. Maybe we should create a shower closer to the campsite. I believe we have pieces in the shuttle that would work."

"That sounds great."

I tentatively step into the water, and the mud washes off, making the water murky around me. I prefer to be able to see what is swimming up to me, so I do this quickly.

♦♦♦♦♦

I finish bathing in the lake, change my clothes in the unit, and lay them out to dry. I look at all the plants and seeds I have with me and think about starting a small garden off to the side of our house. It would be close enough for me to work in without Dalton having to come with me.

Dalton has been a pillar of strength. I know he feels responsible for Ben's death and believes he has condemned me to death as well—but I think this happened for a reason. Not the part about Ben dying of course, but everything else. This is a perfect planet for colonization, and if they ever find us, I will tell them.

I work in my garden the rest of the day and get everything I want to plant in the ground. Dalton comes by with apples from the shuttlecraft.

"I almost forgot I brought these with us. I thought it would be a nice break from the awful powdered rations. Here you go."

"Thank you."

"Your garden looks great. I like the location, nice and close to the campsite."

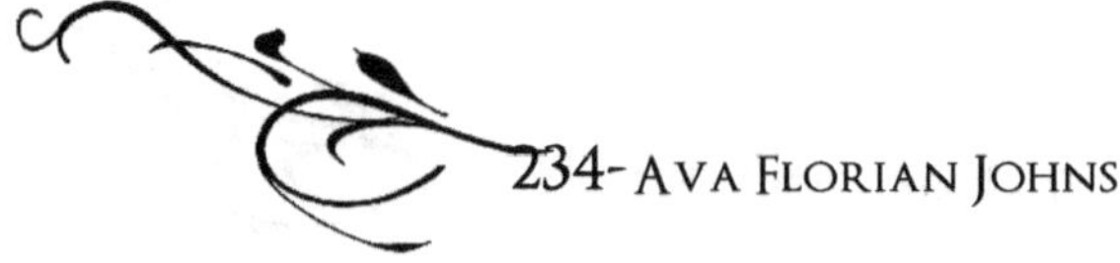

"I knew you would like it so you won't have to come with me all the time."

"Willow, I would go with you anywhere."

When he finishes his apple, he throws the core on the ground off to the side of the garden. Seeing the seeds in the apple core gives me an idea. I hope he is far enough away from me so he won't hear my thoughts.

I want to do something sweet for Dalton. He deserves it after the last few weeks. I carefully take the apple seeds from the core and place them in my hand. I find the perfect place for what I intend to do with the seeds. There is a beautiful clearing not far from the campsite. It is an enormous rectangular piece of land. The only thing on it is some tufts of grass. The soil is perfect here for my seeds.

I make several mounds of dirt in a line on both sides of the rectangle. I use a drop of the sustainability serum we developed for Artona in each pile of dirt. I place one apple seed on each hill and start to communicate with the seeds.

I have never created this many trees at once, but it's certainly worth the try.

I stand in the middle. I wave my hands over the ground in front of me, then up to the sky, telling the seeds what I want them to do. I keep repeating the motion until my arms are tired and there are small trees where the seeds started.

I decide to go into our house before Dalton comes out looking for me. I want to keep it a secret until I finish.

◆◆◆◆◆

I walk into our new home. Dalton is still fiddling with the communication device.

"I thought I would try one more thing on this today, and then I promise I will put it away."

"Why don't we make dinner, then go for a walk. We should come up with a schedule for our days and stick to it, so we don't forget to eat."

"Agreed."

"What should we have for dinner tonight? Apples and protein powder?"

"Let's have apples and the nutrition bars. At least they will have the nourishment we need to survive. Tomorrow let's come up with a menu as well. I think we can do better than the nutrition bars." He says, putting the communication device off to the side.

We walk through the forest to the lake. Dalton still brings his gun everywhere we go. I know that's wise, considering we don't have any idea where we are or what creatures might lurk on this planet. Dalton swears he heard something outside our house last night. All I heard was the beating of my heart.

"Will you tell me what happened to your mother?" I ask, knowing it is a difficult subject for Dalton to talk about. This is the part of him I see is closed off. He is silent for so long it surprises me when he starts talking.

"My mother was an amazing woman. She didn't believe in the Casson way. She taught me to build things with my hands instead of destroying them, and we did everything together when I was a child. My father was away on missions most of the time. When he got back, there was hell to pay. My dad didn't approve of what my mother was teaching me or how she was raising me. They would fight, and he would hit. He found out she was planning to take me to Earth. He was so angry he hit her over and over with his bare hands, never letting up until she was dead. He wouldn't stop no matter how much I begged him to. He beat her to death in front of me to teach me a lesson. I will never forgive myself for not being able to protect her."

Hearing this sad tale breaks my heart and tears start streaming down my face. At that time the rain started coming down again.

"We better get back to the campsite and get out of this rain."

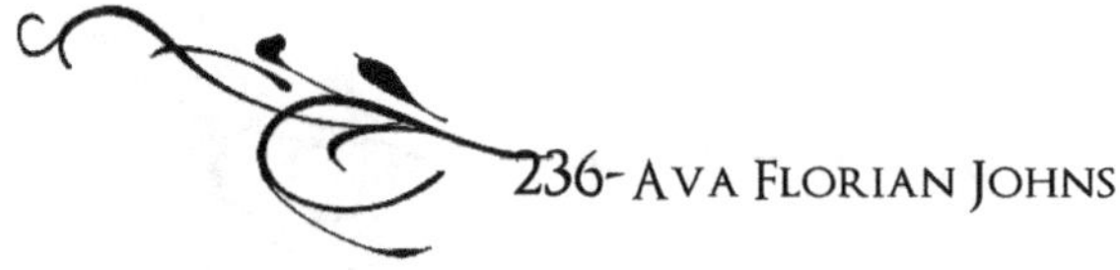

Dalton takes my hand, and we run back to the campsite. By the time we get back to the site, the rain stops.

"I will try to get a fire going, but the wood may be a little wet from the rain," Dalton says, gathering our piled wood.

"I am going to go pick some of the corn I planted today. I will be right back."

I get a few ears of corn and head back to the campsite. I look over at where I plant the apple trees, and they are twice as big as when I left them. Hmmm, that is unusual. I wonder why they continued to grow.

I wonder if my powers are stronger here because of the energy emanating from this planet. It doesn't allow our electrical devices to work, but my mental aptitude seems to be stronger here. It also may be why the connection between myself and Dalton is so strong.

At the campsite, I roast the corn cobs over the open fire. Dalton got the wood to light, and we have flames dancing over the fire pit.

"It will be nice having something warm to eat," Dalton says, eyeing the corn I am cooking.

"Yes, it is only a couple of days, but I miss the meals in the dining hall. They were getting good."

"That's because we had so much fresh produce from you to make the meals better."

"You don't like the protein meals, do you?"

"No, never have."

The first corn cob is roasted, and I hand it to Dalton and start cooking mine.

"This is wonderful. Thank you, Willow."

"You are welcome."

"Can I ask you something?"

"Yes." She says, but she can already tell what he is going to say.

"Have you noticed when you cry it rains?"

"That's probably just a coincidence."

"It has happened twice. Once when we buried Ben and today when I told you the story about my mother."

"I don't know; maybe it's something with the planet. I do feel rather connected to it. It is almost like we are supposed to be here."

"Didn't Dr. Carver tell you your powers could morph and grow into something beyond plants?"

"I guess they could. I will watch things more carefully." I am uncomfortable talking about my powers for some reason.

We finish eating. I clean up and head into the house by myself. I need a couple of minutes alone. I am preparing myself not to have the dream again. I don't want to put Dalton in a position of having to help me. I finally figured it out today, and I know why he tries to keep his distance from me. I remind him of his mother, and he doesn't want to fail me as he failed her. I need to keep my distance from him until I can figure out how to convince him the same thing won't happen. He doesn't have to protect me; I can defend myself.

CHAPTER FORTY

DALTON

I put the chairs away, put the fire out and secure the campsite before heading to the unit. Willow is on her cot, sound asleep. I am glad she is getting some rest. She had a long emotional day today. I know there is some connection with the weather and her powers, but I can't figure out what they are. She doesn't seem to want to discuss it. I think the planet is affecting her more than she is letting on. She doesn't appear to be in any danger, so I will let it drop for now.

◆◆◆◆◆

I wake up again at 0600 hours. I'm glad Willow didn't have any nightmares last night. We both slept through the night. I take a moment to look at her angelic face. When she sleeps, she is so peaceful. I grab my shirt and put it on as I step out the door. Everything with the campsite looks the same as it did last night. I grab a chair and sit down to watch the sunrises. What I wouldn't give for a cup of coffee. Maybe we have some coffee beans in the shuttle, so I'll check on that. If we do, perhaps Willow could plant the beans so that I could have coffee every day.

I meant to bring the communication device outside with me. I know it bugs Willow when I mess with it so much, repeating the same phrase over and over. I have become pretty compulsive trying to fix it.

I can tell she is awake before she comes out of the unit. I can hear her thoughts so clearly now.

"It bothers me that I am trying to start a life here and you seem to want to run away." She doesn't say this out loud; I can hear her thoughts.

"Don't you want to get rescued?" I say out loud

"Yes, but oh, never mind."

I let it drop. I noticed yesterday Willow calls the unit her house or home. She created a garden, and amazingly after only two days she feels connected to this place. I get the impression she has given up on ever being rescued, and I understand now it's easier for her to look forward, while I am still trying to get saved. It is my responsibility to try everything I can to let them know we are alive; it is my duty.

We eat breakfast in relative silence, then we each go off to do our own things. I try to increase the bandwidth even more and attempt a couple more tweaks to the communication device. I try to contact the ship a few more times to no avail.

Willow scampers off to her garden in a white tank dress. She must have thrown that in her pack when she left the ship. It isn't standard Annex or ship wear, but she looks fantastic. I position myself so that I can monitor her work in the garden.

I go into the unit to get another tool for the device. When I come back out, I scan the perimeter. Willow is gone.

"Willow, where are you? Willow, answer me."

No response.

I run to the garden and turn 360 degrees to see if I can find her. I still can't see her. In a panic, I grab my gun and start running toward the grassy clearing where she was yesterday.

I stop short.

Willow is standing in the middle of at least forty colossal apple trees. Her white dress is flowing in the breeze, and her arms extend toward the sky. She looks stunning.

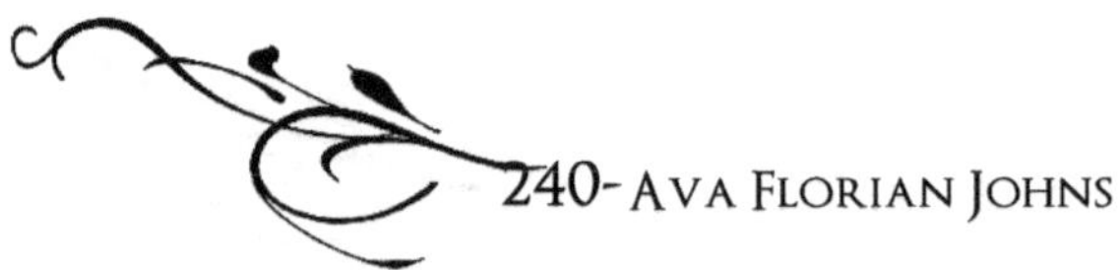

I was upset when I first got there, but my jaw drops when I realize what she did for me. She made an apple orchard.

No one has ever done anything like this for me before. I run to Willow, positioning myself between her and the apple trees. She looks at me as if in a fog. I grab her hands and kiss each one while staring intensely into her eyes. My breathing is coming in short breaths, and my body craves to be near her. I need to take this slow. I want her to know how much I care about her, how much I love her.

She must have heard me think the last part. She pulls her hands away from mine and wraps her arms around my neck and pulls my mouth close to hers. She breathes in, not moving, not touching my lips. Then in an explosion of pure energy, she is kissing me with every ounce of her being. I can hear her thoughts. I have never felt anything like this before. My existence up until this point has been a lonely one. Now I am connected with her, forever.

I know this time I am not going to stop and I am not going to slow down. I am going to show Willow how much I love her, forbidden or not. I am going to have her.

We lower ourselves to the ground. My heart is beating with anticipation. Willow is everything I have ever wanted. With each kiss, I feel like I am whole. She moves to straddle my body and gets extraordinarily close. As close as she can get with our clothes on, she runs her hands under my shirt and tries to pull me even closer.

I can hear the thoughts in her head. She knows there is a part of me still resisting this, still resisting her. Willow takes the next step. She removes her dress and exposes her naked body. She is giving herself to me, and I know what an amazing gift this is.

The next moments are complete ecstasy as we become one.

When I come out of my sensual haze, Willow is curled up on her side and laying on my chest. Our clothes were strewn about on the soft grass.

I am thinking about getting up but hear her thoughts that she doesn't want to.

We remain where we are, in the sun, on the soft grass, with a fresh breeze blowing on our skin.

"I love you Willow."

She looks stunned.

"What?"

"I never thought I would hear you utter those words."

"And?"

"I love you too." She says smiling a wonderfully wicked smile.

CHAPTER
FORTY-ONE
WILLOW

The next two weeks fly by, and we settle into a daily pattern. We get up in the morning, make love, and eat breakfast. I work in my gardens and Dalton creates impressive things. Over this time, we have made a home. Dalton makes furniture out of wooden logs we find in the forest. I tend to my gardens and harvest the grain to make flour for bread. I realize that I have not had a horrible vision since I have been on this planet, I am truly happy here. He has finally given up on the communication device, but I have gotten in the habit of telepathically reaching out to Jax at least once a day. I continue to think if we can connect, I can at least let her know we are okay. Dalton tells me it's a long shot, and I know this, but I try it anyway.

Dalton and I are so comfortable with each other some days we don't even need to speak. We can completely rely on our telepathic communication. It makes it so much easier to connect. We don't even have to be in the same vicinity to hear each other's thoughts.

Dalton loves the orchard I made for him. We spend hours sitting under the apple trees, talking, and kissing. This is the only place I have ever felt "at home," and that is due to one man.

Dalton even rigged up a shower close to our camp. That way we don't have to go down to the lake to get fresh water. The gardens are thriving under my constant supervision, and we are eating like kings.

We even made our temporary housing unit homier by adding a desk where my bed came out of the wall. We both sleep in his bed anyway, so we don't need the second one. Amazingly enough, I have stopped having nightmares.

♦♦♦♦♦

Without warning, we wake to the sounds of our door being broken in. Dalton grabs his gun, which he keeps next to our bed. I scream, and he holds me tight protecting me, and pushing me behind him. Neither of us has any clothes on so the blanket is the only thing covering us. The darkness pours in from outside and bright light flashes in our eyes.

"Commander Alexander, Willow, I am so glad we found you!"

"Captain, how did you find us?"

"I will explain everything. Why don't you get dressed before the rest of the landing party gets here?"

Dalton hands me my clothes. I know he can feel the sadness radiating from my body.

He grabs my hands. "Willow, everything is going to be okay. Please trust me."

CHAPTER
FORTY-TWO
DALTON

I leave our house so Willow can get dressed and gather her thoughts. We have been living in a fantasy world on this planet. I didn't even think about getting rescued anymore. We are both so happy here. There is no way I am going to let that end, whether we are on this planet or the ship, we are together now, and nothing is going to destroy that.

The suns are about to rise, and the Captain is looking at the planet from our backyard as we call it.

"Wow, this place is beautiful. Is it always this perfect?"

"Yes, the weather is mild, the vegetation is bountiful, and the sunrises are amazing."

"I see Willow has been busy."

"Yes, she planted crops, and an apple orchard out of some seeds we had from the apples."

I can tell he wants to address the elephant in the room, the most obvious question.

"Go ahead Captain, ask."

"How long have you two been together?"

"Two weeks."

"So, since you first got here?"

"Yes, is there an issue?"

"No, not with me and there is no rule against it. But I don't want you or Willow to have problems because other crew members think you are showing favoritism."

"Sir, I will not make that an issue."

"Good enough Commander."

"How did you find us?

"Jax."

"What do you mean Jax? Jax found us?"

"Yes, Jax found you. Show me your planet while I tell you the story."

It turns out, ironically, Willow got us rescued. The crew had been looking for us for the last seventeen days, twenty-four hours a day, to no avail. They couldn't get a read on our shuttlecraft or life signs on any of the planets in the area. They never received any of my messages from the communications device.

The Captain tells me Jax has been going crazy looking for Willow. No one could get through to her, so he worked with her and got her to focus her energy. I sense there is more to the story, but I don't want to push it. She had been getting Willow's messages for the last fourteen days, but couldn't figure out where she was. Jax thought she was hallucinating, losing her mind until she realized they were indeed messages from Willow.

The Captain finishes his story. "We hooked Jax up with electrodes and were finally able to trace the location of the telepathic signals. We traced them here."

We walk down to the lake. I think Chris will appreciate the view of the waterfall.

"Wow, this place is fantastic. Too bad it is so hard to get to, or this would be a perfect spot for colonization. We had to work for the last two days to outfit our shuttles to get through the interference in this system."

"It may not be a bad spot if people can't get to us. It is so far away from the PG."

All of a sudden the skies open up, and it starts raining, hard.

"Shoot, Captain, something is wrong with Willow. We have to go."

"Why does the rain mean something is wrong with Willow? I don't understand."

"I will explain as soon as we get to her."

I run in front of the Captain as fast as I can to get to her. She is sitting on the bed in the house, sobbing. I run in and put my arms around her.

"Willow, what's wrong?"

She sniffs, "Nothing."

"Liar."

"Why do you think something is wrong?"

"Well you are crying, and it's pouring outside. That's why. Please tell me what's wrong."

"I am afraid you won't feel the same way about me when we are back on the ship. I fear that we will lose this connection we have. What if we can't communicate telepathically?"

"Willow, I don't love you because we can communicate without speaking. I loved you way before that happened."

"Really, when did you know?"

"The first time I saw your picture on the screen and those beautiful blues eyes. I hadn't even met you yet. I knew you were going to be trouble for me."

She smacks my arm.

The Captain peeks his head through the door he knocked down, "well, it stopped raining, Dalton, are you going to tell me what is going on?"

"Captain, when Willow cries it rains."

"What?"

"I don't know if it is her connection with this planet or if her powers are evolving, but the weather systems take on her moods. If she is happy, it is sunny, if she is sad, it rains."

"How did you figure this out, Willow?"

"When we buried Ben, Ensign Johnson, I was so upset, I caused a major downpour. Dalton, I mean Commander Alexander figured out I could control the weather."

"Can you show me where you buried the ensign? Before we leave here, I would like to exhume the body and have an APA Military memorial service."

We hear the second shuttle land. Kal and his team guard the first shuttle. Williams and the Omega Team came down in the second shuttle.

"The Omega Team is here and will be so happy to see you Willow. I can't tell you how worried they have been. Especially Jax. I will fill you in a bit later about what happened and how she found you but know it was all her. It was Jax."

"Thank you, sir. I am happy to see them too."

"Commander, please fill me in on the rest of your seventeen days. I want to see what you have done and how you lived. I also want written reports from both you and Willow by 1900 hours tomorrow. Willow, you can have a few minutes with your team."

I follow the Captain out as the three ladies on the Omega Team run me over to get to Willow. They race through the door and jump on the bed next to her. All are hugging her and talking at the same time. Jax is crying hysterically.

I laugh as I watch the Omega Team ladies reunite. They are so ecstatic to see Willow.

"They were inconsolable."

"What do you mean Captain?"

"We thought you were dead. Your memorial service is today."

"Oh."

Wow, not much to say after that.

"Must have been hard for you, burying the ensign. The first person you have ever lost on an away mission you led."

I exhale a huge breath, biting the inside of my lip to keep from getting emotional.

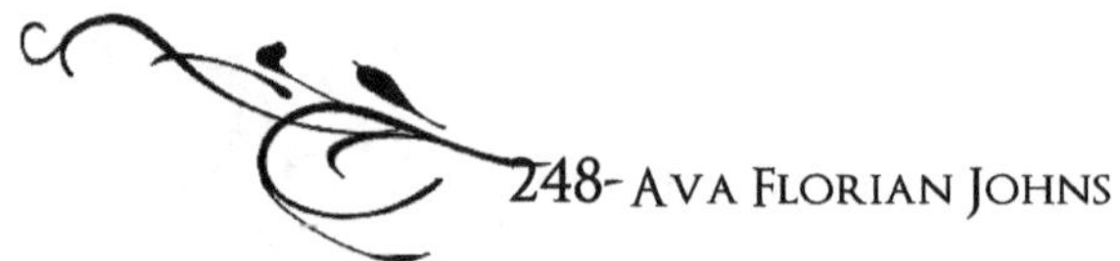

"Yes, especially having to dig his grave. I have never done that before. It is a horrible experience."

"The grave looks good. Why all the daisies? I am guessing they were Willow's doing."

"Yes, daisies reminded Ben of his girlfriend. Willow told me they were planning on getting married after the mission. His girlfriend is waiting for him to return. Willow took it upon herself to write a letter to tell her of his passing."

"I would like to hold a small memorial service here, and one on the ship."

"Thank you, Captain, that will mean a lot to Willow, she and Ben were good friends."

Willow and the others come out of our house. She has gathered everything she can and brings it to the shuttle. She says goodbye to all her plants and picks a few bushels of apples to bring with us. I can feel the sadness radiating from her in droves. The good thing is she isn't crying.

We held the small memorial service for Ben and left our fantastic planet. I have to say I am sad to be leaving it. It is the most beautiful place I ever lived with the most beautiful woman I've ever known.

CHAPTER
FORTY-THREE
WILLOW

I am so sad to be leaving this place; this is my home. Dalton said he loved me here, but will he love me there? On the ship, things are completely different. I will miss this planet with all my heart. I will miss the orchard I planted for Dalton to remind him of his grandfather. I will miss a lot of things.

The Omega Team is happy to have me back. The Captain requested to see me alone before I spoke to anyone else. I guess he wants to debrief about our time on the planet, but I'm not sure why he wants to talk to me. I put all my stuff away in the room that Jax and I share and head back out to see the Captain. He asks to see me in his quarters instead of the bridge.

I get to his door and knock. I hope he doesn't ask me about Dalton. I don't think I could hold it together long enough to explain our relationship. I am still raw with emotion.

"Come in Willow."

"Thank you, sir. You wanted to see me."

"Yes Willow, I want to tell you how we found you, and more importantly what your friend did for you."

"Are you talking about Jax?"

"Yes, of course, your whole team was anxious to find you. But Jax was especially so. She was from the beginning, but after you had started sending the messages telepathically, she became obsessed

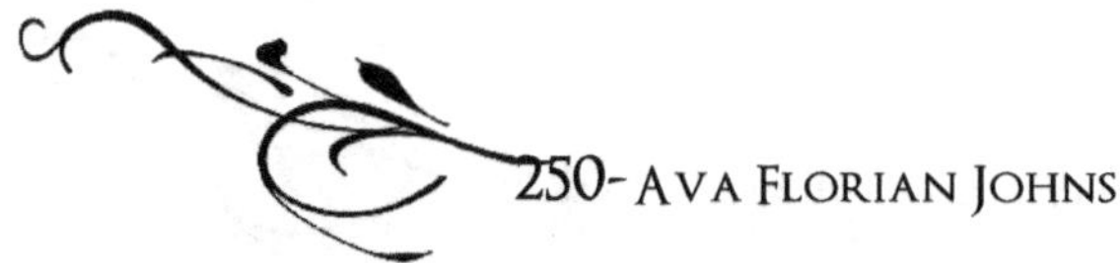

with finding you. She thought she was going crazy and was inconsolable. I want you to know in-case you sense strange behavior from her. I want to make sure she is okay."

Willow senses more from his meaning than merely the concern of the Captain toward a member of the team. She knows he cares for Jax.

"Please tell me the story from the beginning."

The Captain starts the story. "When you didn't meet the ship at the rendezvous time, the crew came to me with a systematic plan of looking for you. Cobalt and Lieutenant Cameron took the lead on this. They used the maps from Elder John and calculated the planets where you could have landed safely. Lieutenant Cameron factored in space debris, including false vacuum fluctuations, and metaphase radiation. We sent away teams down to the five known inhabitable planets in the cluster, unsuccessfully. Every away team who came back without you sent Jax into a downward spiral. She was sure you were still alive. The rest of the crew thought you might have broken up on the impact on one of the planets or moons, but Jax didn't believe them. She poured over maps, studied everything she could study in this area in space. Jax wouldn't believe you were gone. Her nightmares increased, and she was crazed with the thought you were gone. She wasn't sleeping or eating. By the end of two weeks, we could no longer console her or contain her. She was acting crazy. Lieutenant Allium tried everything she could do to help her, but Jax wouldn't listen."

The Captain pauses and takes a drink of water.

"Three days ago, Cobalt, Dharma, and Lieutenant Allium came to me with a plan. They were so worried about Jax. Not knowing how they could help her, they enlisted the help of Chief Medical Officer Laurel Aucuba. She knew Jax's capabilities and background and had a brilliant idea to help her, and help us find you."

"What was the plan Captain?"

"We didn't know if you were reaching out to her telepathically or if she was manifesting this herself. So, in laymen terms, Dr. Aucuba

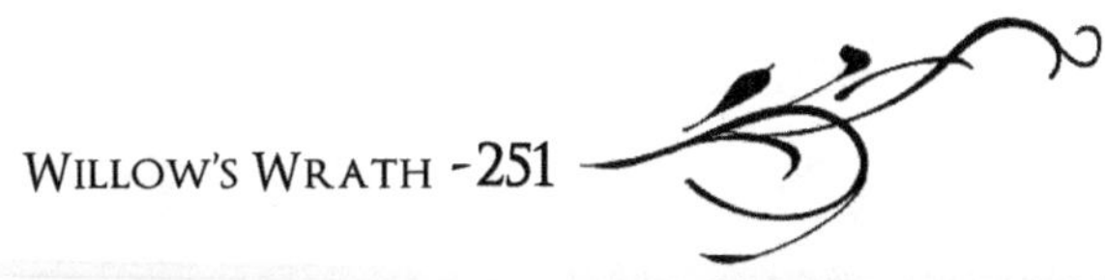

used brain monitors while Jax was sleeping to pinpoint the area of her brain that was receiving the message. Dr. Aucuba is the foremost expert on telepathic dream research. I wish for Jax's sake we would have contacted the doctor sooner."

"Why do you say that Captain? What happened to Jax?"

"Willow, she was fanatical about finding you. We thought she had gone mad. I went to her quarters one night because there were complaints about her throwing stuff around the room. She was acting outrageous, and like I said no one was able to console her."

"But you were able to?"

"Yes, I got her calmed down enough to listen to the doctor's plan to monitor her telepathic dreams. Once she agreed to it, she fell asleep within two minutes. I stayed with her to make sure she stayed asleep as long as possible. We were so worried because she had been acting so irrational. We just hoped the damage to her brain wasn't permanent. I knew that sleep would help at least a little bit."

"Why was she acting so extreme? Was it my fault? Was it my communications?"

"Willow, you could never have known how your telepathic messages would affect her. The doctor surmised it was the combination of your telepathic message and the metaphase radiation emanating from the cluster which caused your message to loop. She was hearing it thousands of times a day. In essence, your message was all she was hearing."

"I am so sorry for what I did to her. I had no idea sending one message a day would impact her as it did. I didn't even want to send it. Commander Alexander kept tinkering with the communications device. So much so he was driving me crazy. I said something to him, and he accused me of not wanting to get rescued. Truthfully, I was happy there. It was the most comfortable I have ever felt anywhere. I wasn't as concerned with finding a way back to the ship as he was. I decided I would prove to him I was as dedicated as he was to getting off the planet. I thought I would try telepathy once a day, just to see if by some fluke Jax would get the message. I never

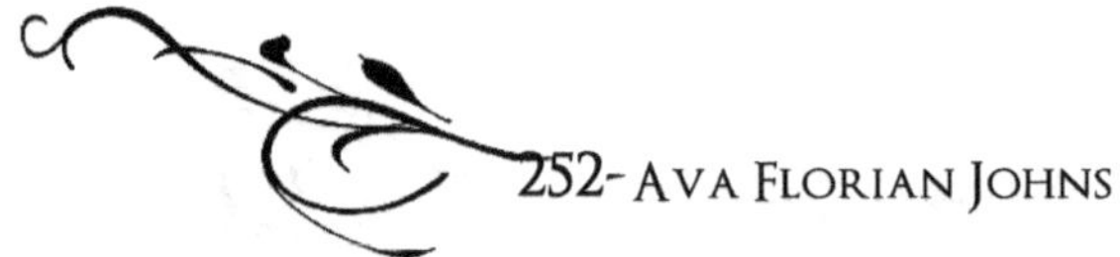

really thought she would. The planet's metaphase radiation or electrical energy had an astonishing effect on my powers. I should have known that something like this could happen. The planet's effect seemed to magnify my abilities exponentially."

"I know you didn't do it intentionally, and Jax knows that too. I knew she would never tell you the story about what happened to her, so I wanted to make sure I did. I wanted you to know what she went through to get you home. I want you and Commander Dalton to write up your reports and submit them to me by 1900 hours tomorrow. Take a day or two and get acclimated to ship life again and you also need to be cleared by medical before reporting back to duty. I want the Science Department to study your increase in power and determine what caused it and if you will still maintain it after we have left this sector."

"Yes sir, thank you, sir."

"We will have a memorial service for Ensign Johnson today at 2100 hours. I am sorry for your loss. Dalton tells me you were friends."

"Yes sir," I say with tears running down my face.

He hands me a tissue.

"I am sorry, these things do happen in space travel. As a Captain, I know I may be sending people to their death on every away mission."

"Do you ever get used to it?"

"No, and if you do it is time to get out."

"I understand."

"Willow, may I ask you one more thing?"

"Yes, Captain."

"Never mind, dismissed."

I know he wants to say something else. I am wondering if something happened between him and Jax. I am not sure about that, but I am convinced I owe Jax a lot for what I put her through the last two weeks. I want to make a grand gesture, but I am not sure what that would be. What do people give someone when they want to express thanks? Flowers? I can do flowers, but it would have to be something more unusual.

♦♦♦♦♦

I leave the arboretum and run into Dalton.

"Hello, Dalton."

"Hello Willow, how are you doing?"

He reaches down and gives me a quick kiss and grabs my hand. It is so good to be with him again. To be intimate, to know he isn't going to pull away once we are back on the ship. It means more to me than anything.

When he is near me, I can hear his thoughts. We had gotten so used to our telepathic connection on the planet, some days we hardly spoke.

"I missed this too," I say as I reach up and give him another kiss. This time it is lascivious. It is thrilling to be with him again, but I am feeling uncensored. I need to reign it in before someone sees us. We start walking toward my room.

"Where are we going, Willow?"

"I am heading back to my room to get Jax. I made a special surprise for her in the arboretum to thank her for all she did to find us. The Captain explained what she went through, and it is more horrible than I ever could have imagined. I didn't realize my telepathic messages mixed with the metaphase radiation would cause such a devastating situation for Jax."

"What happened?"

"I will tell you later. How about we meet at the memorial service tonight. Then we can discuss everything. Also, how much are we putting in our report? The Captain said to include everything. I don't think he wants every little detail, does he?"

"No, I think he has figured that part out. He already questioned me about our relationship."

"What did you tell him?"

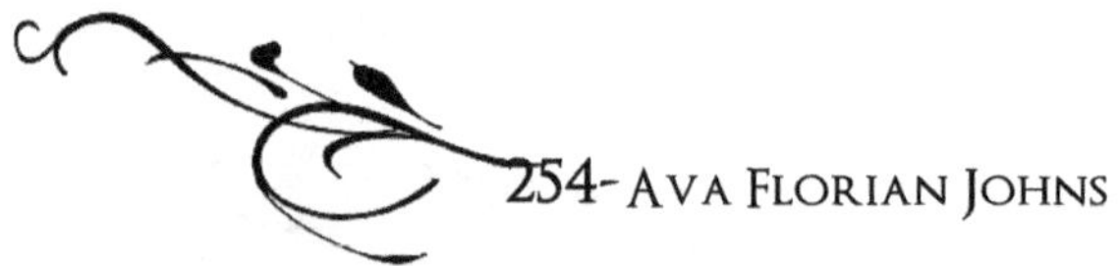

"I told him the truth. I said I wouldn't let our relationship interfere with my duties and I won't show you favoritism over the other members of the crew."

"And he is satisfied with your statement?"

"Yes, he is. Chris has known me a long time. He knows me and knows I mean what I say, and I keep my promises."

"Good. We are here. Do you want to come with us to the arboretum?"

"No, you enjoy your time with Jax. I will see you later tonight."

He gives me a quick kiss on the lips and walks down the hallway. I watch him walk away thinking how much I love him. I know everything will be okay.

I walk into the room. Jax is lying on her bed listening to music on her headphones.

"Hello, Jax," I said telepathically. "I have something for you."

"What?"

"You have to come with me." I don't know why she is sitting in the room. Technically she should have been working in the communications department on her shift. She looks exhausted like she isn't entirely over the trauma I caused her.

"Where are we going?" Jax asks telepathically.

"Arboretum, now come on!" I say out loud

"Okay, give me a second."

I take her hand and make her run with me to the arboretum. I can hear her in my mind complaining the whole time. In a fun way though. I know she isn't serious and I can feel the old Jax coming back to me. When she first saw me all she could do was cry. She hasn't been formulating coherent thoughts for me to read. Her thoughts are chaotic. Captain Holloway explained her condition well. I could feel it when they found us, but now I feel calmness coming from her. I don't sense anxiety or hardship now. It's mostly exhaustion. I wonder if she was on temporary leave.

She answers my question. "They placed me on restricted duty for three days. The only official thing I am allowed to go to is the service tonight for Ensign Johnson."

"Is it okay I pulled you out of the room?"

"I think it's fine as long as I don't get anxious. Are you going to make me anxious Willow?"

"Nope. I have a good surprise. Now get out of my head before you ruin it."

I open the doors to the arboretum. I have created flowers of all sizes and colors, and all together, they spell out "THANK YOU JAX" in beautiful colors.

Out loud I say, "I can't thank you enough for what you did for me, for us. I am so sorry I caused you harm. I had no idea when I sent you the message it would bring you pain. Here is a token of my appreciation. I don't know how I can ever repay you."

I start to cry, and then Jax begins to sob.

"Jax, I apologize, I didn't realize it would make you cry. I am trying to do something nice, to show you how much I appreciate what you did. To say I am sorry for what I did."

"Willow, these are tears of joy. I am so happy I could help find you. Who told you about what happened to me?"

"Captain Holloway called me to his quarters as soon as we got back on the ship. He told me the whole story. He is very concerned about you Jax."

"The Captain is the only reason you are here. I couldn't figure out how to find you. Your messages were replaying over and over in my mind, like a broken record. It was loud and chaotic, like a thousand voices speaking to me at once. I couldn't shut it off, and I ended up going a little crazy. Captain Holloway was able to calm me enough for Dr. Aucuba to help me find you. Oh, Willow, I missed you so much. No one else could understand me. It felt like I would never have the connection we share. I am so glad you are back."

We stay in the arboretum for a while talking and catching up. I can tell Jax has feelings for the Captain. I sense he has feelings for

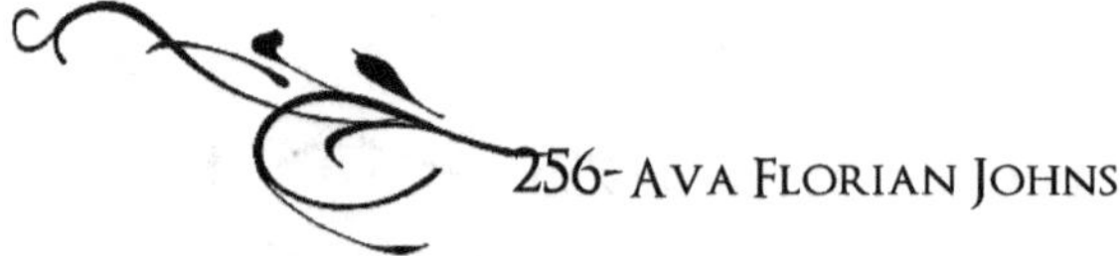

her too, but knowing him, I don't think he will ever act on them. There are married couples on the ship, but I am not sure how well dating on board the vessel would work for the Captain. It's tough enough for the Commander.

♦♦♦♦♦

We are all at Ben's memorial service. I have never been to a military service before, so I am not sure what to expect.

I have the letter with me that I wrote on the planet, and I want to add some more words of comfort for Ben's girlfriend before I send it to her. The body was exhumed from the planet and brought onto the ship. The Commander and Captain decided it would be best if we didn't leave the remains of Ensign Johnson on that world. We didn't leave much of anything there because we thought it best to leave it the way we found it. The only things we left were the orchards and my gardens. The orchards and gardens would have been hard to transport onto the shuttlecraft to bring with us, and they blended in so beautifully with the surroundings, I couldn't think of removing them.

The sound of the bugle calling us to attention breaks into my thoughts, and I look around the room. The entire crew has come in dress uniform. The four of us on the Omega Team are wearing our Omega Team black suits. The body of Ensign Benjamin Johnson is in a space capsule in the center of the shuttle bay with the crew gathered around it. His capsule looks like a giant torpedo. The Captain stands up to say a few words about Ensign Johnson, indicating he made the Alien Planetary Alliance proud and that it was an honor to have him serve aboard the starship Armargosa.

Dalton is standing next to the Captain in his dress uniform. He holds the flag of the Alien Planetary Alliance and drapes it over the top of the space capsule. The whole crew in unison then says a few words in honor of their fallen comrade.

"This flag is presented by a grateful Alliance.

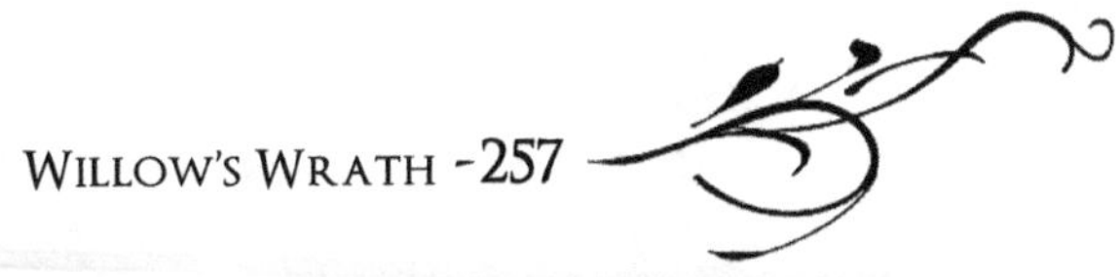

It is an expression of appreciation for the honorable and faithful service you have rendered to the APA.

Godspeed."

The capsule is then loaded into the torpedo tube and shot into space. We watch as Ben's capsule glides through the stars.

"Burial detail dismissed."

There is a gathering in the dining hall immediately following the service. With his head down, Dalton is there with the rest of the crew and the Omega Team. I am glad for this opportunity to find out more about Ben. I want to see if anyone else knows his girlfriend's name. If they don't, I will see if it is in the database or if someone can check his journals for me.

The five of us walk in last.

As Dalton and I walk in the room, the crew stands at attention and salutes our return. It is the grandest entrance I have ever seen. Dalton salutes back, and I stand there with tears in my eyes. The Captain makes a little announcement.

"We welcome the return of our two lost comrades as we mourn the loss of another."

"Here, here."

"Wow. That was touching." I say, wiping the tears from my face.

"The military is not all bad," Dalton whispers. "I know this crew would put their lives on the line for me and I would do the same for them.

"I understand. I have never in my life felt more a part of something, like I do here with this crew. They are amazing."

I start to tear up again.

"No crying allowed. I don't know if it can rain in space, but I don't want to take any chances."

I laugh-snort and swat at him with my hand.

The Omega Team watches our exchange with smiles on their faces. I know they are so relieved to have us back and to have Jax almost back to normal. I also notice the sense of belonging they all have here, not just me. We all sit down at the table with the

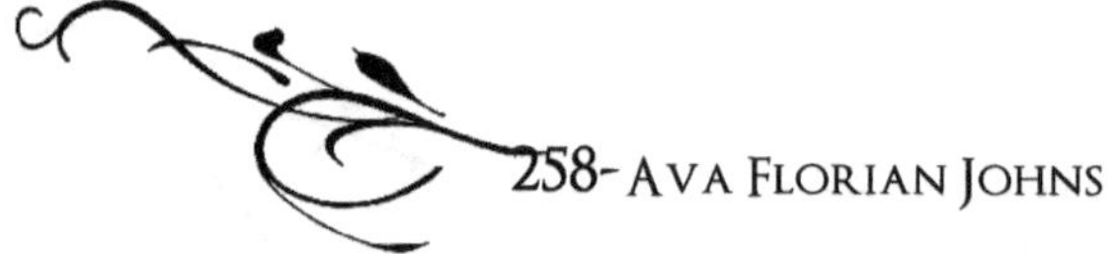

commanding officers. I look around the table. We all finally fit in, and we feel like part of this crew even though we technically are not.

♦♦♦♦♦

Dalton and I excuse ourselves from the table and leave the dining hall. We walk down the hallway, but we are not heading to my room or the arboretum.

"Where are we going, Commander?"

"To my quarters. I want to be alone with you."

"For what?" I asked slyly.

"You'll see."

The second the door closes he is kissing me. I have never been in his room before. It feels so good to be alone with him.

"Why don't you come in and sit down?"

"I have never been in your room before. It is nice—sparse."

"Well, maybe you will have to help me decorate it. I want you to be comfortable here."

"Why is that?"

"Willow, I want you to be a part of my life. I love you. I don't want to lose you because we are back on the ship. I want to ask the Captain if you can move in here."

"I don't know what to say. I am in shock. I thought we would go back to the way it was before. Only seeing you every couple of days, not being seen together. I didn't realize it could be like this."

"This is good?"

"This is great."

"Dalton, I love you too, so much."

We kiss again, and this time it is more passionate. This room's not the beautiful, breathtaking planet we left, but it is home, and I am with the man I love.

♦♦♦♦♦

I leave Dalton's room. I explain to him I need to make sure Jax is okay and I want some time alone to work on my report for the Captain. The Captain asks that we turn it in tomorrow by 1900 hours.

It is getting pretty late. I open the door slowly to make sure if Jax is sleeping I don't wake her. I didn't need to worry. The Omega Team is in my room, sitting on my bed.

"Hey, sexy lady. Where have you been? With your hot bod boyfriend?" Dharma teases, and they all laugh. It is great to hear the laughter again, sharing in the camaraderie. Our planet was like heaven on Earth, but I did miss this.

"Yes, I was."

I jump on the bed and land in between them. They all hug me again. I will never get tired of their love.

"All right before this gets all sentimental and mushy, I am going to go. Luv Ya Willow. Happy you are back," Cobalt says standing up and straightening her Omega Team jumpsuit.

"Me, too," says Dharma. "I figure you want to get some sleep; I guess you didn't get much on the planet."

I throw a pillow at her.

"Out!"

They laugh at me and leave the room. I glance over at Jax. She looks a little sad. I go over and sit on her bed and touch her hands so I can get a better connection.

"How are you?"

"I am getting better. The doctor says my brain activity is almost back to normal."

"You seem sad, are you okay?"

"I feel how happy you and Dalton are, and I wonder if I will ever have anyone who cares as much for me."

"I guarantee you will. I think you already do."

"What do you mean, already do?

"What happened between you and the Captain? He has a very protective vibe when it comes to you."

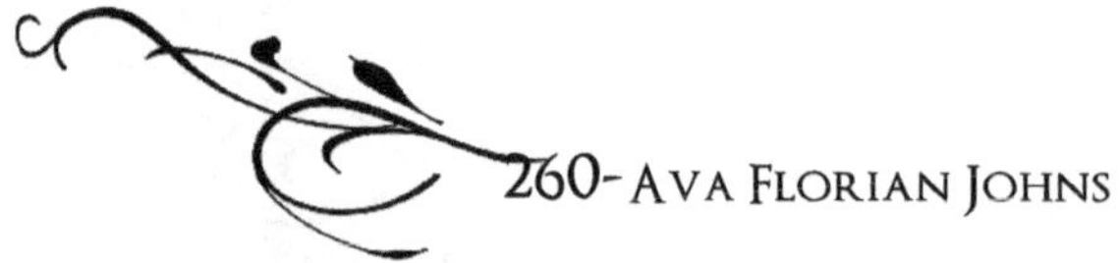

"I don't remember much about the last night before we found you. I was in a rage, smashing things in the room, and then he came in. I don't know how, but he calmed me down enough for the doctor to help me. It was a surreal experience. I woke up, and my head was on his chest, and he was whispering in my ear. He was very reassuring and told me everything would work out fine, and we would find you. He was right."

"I am so glad you are okay. We better get to bed, I will worry about the report in the morning."

♦♦♦♦♦

I am running through the tall yellow sunflowers. The morning sun shines through the flowers in the fields, and it warms my face. Running back toward the farmhouse, I smell smoke and feel the dread wash over me. Hearing the piercing screams of my parents ringing in the air, I know something is horribly wrong. I know it, but my feet will not move. I am frozen in place in the midst of the sunflowers, unable to move, unable to help my parents as flames engulf our farmhouse. I see the military drones fly over me in the smoky sky. I drop to the ground, and bury myself deep in the soil and leaves to camouflage my body. "They" have found them. I never did figure out who "they" were, but heard my parents talking about them several times. I stay hidden for what seems likes hours, and then I slowly walk toward the farmhouse. By this point, our lovely house is a smoldering pile of ashes. I scream out for my mom and dad. Tears are rushing down my face. Dalton is there with his arms extended wide. Holding them out for me, protecting me from the fire. This time I am not a little girl. I am a woman, he picks me up in his arms and takes me away from the farmhouse.

I wake up, not sure if I liked the dream or not. Does Dalton continually have to save me? Did he save me on the planet? What does this dream mean?

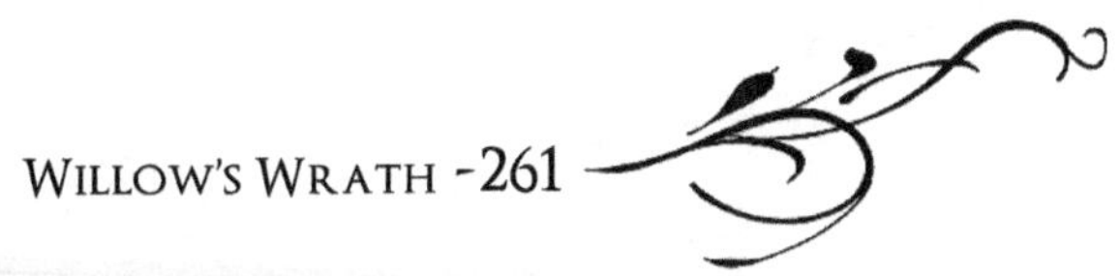

I get out of bed. It is 0500 hours. Too early! I grab my clothes, tablet, and the letter to Ben's girlfriend. We have our daily staff meeting at 0900 hours. I think I can get most of my report done, finish the letter and still have breakfast before the meeting. I head to the dining hall, grab an apple and sit down at a table in the corner.

"Willow, what are you doing up so early?"

"Hello, Dalton," I say a little colder than usual. I am still bothered about the dream. I hate the thought of being the damsel in distress, always being saved by a man.

"What's wrong?"

He grabs my hands.

"Willow?"

I can feel the connection and know he will find out soon enough.

"You had a dream, and now you think I always come to your rescue? Oh please, Willow. Don't you know you saved me? I have never talked about my life with anyone. You helped me see past my horrible childhood and trust again. I trust you Willow as I have never trusted anyone before. Do you think I saved you at the Annex or on Artona? No Willow, you saved yourself. I was just along for the ride."

Wow, I felt so much better. I start to tear up with emotion.

"What did I tell you about crying?"

"These are tears of joy. Thank you, Dalton."

We work together at the table. Dalton looks up Ben's girlfriend's name. Daphne. I finish the letter and get it ready to send. I will need to ask if we have established communication with Earth yet. We finish up and head to the staff meeting.

✦✦✦✦✦

The Captain is the only one in the room.

"Come on in Dalton, Willow; you are a bit early."

The Captain has four large boxes lying on the table in front of him.

"What's in the boxes Captain?"

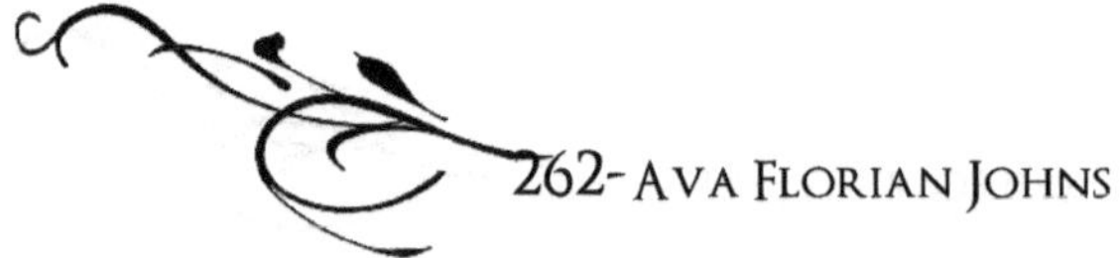

"You will see, Willow."

I reach out to Dalton telepathically, but he doesn't know either.

Everyone else files in the room. Lieutenant Williams walks in and hugs me. "My dear Willow, I am so glad to see you again."

"Thank you, Lieutenant. It is great to see you too."

"All right, now that the hugging is out of the way let's get down to business." The Captain stands.

"First order of business, Omega Team please stand."

We all look at each other, curious. I shrug my shoulders when Jax asks me what is going on.

"Jax, Cobalt, Dharma, and Willow, for exemplary service aboard the Starship Armargosa you are to be promoted to the rank of ensign and officially made members of this crew. You will have all the duties and responsibilities associated with this position. Congratulations Omega Team, I am very proud to welcome you to the crew of the Starship Armargosa!"

The commanding officers stand and salute us. I know I have achieved this on my own and it feels terrific. The Captain hands each of us one of the boxes in front of him.

"Willow, Jax, Dharma, and Cobalt, here are your new uniforms. Wear them with pride. You have earned them."

"Thank you, sir," we all say in unison.

I belong now. I am part of the crew.

CHAPTER
FORTY-FOUR
DALTON

I had no idea Willow is going to be part of the crew. I wonder if the Captain is going to reconsider his statement from the night before. He said he was okay with my relationship with Willow as long as I don't show favoritism toward her.

Well, this may make what I have to ask him after the meeting a little more difficult.

"Second order of business. We need to get Commander Alexander, and Willow caught up on ship business. First, Lieutenant Allium has established communications with an APA-military base about four light years away. It is an outpost in the Calanthe System. The interface strength is spotty at best. We have told them of our situation, and they have communicated our position to APA on Earth. Lieutenant Cameron, do you have an update on the wormhole?"

"Yes, sir. The Engineering Department has researched the maps we received from the Artonians. The closest stable wormhole is only three days' time from here at maximum speed. The wormhole appears every 360 hours, which is fifteen days. We are too far away to see when it appeared last. We will have to go and take a look and wait for the wormhole to appear. This wormhole should dump us out very close to the edge of the APA border. I surmise Elder John wanted us to find it. Our department has researched its validity and

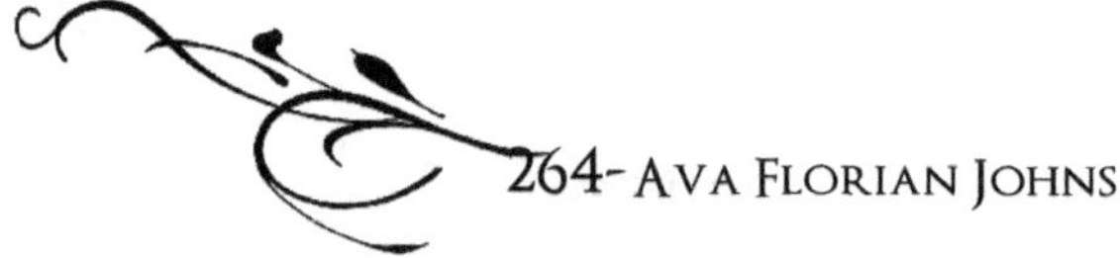

has found it is one of the most stable wormholes we have ever seen. I have given the coordinates of the wormhole to the helmsmen, and we are headed there now."

"Very good, Lieutenant. Thank you. Anything else?"

"No sir."

"Do well, dismissed."

Per usual everyone else goes to the stations. I stay back to speak with the Captain.

"What's on your mind Commander?"

"Willow, sir."

Then I pause, for a very long time.

"What about Willow, Commander, am I going to have to rip it out of you?"

"No, sir. Now she is part of the crew it makes this harder to ask."

"What is harder to ask?"

"Will you marry us?"

He looks stunned. I think he thought I was going to ask if Willow could move in with me. And that was my intention last night. I had a dream we were living on Earth, in a big house, with a bunch of kids running around the yard. And then I knew I couldn't wait. She is the one for me, and that's not going to change. I have been waiting for her to come into my life, I just didn't know it.

The Captain regains his composure.

"Dalton, I would be honored."

"Thank you, Chris."

"When is the big day?"

"I'll let you know as soon as I ask her."

The Captain is still laughing when I shut the door.

♦♦♦♦♦

I have one thing I kept from my childhood. It is a wooden box I made with my mother, and inside I keep her wedding ring. It is the only thing I have of hers. It was her mother's ring, so it meant a lot

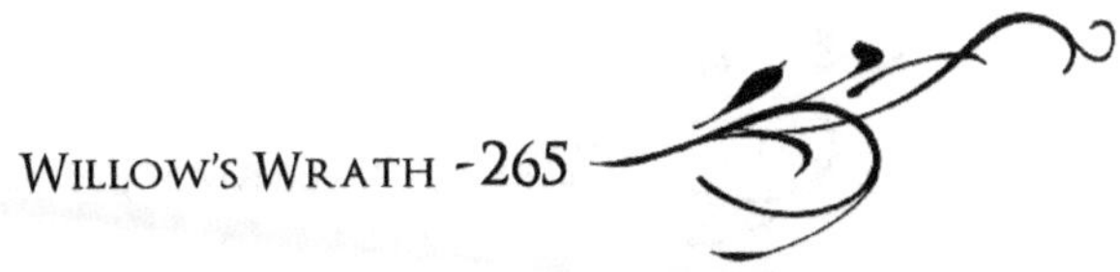

to her, and it has meant a lot to me too. I hope it means as much to Willow.

CHAPTER
FORTY-FIVE
WILLOW

I love my new uniform. I put it on for the first time this morning, and it fits perfectly. I can't stop staring at myself in the mirror. We are to wear the uniform for all ship functions, but we can wear street clothes or our Omega Team jumpsuit during off hours.

♦♦♦♦♦

I decided to research what Dalton and I discussed on the planet. We both could potentially have grandparents living on Earth. I go to the computer lab and bring up the name Edward Clinton, Dalton's grandfather. The screen flashes with information and a photo. He is how I imagine Dalton looking in the future. He is handsome with dark, chiseled features and a light silver dusting in his hair. The screen indicates that he is still alive and farming in Kansas, on Earth.

Now for me. I hesitate with my fingers resting on the keyboard. I am not sure if I want to know if my grandmother is alive or not. I am too scared to know for sure. I key in what I know of her. Her name is Joselin Washburn, and she is from Iowa, USA. Sure enough, the second I hit the enter key, her face comes up on the screen. She looks so much like my mother; there is no doubt about who she is. No surprise, Dr. Carver lied again. I know one thing for sure. Dalton and I need to plan a trip to Earth, in the very near future. I hope we make it through the wormhole, so we get the opportunity to meet our grandparents.

♦♦♦♦♦

I remember that I now have access to all of Dr. Carver's notes. I gained access right before our shuttle crashed, but I never got the opportunity to look at her journal entries. I pull them up on the screen and go to the very first entry, from the year I was born. As I watch them I see a young scientist so full of hope; I wonder what happened to her to make her turn on her best friends. I only get a chance to watch three of the video journals before I need to leave for dinner with Dalton. They don't allude to anything sinister, mainly just talking about the work that she was doing with my parents on the farm. Maybe more information would be in the video from Dr. Carver before she was killed, that Todd and Megan have for me. I just hope I get the chance to see it soon.

♦♦♦♦♦

I finish my report and turn it in early, so I have nothing to do for the whole day. The Captain is giving us a couple of days to acclimate again to the ship. We have to pass a physical and a bunch of medical tests. Doctor Aucuba said everything looks fine, but she wants to be sure, so we are not yet cleared for duty.

Because we don't have anything to do and both of us have already turned in our reports, we decide to have a nice dinner in his quarters and relax. I am very excited that we can have some time alone.

I take my uniform off and put my white tank dress on instead. It's the same one I wore the first time Dalton and I were together on our planet. I walk to his quarters and knock on his door. I can hear music coming from his room, but he doesn't answer. I tap again. "Come in Willow."

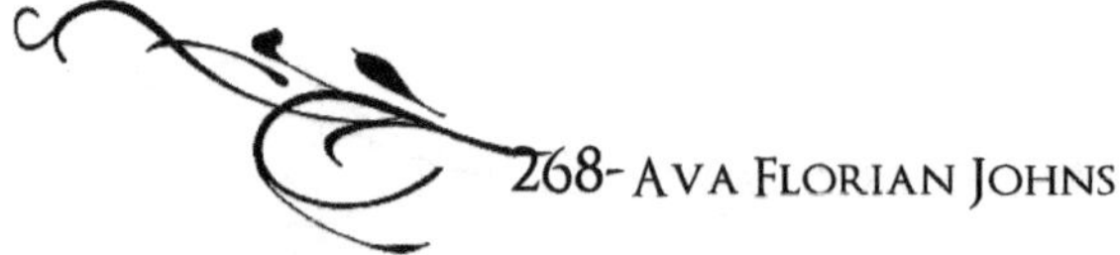

The lights are dimmed, the music is softly playing, and there are beautiful red roses on the table.

"Come and sit down, please."

"Wow, this place looks great. Thank you, Dalton, for making it so special. I have been looking forward to seeing you all day."

"Me, too."

He comes over and kisses me on the forehead. Not exactly what I am hoping for, but it is still nice. We have a great sense of familiarity. I love that we are so comfortable with each other, and he always makes my heart flutter. He is buzzing around the room, looking busy, but not doing much. He seems very anxious.

"Dalton, what are you doing? What's wrong?"

"Nothing is wrong. I better do this now before you tap into my brain and ruin the surprise."

"Do what?"

Suddenly he drops to one knee in front of me. I start to bawl.

"You are breaking my no crying rule."

"Sorry."

"Willow Marie Martin, will you do me the honor of becoming my wife?"

"Yes Dalton, I would be honored to be your wife."

We kiss. This kiss is better than all the others combined. It is an accumulation of everything we have been through together and everything we feel. I know Dalton is the one for me.

♦♦♦♦♦

The next three days go by in a flurry of activity, as the crew is preparing for the entrance to the wormhole. I sincerely hope this works. This crew deserves to find a way home.

The Captain calls all commanding officers and the Omega Team to the bridge. The day we have been waiting for is here. We are close to the wormhole, and now we just have to wait for it to show up.

We position ourselves outside of where it will be.

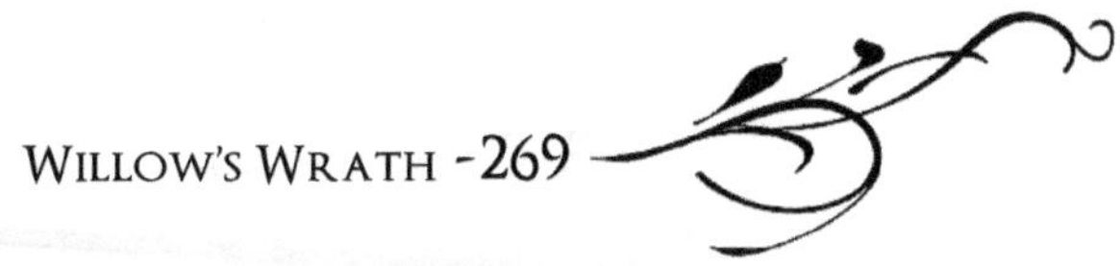

♦♦♦♦♦

We wait for days with no activity. Finally, on the seventh day, we have readings off the port bow.

There it is, our beautiful wormhole.

The Captain orders the helmsman to take us in slowly. We enter the wormhole gradually then speed forward, faster than the ship has ever gone before. All we see are colors and lights in a blur. We hold on to our stations, our chairs, anything we can, so as not to be propelled forward and hit the floor.

We exit the other side of the wormhole.

The bridge crew cheers.

"Sir we are receiving a transmission." Lieutenant Allium says calmly from her communications station.

"On speaker." We all wait with breathless anticipation for the message to start. It is four simple words.

"Starship Armargosa, Welcome Home!"